love you madly

MEN OF THE MIDWEST
BOOK 1

SAMEE MICHELLE

Copyright © 2024 by Samee Michelle

All rights reserved.

No part of this book may be reproduced in any form or by any electronic or mechanical means, including information storage and retrieval systems, without written permission from the author, except for the use of brief quotations in a book review.

This is a work of fiction. Names, characters, places, and incidents, while potentially inspired by real life, are ultimately either the product of the author's imagination or are used fictitiously. Any resemblance to actual persons, living or dead, events, or locales is purely coincidental.

Cover design by *Small Fry Marketing*.

*For all the sad bitches
who don't know
they're bad bitches.
This one's for you.*

trigger & content warnings

- Death and Grief - off the page
- Divorce
- Emotional Abuse
- Explicit Language
- Explicit Sexual Content
- Financial Abuse
- Gaslighting
- Honorifics
- Infidelity - not between MCs
- Manipulation
- Mental Health Struggles, including Anxiety & Depression
- Pregnancy
- Pregnancy Complications not resulting in death
- Substance use and Numbing
- Toxic Relationships

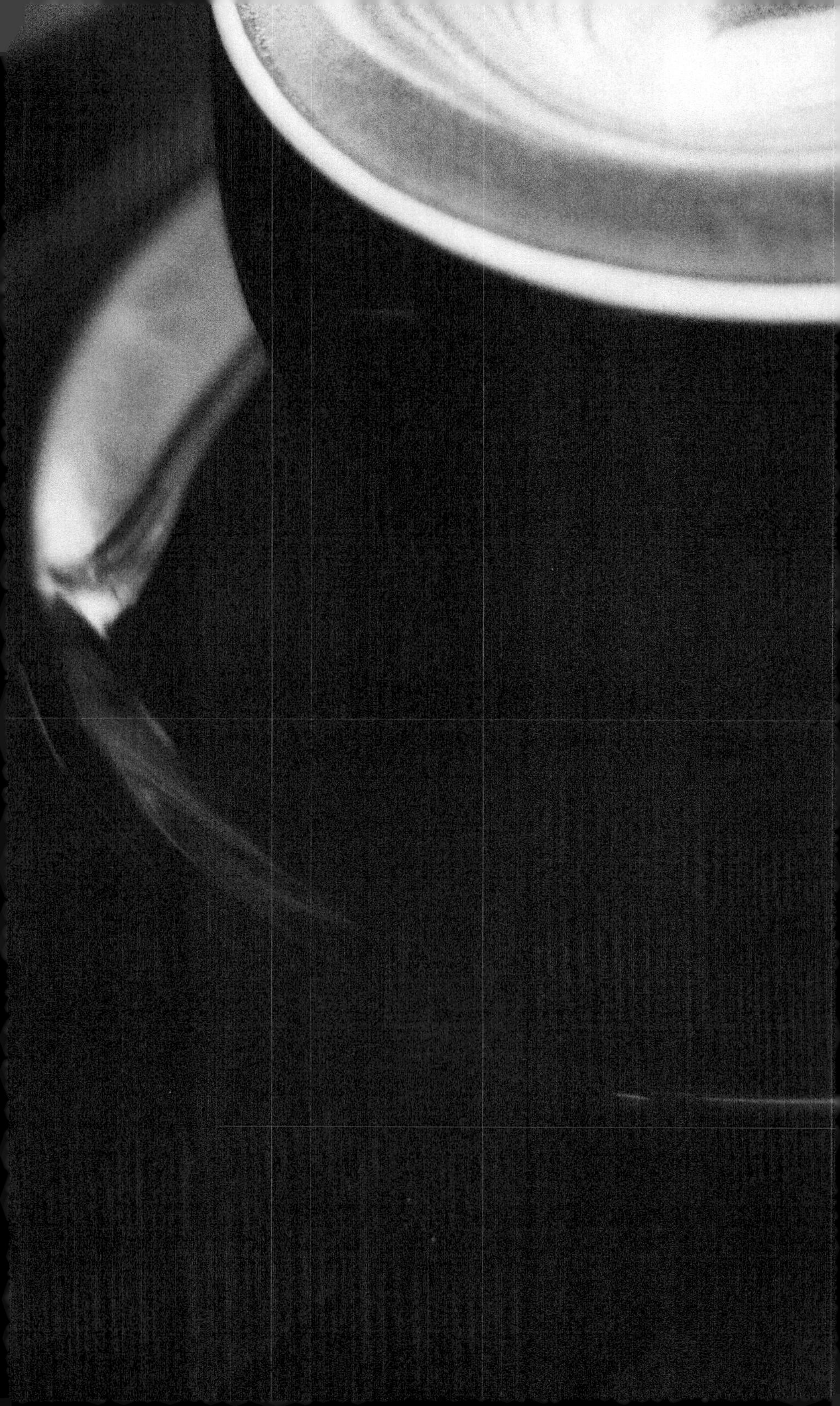

author's note

For legal reasons,
this is a joke.

And if you don't like this FMC,
it's okay... I hated that bitch too.

playlist

Believe - Staind
A Thousand Years - Christina Perri
Bring Me to Life - Evanescence
Wake Me Up - Avicii
Love / Hate Heartbreak - Halestorm
Somebody That I Used to Know - Gotye feat. Kimbra
Love the Way You Lie - Eminem feat. Rihanna
Do You Realize - The Flaming Lips
The House That Built Me - Miranda Lambert
Dog Days Are Over - Florence + The Machine
Consider Me Gone - Reba McEntire
The Crossroads - Bone Thugs-N-Harmony
A Little Bit Stronger - Sara Evans
Breakeven - The Script
She Will Be Loved - Maroon 5
The Bad Touch - Bloodhound Gang
Call Me Maybe - Carly Rae Jepsen
Pinch Me - Barenaked Ladies
I Wanna Dance with Somebody - Whitney Houston

PLAYLIST

I Wanna Know - Joe
So Contagious - Acceptance
Use Somebody - Kings of Leon
Back to December - Taylor Swift
Impossible - James Arthur
Breathe (2 AM) - Anna Nalick
Wonderwall - Oasis
Say Something - A Great Big World feat. Christina Aguilera
Payphone - Maroon 5 feat. Whiz Khalifa
Who Knew - P!nk
Ain't No Rest for the Wicked - Cage the Elephant
Almost Lover - A Fine Frenzy
Not Over You - Gavin DeGraw
I Touch Myself - Divinyls
Over My Head (Cable Car) - The Fray
Clumsy - Fergie
Just a Dream - Nelly
Waiting for Superman - Daughtry
Blurred Lines - Robin Thicke, T.I, & Pharrell Williams
Lego House - Ed Sheeran
Count on Me - Bruno Mars
Stay - Rihanna feat. Mikky Ekko
Girl, I Wanna Lay You Down - ALO feat. Jack Johnson
Why Can't I? - Liz Phair
Everything You Want - Vertical Horizon
A Thousand Miles - Vanessa Carlton
Love You Madly - Cake
Kiss Me - Sixpence None The Richer
Suffocate - J. Holiday
Doin' It - LL Cool J
Gold Digger - Kanye West
It's Not You - Halestorm
Better Together - Jack Johnson

x

PLAYLIST

The Boy Is Mine - Brandy & Monica
I Love You - The Bees
Never Again - Katie Clarkson
Slow Motion - Trey Songz
Birthday Sex - Jeremih
All In - Lifehouse
You'll Be in My Heart - BOYS LIKE GIRLS
I Wanna Be Yours - Arctic Monkeys
I Choose You - Sara Bareilles
He Didn't Have to Be - Brad Paisley
Ruby - Kaiser Chiefs

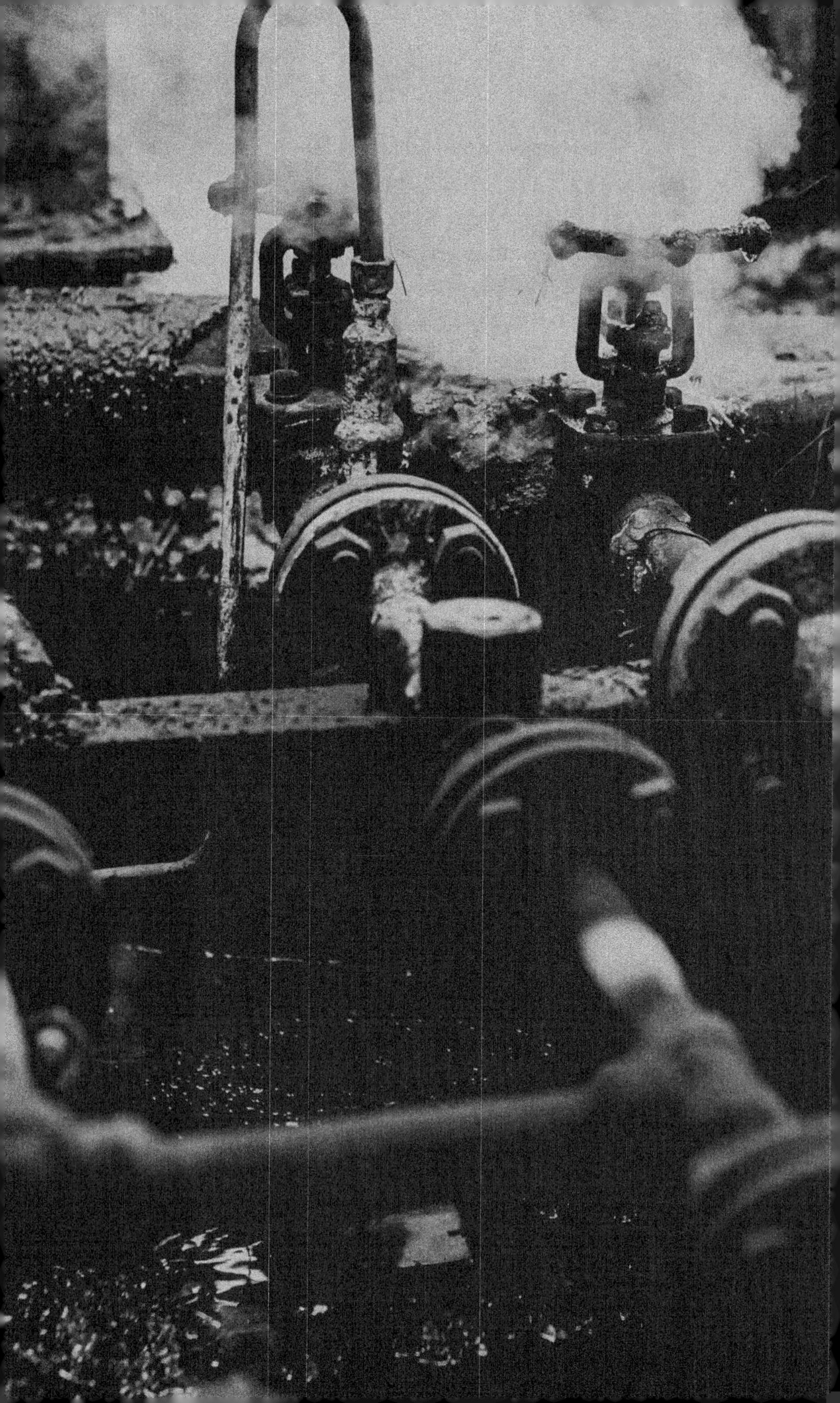

believe
STAIND

Believe in me.
Sometimes the weak become the strong.
Believe in me.
This life's not always what it seems.
Believe in me.
'Cause I was made for chasing dreams.

Written by: Aaron Lewis, Johnny April, Jon Wysocki, & Mike Mushok

Produced by: Aaron Lewis, Johnny April, Johnny K, Jon Wysocki, & Mike Mushok

The Illusion of Progress, 2008

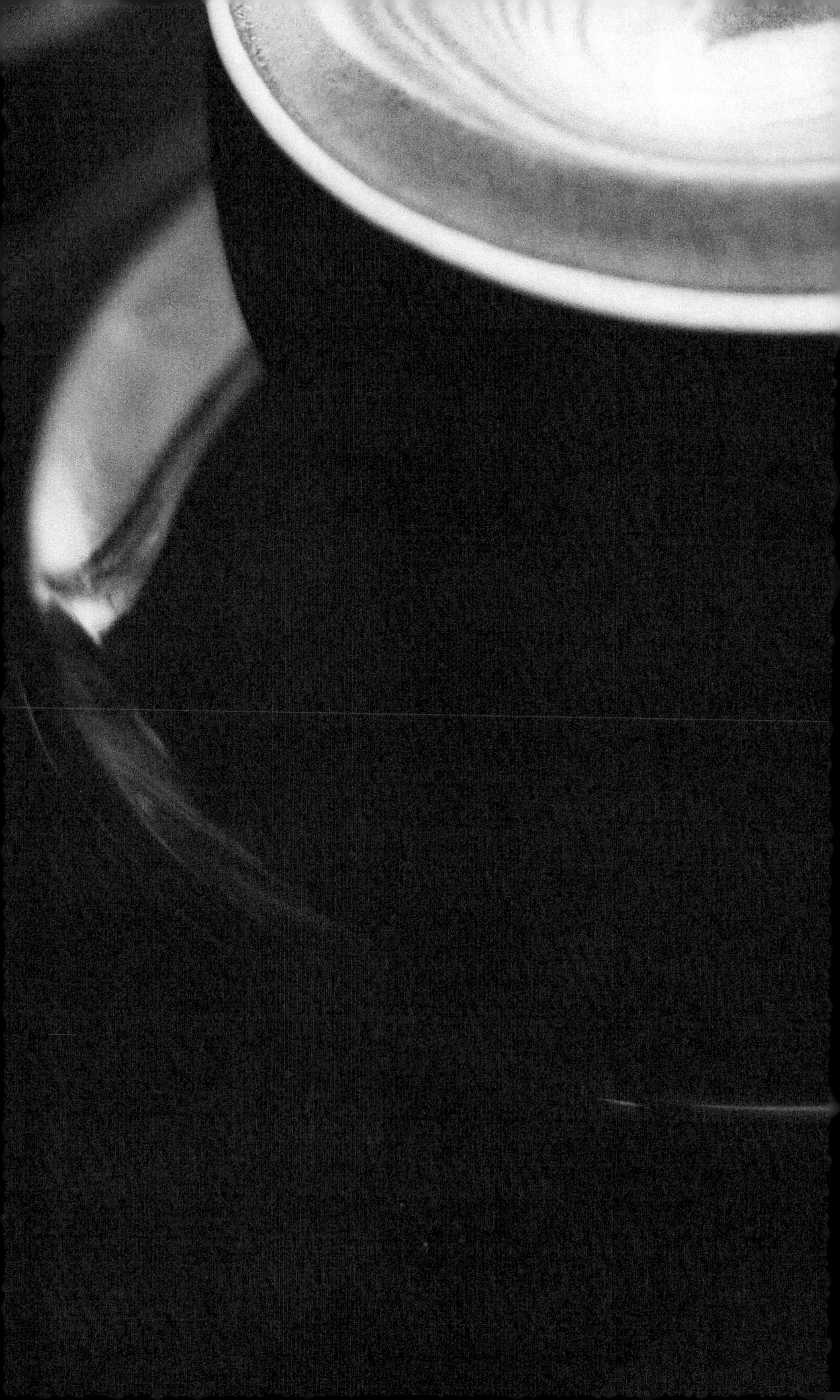

prologue
A THOUSAND YEARS - CHRISTINA PERRI

CALLIE - JULY 26, 2014

I never imagined I would find myself here again, especially not like this. After the mess that was made of me the first time around, I swore I'd never get married again. And honestly, I didn't think anyone would want me after what I'd been through. I was damaged goods... A woman with two children and a reputation that's seen better days (especially in this goddamn town). Who would sign up for that?

But I suppose he did. I suppose that's exactly what he signed up for. This. Fucking. Man. It's remarkable how quickly "never" turned into "forever" when I met him.

When I stretch out on the window seat in my childhood bedroom at the Van Damme Hawkridge estate, it all feels so surreal. This home has been in my mother's family for generations, but it feels like I'm watching someone else's life unfold. The buckeye tree I used to climb as a child remains tall and steadfast, a silent witness to years gone by.

Down the hall, I can hear the rapid pitter-patter of little feet and giggles approaching. "Sara, please! We need you to cooperate," my mother, Rita, pleads with my little girl. She sounds exasperated. It's clear my mom and sister are struggling to wrangle my two-year-old.

It's not surprising when the doorknob jiggles a moment later. Sara's tiny voice pierces through the door, "Mama! Mama!" she yells, banging on the door with all the impatience only a two-year-old can muster.

I can't help but laugh as I crack open the door just as my niece, Ava, catches up to Sara. "Coast is clear! He's already outside and won't be able to see you. Can we come in?"

I nod, opening the door further. I managed to sneak out of bed this morning without waking him, and I would be heartbroken if he caught sight of me this close to the ceremony. I want our photographer to capture his expression when he sees me in my dress for the first time. I also don't want to risk tempting fate to throw bad luck my way today. I've stumbled into that more often than I care to admit.

It seems my luck has changed, though. But maybe I shouldn't even think that, in case I jinx myself. God, anxiety sucks. Feeling anxious and superstitious at the same time? Super fun!

Sara's eyes are brimming with excitement. My mischievous toddler looks so sweet in her navy flower girl dress, her hair adorned with tiny silk sunflowers. As I stare down at my darling daughter, I can now see her pretty hairstyle is already disheveled.

It makes me chuckle and reminds me of the day I met my stepdad, Wayne, with untidy hair. Mom had brought Wayne to meet my sister and me when I was around the age of five. I couldn't find the Lego piece I was looking for and had gone diving under my bed to find it. When I came out, my hair got stuck in the bottom of the box spring and was sticking straight in the air by the time I'd gotten myself loose... Shout-out to my big sister for cutting my hair for me to free me from the box spring death trap.

"You girls look beautiful." I wrap them up in a miniature group hug and smile before turning to my oldest daughter and picking her up. "Where's baby sissy?" She absentmindedly fiddles with the necklace he got her to wear today before answering.

"Sissy's sweeping," Sara says.

"Sl-ee-p-ing," I say, enunciating the word to help Sara repeat it back to me correctly.

"That's what I said, Sissy's sweeping," Sara says, matter-of-factly.

Ava giggles. "Grammy wanted to let her take a nap before the ceremony. My mom said that's probably for the best so she's not crabby later, but I can get the baby if you want me to."

"No, that's okay, honey. Your mom and Grammy are right... Just don't tell them I said that," I say with a mischievous wink.

Ava sticks out her smallest finger to initiate our super-secret pinky swear, and I loop mine into hers. We kiss our fists to seal our secret tight. "Thank you for your help today, Ava Bug. You look absolutely beautiful and mean so much to me."

"Can you please take Sara back downstairs and let Miss Vicki know that I'm ready for her to finish my makeup?"

"Sure can!" Ava says with an excited pep in her voice. She takes Sara's hand ready to lead her out of the room as I kiss them both quickly on the forehead. They walk back out the door, leaving it wide open behind them. *It's a good thing he's already outside, or these two girls would have me busted long before the ceremony starts.*

I choose to leave the door open for Vicki and hear Sara

speak up a couple of minutes later. "Auntie Tay Tay!" she shouts, "Mama said you was right. Let Sissy sweep!"

I can't help but laugh as I hear Ava scold Sara for telling our secret and cringe, knowing that both my sister and I want to amend Sara's grammar, but today is not the day for that battle.

I turn back to the mirror, taking in my reflection. It's hard to recognize the woman staring back at me. There's a strength in her I never thought I would have. The simple elegance of the dress, the way my green eyes shine with a bundle of nerves and excitement.

I reach for the rose quartz plugs on the dresser, slipping them into my stretched earlobes. The cool, smooth stone against my skin is calming, a reminder of the love and positive energy I want to carry with me today and always. The choice of rose quartz, the stone of unconditional love, feels perfect at this moment because that is exactly what this man has given me and my daughters.

I'm so glad I've found this man. He has stepped up in ways I never imagined anyone would for me. I had a great stepfather example, but I never thought I'd be so lucky as to find a partner who would be willing to be that for my girls.

Tears fill my eyes as I slip on the bracelet my new bonus son got me for Christmas. I never thought that I could love a child that didn't start off as my own as much as I love that sweet, handsome little boy. He is the spitting image of his father, and I feel so grateful to call him my son.

The bracelet sits over the tattoo on my wrist. It is a script of the word "love" along with a date that has become very special to me. The tattoo pays tribute to the organization *To Write Love on Her Arms*, which rescued me from a very dark place as a teenager. The date reflects the last time I allowed myself to be nearly too far gone.

I'm so grateful my attempts were unsuccessful. Especially now.

Staring at myself in the mirror, I take in the tattoo of a large cherry blossom tree that climbs my right arm from elbow to shoulder. The pink blossoms cascade down my arm, signifying the strength and resilience I've found in myself as a mother. The tattoo means so much to me because I got it after I had to give up breastfeeding Sara when my body couldn't keep up with the supply she needed. I felt like a complete failure. Each bloom represents the moments that brought me here–good, bad, or otherwise. The tree's roots represent strength and stability, the foundation I've built for my children.

It's been a year and a day since I told him I was going to refer to him as my boyfriend when talking to my mother because "this guy I've been seeing exclusively for a while but met online a few months ago" was too long.

Three-hundred-sixty-six days.

It seemed fated as I was looking for something unique to add to our ceremony, I discovered handfasting rituals typically take place a year and a day after a couple has committed to one another. And our year and a day just so happens to be a Saturday. Today.

Although I've never been particularly religious, pagan and Celtic traditions have always fascinated me. I was a solitary practitioner for years, so the rituals, symbolism, connection to the universe, and idea of karma feel more like home to me. Which is the exact opposite of how I feel about the rigid Catholic traditions my mother's family clung to. So, as I prepared for this day, I couldn't help but subtly infuse my own beliefs into our celebration. It has given me the opportunity to embrace my true self.

My hair will be braided for the ceremony, each twist symbolizing a bond–past, present, and future–as is the handfasting cord that will bind our hands together during the ceremony. The cord is braided with threads of green, gold, red, pink, brown, purple, and light blue–each color chosen with intention. Green for prosperity, gold for longevity, red for passion, pink for romance, brown for encouragement, purple for growth, and light blue for patience and devotion.

Our handfasting will be a quiet, personal moment during the ceremony, a nod to the ancient tradition that resonates with the connection we've built–a bond that feels as though it's been tied over lifetimes. The knots of the handfasting are meant to showcase our commitment to each other, our future, and the family we are building together.

I didn't think this could become my reality. But I am here, standing on the precipice of a new beginning, with the man who made me believe in forever again and the children who have become my entire world.

Our entire world.

I take a deep breath, ready to embrace this new chance at life and remind myself I deserve to be happy. And I know, with every fiber of my being, this is just the beginning.

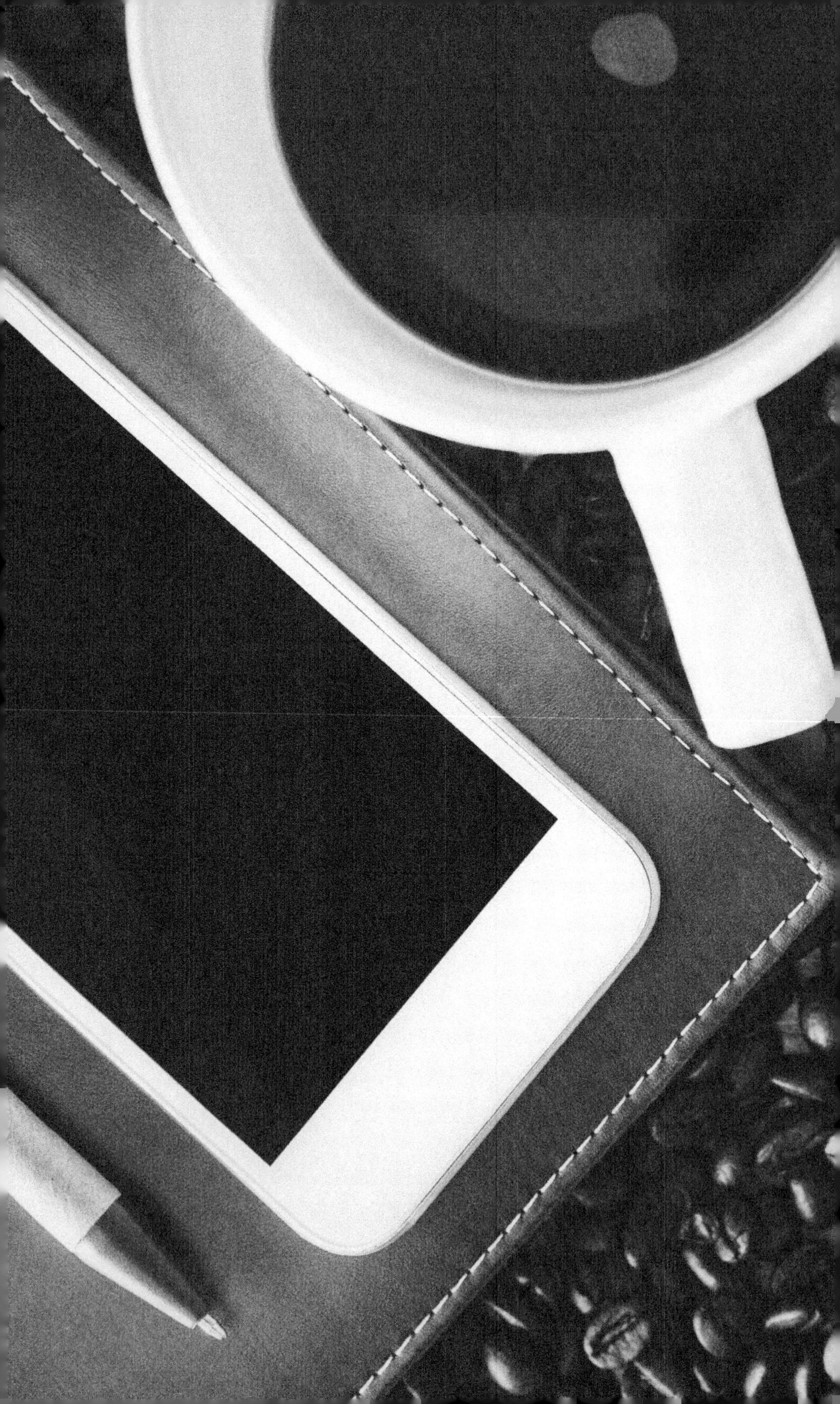

part one

SIXTEEN MONTHS EARLIER

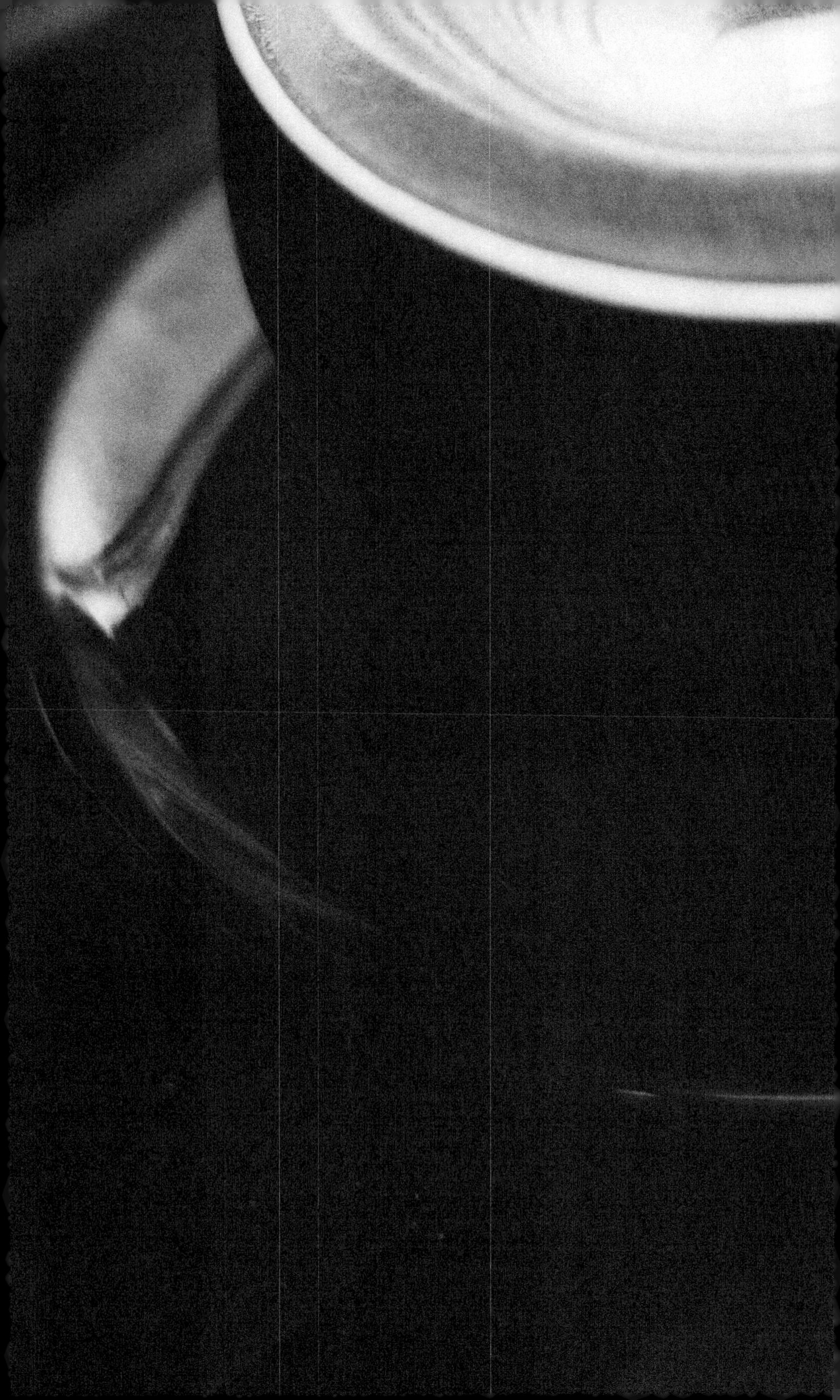

one

BRING ME TO LIFE - EVANESCENCE

CALLIE - MARCH 12, 2013

"You have got to be fucking kidding me!" I whisper-shout, staring at the positive pregnancy test in my hand. My bathroom feels smaller, closing in on me as I try to process the reality of the situation. I try to stay calm because my eight-month-old daughter, Sara, is napping nearby, but internally, I'm screaming.

What. The. Actual. FUCK.

Since Sara was born, I've had sex with that asshole precisely one time. Once! The obligatory "Babe, come on, it's Valentine's Day!"

Cupid can suck it. I hate that chubby fucking cherub. Almost as much as I hate my husband.

As the word "pregnant" flashes on the test's display, I can hear the voice of my ninth-grade sex education teacher, Ms. Reyes, resonating in my ear, much like the voice of the teacher from Charlie Brown. *Now, remember, class: It only takes one time to get pregnant.*

This is what I get for constantly chasing a romantic high. I loved love, and it bit me in the ass every time. Why on earth I thought Adam would be different is beyond me. To be honest, I wasn't the best wife either. But fuck, at least I tried.

I met Adam in my first year of high school; he was a senior in my sister Taylor's class. We bonded after I kicked the shit out of the vending machine that was holding my cosmic brownie hostage, and he helped tip the machine to shake it loose. He turned eighteen early in his senior year and enlisted in the military, planning to leave for boot camp after graduation. Adam took on the role of my enforcer, consistently watching out for me.

We were flirtatious friends, but I was only fourteen when we met. We never crossed the line because I knew he would be leaving. Adam was my best friend and nothing more—or so I thought.

The day he and my sister graduated, I realized my best friend was slipping away from me and mistook that for some "Oh my God, I'm in love with him" movie moment. You know, like the one in *Clueless* where Alicia Silverstone is standing in front of the fountain, and it lights up purple as she realizes she's in love with Paul Rudd? Yeah, I thought I was majorly, totally, but crazy in love with... Adam. Oof.

I had to write him a note and tell him by slipping it to him at his graduation party where his girlfriend was standing outside even though my sister could see it coming from a mile away and told me not to be Chaos Callie and just let him be. Why would I do that? That would have been entirely too reasonable. And ethical.

He ended up breaking up with his girlfriend that night. And... two months later, I wrote him a *Dear John* letter while he was at boot camp. By then, I was fifteen and had a can't be held back attitude. God, I was such an asshole. But also... he was a full-blown adult, so... Ew.

Perhaps this is my karma, right?

I don't know if it was my daddy issues or mommy issues, but I was always chasing the feeling of being needed. I became quite the little trollop, an awful girlfriend to almost everyone I dated. I sought attention and validation desperately, going wherever I felt needed and ignoring the wreckage I had left behind.

After high school, I vowed I was going to be different. I'd gotten into a lot of trouble at the end of my senior year, and it was a severe reality check for me in many ways. Turns out, if you sleep with the wrong person, you may get your ass beat. If only I could go back in time and convince my younger self sleeping with my best friend's baby daddy was not quite the plot twist I should have been looking for in my life.

I know most teens grow up and say they cannot wait to leave their hometowns. That was me, without a doubt. I started focusing my energy on ways to get out of Hawkridge. And I certainly wasn't going to be dating any more guys from my hometown because, well... fuck them.

When I met a guy named Johnny through a mutual friend, it didn't take long for me to uproot my life and move to Ohio to be with him. I wanted to escape from the reputation I had built for myself, which was starting to catch up with me.

I thought Johnny was going to be my redemption arc. Have you ever experienced that part in a book or movie where a character you detest suddenly turns into a respectable human being? This was going to be my fucking moment.

Except it wasn't.

Johnny proposed to me on our six-month anniversary in front of a crowded restaurant when we went to dinner with friends. I thought he was just the greatest ever. I'll never understand why on earth I thought it was a good idea to get engaged at barely twenty years old to a free-loader who couldn't hold a job for twenty-four hours. A month after Johnny proposed, I found out he had been cheating on me the entire time we were together.

I'd say, "Fuck you, Karma," but I don't think I want to risk pissing her off further. I can't take much more of it at this point. I went from being the walking Red Flag to collecting red flags like it's my fucking job and I need a pay raise plus commission.

After I moved back home to Hawkridge from Ohio, Adam and I reconnected through social media after not talking in years. He told me he had gotten discharged from the military and had just gone through a major surgery and a divorce from his first wife two years before that. When Adam offered to buy me a plane ticket to Seattle a few days after we reconnected, I jumped at the opportunity to get the hell out of Hawkridge for a while, fully expecting our relationship to remain platonic.

I was a shell of a human, and he was offering me a safe haven. I thought he was picking up the pieces to make me whole again. You know… because it had been six weeks since my sister and her husband, Nick, were picking me up in Cleveland. Why wouldn't I hop my dramatic ass on a Boeing seven-eighty-seven to Seattle on a whim?

I was supposed to return home after two weeks, but instead, I skipped the flight home as Adam promised stability, a family, and everything I thought I wanted. Blinded by desperation and my deteriorated mental state, I was married to Adam within six months of moving to Seattle.

Do you see a pattern?

You know how the definition of insanity is repeating the same thing over and over and expecting different results? Nailed it!

I was thousands of miles from home (again), and all my friends were Adam's. I hadn't yet realized the more I was fused into Adam's world, the more I lost touch with reality. I didn't even know I'd stopped talking to most of the people from Iowa shortly after I moved to Seattle to be with Adam.

In hindsight, I made a foolish and hasty decision when I married Adam almost two years ago. However, I convinced myself our story was some exceptional romance back then.

Despite his promises of the world on a silver platter, I was unable to see how Adam took advantage of me, blinded by my deteriorated mental state. But when you're twenty years old and don't know any better, a guy flashing nice cars, a motorcycle, a house, and money when you were just with someone you had to be the provider for, I thought THIS was how it should be. He was the total opposite of Johnny. So, Adam must be the answer to my prayers, right?

The fucking crotch rocket he owned but never actually rode should have been my first clue. But it wasn't.

Red Flag #87.

I was so delusional, but Adam seemed like everything I needed. He was financially stable for someone in his mid-twenties, unlike Johnny, who stole from me and didn't have a job for the entire eight months we were together. So, Adam seemed like a dream.

Adam was supposed to be my knight in shining armor who rescued me from my evil, thieving ex-fiance. And we would live happily ever after.

Turns out...

The bar was on the fucking floor. And he was the *Great Value* version of the Tin Man.

At first, everything seemed to be perfect. Adam was attentive and caring. He showered me with gifts and nice dinners. If only I knew what love-bombing was back then. Once the excitement of the pregnancy wore off, his true colors showed. He didn't want me to work, claiming the stress would hurt the baby. *That's rich coming from him.* I reluctantly quit my job even though it was the only way I'd made any friends who weren't already his friends in Seattle. At this point, I've been without work for two years.

After a couple of months of marriage, he made jabs at me about me not contributing and "his money." It was his fucking fault I didn't have a career in the first place, but he had no trouble blaming me for money woes.

Red Flag #127.

Months later, he slipped up and told me he didn't like where I was working at the time because he thought something was going on between me and one of my coworkers… even though he was the one who showed up to my place of employment with one of his female "friends" on the back of the motorcycle he owned for a very short amount of time. I guess he rode the stupid thing after all, just not with me.

Oh, the hypocrisy.

I knew I shouldn't have stayed with him when he begged me to after yet another screw-up. I should have taken Sara and gotten the hell out of this complete fucking joke of a marriage. But I didn't. He rattled on about how he'd made mistakes and vowed to make it right. All things I'd heard a million times before. I was tired. So, he wore me down again, just like he always had. I brushed off all the red flags even though they were so glaringly obvious that they could probably be seen from freaking Jupiter.

I'm grateful to be back home in Iowa instead of Seattle, where I was when Adam and I learned I was pregnant with Sara.

Now, I'm standing here, staring at this goddamn test, and I feel like the universe is playing some cruel joke on me. *Am I being Punk'd?* Because that's what it feels like! How did I let it come to this? Like a complete moron, I wanted to believe he could change, that he would be the man I needed him to be for Sara. But deep down, I knew it was a lie. I knew he was never going to change.

As I stand here, the realization that I'm carrying another one of his children sinks in. I don't want to raise another baby with a man who only brings me pain—my mind races with the possibilities and the consequences. I have no idea how I'm going to get through this. How the fuck am I going to explain this to everyone? And, more importantly, how am I going to protect my poor babies from the catastrophe known as my husband?

Maybe I should just run... Yeah, right. Where the fuck would I even go?

I take in a deep breath, trying to steady myself. I have to be strong—not only for myself but also for Sara, and the new life I now know is growing inside me. I am going to have to make a tough decision. I wish I had done this a long time ago. I can't keep letting Adam dictate my happiness. This could be my chance to break free, to build a life for my children that won't be overrun by his toxic presence.

I would love to have more children, but I don't want to have more children with him. I feel so guilty for the new life growing inside me, knowing this baby deserves better than the pain my relationship with Adam causes.

I quickly wipe away my tears, silently vowing to myself and this tiny life inside me that we will get through this. We will be okay. Looking down at the pregnancy test in my hand, my head is spinning. Just as I'm about to stash the test away before anyone finds it, the bathroom door creaks open slightly.

"What's going on?" he asks, his voice laced with suspicion.

I quickly shove the test behind my back, but it's too late.

Adam's gaze shifts to the discarded box on the counter. His eyes widen, and a strange, almost triumphant smile spreads across his face.

"Are you...?" He steps closer, his hand reaching out to touch my arm. "Are you pregnant?"

I nod, unable to find the words. My husband's reaction is not what I expected. Instead of concern or guilt, he looks almost... pleased.

"This is great news, babe!" he exclaims, pulling me into a tight hug. I stand there, stiff and unresponsive, the reality of our situation crashing down on me even harder.

"Great news?" I finally manage to say, pushing him away gently. "How is this great fucking news, Adam? We're barely holding it together as it is."

He steps back, his expression hardening. "Come on, Callie. This is our chance to start over. A new baby could bring us together. It's a sign, don't you see?"

"A sign?" I repeat warily. "A sign of what? That we're stuck in this toxic cycle?"

It's like no matter what I do, he always sucks me back in. And I am too exhausted to fight anymore. *Jesus fucking Christ, he sounds like a teenage girl that's just made good on a pregnancy pact with her besties.*

Adam's jaw tightens, and for a moment, I think he might actually acknowledge the truth. But he shakes his head, a determined look in his eyes.

"No, babe. It's a sign that we truly have something beautiful here. Please, Callie. Just give it a chance. Give us a chance. For Sara's sake. For the baby's sake."

I turn to face the bathroom mirror again and grab a baby wipe to remove the black streaks of mascara from my tear-stained cheeks. He stands behind me, wrapping his arms around me, his right palm flat against my lower belly. I do my best not to recoil from his touch. I never expected that this would be his reaction. If anything, I thought he would think I was the one trying to trap him. Something about this doesn't feel right.

"We can make this work, baby. I promise."

I look up at his reflection in the mirror, his blue eyes glimmering and glossed over with his own tears. As our eyes connect, I search for any hint of sincerity. But all I see is desperation. Desperation to hold on to the illusion of control, of a perfect life that never existed.

Right now, my options are pretty limited.

If I leave, I'll lose my insurance. At this point, this really is a marriage of inconvenience. Having a baby without health insurance in America is not exactly the best-case scenario. And my pride won't let me tell Mom and Wayne just how bad the situation really is.

"Okay," I say softly, more to myself than to him. "I'll think about it."

Adam's face lights up with relief, and he turns me around to face him, pulling me in for another hug. "Thank you, Callie. You won't regret this, I promise."

I feel myself physically holding back from laughing at his words and plastering on a fake smile. I can't think of a single promise this man has made me that he's kept aside from providing for me financially. But he always made sure to remind me that it was his money. And without him, I would have nothing.

I got my associate's degree a few years ago, but I don't have much job experience besides working as a waitress. I've always had a hard time figuring out what I wanted to do when I got older for a career. Outside of being a mom, I never knew what I wanted for myself.

I also didn't want to rack up more student loan debt trying

to figure it out, so I decided to wait to go for my Bachelor's degree until I was more sure of myself. However, nothing ever really clicked for me. That's when Johnny happened. And when Johnny stopped happening, Adam happened.

Sure, I'd worked at a crooked as fuck furniture rental place for a couple of months after moving to Seattle, but since Adam had convinced me to quit my job when I found out I was pregnant, that all tallied up to maybe nine months of work experience since I'd finished community college.

"Can you explain this gap in employment history, Mrs. Graham?"

"Sure, my husband is a piece of shit that claimed he wanted me to not work for the sake of the baby, but really, it was so he could have control over me."

I'm sure that interview response would go over swimmingly. Maybe someone would find pity on me enough to give me a job washing dishes.

As he walks out of the bathroom, I'm stuck here, along with my thoughts and the overwhelming weight on my shoulders, which makes it feel like I'm balancing an elephant on each shoulder. Can I really trust him to change?

I mean... I know people change. I remained faithful in multiple relationships after being a serial cheater. So, if I could change, that means he can too... right?

I look down at my belly, a massive ache forming in my heart. "I'm so sorry, Little One. I'm so sorry for bringing you into this. I'm sorry that this is the life you and your sister were brought into."

I have to figure out a way to protect my children. And if that means leaving Adam for good, then so be it. But first, I need a plan.

I'm determined to make sure my kids know they shouldn't be getting married if they cannot have champagne at their reception. Just because you can do something doesn't mean you should. Hell, they probably shouldn't get married if they aren't old enough to rent a vehicle. Actually, fuck that. I'm going to tell them that they shouldn't get married until they are old enough to run for President. Yeah, thirty-five, that should do the trick. That is assuming my children listen to me better than I listened to my parents... Fat fucking chance.

two
WAKE ME UP - AVICII

OWEN - MARCH 21, 2013

I find myself back at my uncle's farm, in that same old fishing spot we used to visit every chance we got. The trees stretch high, their branches interwoven like the arches of a cathedral, creating a canopy of shifting light and shadow. The air is eerily quiet, the only sound the rustling of leaves in the faint breeze. I'm hit with a wave of nostalgia, memories pouring over me. As a kid, I remember how my dad would get home from work, barely taking a breath before loading me up in the truck and driving us out here to our favorite fishing hole.

Darling Ridge Farms is a patchwork quilt of memories. It feels like I've been here a million times. I'm surrounded by the fields dotted with wildflowers. In the near distance, I can see the weathered barn with its chipped red paint where my cousins and I used to play hide-and-seek in the lofts.

Each corner of this place holds a piece of my childhood. I remember running through these fields, the taste of the fresh apples picked straight from the orchard, and the comforting smell of hay in the barn. This place is a sanctuary—the place where the world seems simpler and my worries are far away.

It's been nine years since I first had this dream, but the details keep shifting. Each change is subtle, sometimes so slight I barely notice. I feel a strange sense of anticipation, knowing that she will be there, waiting for me. Alongside that anticipation is a gnawing guilt, a heavy weight on my conscience that I can never shake.

I turn away from the lake and walk down the path to a clearing. My heart pounds in my chest, a mix of excitement and dread coursing through me. There she is, standing with her back to me. Her hair's so dark that it's almost black. As she turns to face me, her green eyes lock onto mine. Those eyes pierce straight into my soul and fill me with a warmth I've never known before–a warmth I only ever find in these shared moments with her. The irises are dark around the edges, and when the sunlight hits just right, hints of purple shimmer within the green, like a hidden amethyst.

Wait... Have I noticed that before?

I feel the familiar pull overtaking me, the inexplicable connection that has haunted my dreams since the day before my wedding. She appeared out of nowhere for the first time, and since then, she's been a constant presence in my dreams. The intensity of my emotions surprises me every time—the longing, the yearning, the ache to be near her. And with each longing glance, each moment spent in her presence, the guilt intensifies.

The problem is... she isn't my wife.

"Who are you?" I ask, knowing she won't answer. She never does. Her gaze is intense and unwavering, as if she holds a secret just out of my reach. The amethyst ring around her iris is deeper and more vivid now.

Silence lingers in the surroundings. I can see every detail of her here—the subtle curve of her lips into an enigmatic smile, the hidden pain reflected in her eyes. It's like my own version of

"Groundhog Day," but instead of reliving the same day, I'm trapped in this recurring dream with her, and I never want to wake up. Phil Connors had it easy; he knew what to expect. She changes the game, and I never know what the dream is going to reveal to me next.

Is she trapped here too?

I take a step closer, the crunch of leaves underfoot echoing my unanswered questions. "Why are you here?" I ask, moving as close as she allows. "Why are you doing this to me?" My voice cracks with pain, desperate for her response. My heart breaks every time I wake, knowing I have to wait to sleep again to see her. I'm desperate to hear her voice, to break this cycle that has gnawed at me for years.

She tilts her head slightly, her expression softening, as she absorbs my frustration. But she remains silent. No whispered words, no murmurs, not even a sigh. Her presence is both a comfort and a torment, a reminder of something elusive. There's a part of me terrified of what I might discover if she ever speaks. And then there's the part of me that feels like I'm betraying my wife. Every time I yearn for this mysterious woman, every time I hope for her to break the silence.

In the dream, time seems fluid, stretching and slowing in defiance of logic. I could stand here for hours, lost in her eyes, yet it feels like moments... and it's never enough. Each time I think I'm close to understanding, the dream ends abruptly, leaving me with more questions than when I first spotted her in the clearing years ago.

I reach out, desperate to touch her, to know if she's real. But as my fingers brush hers, the dream fades. Tears fill my eyes as she slowly disappears, leaving me with an ache that lingers long after I wake—an ache compounded by the guilt of pining for someone who isn't my wife.

As the clearing dissolves into darkness, I wake up, my heart pounding against my ribs. I lie in bed, staring at the ceiling, the image of her eyes burning in my mind. Each time I have this dream brings me the same torment, and yet, I'm no closer to understanding her hold over me.

The dream is a twisted form of hell, a relentless repeat with no apparent escape. I'm trapped in this cycle, waiting for answers that never come. I can only hope one day, she'll reveal the truth behind her haunting presence.

Waking up without Sabrina next to me is a relief. I always felt a heavy burden of guilt after dreaming about another woman while my wife was sleeping next to me. Despite our divorce being finalized two years ago, waking up alone after these dreams remains just as difficult. I remind myself that I'm not married anymore, so I don't have to feel as guilty about the dreams. And even when I was married, it's not like the dreams are something I had control over. Yet, the sense of relief quickly fades, and the feeling of loneliness persists as a constant companion.

As messed up as it sounds, my ex-wife's presence used to offer me solace, anchoring me in reality, a reminder that I wasn't completely alone. I've tried to find ways to move on both from Sabrina and the enigmatic smile of the girl who invades my dreams. We'd been together since high school, dating for seven years and married for almost another seven.

Almost.

Even though I'm no longer married to Sabrina, I still wrestle with my conscience. The woman in my dreams only ever appeared in my sleep, but it feels like I had an emotional affair while I was married. The guilt lingers, a shadow over every dream, every longing glance at the mysterious woman.

The fact is, I fell in love with another woman while I was

married to Sabrina. And I've never even met her. I don't even know if she's really out there somewhere.

I questioned myself constantly: Did these dreams affect my marriage? Was I unfair to Sabrina, emotionally connected to someone who wasn't real? The answers never come, and the doubts gnaw at me, a reminder of the unresolved conflict within. I try to remind myself that, in the end, Sabrina and I didn't have a happy marriage and my guilt starts to subside.

FEBRUARY 17, 2011 - TWO YEARS AGO

Our marriage was a societal expectation, a natural progression after college. I could almost hear my ex-mother-in-law's shrill voice insisting that marriage was the next logical step. God, that voice was the stuff from nightmares. But, alas, I followed the script. But after five years of marriage and a year of parenthood, I grew weary of the routine. Fatherhood shifted my perspective, and I didn't want my son to witness a relationship that felt empty, devoid of the passion and connection I wanted to model for him.

I did love Sabrina. How could I not? I'd known her for fourteen years. But I also couldn't stand to be around her. Not in the typical "they drive each other crazy but are deeply in love" way. I genuinely couldn't stand her presence. I didn't want to be near her or share her company. My feelings for her had evolved into a complex mix of love tinged with resentment, a stark departure from the affection I once felt.

I even started working third shift just to avoid her. It allowed me to spend my days with Barrett while he was a baby, and we saved on childcare since Sabrina got home most days before I had to leave for work except for my every-other Friday double shift when I had to be in at Noon. The more time I spent away from Sabrina, the clearer it became that I couldn't spend the rest of my life this way.

Growing up in Cedar Bluff, I watched my parents fight constantly. They stayed together "for the kids," but their marriage crumbled soon after I married Sabrina. Nearly thirty years together, and it ended in a hollow, anticlimactic separation. I didn't want that for myself. I couldn't imagine enduring a lifetime of trying to force something that was never meant to work. Surely, Sabrina wouldn't have wanted that either.

I pulled away, bit by bit, until one day, I did the most fucked up thing I could have done. I left. While she was at work, I packed my stuff, dropped Barrett off at her parents' house—just like I did every other Friday when I had an early shift-and went to work. Her parents didn't think much of it; they always watched him two Fridays a month. But that day, I turned my phone off.

I left a note for Sabrina, explaining that I needed time to clear my head. Leaving a note means I wasn't a total monster, right? It's not like I said that I was going out to get a pack of cigarettes or a gallon of milk and then just dipped out forever. I promised I'd be back on Monday to watch Barrett when she went to work. Our marriage might have been coming to an end, but there was nothing in the world that would make me walk away from my son.

It wasn't just a Post-it note either; I poured out everything, telling her we both knew we weren't happy and it was only a matter of time before everything imploded. I just happened to be the one to say out loud what we had both undoubtedly been thinking for quite some time.

When my shift ended at five in the morning, I turned on

my phone and was greeted by a flurry of texts pinging one after another and a missed call from Sabrina. The first one was clueless, not realizing yet that I had left. Then came the furious string of pings on my phone as her messages came through.

SABRINA:

> Making "Breakfast for Dinner" in case you want leftovers after your shift. Have a good night at work. Text me when you can. I love you.

I felt a pang of guilt reading that. She had no idea what was coming. I knew it was cowardly, but leaving a note seemed like the only way I could go through with it.

I clocked out and walked to the truck, my feet dragging with the weight of the night's events. The parking lot was nearly empty, the dim streetlights casting long shadows. I got into my car, started the engine, and let out a deep sigh as the texts continued to pour in.

I opened them, knowing I was probably in for a Grade A ass-chewing as I started to read the rest.

Ping. Ping.

SABRINA:

> Found your note. What the hell, Owen?! Call me.

> Straight to voicemail, really? You shut your phone off? ARE YOU FUCKING KIDDING ME?

She was right to be angry. Fuck, I was a coward. I should have handled this whole situation differently.

Ping. Ping. Ping. Ping.

> SABRINA:
>
> Please tell me this is a joke. Fourteen years together and you leave me a note?
>
> How the fuck did we get here?
>
> Going to bed. Text me when you get back to your dad's. Don't put me through this and then die on the way home. If anything is going to kill you today, it's going to be me.
>
> I was joking earlier, by the way. Hey cops, if he died and you're reading this, I didn't actually kill him.

Her attempt at humor stung me more than her anger. It reminded me of better times when we would joke to diffuse tension. But this wasn't something a joke could fix.

Ping. Ping.

> SABRINA:
>
> Didn't tell my parents. Your note said you're staying at your dad's. Please ask him not to say anything until after we talk. I love you, Owen. But I think maybe you are right.
>
> I hope you know that even though you're the World's Shittiest Husband right now, I'd never keep Barrett from you. You're a good father and he needs you.

Maybe she was starting to understand, even if it was just a little. Relief washed over me. Barrett was my world, and the thought of being separated from him has been one of the hardest parts of this decision. I was terrified that she would use him as a way to punish me for leaving.

Apparently, she went through every stage of grief while I was gone and landed on acceptance just in time for me to avoid a full blown confrontation when I got off work.

> **ME:**
> Just got off work. Hope this doesn't wake you. I'll text you when I get back to Dad's.

> **SABRINA:**
> Thank you.

> **ME:**
> I'm sorry it had to be this way. I couldn't face you. I knew if I did, I would never be able to go through with leaving.

I pulled out of the parking lot, gripping the steering wheel tighter than necessary. Her words cut deep, but I knew she was right. I made this choice, and now I had to live with it.

The roads were quiet, only a few other cars passing by this early on a Saturday morning. The silence was oppressive, giving my thoughts too much room to roam.

She deserved so much better than this, better than me. I had thought about what to say a thousand times but could never find the right words. Maybe that's because there weren't any.

As I drove, memories flooded back—our wedding day, Barrett's birth, the countless little moments that had once made us inseparable. Now, those memories felt like a cruel joke. How had we come to this? Was there a moment when everything had gone wrong, or was it a slow, inevitable decay?

My phone buzzed again with a text I was sure came from Sabrina. It would be another twenty minutes before I could look at it, though.

When I pulled into my dad's driveway, the sky was beginning to lighten with the first hints of dawn. I turned off the engine and sat there for a moment, gathering the strength to face whatever happened next. Hesitantly, I looked at the last text I'd received while I was driving.

SABRINA:
It didn't have to be this way, Owen. You made it this way. And you're an asshole for it.

She wasn't wrong. I made this choice, and now I had to live with it. I texted her back as I walked up the sidewalk, the cool morning air biting at my skin.

ME:
I know... I just pulled into Dad's. Do you need me to come get Barrett so you can get some sleep?

I opened the door as quietly as I could, trying not to wake my dad and his wife, Beverly. The house was dark and silent, the only sound was the creak of the floorboards under my feet. I made my way to the guest bedroom, my old room now converted into storage space for old furniture, forgotten memories, and Dad's coin collection. I set my bag down and sank onto the bed, exhaustion hitting me like a wave. My phone buzzed again.

SABRINA:
No, that's okay. Thank you though.

ME:
It's the least I can do. Let me know if you change your mind and need help with him this weekend. Hey cops, if I die today, she 100% was the culprit.

SABRINA:
Too fucking soon for jokes, Dickweed.

ME:
That's fair. I really am sorry, Sabrina.

SABRINA:

It's not okay. 😳 See you Monday.

three

LOVE / HATE HEARTBREAK - HALESTORM

CALLIE - MARCH 21, 2013

The uncertainty is consuming me, coiling around my thoughts like a vice. Adam strides into the room with a determined look on his face, disrupting my silent turmoil. I stare out the window, watching the trees sway in the spring breeze, trying to make sense of the whirlwind that has become my life. It's been a little over a week since I found out I am pregnant, and I still do not know how I am going to get through this.

"Callie, we need to talk," he says, his tone more serious than usual.

Red Flag #750.

He takes a deep breath as if gathering his strength. "I've been thinking—"

"Don't hurt yourself," I retort. My patience with him is nonexistent at this point. Whether it's the pregnancy hormones or the years of accumulated resentment, I am nearly over it. When I found out that I was pregnant with our second child, I vowed I wouldn't let him have this hold over me anymore, and yet... Here I sit, trapped in this conversation.

He shoots me a glare, his eyes narrowing. "Can you please not? I'm really trying here... I think maybe we need a fresh start. A new place. Somewhere, we can leave all this behind and try to make things work again."

Part of me is certain this is a terrible idea. However, we have been living with my mom since moving back to the Midwest, and I know that thanks to the lack of privacy isn't helping our situation. My mother isn't the easiest woman to get along with, and she has too much to say about how we parent Sara. This is only going to get worse as Sara gets older.

"Okay," I say hesitantly. "I'm listening..." Maybe this talk won't be a red flag after all.

"I found a house in Burlington we can rent until I get the house in Seattle sold, and we are ready to buy a new one. It's not very far from here. And it's available on the first of April. That's a little over a week from now. The timing is perfect. We will still be able to visit Hawkridge easily, but it will also give us a change of scenery. A chance to start over."

I feel my stomach tighten as a knot of anxiety coils in my stomach. I feel like I'm going to be sick, and I don't know if it's because of the pregnancy or his words still hanging in the air. A change of scenery? Really, because clearly, all our problems stem from the view out the window. I can't shake off the skepticism that prickles under my skin. But even as I cross my arms, shielding myself from the pain he has caused me before, a tiny flicker of hope flutters in my chest. Maybe he is right; a new place would make things more bearable.

We've been staying with my mom because Adam hasn't been able to sell the Seattle house. I wasn't on the mortgage and can't afford a place here alone. So until it's sold, we're stuck either renting or living with Mom.

This would ensure that Adam moves out of my mother's house in case I ever need to return here alone.

"Adam, I don't know–" I start, but he cuts me off.

"Look, I know things have been rough. I know I've made mistakes. But I want to make it right, Callie. We were best friends once," he reminds me.

Green Flag #1.

Wait... Green flag... Do they make those?!

"I can't help but think we can get back there," he continues, his voice softer now. "I want us to be a family again. For Sara and the new baby's sake."

"Yes, because dragging two innocent babies into our mess has been working out so well so far," I mutter, glancing over at Sara, who is now playing innocently on the floor with her favorite giraffe toy. Our sweet baby girl is blissfully unaware of the circus her parents are running. She deserves better than this chaos.

"Okay," I finally say, my voice barely above a whisper. "I'll try it. But this is your last chance, Adam. If things don't change, I'm done."

He beams as if I have just given him a get-out-of-jail-free card. "Thank you, Callie. You won't regret this, I promise." The gleam in his glacier-blue eyes gets me every time. *God damn it, Adam.*

I nod, forcing myself to cling to some shred of belief, but it's a lie I can't fully swallow. Deep down, I know the truth. Actions always speak louder than words, and Adam's red flags scream at me. Still... here I am. I haven't walked away. I'm still pretending, still hoping—because maybe, just maybe, this time will be different. Maybe he'll prove me wrong. But the ache in my chest tells me I already know how this will end.

That night, Adam does something unexpected. He comes home with a bouquet of roses—roses he thinks are my favorite.

I've never had the heart to tell him I hate roses because they feel thoughtless, but tonight, I force a smile as their overly sweet scent fills the room. He also brings takeout from the little Chinese restaurant I love–the one I always missed when we lived in Seattle. He sets the table meticulously, lights candles, and even puts on some soft music.

Green Flag #8.

"Callie," he pauses, eyes locking onto mine. "I know I've messed up a lot." His voice is heavy with sincerity, begging me to believe him. There's a rawness in his tone, a desperation tugging at something rooted deep inside me. His usual confidence wavers, replaced by vulnerability. "But tonight, I just want us to have a good evening together. No fighting, no talking about problems. Just us."

I'm taken aback. It's been so long since we had a moment like this. When was the last time he did something sweet for me? A flicker of the Adam I fell in love with shines through his eyes, tugging at my heart.

As we sit down to eat, he reaches across the table and takes my hand, his touch gentle and warm. His fingers wrap around mine. At that precise moment, I sense a delicate connection forming between us, but I remain doubtful. "I'm really trying, babe. I want us to work. For real this time."

I let myself believe him. We talk about anything but our problems. It feels easy. His laughter is genuine; for the tiniest, briefest second, we're just like we used to be. I sit there watching these fleeting glimpses of the man I once adored, and it stirs something inside me—something I thought I'd buried a long time ago.

Once Sara has fallen asleep, we sit on the porch, swinging, talking, wrapped in my favorite green blanket—the one that's always brought me comfort.

He draws me close and kisses my forehead, his warmth

seeping into my skin. It's a tender gesture that makes my heart ache. *Damn hormones.* I relax against him, feeling fragile—as if I'm holding my breath. Even if it is just for tonight, this feels right.

Green Flag #9.

"I love you, Callie," he whispers, his voice barely audible over the rustling leaves. "And I'm going to prove it to you."

Unable to speak, I nod, swallowing down the lump in my throat. Maybe there's hope for us after all. Maybe this pregnancy will be different.

The next week is a blur of packing and planning. We sort through our belongings, deciding what to take and what to leave behind. Each item packed feels like a step towards something new.

He has been extremely sweet to me since he approached me about the house in Burlington last week. The landlord agreed to let us move things in over the weekend since our official lease date is on a Monday this year, and the prior tenants have already moved out. I can't help but feel like it's too good to be true. But there is another part of me that just cannot shake the thought if I don't give him this last chance, I'm going to wonder what could have been.

As we load the last box into the truck, I take a look behind us at the house that built me. The good, the bad, and the downright ugly. I silently pray to a God I don't believe in that this time really will be different. I will be different. Stronger, more vigilant. For my children's sake, if not my own.

Thankfully, Mom has already let me know Sara, and I can come back if this doesn't work out. I can tell she's conflicted because she knows Adam hasn't been a great husband to me, but she also doesn't want to see me go through a divorce— Catholic guilt and all that.

Adam starts the engine, and we pull away, uncertain of the

road ahead. But for now, it's a chance for something new. A chance to escape the shadows of our past and find a little light.

As we drive toward our new home, I can't shake the feeling this move is just another one of Adam's desperate attempts to fix something already broken beyond repair. I try to put the thoughts out of my mind and hold on to the sliver of hope maybe this time will be different. Because if it isn't, I'm finally done playing this game.

We pull up to the new house just as the sun sets. It's a charming little place with a wraparound porch. Just like he always promised me, we would have. The kind of house that promises a perfect life. Too bad that's not what's waiting inside.

Adam exits the truck, stretching and grinning like he's just won the lottery. "What do you think, Callie? Isn't it great?"

It brings back memories of when Adam dropped hints about liking me in high school. We listened to music, and the song *Paint Me a Birmingham* by Tracy Lawrence came on the radio. I told Adam I hoped to have a house like the one described in the song one day. He promised me I would. It feels strange to reflect on the dreams we used to share.

I force a smile. "Yeah, it's something."

We unload the boxes, each one feeling like it's filled with more than just our belongings. By the time we're done, I'm exhausted in every way possible.

Adam heads to the shower, and I'm left to unpack in peace. I search for suitable spots to showcase Sara's baby pictures and contemplate reframing our wedding photo for the fireplace. Maybe this move could be a fresh start. But that hope feels fleeting.

four

SOMEBODY THAT I USED TO KNOW - GOTYE
FEAT. KIMBRA

OWEN - MARCH 21, 2013

I lie awake, pushing thoughts of the past aside. They haunt me like ghosts, leaving me to wonder if I'll ever break free from this endless cycle.

I remind myself I've come a long way since then. Yet, here I am, staring at the ceiling of my bedroom in my mostly empty apartment questioning everything that got me to this point. Why does it feel like I am as lost as ever? I sit up, rubbing my face, trying to shake off both the fragmented pieces of the dream and the memory of one of the hardest days of my life– the day I left Sabrina.

My body is drenched in sweat, and my heart's still pounding, the image of Dream Girl's eyes lingering in my mind. I glance at the clock on the nightstand: 6:15AM. It's too early to be up on a Saturday, but I am certain that I won't be able to fall back asleep. I swing my legs over the side of the bed and stand, stretching. The apartment is quiet, with only the faint hum of the refrigerator in the kitchen.

I walk to the bathroom and splash cold water on my face, hoping it will somehow wash away the heaviness clinging to me. When I look up at the reflection in the mirror, he's just as haunted as I feel—dark circles under my eyes, a weariness that no amount of sleep can fix.

With a sigh, I move to the kitchen to start the coffee maker. The familiar aroma of freshly ground beans fills the air, offering a small flicker of comfort, even if it's only a temporary distraction from the storm raging inside me.

As I wait my thoughts drift back to Barrett. He's the one constant in my life, the reason I push forward. His laughter, his innocence–it's all been worth it, for him. I think about how he looked at me yesterday, his eyes wide with excitement as he showed me the drawing he made at preschool. His joy is a beacon of light in my otherwise dark and complicated world.

I take a deep breath and let it out slowly, trying to center myself. The past haunts me, but I know I have to keep moving forward, for Barrett's sake and mine. The dreams, the guilt, the longing–they are all part of my journey, but they don't define me.

I pour myself a flavored cup of black coffee and take a sip, feeling the warmth spread through me. This particular blend was one I'd found at a grocery store here in Mount Vernon shortly after I moved into my place. I happened to grab it one morning from a display by the checkout line after forgetting to grab my usual Folgers Breakfast Blend from the shelf, not wanting to lose my spot in the line by going back through the store.

It turned out to be the best thing I could have done for my coffee taste because it was perfect. I haven't bought Folgers since. Thankfully, the new stuff was kept stocked in a Farmer's Market-style display at the grocery store.

I moved to Mount Vernon after a six-month stint at my

dad's place in Cedar Bluff. Things were tense with my stepmom, Bev, who was overbearing and kept giving unsolicited advice about my divorce and custody arrangement with Sabrina. Bev even insisted I should fight for full custody of Barrett, but I disagreed since I was working so much.

Around the time my divorce was finalized, I found out my mom needed a roommate after leaving her second husband. She had just gone into remission from breast cancer and was hoping to pay off her medical bills more quickly. Since killing my step-dad wasn't an option, I opted to be my Mom's roommate as a way to help her out instead.

Sabrina and I worked out a one week on, one week off arrangement for Barrett, and I agreed to handle pick-ups and drop-offs. My project in Iowa City was going to take at least a year, and Mount Vernon was closer. Mom worked part-time in Iowa City, so we commuted together, and the hospital had a great daycare for Barrett. The arrangement was perfect aside from the long drives to Cedar Bluff.

Mom and I lived together for over six months, but a smaller unit became available in our building, so she moved. I'm now riding out the last few months on the lease and will decide where to go when it's up in June. The landlord agreed to let me stay month-to-month until someone expresses interest in the apartment.

I walk to the living room, where the early morning light casts long shadows across the floor. The photos on the mantle catch my eye – pictures of Barrett at various stages of his young life, smiling and carefree. My goal is to be back in Cedar Bluff permanently around the time Barrett gets to kindergarten but I'm not sure if I will be able to because of work. I pick up one of the frames, tracing the outline of his face with my thumb. Setting the frame back down, I sip my coffee, trying to shake off the lingering unease from the dream.

Shortly after six in the morning, I grab my phone and see a text from Sabrina, probably about the weekend plans for Barrett. We've managed to keep things amicable for his sake, a small mercy I don't deserve in the aftermath of our split. I open the message.

SABRINA:
> Morning. Barrett wants to know if you can take him to the park later. We're free after 10 if that works for you.

A small smile tugs at my lips. Apparently, I wasn't the only early bird this morning. He'd probably been awake since before I was. I type back a quick response.

ME:
> Of course. I'll pick him up at 10:30. Tell him I'm looking forward to it.

SABRINA:
> Will do. Thanks, Owen.

Feeling a bit more grounded, I finish my coffee then head to the shower, letting the hot water wash away the remnants of the dream. I grab my keys, wallet, and phone, and head out the door for the drive to Cedar Bluff.

The drive to Sabrina's is familiar, the route etched into my memory after countless trips. The rolling countryside of Iowa passes by, the fields of corn and soybeans stretching out to the horizon. The drive helps me think and mentally prepare for the day. I pull into Sabrina's just before ten-thirty and park the car.

I reach to knock on the door just as it swings open, and I am greeted with my son's wide grin, his excitement palpable.

"Daddy!" he exclaims, throwing himself into my arms. I scoop him up and hug him tightly, feeling the weight of the world lift slightly with his embrace.

"Hey, buddy," I say, setting him down. "Ready for the park?"

He nods enthusiastically, and we head out. Sabrina waves from the doorway, a small smile on her face. We've made a lot of progress since our divorce, but we still have a long way to go in terms of a healthy co-parenting relationship. Her call to pick him up on a non-designated day feels like progress.

We spend the next few hours at the park, Barrett running around and playing while I keep a watchful eye. His laughter fills the air, a soothing balm for my restless mind. At lunchtime, we head to a local ice cream shop and share some lemon ice cream. His face lights up with every bite, and I can't help but smile at his joy.

Afterward, we stop by my dad's house. Dad opens the door, his eyes lighting up when he sees us.

"Papa Henry!" Barrett shouts, running to him.

My dad crouches down and scoops Barrett into a hug, lifting him off the ground. "Hey there, champ! I've missed you," he says, ruffling Barrett's hair.

Barrett giggles, wrapping his arms around Dad's neck. "I missed you too, Grandpa. Look, I brought my new toy car!"

Dad chuckles and sets Barrett down gently. "Well, let's go see how fast that car can go, shall we?"

We step inside, and I'm immediately struck by how different the house looks. It's the same house I grew up in, but Beverly's touch is everywhere—new furniture, fresh paint, and different photos on the walls. Among the photos on the wall are a picture of me and my stepbrother Luke at Dad and Beverly's wedding. We were more than a little drunk and had the orange slices from our beers covering our teeth to make huge smiles—it's one of my favorite pictures.

"Come on in, make yourselves at home," Henry says,

leading us into the living room. Beverly is in the kitchen, and she comes out to greet us, wiping her hands on a dishtowel.

"Hello, Owen. Hi there, Barrett!" she says warmly, bending down to give Barrett a hug. "I just baked some cookies. Would you like one?"

Barrett nods eagerly, and she laughs, ruffling his hair. "Let's get you a cookie, then."

We spend the afternoon there, talking and catching up. Dad and Barrett play with some toys in the living room while I watch, feeling a sense of peace I haven't felt in a long time. Dad gets down on the floor with Barrett despite having had a knee replacement not too long ago. They build a fort out of couch cushions and blankets. Barrett's giggles fill the room as they crawl inside and pretend it's a secret hideout.

I look around the living room, noticing some of the more recent changes Beverly has made. The house feels brighter, more eclectic, but it still holds echoes of my childhood.

Beverly and I sit at the dining table, sipping iced tea. "How have you been, Owen?" she asks, her eyes kind and concerned.

"I've been okay," I reply. "Work's been busy. I'm pretty close to the number of hours that I need to complete my apprenticeship so I'm looking forward to that. I'm still trying to figure out where I'll be living long-term. But things are good with Barrett, and that's what matters most."

She nods, understanding. "You're a good father, Owen. Barrett's lucky to have you."

As I thank her for her kind words, Dad emerges from the fort, laughing as Barrett pretends to be a superhero, saving the day. "He's got quite an imagination," he says, catching his breath.

"He sure does," I reply, watching my son destroy the fort from the inside out with dramatic "POW!" and "Boom boom!" chants.

As the hours pass, I start to feel the weight of the days' events catching up with me and know it's time to head home. I gather our things and we say goodbye to Dad and Beverly. Dad hugs me tightly, a silent understanding passing between us.

We leave Dad's house, and I drive back to Sabrina's to drop Barrett off. By the time I'm on the road back to Mount Vernon, it's close to 6 PM. The sky is starting to darken, the sun dipping low on the horizon, casting long shadows across the fields.

About fifteen minutes from home, my phone rings. It's Mom.

"Hey, Mom," I answer, keeping my eyes on the road and rolling up the windows in the truck so I can hear her better.

She hesitates. "Owen, can you call me back when you're not driving?" she asks, her voice tense.

"Mom, just tell me now," I say, feeling a knot of anxiety forming in my stomach.

She takes a deep breath. "Your Uncle Teddy just passed away, baby."

The words hit me like a punch to the gut. I swallow hard, trying to process the news.

"What happened?" I manage to choke out.

"He had a heart attack," she says softly. "It was sudden."

"Do you know if anyone has gotten ahold of Dad yet? I was just with him a little bit ago. I can try to call him," I offer.

"You don't have to do that, honey. Henry was already informed. Teddy's wife called him on their way to the hospital. Your dad and Beverly made it there pretty quickly since he lives so close. But Teddy had already passed, baby. I'm so sorry."

The grief comes in waves, overwhelming and suffocating. I grip the steering wheel tightly, trying to keep my emotions in check. "Thanks for letting me know, Mom. I'll call Dad to check on him when I get home."

"Be careful, honey. Are you close to home?" she asks.

"Yes, about ten minutes out. I'll be okay."

"I love you, O."

"I love you too, Mom."

I hang up and drive the rest of the way home in silence, the weight of the news settling heavy on my shoulders. The familiar streets of Mount Vernon blur past as I navigate through the small town, my mind reeling with memories of Uncle Teddy–his laugh, his advice, the way he always seemed larger than life. Now, he is gone, and the world instantly feels a little dimmer.

And I know the dreams are going to hurt even more now that he's gone. Because it won't just be the girl in them I miss every time I wake up. It will be Teddy too.

five
LOVE THE WAY YOU LIE - EMINEM FEAT. RIHANNA

CALLIE - APRIL 4, 2013

Before I found out I was pregnant with Sara, Adam was obsessed with trying to get me to bring women home. He'd constantly push for threesomes, saying things like "You like girls, anyway. It would be so hot." Typical. Just another guy trying to fetishize my sexuality. How original.

Red Flag #302.

I caved more than once, but only after numbing myself with alcohol to get through it. He took it a step further and asked if I would be interested in swinging and introduced me to a couple he'd found online. To add insult to injury, I didn't find either person remotely attractive. The moment I saw Adam with the woman, I felt sick. I kicked them out and locked myself in the bathroom, sobbing until I was so exhausted I fell asleep on the floor.

Red Flag #323.

The following day, he acted like nothing ever happened. He

stopped pushing the issue for a while and things went back to normal. *What the fuck was I still doing with him?*

Red Flag #326.

Not long after that night, I found out that I was pregnant with Sara, and I was ecstatic. But then I borrowed Adam's laptop and found Skype calls between him and a woman from one of the couples we knew. He claimed he was helping plan her fiance's bachelor party, which made no sense. Adam had never planned a party in his life, wasn't close to the groom, and was only in the wedding because of his friendship with the bride.

Maybe even a little too close.

Red Flag #400.

My rose-colored glasses were extra hazy, apparently. Becoming a mother was supposed to fulfill all my dreams. I had the house, the husband, and soon, the perfect little family with two-point-five kids and a dog. Isn't that the dream I was chasing?

When we moved back to Iowa from Seattle, Adam told me he wanted to have an open marriage. I told him I wanted a divorce or, at the very least, a trial separation. The expectation during the separation was for us to keep things quiet until we figured out what we wanted. I was so embarrassed at the idea of my family finding out.

As a result... he started looking for hookups on Craigslist.

Red Flag #704.

This wasn't the first time I'd seen this side of him. And apparently, won't be the last.

It's been three days since we moved in, and the new house is slowly starting to feel like home. Sara's giggles echo through the rooms, and even Adam has been more helpful than usual. There's a cautious sense of optimism in the air, but it feels fragile, like it could shatter at any moment.

Then I see it—Adam's phone, left carelessly on the kitchen counter, lighting up with a new notification. My heart sinks. He never leaves his phone unattended. It's practically daring me to pick it up.

I know it's wrong, an invasion of privacy. But after all the times he's broken my trust, the resentment burns hotter than the guilt. Screw it. My hands tremble as I grab the phone and check the notification.

There it is–FlameFinder, a dating app, bold and blatant on his screen.

Red Flag #751.

My heart sinks, but anger surges even faster. Really, Adam? Not even a week into our new home, and you're already looking for your next fling?

I stand there, frozen in disbelief. Maybe I'm overreacting. Maybe he just hasn't deleted the app since we moved in. I knew he had it during our trial separation, but now? Now, when we're supposed to be rebuilding? I don't know his password, so I can't check the details. All I see is that flame icon, a symbol that now haunts me. I have no proof he's using it, but the doubt gnaws at me, eating away at whatever hope I have left.

I take a deep breath, trying to calm the storm inside me. Logic tells me to confront him, but fear and frustration hold me back. Instead, I download the app on my phone and create a profile. I upload a recent selfie and add a headline:

I'm just waiting to see how long it takes for my husband to figure out he's been caught.

Subtlety has never been my strong suit.

Throughout the day, Adam is his usual self, even sweeter than normal. He makes breakfast for Sara and me, and for a brief moment, it almost feels like we're a happy family again. But the sight of his phone sitting on the counter nags at me, a relentless reminder that things are far from perfect.

Later that evening, while Adam is in the shower, his phone lights up again with another notification from FlameFinder. My patience is wearing thin—I can't keep pretending nothing's wrong.

I head into the bathroom, determined to confront him, but as soon as I open the door, I'm met with the unmistakable sound of his fist slapping against his own wet skin. His back is to me, but it's obvious what he's doing, even through the steam clinging to the glass shower door.

The pit in my stomach deepens, but this time, it's not just disappointment–it's rage.

You'd think I'd want to join him, maybe take care of him. Nope. I'll see myself out. I don't need to see anything more than that. No, thank you. It hits me in that moment just how much I'm no longer attracted to my husband—in any way.

The next morning, Adam is up early, heading out to do who-knows-what, leaving me alone with my thoughts. I spend the day unpacking, but the weight of his potential betrayal hangs over me like a dark cloud. Every time I hear his phone beep, my stomach tightens into knots.

Days blur together, each one indistinguishable from the last. Adam continues to play the role of a devoted husband, but the cracks are starting to show. Then, out of nowhere, he asks if I'll go with him to a funeral visitation. Apparently, his high school friend's dad passed away. We went to high school with the same crowd, but I don't recall anyone losing a parent recently.

Turns out, it's Janelle's dad—Janelle, the girl he dated all through high school. The girl he broke up with just before he and I started dating the first time.

"Adam," I say cautiously, the unease clear in my voice. "I don't think Jess would be comfortable with me going. If you want to attend, I won't stop you, but it feels inappropriate for me to tag along."

I never really knew Janelle VanPelt. She was homeschooled, and our paths never crossed. Still, I remember their breakup wasn't exactly amicable, and she definitely didn't appreciate finding out that Adam and I got together soon after.

"I already talked to her about it," he says casually. I wasn't aware they still spoke, and the thought unsettles me. "She said it would be okay. I think she would actually appreciate it if you came with me."

A knot forms in my stomach, but despite my reservations, I reluctantly agree to go.

A few days later, we attend the visitation. It's awkward—funeral visitations always are, especially when you didn't know the deceased. I hang back, trying to offer Adam whatever support he needs. He holds my hand as we go through the line, and Janelle isn't outwardly rude, though the tension between us is palpable. Of course, she has other things on her mind, but the undercurrent is undeniable.

Ten days after we moved in, I saw the messages. Explicit. Intimate. Unmistakable. He hasn't just been talking platonically with Janelle—they've been having an affair. And it's been going on since before we moved back to Iowa. She's been right here, in Burlington, this whole time.

He moved our family to Burlington at the recommendation of VanPelt Realty. As in Janelle fucking VanPelt. How I didn't make that connection when I saw the listing just further solidifies how blind I was to all the shit Adam was pulling behind my back.

That night, when he got home, I didn't hold back. "Care to explain these?" I asked, my voice calm in a way that scared even me. The laptop sat next to me, the messages pulled up from his Skype account, synced across all his devices. I watched his face drain of color as he saw the undeniable proof of his betrayal. You would think that considering I've caught him using this account for things like this before, he would have changed his methods. He obviously didn't care enough to try and hide it more.

He stammered, "It's not what it looks like, I swear. Those are old messages from when you and I were separated."

A bitter laugh escaped my throat. "Don't insult my intelligence, Adam. I've seen the dates on these messages. They're recent. Some of them are from after I went with you to her dad's funeral visitation. I won't even start on how fucked up it is that you're screwing around with someone who just lost her father. But the bottom line is—you're still cheating on me."

Why am I even defending Janelle? She knew he was married, she's just as guilty in this mess. This has all been going on since long before her dad died. But I can't unpack that right now—there's too much rage boiling inside me.

Adam stepped closer, reaching out as if his touch could somehow fix the damage. "Baby, please. Let me explain. I love you. I'm trying to make things right." The words hung in the air, empty and meaningless. He was still trying to play the part of the devoted husband, but I wasn't falling for it anymore. Not after everything.

I step back, shaking my head. "You've had plenty of chances to make things right. I'm done. This was your last chance, and you blew it."

His face hardens, the desperation shifting into anger. "You're overreacting. We just moved here. We're supposed to be starting fresh. Why are you doing this?"

"Because I deserve better. Sara and I deserve better. I won't let you keep hurting us."

He scoffs, trying to brush it off. "You're overreacting. We're just catching up."

"Catching up? Really? Because it looks a lot more like catching feelings."

He denies it, of course. Gaslights me, like he always does. But this time, I'm not backing down. "Since when does catching up include seeing what her fucking tits look like these days?"

He storms out, slamming the door behind him, leaving me seething in the wreckage of my anger and frustration. I grab my phone and call Brooke, telling her everything. She's furious, livid on my behalf, and she promises to do some digging of her own.

Adam doesn't come home that night. Which is probably for the best because I really don't want to have this baby in prison.

The next morning, Brooke calls me, her voice tight with disbelief. "Callie, I'm on my way to an appointment, and guess whose truck is parked outside the VanPelt house? Adam's. He's there right now. At her mom's."

That's all it takes. I pack our things, my emotions swinging wildly between heartbreak and pure rage. And then I do what any rational woman in my position would do—I drive straight to Janelle's family home, heart pounding with fury and resolve.

He must have gone to her parent's house in Hawkridge to hide out last night. Why he would go to her parent's house rather than the house she owns in Burlington is beyond me.

When I pull up, Adam's obnoxiously huge F-350 is sitting there in the driveway, as if it's mocking me, as if everything I feared has been right in front of me all along. I walk up and knock on the door, my hands trembling with adrenaline.

Janelle opens the door, and her stupid big, pretty eyes widen in surprise. "Callie? What are you doing here?"

For a moment, I can't even speak. I just point to Adam's "I have a small dick so I drive a huge truck to overcompensate" monstrosity still parked in the driveway.

Red Flag # I don't even fucking know anymore.

God, why is she so fucking pretty? It's almost unbearable. She looks like a Disney villain—Vanessa from The Little Mermaid, the human version of Ursula. Or worse, like Janelle Rabbit with jet-black hair. Hell, she's probably named after that damn cartoon.

Why can't she be as ugly on the outside as I now know she is on the inside? If there's a God, he's got a seriously twisted sense of humor. It's no wonder Adam's so drawn to her. And honestly, if things were different, she's probably exactly the type of girl I'd go for.

Mother fucking fuck. Get your shit together, Callie!

"I'm here to see my husband. I'll be in my car," is all I manage to get out, my voice sharp, controlled, but seething beneath the surface. This fucking succubus is so infuriatingly beautiful it makes me want to scream. And I can guaran-fuck-ing-tee Adam slept in her bed last night, not mine.

After what feels like an eternity, Adam finally slinks out of the house, looking as guilty as sin. He walks up to the car, panic flashing in his eyes. "Callie, it's not what you think—"

"Oh, it's exactly what I think," I snap, the rage bubbling

over. "I warned you, Adam. We are done. You can keep your lies, your fancy new house that she picked out for you, and your fucking girlfriend. I'm taking Sara and going to my mom's. Don't you dare try to stop me."

I drive in silence, Sara asleep in the backseat, a determination rising inside me like a fire that won't be snuffed out. This is the beginning of a new chapter—for me, for Sara, for our future. One where Adam's deceit no longer has a place. One where I am in control, not his lies.

When we arrive at my mom's house, she opens the door and embraces us with warmth and love. "I knew this was coming, sweetheart. I'm so proud of you for standing up for yourself."

"A heads up would have been nice then, Mom. I don't need an 'I could have told you that,' right now."

"Honey, do you have any idea how stubborn you truly are? If I had told you that I thought it was a bad idea for you and Adam to get a new place together, you would have done it just to spite me."

Okay, she's not wrong.

"You're strong, Callie. You'll get through this," she continues. "But you had to get there on your own. You had to make this decision by yourself. No one could make this choice for you, my sweet girl."

I nod in understanding, tears streaming down my face. "Thank you, Mom. I'm just... so tired."

She hugs me tighter, her voice soft and comforting. "I know, honey. I know. Wayne and I are here for you. Every step of the way."

I take a deep breath, feeling a glimmer of peace. This is the start of a new journey. It's not the new journey I thought I was starting ten days ago. But it's one where I'll find my own strength and build a better future for myself and my children.

As I settle into my old room at my mom's house, a wave of relief washes over me. Despite the circumstances, I feel grateful that I at least got what I wanted by temporarily moving with Adam to the new house. Now, I can stay here at my mom's with Sara and not have to worry about seeing him. It's a small comfort in the midst of this chaos, but I'll take it. My mom and Wayne are a steady presence, offering support and understanding without judgment. It's a stark contrast to the tumultuous relationship I had with Adam, and I find solace in the familiar surroundings of my childhood home.

six

DO YOU REALIZE - THE FLAMING LIPS

OWEN - APRIL 14, 2013

The day of Teddy's funeral feels like another punch to the gut, one I've been dreading since the moment Mom called to tell me he was gone. We put off the funeral as long as we could, not just to get the logistics in order, but to give ourselves time to breathe. But there's no time long enough to prepare for this. My uncle, the man who was like a second father to me, is gone. And now I'm standing outside this church, feeling like a fraud, about to walk in and say goodbye to someone I can't imagine living without.

I lean against the cool stone of the church, trying to steady my breathing. I've never been a religious person, and Teddy wasn't either, not really. But this was his request—a simple service at a place he rarely stepped foot in. The irony isn't lost on me. I glance at the sky. At least the weather is decent, which feels like a small mercy. Midwest springs are unpredictable at best, but today the sun is shining, a calm backdrop to the storm raging inside me.

People filter into the church, familiar faces I can't quite focus on. I catch a glimpse of Debra standing near the entrance, her face tight with barely-concealed frustration. She's been on edge since Serena showed up. Debra hasn't said a word, but the tension between them is palpable. I can feel it from across the parking lot.

Serena—my aunt, Teddy's ex-wife—has every right to be here. She and Teddy may have divorced years ago, but they shared a life and two children. She's part of this, whether Debra likes it or not. But Debra's hurt, and I get that too. Teddy found a second chance at happiness with her, and now it feels like Serena's presence is muddying those waters. It's complicated, like everything in this family.

I quit the tranquilizers a few weeks ago, not long after Teddy passed, thinking I needed to feel something, anything, even if it hurt. But now, standing here, I'm starting to regret it. Every emotion is raw and sharp, threatening to pull me under. My heart is pounding, my hands clammy as I shove them into my pockets. My throat feels tight, like there's not enough air in the world to fill my lungs. It feels like I'm drowning, like the weight of everything is pressing down on my chest.

I take a deep breath, trying to focus. Five things I can see. Four things I can touch. But all I can feel is the crushing weight of this day, the panic lurking just beneath the surface. I can't fall apart. Not here. Not now.

Across the parking lot, I see Dad with Beverly. He's comforting her, even though he's the one who should be getting support. Dad and Teddy were brothers-in-law for thirty years, and here Beverly is, soaking up all the sympathy like she's the only one who's lost something. I bite back the bitterness, knowing it won't help. Grief makes people act in strange ways. I can't blame her for falling apart, even if it annoys me. Everyone handles loss differently, right?

Inside the church, everything feels too close, too stifling. The scent of lilies is overpowering, clinging to the air along with the faint aroma of incense. It's strange to be here in this church, listening to the priest drone on about a man who rarely set foot in a place like this. Teddy wasn't religious—he was more comfortable out on the farm, surrounded by animals, or cracking open a beer at family barbecues. But this is what he wanted, and so here we are.

Teddy's urn sits at the front, a simple thing. No coffin, no heavy rituals. Just an urn, and a priest reciting verses that feel disconnected from the man I knew. The real goodbye will come later, when we scatter his ashes at the farm—his true resting place. This service feels like a formality, something we're doing for the sake of tradition, even though none of us truly belong here.

The slideshow starts, images of Teddy flickering on the screen—moments frozen in time. Teddy laughing at the lake, Teddy holding a newborn puppy at the vet clinic, Teddy with a beer in his hand, smiling like the world hadn't thrown him any curveballs. Each picture is a punch to the gut, a reminder of everything we've lost. The knot in my chest tightens, and I find myself blinking back tears I promised I wouldn't shed.

I glance over at Vince and Malcolm. They're sitting a few rows ahead, stiff and silent, their faces unreadable. This is harder for them than anyone. They've lost their dad. No matter how close I was to Teddy, I can't touch the depth of what they're feeling. I want to be there for them, to help hold them up, but I'm barely keeping myself together. The grief is too thick, too overwhelming.

The priest is still talking, and I can't focus. His voice fades into the background as I lose myself in memories of Teddy— his rough laugh, the way he'd ruffle my hair and tell me everything would be alright, even when it wasn't. He was always there when Dad wasn't, filling in the gaps, making me feel like I mattered. Now, there's just this empty space, and I don't know how to fill it.

I feel a tear slip down my cheek, and I wipe it away quickly, hoping no one noticed. The pressure in my chest builds, the familiar grip of panic wrapping itself around my lungs. I try to breathe through it—in for four, hold for four, out for four—but it's not working. The walls are closing in, and the urge to run is overwhelming. But I can't. Not yet.

In the basement of the church, the reception is as awkward as I expected. The air is thick with the smell of casseroles and cheap coffee, and people mill about, talking in hushed tones like they don't know what else to say. The slideshow from the service continues to flicker across the screen, images of Teddy cycling in and out of view, a never-ending loop of his life. It feels surreal, like we're all just going through the motions.

I spot Vince at the back of the room, standing alone, staring at a picture of him and Teddy from years ago. He's holding his newborn daughter, the look of pride unmistakable on his face. His jaw is tight, his eyes red-rimmed but dry. "Doesn't feel real, does it?" he mutters as I walk up, his voice rough from holding it all in.

"No," I manage, my throat tight. "It doesn't."

Malcolm joins us, a beer clutched in his hand that he hasn't even touched. "This sucks," he mutters flatly, staring at the floor. "Feels like we're all pretending to be okay, but none of us are."

I nod, the words catching in my throat. Everything about this day feels wrong. The bright lights of the reception hall, the muted chatter, the smell of casseroles—it all feels out of place, like it belongs to someone else's grief, not ours.

Across the room, Dad is talking to someone, his face composed but strained. Beverly is still flitting around like she's trying to fix things, as if organizing a buffet can somehow make this better. And then there's Debra, sitting alone, staring into the distance. Her grief is like a raw wound, and it's impossible not to feel it radiating through the room. Even though I don't agree with her anger over Serena being here, I understand it. She loved Teddy, and now he's gone. There's no right way to grieve that kind of loss.

The slideshow shifts again, another photo of Teddy grinning at some long-ago family picnic. My chest tightens, and for a moment, I feel the panic creeping in again, threatening to take over. But I focus on the sounds around me—Malcolm's quiet muttering, the clink of dishes, the low hum of conversation. It doesn't take away the pain, but it's enough to pull me back from the edge.

Vince shifts beside me, his eyes still on the screen. "We'll scatter his ashes next week," he says quietly. "At the farm. That'll be the real goodbye."

I nod, knowing that's when it will hit me for real. This... this is just the prelude. The real mourning comes later, when we say our final farewell.

seven

THE HOUSE THAT BUILT ME - MIRANDA LAMBERT

CALLIE - APRIL 14, 2013

When I wake to the distant rumble of the Amtrak train passing outside the window on Sunday, a wave of nostalgia washes over me. That sound used to lull me back to sleep as a child, but now it stirs something deeper—memories of simpler times, when life felt more secure. The early morning light seeps through the curtains, casting a soft, comforting glow across the room. As the train fades into the distance, I hear the familiar sounds of Mom bustling in the kitchen and Sara's laughter echoing from the living room. It grounds me in the present, even as the weight of everything that's changed presses down on me.

I get dressed and head to the kitchen, where the smell of freshly brewed coffee greets me. It's a welcome shift from the West Coast, where I used to have Brooke ship me coffee just to get through the day.

Mom is at the stove, humming softly as she cooks breakfast. It's strange to see her like this—relaxed, taking her time in the kitchen. When I was growing up, she was always in a rush, and breakfast was a quick bowl of cereal before I darted out the door to catch the bus. Seeing her now, so at ease, is a stark reminder of how much time has passed.

I've always wondered if Mom's reluctance to cook stems from her own childhood in this house. Her mother—my grandmother—died here in the kitchen when Mom was just thirteen, baking an apple pie on Christmas morning. I suppose that's why cooking felt more like a burden to her than anything else when I was younger. She was thrust into the role of preparing meals for herself, Grandpa, and whichever of her twelve siblings still lived at home after Grandma passed.

"Morning, sweetheart," Mom says with a warm smile, flipping pancakes at the stove. "Did you sleep well?"

"Better than I have in a while," I reply, pouring myself a cup of coffee. I lean against the counter, savoring the moment. "Sara seems happy to be here."

"She loves it. And she loves having her Grammy doting on her," Mom says with a chuckle. "We're glad to have you both here."

I nod, a wave of gratitude swelling inside me. "Thanks, Mom. I don't know what I'd do without you."

Mom waves her hand dismissively, her eyes soft. "You'd do just fine, Callie. You're stronger than you think."

It's been a week since I moved back in with Mom, and I'm praying I can find an apartment before the end of April, so I don't overstay my welcome. I know she means it when she says I'm always welcome here, but I can only take so much before her well-meaning comments about how I don't really need to eat for two start gnawing at me. But finding a place means finding a job first, and I know that's the next hurdle.

For now, though, I take a sip of my coffee, letting the

warmth of the moment settle inside me. I'll figure out the rest—just not today.

Later that morning, just as I'm getting lost in Virgin River by Robyn Carr, a knock on the door interrupts my escape. I shuffle to open it and find Brooke standing there with a tray of her famous cinnamon rolls, looking like she just stepped out of a Pinterest board.

"Good morning! I thought I'd bring some treats from the shop," Brooke chirps, her grin wide enough to rival the Cheshire Cat's as she breezes past me into the house.

"You're a lifesaver! Just don't tell my mom I'm having a second breakfast. She doesn't believe in the whole 'eating for two' thing," I say, grabbing the tray and inhaling the sweet, cinnamon goodness like it's the answer to all my problems. "Come in, let's catch up."

We settle at the kitchen table, the smell of coffee mixing with the scent of cinnamon rolls, making the kitchen feel cozier than it has in years. Sara's playing nearby, occasionally running over to show us a toy, her enthusiasm infectious as always.

Brooke takes a sip of her coffee, eyeing me over the rim of her mug. "So, how are you holding up?" she asks, her voice cutting through the small talk.

"It's been tough," I admit, tearing off a piece of cinnamon roll and savoring the sticky sweetness. "But being here helps. With family and all. I'm just glad I'm not still in Seattle."

Brooke nods, sympathy softening her features. "I'm glad to hear that. But listen, I've been meaning to ask you something. The coffee shop's been crazy busy, and I could really use some help. I thought... maybe this could be good timing for you too?"

I nearly choke on my coffee. A job. An actual job. My way out of my childhood bedroom and a chance at real independence. The idea is thrilling and terrifying all at once. On one hand, I desperately need the money and something to do other than stare at my mom's Americana decor, wondering if it was always this ugly. But on the other hand, I haven't worked in ages, and the thought of messing up someone's triple-shot, half-caf, no-foam, extra-hot latte with oat milk makes my stomach turn.

"I'd love to, but are you sure?" I ask. "I don't want to disappoint you or, you know, cause a caffeine riot. You've seen me operate a blender, right?"

Brooke waves me off. "Callie, you're more than capable. And honestly, it'll be good for you to have something else to focus on besides... everything. Plus, we can laugh about it when you inevitably mess up and someone storms out in a huff. I'll even throw in extra cinnamon rolls as peace offerings."

Before I can respond, Mom enters the kitchen, her eyes immediately narrowing at the sight of the cinnamon rolls before landing on us.

"What are you two up to? Not planning to break out my window screen and run off to see boys at the rock quarry, I hope," she jokes with a wink.

"Brooke offered me a job at the coffee shop," I explain, quickly wiping icing off my mouth, silently hoping Mom won't mention the extra weight I've put on.

"That's wonderful, sweetheart! Something to get your mind off things. And I've seen how busy that shop gets," she says with a tone that's half-supportive, half-condescending. "You'll definitely get your steps in. The exercise will be good for you and the baby."

I take a deep breath, biting back any snarky retort. My mom means well, after all. Her support, while sometimes backhanded, is still a relief. I turn back to Brooke with a smile. "Alright, Boss Lady. When do you want me to start?"

Brooke beams, excitement lighting up her face. "How

about tomorrow morning? You can just come in for a couple of hours, and I'll show you the ropes. And don't worry, we'll keep the blender far away from you. No blended coffees until you've been there at least a month."

I glance at Mom, silently asking if she can watch Sara. She nods, already heading back to her crossword puzzle, clearly satisfied.

"Guess that means I'll be there!" I say, feeling a mix of nerves and anticipation bubbling up. Maybe this is exactly what I need–a new start, a new routine, and Brooke's fresh cinnamon rolls every day.

eight

DOG DAYS ARE OVER - FLORENCE + THE MACHINE

OWEN - MAY 17, 2013

The final day of my Steamfitters apprenticeship arrives, not with ease, but with a tension that buzzes beneath my pride. The last two months have been a whirlwind—late nights, grueling hours, every task piling up on the weight of the one before it—all leading to this moment: the day I become a Journeyman.

I stand on the job site, hands rough and calloused, marked by years of labor. The sun beats down relentlessly, casting long shadows over the construction site. Around me, my coworkers are busy putting the finishing touches on the new cancer center for the children's hospital in Iowa City. The building, a gleaming mix of steel and glass, reflects the sun's glare like a beacon. It's beautiful, yes, but there's something else—something raw about knowing what this structure represents and the lives it could change.

As I tighten the last bolts on the high-pressure steam line, a knot tightens in my chest, winding tighter with each turn of the wrench. This shift marks the completion of my eighty-five-hundred hours for the Steamfitters Local. I've poured five years of sweat and grit into this apprenticeship, but the gravity of this moment? It feels too big to grasp. Over four years of relentless working hours, testing my limits both on the job and in the classroom since I first applied back in 2008. Now, standing here, the weight of it all hits like a punch.

The past two months have pushed me harder than I ever imagined. Endurance. Skill. I've been navigating the labyrinth of this cancer center job—blueprints, welding, pipe fitting—everything a test of my mettle. I learned from seasoned journeymen, soaked in their knowledge like my survival depended on it. My best friend Will convinced me to start this journey five years ago, stood by my side through it all, showing me the ropes, pushing me to be better, faster, sharper.

And now it's finally paying off. Literally. When I clock in on Monday, I'll be walking in as a Journeyman pipefitter—five dollars an hour richer, but that's not what's making my heart race. It's the finality, the pressure, the realization that after all these years, all the sweat and stress, I'm stepping into something bigger. Something I can't afford to fail at.

"Congratulations, Owen," my supervisor Tim says, clapping me on the back. His hand is heavy, solid, like everything about him—burly, thick beard, gruff voice that commands respect. "You've earned this."

I nod, swallowing the mix of pride and relief swelling in my chest. This is it—the moment I've been working toward for years. With my journeyman's card, I'll have more responsibility, more opportunities, and most importantly, I'll be able to provide a better life for Barrett. Everything I've pushed myself through has been for him.

But as I pack up my tools, ready to leave the job site behind, a strange hollowness settles over me. There's a sense of accomplishment, sure, but it feels incomplete. Despite the long hours, the sweat, and the physical exhaustion, she's still there—the woman with dark hair and piercing green eyes. She's been haunting my thoughts, visiting me every night in my dreams. No matter how hard I try to shake her off, she lingers in the back of my mind, an ache that won't fade.

I push the thought away as I head home to clean up. Tonight's supposed to be about celebrating, about forgetting everything for a while. Will and I made plans with my stepbrother, Luke, and they've both promised me free drinks in honor of my journeyman status. It's the perfect excuse for a low-key night with the guys—something I've been looking forward to for weeks.

Even as I think about the drinks and the laughter, that sense of something missing gnaws at me. It's been there for a while, growing louder with each passing day. And no matter how much I try to drown it out, I can't shake the feeling that this is just the start of a much bigger battle. One that has nothing to do with pipefitting.

As I walk toward the Black 'N Gold Bar & Grille, the sounds of laughter and music grow louder, pulling me out of the quiet weight of my thoughts. It's a stark contrast to the suffocating silence of my apartment—when Barrett isn't there, at least. Up ahead, Luke and Will are already waiting, leaning against the brick wall like they've been up to no good. Luke, with his shaggy blond hair and those mischievous gray eyes, looks particularly pleased with himself.

I raise an eyebrow, suspicion creeping in. "What's going on?" I ask as I approach.

"We're just here to celebrate, buddy," Will says, clapping me on the back, his voice full of reassurance. He's tall, broad-shouldered, always the steady one.

"Yeah, we figured a few drinks would be a good start," Luke adds, his grin widening into something more dangerous.

I nod, a half-smile tugging at my lips. "Sounds good to me." But in the back of my mind, I'm bracing myself. Knowing these two, there's no way this night ends without some kind of chaos. If they've hired a stripper for my turnout day, I swear I'm gonna kill them both.

We push through the door, and the noise hits me like a wave. The dimly lit bar is packed, the smell of alcohol thick in the air, the hum of rowdy conversation filling the space. It's the kind of place where the energy is electric, where people come to forget, to let loose. The jukebox in the corner is blasting some classic rock, the bass heavy and relentless. My eyes catch on a sign above it, glowing under the backlight:

DO NOT play Creed on this jukebox. Your song will be skipped. NO REFUNDS! I fucking hate Creed.

- Hunter Holloway, Owner

We will also skip Nickelback, Hoobastank, Matchbox 20, Hinder, Buck Cherry, Def Leppard, the song "Wagon Wheel" or any other overplayed terrible music.

Thank you for your understanding and remember, no Creed.

- Mandee Holloway, Owner's Wife

The note on the jukebox makes me laugh—who doesn't hate Creed?—but it reminds me how much I've missed the little things, like hearing "Wagon Wheel" on repeat. Barrett's been obsessed with that song and the thought of seeing him tomorrow tugs at my chest. The past few months have been brutal, not just because of work but because of all the time I've missed with him. Now, I finally have a whole week with just the two of us, and I'm counting down the hours.

I smirk at the sign, but a gnawing feeling stays at the edge of my mind. The loud, carefree atmosphere should distract me, but instead, it amplifies the unease lurking in the back of my head. I feel it tightening, that unresolved tension pulling at me. Luke and Will joke around, already talking about shots, but my mind drifts back to the woman with green eyes.

Her image feels too close, too real, even now.

"Come on, man, you're too quiet tonight!" Luke nudges me, pulling me back to the present. "This is a night to celebrate, not stand there like you're about to bury a body."

I laugh, forcing myself to join in, but that nagging feeling won't let go. Something's off.

I push thoughts of her aside for now and follow Luke and Will toward the back patio. The bar's warm and familiar, walls covered in old photographs and sports memorabilia—mostly for the Hawkeyes, of course. Comfortable booths line the edges, and high-top tables fill the center. The bar itself gleams, polished wood and rows of craft beers on tap. It should feel like a place to relax, but there's this underlying tension in me, something pulling at the edges of my thoughts.

As we approach the patio doors, I start to notice familiar faces. People from my apprenticeship class, coworkers from the hospital job, and then, to my surprise, family—Dad, Beverly, even Mom. My heart skips a beat when I spot Sabrina and Barrett. They're here. They're really here.

My heart swells with gratitude and something else—something I can't quite name. I had no idea they were planning this. But if Barrett's here, I silently pray Luke and Will didn't get any ideas about strippers.

"Surprise!" The shout hits me as soon as we reach the table. The room explodes with cheers and applause, and I'm caught off guard, grinning despite myself. The feeling is overwhelming—like the ground underneath me is shifting in the best way possible.

Sabrina comes up with Barrett by her side. Her auburn hair falls softly over her shoulders, and her kind smile—the one I fell for years ago—still lights up her face. "Owen, we just wanted to show our support. We can't stay long, but Barrett's really proud of you. So am I. I know how hard you've worked for this."

I crouch down and scoop Barrett into a hug. "Thanks for coming, buddy. It means everything to me that you're here."

Barrett's eyes shine up at me, big and brown, full of that innocent admiration only kids have. "Mommy says you're a real big deal now, Daddy. And I'm supposed to say, 'Comgratuwations.'"

"Thanks, kiddo," I say, laughing as I ruffle his hair. We do our secret handshake, but before I know it, he's bolting toward my mom, calling for Nana like he always does. The joy in his voice echoes through me, grounding me, but at the same time, the tension in my chest tightens.

I stand up, watching him disappear into my mom's arms, and a strange feeling washes over me. Gratitude, pride… but also something darker, something lurking in the corners of my mind that I can't quite shake. Even with everyone here, celebrating my success, there's still a part of me that feels… unsettled.

Sabrina smiles warmly. "You've earned this, Owen. Enjoy

your night. I'll stick around for a bit, but just so you know, Barrett is spending the night at your mom's. That way you won't have to drive all the way back to Cedar Bluff in the morning."

I nod, feeling an unexpected swell of emotion. "You can stay as long as you want, Sab. I appreciate you being here. And for everything while I finished out the apprenticeship—changing schedules, being flexible... I can't even begin to tell you how grateful I am. And thank you for letting Barrett stay with Mom tonight. I know you didn't have to."

She smiles again, but there's something else in her expression, something hesitant, as if she's weighing her next words carefully. "I'll always be here for you, Owen. You know that. And after everything your mom's been through, I'll never stand in the way of her spending time with Barrett."

We share a friendly hug, but as she pulls back, she lowers her voice to a whisper so soft I have to strain to hear her in the noise of the crowded bar. "I'll have to leave soon, though. I have a date with Alex tonight," she says, her smile beaming.

Her words hit me harder than I expect. I'm genuinely happy for her—Sabrina deserves to find someone who makes her smile like that. But there's also a sharp twist of something else, something I wasn't prepared for. A kind of wistful nostalgia as I realize that the giddy side of her, the one I used to bring out, is now shining for someone else. "I'm glad you've found someone, Sab. I really hope he treats you well."

She nods, relief flooding her features. "Thanks, Owen. It means a lot, hearing that from you. Alex is going to be great with Barrett too. I've been thinking... maybe I could introduce him to Barrett soon? But I wanted to run it by you first. Maybe you should meet him before that happens?"

Her words settle uncomfortably, a reminder that things are moving forward, that the parts of our lives that used to overlap are separating more and more. I push past the unease and nod. "Yeah, I'd like that. I'd like to meet him first."

Sabrina smiles a mix of gratitude and understanding in her eyes. And while I know this is the right thing, a part of me can't quite shake the strange sense of loss creeping in, like I'm watching a door slowly close on a chapter I wasn't fully ready to end.

But it has ended.

So, I fake it.

"Actually, you know what? If you think he'll be great with Barrett, I trust your judgment. After all, your track record with men shows you have impeccable taste." I let out a laugh. "Well, except for that Owen guy. Yeesh! What a tool. Although, he was pretty hot."

Sabrina shakes her head, laughing despite herself. "Modesty was never your strong suit, Owen. Good to see some things haven't changed."

I give an exaggerated stage bow. "Why, thank you. I aim to please."

"You're impossible," she says, still fighting off laughter. "No wonder there's a line of suitors out the door for you tonight."

I roll my eyes and look toward the door in mock astonishment and let out a gasp as if I'm appalled.. "Listen, I got married once and it turns out, I wasn't very good at it. I don't see that ever happening again. I have Barrett, and I work all the time. Marriage just isn't in the cards for me again. You have at it though. Now that you got that Practice Marriage out of the way, you should be good to go for the next round."

She slaps me on the shoulder, laughing. "I'm not talking about either of us getting married again, Owen. I'm just saying... your charm is... an acquired taste. There might actually be someone out there who can keep you around. And put up with your bullshit."

Her words land harder than I think she means them to, a quick sting that I try to shake off. Sabrina's always been blunt—one of the things I've always loved about her—but sometimes, the truth hits a little too close to home. Still, I force a grin. This is a good night, and I'm not about to let a moment of honesty derail that.

Just then, the patio doors swing open, and the bartender steps out with a tray of shots. As she passes, I quickly grab two—one for me and one for Sabrina—silently thanking whoever decided to buy this round. I hand her the glass with a smirk.

"Only one shot," I remind her, "and you're staying long enough for it to clear your system before you head out. Besides, maybe it'll take the edge off before that hot date tonight."

We laugh, clinking our glasses together before downing the shots. The whiskey burns as it slides down my throat, and as the familiar sting hits, I realize it's the same whiskey I had way too much of on our wedding night. Talk about full circle.

"Here's hoping this night ends better than the last time I had too much of this stuff," I say, wiggling my eyebrows at her.

Her cheeks flush pink, and she punches me lightly in the arm. "Shut up," she says, her tone playful but warning. She's never been a fan of my humor when it teeters on the edge of crude, but I can't help but laugh at her reaction.

In this moment, the weight of everything—our shared past, the path we've taken to get here—seems to hang between us. But instead of it feeling heavy, it feels... lighter. Like we're both finally on the other side of something we never thought we'd get through.

It's then that I notice the bartender standing across the room, still working but clearly keeping an eye on me. She's pretty, around my age, with curly blond hair that frames her bright blue eyes. She's wearing an Iowa Hawkeye jersey, tied up just enough to show a hint of skin above her low-slung jean shorts. She's not my usual type—I tend to lean more toward curvier women—but there's no denying she's beautiful. I grab my beer from the table, raising the bottle in a silent "cheers" with a wink in her direction.

Sabrina catches the exchange, and as we part ways, she mutters something that sounds an awful lot like "shameless flirt" under her breath. I chuckle, shaking my head as she heads out. The rest of the night is spent surrounded by friends and family, celebrating this milestone in my life. As I look around at the smiling faces, hear the laughter and clinking of glasses, I feel a deep sense of gratitude for everyone who's been by my side through it all.

As the party starts winding down, my phone buzzes with a video call from my cousin Vince. He looks exhausted, his eyes heavy from working double shifts at the prison. His girlfriend is pregnant with their third kid, and he's been pulling extra hours before his paternity leave kicks in. "Sorry I couldn't make it, man. Just trying to get everything squared away before the baby comes," he says, rubbing the back of his neck.

"No worries, Vince," I assure him. "You've got a lot going on, and we'll catch up soon. Take care of yourself."

After the call, Sabrina gives me a quick hug goodbye, followed shortly by Mom and Barrett. I wave them off, my heart full as I watch them go. Dad and Bev hang around a little longer, but they eventually head out too, making the drive back to Cedar Bluff. Despite the tension between Bev and Sabrina—and the mountain of unsolicited advice Bev has offered over the years—I appreciate that they made the effort to come.

I'm also grateful that Sabrina held her tongue tonight,

probably knowing I'd already had enough awkward moments to last a lifetime.

The night at the bar stretches out longer than I've stayed out in years. We drink, laugh, and reminisce about the journey that has led me to this moment. Despite the late hour, the guys show no signs of slowing down. As the rest of the crowd begins thinning out, it's just Will, Luke, and me left at a high top table on the patio. We decide to venture into the main bar where it's quieter now, the buzz of conversation reduced to a low hum. And no Creed, thankfully. The bartender wipes down the counter, glancing over at us with a tired but amused expression.

Luke leans back in his chair, his eyes slightly glazed from the alcohol. "So, Owen, now that the apprenticeship is done, what's next for you?"

"Honestly, I'm not sure," I say, fidgeting with the label on my beer bottle. "I thought about getting back on FlameFinder, but I don't know." I pause, noticing the label reads Apple of my Hawk-Eye, and the corniness of it makes me laugh mid-conversation.

"I hate dating," I admit after composing myself. "I just miss having someone to talk to and spend time with. I guess dating is a necessary evil, but with work and Barrett... I don't even know if I have time to really get to know someone."

I shake my head, looking down at my beer as I swirl the liquid inside the bottle, peeling off the label completely. The bar has a wide variety of craft beers, including local favorites, and I mentally note to check if Hunter Holloway runs a brewery nearby. I need a distraction, and that seems like a good one.

Will leans in, his voice steady. "I get that. And listen, I know you've been through a lot, but you deserve to be happy too."

"And if that happiness just so happens to involve a cute little bartender with blond curls who's been giving you the 'fuck me' eyes all night, then so be it," Luke chimes in, casting a knowing look toward the bartender, a bemused grin on his face.

I think back to Sabrina's earlier comment and decide that if anyone is the shameless flirt here, it's Luke Olsen.

"It's not that simple, Luke," I reply, more serious now. "I can't just bring anyone into Barrett's life. I made that mistake with Brittany a couple of months ago. I let her convince me to bring her kids over for a 'play date' with Barrett, right after Mom moved out of the apartment. I had a strict no PDA rule because I wasn't ready to introduce her as my girlfriend yet."

Brittany Stone was a nightmare, plain and simple. Her two boys—six and eight years old—were little terrors who ganged up on Barrett every chance they got. When I confronted her, irritated beyond belief, she brushed it off with a smug, "Boys will be boys," and had the audacity to suggest I didn't understand because I "didn't have enough experience as a parent yet." That was the last straw. I told her to kick rocks and never looked back.

Will nods thoughtfully. "I get that, man. But you need to remember, not every woman is Brittany."

"Thank fuck," Luke and I say in unison, the words a shared breath of relief.

We sit in comfortable silence for a few moments, the weight of the conversation hanging in the air. Their concern for me is obvious, and though I'm not sure how to act on it yet, I appreciate it. I know they're right. I just don't know what my next step should be.

The blonde bartender walks over, a friendly smile lighting up her face. Luke wasn't wrong—she's pretty damn cute. "Last call, gentlemen. Can I get you anything else?"

I glance at Luke and Will, shaking my head. "I think we're good, thanks."

She nods, collecting our empty bottles. Her smile lingers, a little flirtatious now. "I hear congratulations are in order. What's the occasion?"

Luke jumps in before I can say anything, slapping me on the back so hard I almost choke on the last sip of my beer. "Our buddy here just finished his Steamfitters apprenticeship. He's a big shot now, making the big bucks."

The bartender laughs, glancing at me. "Well, congrats on the big bucks, then. Be safe getting home, boys." She walks away, and Luke, ever the smooth operator, leans so far back in his barstool, checking out her ass, that he almost tips over. At the last second, he catches himself, grabbing the edge of the table before completely toppling over.

"You are ridiculous, Luke," I say, shaking my head. "Keep it in your pants, or I won't be the only one at this table with a kid running around. I think it's time to call it a night."

Will nods in agreement. "Yeah, we can't party like we used to."

"Speak for yourself," Luke says, his words starting to slur and holding up a napkin I didn't notice was even put on the table. "Looks like you've still got it, man."

He hands me the napkin and sure enough, it has the name Heather written on it with a phone number and a simple "text me sometime," note scrawled on it.

"Yep, that does it. You're sleeping on my couch tonight, bro. Not a chance in hell I'm letting you get on your bike," I say with a warning. Will is already planning on staying at my place tonight so he doesn't have to take a twenty-five mile rideshare back to Iowa City.

As we stumble out of the bar, the cool night air hits me, clearing my head slightly. Will and Luke are both grinning like fools, clearly enjoying themselves. I smile, feeling a sense of gratitude wash over me. As we walk back to my apartment, the streets are quiet, the only sound is our footsteps echoing off the buildings. I feel a sense of peace settle over me, a rare moment of calm in the chaos of my life.

When we reach my apartment, we opt for a nightcap, and we settle in the living room, nursing our drinks and talking about everything and nothing.

As it turns out, Luke did, in fact, want to hire a dancer for the party tonight. Thank fuck Will thinks with the head on his shoulders instead of the one in his pants and reminded Luke that I have a kid that would be there.

Luke laughs, looking unrepentant. "Hey! I didn't know that you'd already told Sab we were throwing a party for him. Besides, I just wanted you to celebrate properly and, you know," he shrugs, "see some titties!"

I laugh, shaking my head. "I assure you, if I was that worried about seeing titties, I can find them myself."

I lean back, taking a sip of my drink. I had the stereotypical after-divorce hoe phase but the fun wore off after about three months and just left me feeling numb. It's been a long time since I actually dated anyone.

At one point after the divorce, I downloaded some dating app Luke suggested and it was great for the no-strings-attached flings but I can't imagine finding someone real through one of those matchmaking sites.

As the night wears on, we continue to talk, the conversation eventually turning to lighter topics. We share stories from the job site, reminisce about old times, and laugh until our sides hurt. It's moments like these that remind me of the importance of having friends who have been through the ups and downs with me.

Eventually, the energy in the room starts to wane, and we all exchange knowing looks.

"I think it's about that time," Will says, stretching his arms over his head with a yawn.

"Yeah, we've had enough excitement for one night," Luke adds, though he doesn't look too eager to leave the comfort of the couch.

As we all stand, gathering our things, Luke looks at Will and says "So, who's getting Barrett's bed?"

Will smirks. "Rock, paper, scissors?"

Luke beams with excitement. "Lizard, Spock?!"

I burst out laughing. "You guys watch way too many episodes of *The Big Bang Theory*."

"There's no such thing as too much of that show," Will protests.

"Yeah, Leonard," Luke says, nudging me with a grin, "you know this is the only way we settle things."

With dramatic flair, they play out the game. After a few intense rounds, Luke triumphantly declares, "Lizard eats paper! Barrett's bed is mine, Mother Fucker!"

Will shakes his head, laughing. "Well played, sir!"

As I make my way to my bedroom, still chuckling, I can't help but feel a deep sense of gratitude for their friendship.

nine

CONSIDER ME GONE - REBA MCENTIRE

CALLIE - MAY 17, 2013

The thought of moving out of Mom's house and into my own space is both exhilarating and terrifying. It's my first real taste of independence—living alone for the first time in my life. Well, technically, not alone since I'll have Sara, but still, the reality that I won't have another adult around is daunting. I stand outside the yellow brick building that's about to become my home, my heart a mix of excitement and anxiety.

When I found out the apartment was available, I was thrilled. It's only a couple of blocks from the coffee shop, and I'm terrible about getting exercise, so the proximity gives me an excuse to walk on nice days. The apartment itself is small—a one-bedroom that I plan to make work by sectioning off part of the living room to give Sara her own "room."

But despite my efforts to feel optimistic, there's a gnawing feeling in the pit of my stomach. This will be the first time I'm entirely on my own. No man, no family, just me, and Sara. A wave of fear hits me, and I make a mental note to find my old baseball bat in Mom's attic. Maybe that will help calm the gnawing anxiety. I've done all the "right" things for a single woman to feel secure—installed extra locks, picked an apartment in a relatively safe neighborhood—but my paranoia never lets me rest. The truth is, I've always been afraid of the dark.

I still remember running from the car to Mom's farmhouse at night, especially with the nearby train tracks echoing through the fields. Every time the train rumbled by, I'd picture that scene from *Dennis the Menace* where the creepy drifter played by Christopher Lloyd promises to take Dennis hostage on the midnight train. I know it's irrational, but some childhood fears never quite go away.

The movie came out when I was three years old and since Taylor knew it terrified me growing up, she would slice apples with a paring knife and eat the slices straight off the blade like a fucking psycho just like he did in the movie.

But yeah, I'm sure living alone is going to go great.

I unlock the door, and a wave of nostalgia hits—though not the good kind. This is the same apartment I used to hang out in during high school, partying with guys who had no business spending time with teenage girls. Back then, this place was a symbol of rebellion. Now, it's a symbol of something entirely different—my stubbornness to refuse more help from Mom and Wayne, my determination to make this work on my own, even if it gives me the creeps.

I start unpacking for what feels like the hundredth time in the last few months. Clothes go into the closet, furniture is arranged, and I do my best to make the space feel like a home. But the walls are thin. I can already hear my upstairs neighbors stomping around, and I realize this place might come with more challenges than I bargained for. Still, it's a stepping stone, a temporary situation until I can save enough for something better. It'll do for now.

The first month at the coffee shop flies by. Brooke's a great boss, and the work is a welcome distraction. It feels good to be busy again, to have a routine, and I start to recognize the regulars, remembering their orders and making small talk. I still feel guilty for moving out of the farmhouse so quickly, especially since Mom and Wayne have been so generous about watching Sara. But I need this space, this chance to rebuild.

Today, I'm heading to my first OB/GYN appointment with my new doctor. The thought makes me both nervous and hopeful. As I fill out the paperwork, my hand shakes slightly as I sign my name—still Adam's last name for now. I've been debating whether to keep it for the kids' sake, but the weight of it feels heavy.

"Callie Graham?" a nurse calls, and I follow her back to the examination room. Dr. Everett is kind, with a reassuring smile that puts me at ease. She asks me about my medical history and how I've been feeling. We discuss my plans and the importance of prenatal care.

Adam offered to come with me to this appointment but I wanted to be able to speak freely with the doctor and I wouldn't have been able to do that with him here. I assured him that I would make sure I kept him informed of appointments and that he could still come with me when we get to the point where we are going to find out the biological sex of the baby. Thankfully, he didn't fight me too hard on it and offered to keep Sara overnight instead of her going to my mom's.

I lie back on the examination table, she performs the ultrasound. The sound of the baby's heartbeat fills the room, a steady thump-thump that brings tears to my eyes. It's real. This baby is real, and despite everything, I feel a sense of hope.

Leaving the clinic, I head back to the coffee shop for my shift. The familiar aroma of freshly brewed coffee greets me as I step inside. Brooke waves from behind the counter, and I slip into the routine of taking orders and making drinks. I show Brooke the ultrasound pictures and we cry together a bit. The hours pass quickly, and before I know it, it's closing time.

As I lock up and head back to my apartment, the noise from upstairs is already starting. I sigh, knowing I'll have to talk to the landlord about it soon. But for now, I focus on the positive. I have a job I enjoy, a place of my own, and I'm doing what it takes to survive.

I flop onto my bed, exhausted from the day, grateful that Sara is staying with Adam tonight. As I stare up at the ceiling, I try to quiet my mind. There's so much to figure out, but I'm determined to make this work. This is my new beginning, even if the road ahead feels long and uncertain.

I pull out my phone, mindlessly scrolling through social media to unwind. But my thumb freezes when I see his profile. My heart clenches as I notice the change in Adam's relationship status—from "Married to Callie Graham" to "In a Relationship with Janelle VanPelt."

The words blur as betrayal and anger course through me. I hadn't expected this. I didn't think Adam would make it public so soon. He didn't even have the decency to unfriend me before broadcasting his new relationship to the world.

Their smug faces stare back at me from matching profile pictures—dressed up, smiling like they don't have a care in the world. The comments beneath are a sickening mix of congratulations and heart emojis. My fingers tighten around my phone, and for a moment, I consider blasting him in the comments. But I won't give him the satisfaction.

Tears sting my eyes, but I refuse to cry. This isn't just betrayal—it's public humiliation. I take a deep breath, block them both, and quickly change my name on all my social media back to Callie Madden. If Adam wants to flaunt his new relationship, I'll be moving on too. I immediately start searching for divorce attorneys.

But as the anger simmers, an idea forms. I need to get away. Put some distance between myself and this mess. My mind drifts to New Orleans, to Dad and Shelly. A trip might be exactly what I need.

Memorial Day weekend is coming up, and it feels like the perfect excuse. I call Brooke to make sure I'm not needed that weekend, and luckily, she has it covered. It's settled. I'll head to New Orleans. I just need to convince Taylor to come with me. I've never been great at long-distance driving, and Taylor is the queen of road trips.

As I crawl into bed, I shoot off a quick text to Dad and Shelly.

ME:
> Are you guys up for Memorial Day weekend? Thinking about planning a trip down with Sara.

DAD:
> We would love to have you both. Maybe Taylor could come with you?

SHELLY:
> That would be amazing, sweetie.

That was the easy part. Now I just need to convince Taylor. She's always been the adventurous one, and I know she won't pass up a chance for a road trip.

As I close my eyes, I can't help but smile. Despite everything—Adam's betrayal, the stress of figuring out my life—there's a part of me that's ready for this new beginning. Maybe it's time to embrace it. Time for Taylor and me to start our own tradition, just like Mom and her sisters had their "Sisters' Weekends" when we were kids. Maybe this trip is exactly what I need to clear my head and move forward.

ten

THE CROSSROADS - BONE THUGS-N-HARMONY

OWEN - MAY 18, 2013

The morning after my turnout party, sunlight filters through the blinds, casting a soft glow across the room. I stretch, the dull throb of a slight hangover reminding me of last night's celebration. It's a small price to pay for the overwhelming sense of accomplishment and the camaraderie that filled the air.

I shuffle to the kitchen, making a cup of my favorite coffee from BB Coffee Co., letting the rich aroma wake me up as I settle at the table. As the hot liquid slides down my throat, I scroll through my phone, catching up on the flood of messages from friends and family congratulating me on completing my apprenticeship.

I shoot off a quick text to Mom, letting her know I'll come get Barrett in about an hour, giving him some extra playtime before we meet for lunch. I take another sip of coffee, savoring the quiet before the day starts. Then, my phone buzzes with a message from the group chat.

LUKE:

Hey, fuckers! Sorry I had to bail out before you could buy me breakfast. Got called to an outage in Davenport around 7:30 this morning. They had some pretty rough storms last night so it's all hands on deck.

ME:

I'm shocked you were able to get up this morning. Were you even sober when you woke up?

WILL:

Your dumbass better not have gotten on that motorcycle still drunk.

LUKE:

Chill out, Daddy Dearest. Gotta make that money! 🤑

VINCE:

PREACH! Wish I could've been there last night, but kids aren't cheap, and I can't pass up doubles. Sorry I missed it, Owen.

LUKE:

And, for the record, I was good to go after I downed some water and ibuprofen before I took off. Sooo, Owen… what about Heather? Are you going to text her or what?

WILL:

For fuck's sake, Luke. Leave the man alone.

LUKE:

Fuck you, Will. 🖕

VINCE:

Wait! Who's Heather?! 😏

LUKE:

A fucking dime piece that slipped Owen her number at the bar last night.

> **ME:**
> Luke, don't you dare text her. I know how you are with numbers and I guarantee no matter how drunk you were last night, you remember the phone number on that fucking napkin.

> **VINCE:**
> Haha! Called you out man!

> **LUKE:**
> Maybe... 😼 Does that mean that you're going to text her?

I groan, shaking my head with a smile. Luke can't help himself. He lives for this kind of teasing.

> **ME:**
> I'll think about it... But she didn't give you her phone number. So don't be a douche canoe.

> **WILL:**
> He's already a fucking douche canoe.

> **LUKE:**
> Again, fuck you, Will!

Luke's text is quickly followed by him sending a series of middle finger emojis in Will's direction.

> **LUKE:**
> And fine, I won't text her until she gives ME her number. KIDDING. Just don't overthink it. Life's too short, man.

I stick my phone in my pocket only to have it buzz again a moment later. I reopen the group chat to see Luke has sent a GIF of Rob Schneider from *The Waterboy* popping up on my screen, his iconic "You can do it!" on repeat.

I roll my eyes before typing out a reply.

> ME:
> Wow, Luke, truly inspirational. Now, I'm ready to take on the world. 🙄

Just as I hit send, there's a knock at the door. I open it to find Will, grinning like an idiot, holding a bag of takeout from Cedar Bend Bistro.

"Morning, sunshine," he says, lifting the bag in greeting. "Thought you could use some hangover food, so I grabbed you a breakfast burrito."

I laugh, stepping aside to let him in. "You know, if you keep bringing me breakfast, I might not have to start dating again."

He chuckles, setting the bag down. "Wouldn't want to deprive you of that, but I can't have my best friend starving. Plus, who else would listen to my dating disasters?"

We sit down at the table, the aroma of fresh food filling the room. The burrito is exactly what I need, hearty and comforting. Will's presence is steady, the kind of support you don't always realize you need until it's right in front of you.

"So," he says, biting into his burrito, "what's the plan for today?"

I shrug, swallowing a mouthful of food. "Not much. I'm picking up Barrett from Mom's soon, maybe taking him to a movie or something later."

"Ah yes, the thrilling life of a single dad," Will says with mock sympathy. "I bet the laundry and dishes are just begging for your attention."

I smirk. "You know it. I've got a hot date with the vacuum cleaner."

Will snorts, nearly choking on his coffee. "Call me if it gets too wild. I'll bring reinforcements—maybe a mop and some disinfectant."

"Don't forget the French maid costume," I joke, rolling my eyes.

He grins, leaning back in his chair. "Speaking of hot dates, did you ever decide what to do with Heather's number?"

I glance at the napkin still on the table, feeling the weight of his question. "I'm on the fence about it."

Will raises an eyebrow, smirking. "On the fence? Dude, you've got nothing to lose. Worst case, she doesn't respond. Best case? You have a good time."

"Yeah, yeah," I mutter, waving him off. "I know. It's just… I don't know. It's been a while."

"Exactly why you should do it," he says, pointing at me with his burrito. "You can't spend your nights romancing your vacuum cleaner forever."

I laugh, feeling the tension ease a little. "Fine, I'll give it a shot. But if it crashes and burns, I'm blaming you."

"Deal," he says, clinking his coffee cup against mine. "Now let's finish this before it gets cold."

We eat and swap stories, mostly about Will's disastrous dating life, which doesn't exactly ease my hesitation about jumping back into the scene. The conversation flows easily and comfortably. Eventually, he glances at his watch.

"I should get going," he says, standing up. "Got a few errands to run before the day slips away."

"Thanks for breakfast," I say, walking him to the door.

"No problem. Take it easy, alright?" He gives me a quick, one-armed bro hug before heading out.

I sit back down on the sofa, eyes drifting to the napkin with Heather's number. Luke won't let me live it down if I don't at least try. Screw it. I pick up my phone and type out a message.

> **ME:**
> Hey, Heather. It's Owen. Just wanted to say thanks for putting up with us last night. Want to grab coffee sometime?

I hit send before I can overthink it, trying to brush off the nerves bubbling under the surface. It's just a text, right? No big deal. I distract myself by tidying the living room, but my phone buzzes only a few minutes later. My heart jumps.

> **HEATHER:**
> Hi, Owen! It was great meeting you last night. I'd love to get together sometime but I actually don't drink coffee. Maybe we could go see a movie sometime?

I stare at the message, thrown. Who doesn't drink coffee? And a movie for a first date? Isn't that a little... impersonal? How are we supposed to get to know each other sitting in the dark?

I sigh, rubbing the back of my neck. Maybe I'm overthinking this. Maybe it's not a big deal. With a resigned breath, I pick up the phone again.

> **ME:**
> A movie sounds good too. Maybe we could grab a bite to eat before or after? Also, I have to say, I'm not sure I can trust someone who doesn't drink coffee.

Trying to keep busy while I wait for her response, I flip through the channels, but nothing holds my attention. Eventually, I settle on organizing some old photos on my laptop to pass the time.

My phone buzzes again.

HEATHER:

Haha, fair enough! I guess you'll have to get to know me and find out if I'm trustworthy. Dinner before the movie sounds perfect! How about Friday evening?

A smile tugs at my lips. At least she has a sense of humor.

ME:

Sounds like a plan. I can come pick you up after I drop my son off with his mom on Friday before dinner.

HEATHER:

Great! Your son is the little boy that was at the party last night, right? He's adorable. Just like his Dad. 😊

I chuckle, shaking my head. This might actually be fun. Although, I don't think I've been called adorable in nearly three decades.

ME:

Haha! Thanks. I'll pick you up around 7.

HEATHER:

Sounds good. I live in the apartment above the bar so I'll just meet you downstairs.

ME:

It's a date.

The rest of the afternoon passes in a blur, and I walk downstairs to Mom's to pick up Barrett. The weather's too nice for a movie, so we hit the park instead. As I tuck Barrett into bed later that night, his sleepy eyes looking up at me with trust and love, I make a silent promise to him—and to myself.

No matter what happens, I'll always be the best dad I can be. And maybe, just maybe, I'll figure out how to be happy again.

eleven

A LITTLE BIT STRONGER - SARA EVANS

CALLIE - MAY 23, 2013

After a brief, exhausting argument with Adam about taking Sara out of state, I'm finally all set for my mini-vacation to New Orleans. The thought of getting away feels like a breath of fresh air, even if it meant one last round of tension with Adam. He never makes things easy. I've always hated driving on the interstate, convinced that if I die young, it'll be from a head-on collision with a semi.

Thankfully, my sister Taylor loves road trips and volunteered to come with me since her daughter Ava is spending the week with her dad. Taylor has been my rock through all of this. She's three years older, and honestly, more like a second mom. With Mom and Wayne constantly working or Mom going back to school when I was little, Taylor was the one who held things together. That closeness, though, came with its share of fights. For a long time, we butted heads—constantly. But after everything we've both been through, she's the only person who really understands what I'm going through.

Taylor's been down this road, too. When she told me she and Nick were divorcing, my heart broke for her. Ava was barely two, and her marriage was falling apart. They were complete opposites, and from the moment I met Nick, I remember thinking he was someone I'd date, not her. Covered in tattoos, spiked red hair—he was more my type than hers. But somehow, their chemistry just worked.

Until it didn't.

On Thursday morning, just as the sun rises, we hit the road south. The landscape shifts slowly, from the familiar farmlands of Iowa to the green hills of Missouri, to the worn, bumpy roads of Arkansas. Even with the rough ride, it's oddly calming, almost meditative. The kind of silence I need to reset.

Sara's fast asleep in the backseat, curled up with her favorite stuffed bunny. I glance back at her, feeling that mix of guilt and love that hits me every time I think about this trip. It's for her as much as it is for me—to show her the family bonds I'm desperately trying to hold onto.

Taylor drives, her hands steady on the wheel, her chestnut hair catching the sunlight as we go. She's calm, collected, the way she always is. Even with everything she's been through, Taylor radiates strength. It's something I've always admired, even when we were kids.

When Sara wakes up, we crank up the music, singing along to Michael Bolton, Celine Dion, and, of course, Reba McEntire. No road trip would be complete without Reba. The car fills with laughter and our horribly off-key harmonies, making the miles fly by. For a moment, things feel normal, like they used to before life got so heavy.

"How are you feeling, Callie?" Taylor asks, her voice breaking the comfortable silence that's settled after our latest rendition of "Callin' Baton Rouge." Sara, somehow, managed to fall back asleep despite our screaming, but now the quiet is thick with something unspoken.

I shrug, staring out at the rolling fields. "Anxious, I guess. I'm hoping this trip helps clear my head."

Taylor nods, her eyes on the road. "You're allowed to feel anxious, Callie. But just remember—you're not broken. You're pregnant, going through a divorce, yeah, but you're stronger than you think. You'll get through this."

Her words make something in my chest loosen, and I manage a small smile. "Thanks, Tay. I needed to hear that."

As we drive, my mind drifts back to my recent OB/GYN appointment. Everything went well, and I'm scheduled to find out the baby's gender after this trip. It's a small relief amidst the chaos. The thought of a new life growing inside me fills me with a jumbled mix of excitement, fear and hope.

As the drive continues, my mind drifts back to my OB/GYN appointment. Everything was normal, and after this trip, I'll find out the baby's gender. That thought alone brings a swirl of excitement, fear, and hope. I've always wanted a little boy, but at this point, a girl would feel like less pressure. At least I could reuse all the baby stuff from Sara—except for that godawful camo and mauve crib set Adam insisted on. What the hell was I thinking letting him choose that?

I shake my head, silently vowing to make better choices this time around.

"How've you been, really?" I ask, wanting to dig a little deeper. "You never really talked about what happened with Nick."

Taylor's fingers tap lightly on the steering wheel, her jaw tightening. "It was complicated, Callie. We were always different, but after Ava was born, it became impossible to ignore. I was struggling with postpartum, and he just... wasn't there for me. It felt like we became roommates. I didn't feel wanted, and he didn't understand why that mattered. I don't really want to get into it, though."

I nod, the weight of her words sinking in. "I'm sorry for prying. I just... I just want to make sure you're okay. I wasn't sure if it was something Nick did or if things just... fell apart."

"It wasn't like he did anything horrible," she admits, her voice soft. "He didn't cheat or anything. He just wasn't giving me the attention I needed. It's hard enough for me to be intimate with anyone after... everything that happened when we were kids. I just wanted him to show me that I was still desirable, still loved."

I feel a lump in my throat, struggling to find the right words. Taylor's been through so much, and hearing her talk about this is heartbreaking. I glance over at her, but she doesn't look back. Instead, she stares straight ahead, her expression unreadable.

In a way, her confession makes me think about my own situation with Adam. By the end, our sex life was non-existent, but unlike Taylor, I wanted it that way. His presence repulsed me. But it wasn't about my insecurities—it was because of his betrayals, his selfishness. It's not the same thing, I remind myself, pushing the fleeting sympathy for Adam out of my mind.

"Don't feel bad for me, Callie," Taylor says, her voice firm, but there's a softness there too. "I hate that pity shit."

Her words hit me hard, and I blink back the tears that threaten to fall. I've leaned on Taylor so much these past few months, probably more than she realizes. Her strength has kept me grounded. If she can survive everything she's been through, maybe I can too.

twelve
BREAKEVEN - THE SCRIPT

OWEN - MAY 23, 2013

The week with Barrett flew by in a blur of laughter, activities, and stolen moments of joy. I had the week off from work, and I was determined to make the most of every second with him. We spent our mornings at the park, where Barrett's little body zipped up and down the jungle gym, his dark hair flopping into his eyes as he climbed higher. His bright smile grew with every daring move, his eyes sparkling with excitement.

In the afternoons, we took bike rides down winding nature trails, exploring every twist and turn like adventurers on a quest. One day, we visited the zoo, where Barrett was mesmerized by the lions and practically dragged me back to the reptile house for a second round of snakes and lizards. Evenings were quieter—movie nights on the couch and LEGO towers that became more elaborate as the hours slipped by, the soft glow of the floor lamp casting warmth over our little sanctuary.

On Thursday, we visited Mom. She was thrilled, as always,

to see us, but especially Barrett. Her living room, always smelling faintly of lavender, quickly became an impromptu art studio. Barrett busied himself with crayons, markers, and stacks of construction paper while Mom fussed over him, bringing out cookies and milk like it was her mission to spoil him rotten. By the end of the visit, he had a towering pile of colorful drawings.

"Daddy, can I take these home to Mommy?" Barrett asked, holding up one particularly bright piece—a family of dinosaurs, I think?

"Of course, buddy. I'm sure she'll love them," I said, ruffling his hair.

Friday came too quickly, and it was time to take Barrett back to Sabrina's. As we pulled into her driveway, the late afternoon sun casting long shadows across the pavement, I noticed a car I didn't recognize parked out front. Must be Alex's. Sabrina had mentioned introducing Barrett to Alex and had texted earlier to make sure I was still okay with it. I told her it was fine, but now, seeing the car, it hit differently.

Barrett, though, was buzzing with excitement, his drawings clutched tightly in his little hands. "Mommy's gonna love these!" he exclaimed as we walked up to the door.

Sabrina answered almost immediately, her face lighting up as soon as she saw Barrett. She looked radiant—her chestnut hair falling in soft waves, her warm brown eyes sparkling with joy.

"Hey, little man! I've missed you!" she said, scooping him into a big hug.

"I missed you too, Mommy! Look, look at my drawings from Nana's!" He thrust the papers toward her, beaming with pride.

Sabrina smiled, though I caught the brief look of confusion as she eyed the abstract art in her hands. "They're wonderful, sweetie." She shot me a look that screamed, What on earth is this? I just chuckled under my breath.

"Why don't you come inside?" she said, stepping aside. "There's someone I want you to meet."

We walked into the living room where a tall, clean-cut guy stood up from the couch. He had sandy blond hair and an easy smile that seemed genuine enough.

"Barrett, this is Alex," Sabrina said gently. "Alex, this is my son, Barrett."

Alex crouched down, meeting Barrett at eye level. "Hi, Barrett. It's nice to meet you. I've heard a lot about you."

Barrett looked up at me, then back at Alex. "Hi. Do you want to see my drawings?"

This right here, I thought, was the test every single parent faces when they introduce someone new to their kid. Forget dinner dates—how someone reacts to your kid's artwork is the real litmus test.

"I'd love to," Alex said, taking the drawings from Barrett and examining them with interest. "These are fantastic! You're quite the artist."

Well, looks like he passed that test. Barrett beamed with pride before running off to hang the pictures on the fridge.

"Hey, Owen," Alex said, standing to his full height and extending his hand. "Nice to meet you."

"Nice to meet you too," I said, shaking his hand.

Barrett, still full of energy, ran back over, looking up at Alex with wide eyes. "Do you want to see my playroom too?"

"Sure thing, buddy. Lead the way," Alex replied, following Barrett toward the back of the house.

Sabrina and I lingered in the living room for a moment, the sunlight streaming through the windows, casting a golden glow on the hardwood floors. "Thanks for bringing him over," she said softly. "Got any plans for the weekend?"

"Actually, yeah. I've got a date tonight," I said, feeling a little awkward.

"A date? That's great! Who's the lucky lady?" Sabrina asked, her smile genuine.

"Remember the blonde bartender from the night of the turnout party?" I asked, raising an eyebrow.

Her eyes lit up in recognition. "Yes!"

"We're having dinner at Monica's in Coralville," I said, trying to sound more relaxed than I felt.

"Well, I hope it goes well," she said sincerely.

"Thanks," I replied. "I should get going—don't want to be late."

Just then, Barrett came bounding back into the room, a stuffed dinosaur clutched in his hands. "Mommy, look! It's my T-Rex! Just like my drawings!"

So they were dinosaurs.

"That's awesome, sweetie!" Sabrina said, her eyes twinkling. "Did you show Alex?"

"Yep! He knows all about the dinosaurs," Alex said with a grin, walking back in from the playroom.

"Hey, buddy," I said, crouching down to Barrett's level. "I've gotta go now. Can I get a hug?"

Barrett flung his arms around my neck, squeezing tight. "Bye, Daddy! I'll miss you!"

"I'll miss you too, kiddo," I said, my voice thick with emotion. "I'll see you next week, okay?"

"Okay, Daddy," he mumbled into my shoulder before letting go.

I gave him one last squeeze, then stood to leave. Sabrina and I exchanged a brief look—one filled with understanding—before I headed back to my truck.

Just as I was about to open the door, I heard Alex's voice behind me. "Hey, Owen, before you go…"

I turned to face him.

"I just wanted to say thanks. I know meeting Barrett's a big deal, and I appreciate you being so understanding."

"No problem," I said, giving him a nod. "As long as you're good to him and Sabrina, that's all that matters."

He smiled, looking genuinely appreciative. "Absolutely. Have a great night, man."

"You too," I said, before finally getting into my truck and driving off.

As I made my way from Cedar Bluff to Coralville, I couldn't help but reflect on the day. Seeing Sabrina with someone else was strange, but it was also a relief knowing she was happy. Barrett seemed to like Alex, and that's what really mattered.

I hadn't done much dating since my divorce, aside from that regrettable post-divorce fling phase, but this felt different. Excitement mixed with nerves fluttered in my chest. And maybe a little guilt too. Was I really ready for this? Was Heather just a test run?

By the time I arrived at Monica's, the sun was dipping low, casting a soft golden light over the quaint little restaurant. I texted Heather, letting her know I'd be a little late, but she didn't seem to mind. She was waiting at a table by the window when I walked in, looking elegant, her blonde curls framing her face as she smiled up at me.

"Hey, Heather," I greeted her, sliding into the seat across from her. "Sorry if I kept you waiting."

"Not at all," she smiled warmly. "I just got here."

We made small talk as we ordered, but there was a lingering awkwardness that neither of us could seem to shake. Conversation came in fits and starts, and I found myself distracted, my mind wandering to the dark-haired woman I couldn't stop thinking about.

"So... you don't drink coffee, huh?" I asked, trying to find some common ground.

Heather laughed, but it felt a little forced. "Nope, more of a tea girl."

"Tea, huh? I guess I can tolerate that," I joked, but it didn't land.

As dinner arrived, we both made attempts at polite conversation, but the connection just wasn't there. She was kind, smart, and attractive, but there was no spark. I was somewhere else, my thoughts adrift, and I think she sensed it too.

When she suggested a movie after dinner, I hesitated. I didn't want to keep forcing something that wasn't working.

"And you feel obligated because we made plans, but super awkward because this whole thing's been weird, and you've probably thought about bailing more than once?" Heather said, breaking into my thoughts.

I blinked in surprise, then laughed. "Yeah, nailed it."

Heather nods, looking relieved. "Oh, thank God! Look, Owen, I know that you're just starting to date again and I think that maybe we are just at different points. It seems like you're putting a lot of pressure on yourself and I was really hoping for something more laid back and fun."

I nod, feeling a weight lift off my shoulders. "I completely understand. I'm sorry if I seem a bit off tonight. It's been a while since I've been on a date, and I guess I was just overthinking things."

Heather smiles sympathetically. "No worries, Owen. It happens to the best of us. I'm sure you'll find someone who's the right fit for you."

As we go to part ways outside of Monica's, a thought occurs to me, "Hey Heather, at the risk of making tonight even more awkward, I have a question."

She smiles, "Go for it."

"Well, you mentioned that you were hoping for something more fun, right?"

She nods, hesitantly.

"It's just that... Well, do you remember the two guys that were with me at the bar last week?"

Her smile beams almost instantly.

"One of them–the blond–is my younger brother and probably more your speed. Mind if I give him your number?"

thirteen

SHE WILL BE LOVED - MAROON 5

CALLIE - MAY 23, 2013

With only a few hours left in our trip, Taylor cranks up a family road-trip classic—Hanson's *Snowed In* album. It's a bizarre choice for an eighty-five-degree day at the end of May, but it doesn't matter. We're belting out Christmas carols like it's the middle of December, not caring that we're sweating under the hot sun. The windows are down, and the wind whips through my hair, carrying away the heat of the afternoon. For a while, I let myself get lost in the rhythm of the music, my voice blending with Taylor's in a way that feels effortless, familiar, like we're those two carefree girls again, road-tripping without a worry in the world.

As we laugh through the final chorus of "What Christmas Means to Me," I feel a stitch in my side from all the singing. I let my voice trail off, leaning back in my seat to catch my breath, and the reality of everything begins to creep back in—the growing weight of my belly, the uncomfortable tightness of my clothes. I shift in my seat, suddenly aware of the contrast between this fleeting moment of joy and the heavier, more complicated reality that's waiting for me when the music stops.

Taylor seems to sense the change in my energy, her voice fading as she lowers the volume on the stereo. There's a beat of silence, the kind that only happens between people who know each other well enough to feel when something shifts beneath the surface.

"We've still got it," Taylor says with a grin, glancing at me out of the corner of her eye.

I laugh, shaking my head. "Yeah, but I'm not sure my lungs can handle it like they used to. I feel like an out-of-shape Santa Claus over here."

"Cutest Santa ever!" Taylor giggles, her eyes twinkling amusement. I can't help but smile at her playful tone. After a moment, she sighs, her fingers tapping absently on the steering wheel. "I've missed this, you know?" she says, her voice almost nostalgic. "Just us, singing our hearts out like nothing else matters. Adam never really let you talk to me when you were together. There was always something more important he needed you for when I tried to call."

My heart sinks a little at her words. She's not wrong. My relationship with Adam isolated me from almost everyone unless he was able to find the person useful. A part of me feels like I'm still mending my relationship with my sister after a falling out she and I had thanks to Adam and her ex not getting along. "I've missed you too, Taylor," I assure her. "I'm sorry for everything."

"You don't have to be sorry," she says. "Just... don't disappear on me again, okay?"

"Sisters over misters," I say, holding up my pinkie. Taylor smiles softly, reaching over to loop her little finger in mine. We lean toward one another, pressing our fists together to lock in our promise, just like we've done since we were kids.

For a moment, the mood feels lighter, but when she glances back at me, her expression grows more serious. She turns her attention back to the road, her grip on the wheel tightening just a little. "I just don't want you to lose yourself, Callie. You deserve to be happy."

Her words catch me off guard, and I shift uncomfortably in my seat, not sure how to respond. It's like she's saying what I've been too afraid to admit to myself. I clear my throat, searching for the right words. "I'm getting there," I finally say, though it feels like a half-truth. "It's only been six weeks since I found out Adam was messing around with Janelle and that stupid FlameFinder profile of his."

Taylor gives me a mischievous look, her mood lightening again. "Speaking of which, did you ever delete that profile you made to catch his attention?"

I groan, rolling my eyes as I lean my head back against the seat. "Honestly, I forgot it even existed," I admit, but the moment the words leave my mouth, I know I've opened the door for whatever Taylor has in mind. Her grin widens, and I know I'm in for it.

"Well, well, well," she teases, her voice playful but with that familiar undercurrent of mischief. "You know, just because you're pregnant doesn't mean you can't let loose and have a little fun."

I laugh, feeling a blush creep up my neck because I know exactly what she's hinting at. These pregnancy hormones have been no joke, and I've almost considered buying stock in AA batteries. "Oh yeah? What do you suggest, wild one?" I ask, pretending to be serious, though we both know Taylor's always been the more reserved one between us.

I shake my head but that doesn't seem to deter her interest

in the subject. "I can't imagine anyone would want me right now," I say looking down at my growing belly. "Look at me!"

"So you never deleted the profile?" she asks, raising an eyebrow.

"No," I admit hesitantly. "But I haven't logged in since the day I made it. Never even turned on notifications."

Taylor's grin widens. "Well, why not log back in and update it? Use it to meet some people. You deserve to have fun too, Calico Cat," she says with a wink, reviving my old nickname from when I was more chaotic and carefree.

I'm a little taken aback, not used to my sister being the one to push for this kind of thing. She's not prudish, but we've never really talked about stuff like this so openly. "I don't know, Tay... it feels kinda weird," I say, half laughing, half genuinely nervous.

She nudges me, undeterred. "Come on, what's the harm? You don't have to take it seriously. Think of it as a confidence boost. Besides," she pauses, her grin now full-on mischievous, "it's not like you're gonna get pregnant."

"TAYLOR!"

She's cackling now, tears practically forming in her eyes. "What?! It's true!" she says, her face turning red from laughter. "Seriously, Callie. I'm not saying go full 'post-divorce-hoe-phase,' but you can have fun. At the very least, log in and read the messages. I guarantee your inbox has been blowing up since you made that profile. I bet it's full of cringy gold."

She glances over at me, eyes twinkling with mischief. "Well? What are you waiting for? Chaos Callie wouldn't have given this a second thought back in the day."

I cringe a little at the mention of my old nickname. Chaos Callie was what I dubbed myself back in high school when everyone was calling me a mess. Instead of letting it get to me, I embraced it—probably more than I should have. "Well,

Chaos Callie wasn't a mom," I point out, trying to sound more responsible than I feel.

"Callie, men do this crap all the time and get high-fives for it," she says, her voice carrying a hint of frustration, like she's giving herself the same pep talk she's giving me.

She has a point. Why can't I have some fun as long as it's safe, sane, and consensual? After a moment of hesitation, I shrug. "Fuck it, I'm in," I say, pulling out my phone.

Taylor cheers beside me as I log into the account, already laughing at the ridiculousness of it all. Sure enough, my inbox is full of messages—some of them beyond cringeworthy. One particularly charming message from Slay_N_Pussy69 reads: "Well, if your husband's on here, you might as well have some fun too, baby." Gross. Thank God this app doesn't allow picture messages, or I can only imagine what horrors would be waiting for me.

"I cannot believe I let you talk me into this," I say, mass deleting everything in the inbox so I can start fresh.

Taylor laughs, throwing me a knowing look. "Oh please, Callie, it didn't take that much convincing. Don't act like you're not dying for a little... excitement. You've forgotten I know what pregnancy hormones are like!"

It's so strange hearing my sister talk like this—about sex, no less. She's always been the one with a spotless reputation, while I've been the one causing trouble and making questionable life decisions. But here she is, encouraging me to let loose, to reclaim a part of myself I thought I'd buried.

With her encouragement, I update my profile, adding some new photos and tweaking my description. And as a final act of rebellion, I change my username from Callie_co to ChaosCallie, fully embracing my old persona. It feels oddly liberating, like I'm reclaiming a piece of myself I'd lost somewhere along the way.

The profile reads:

Not looking for another Baby Daddy. I already have one that I can't stand.

Age: 22
Location: Hawkridge, IA
About Me: Hey there! I'm Callie, a mom of an adorable little girl and a soon-to-be mom of another bundle of joy. I'm rediscovering myself and not really looking for anything other than someone to talk to and share laughs with. I'm trying to learn not to take life too seriously. I love reading, coffee, and indulging in spontaneous dance parties in the living room.
Occupation: Barista
Favorite TV Shows: One Tree Hill, Friends, That 70s Show and Sons of Anarchy
Fun Fact: I'm pregnant. Yes, I'm serious. And no, you are not the father! *insert best Maury impression ever*
Looking For: Someone to have intelligent conversations with. I won't respond to any messages if you just start with a "Hey girl," or try to get in my pants.

If you're interested in actually getting to know me, send me a message!

By the time we reach New Orleans, the sun is setting, painting the sky with brilliant hues of orange and pink. The French Quarter is alive with music and laughter, its ironwork balconies and vibrant colors a feast for the eyes. The aroma of Cajun spices fills the air, mingling with the sound of jazz spilling out from nearby bars.

This city has a heartbeat all its own, and for the first time in a long time, I feel like I might just find mine again here.

Our dad, Edward, is waiting for us on the porch of his weathered house in the Marigny district, the kind of place that feels like it holds centuries of stories. As we pull up, his broad smile is the first thing we see. He strides toward us with open arms, his laughter ringing out like music, making everything feel lighter, if only for a moment.

"Welcome, my girls!" he exclaims, his eyes gleaming with joy as he pulls us into a bear hug. His warmth is infectious, the kind of embrace that promises everything's going to be okay, even when it isn't.

Inside the house, the scent of gumbo bubbling away on the stove fills the air, mixing with the scratchy sounds of Dad's old vinyl records playing in the background. It's like stepping back in time—before everything got complicated, before the heartache and the mess of adulthood. The weight I've been carrying around feels a little lighter, just being here.

Friday morning, we venture into the vibrant streets of the French Quarter. The city hums with life—street performers fill the air with music, and artists sketch passersby with quick strokes of charcoal. The unmistakable scent of beignets from Café du Monde floats through the air, sweet and rich, tempting us at every corner.

Sara's eyes are wide with wonder, taking in the kaleidoscope of sights and sounds, and I tighten my grip on her tiny hand, feeling that fierce pull of love and protectiveness. This trip isn't just for me; it's for her too—a glimpse into a world beyond the walls of our messy, broken home.

At Jackson Square, we weave through artists' stalls filled with vivid paintings, pausing every so often to watch horse-drawn carriages clatter by. The city's pulse beats around us, each moment more alive than the last. Taylor and I take turns snapping pictures of Sara, capturing the pure joy that dances in her eyes. I can feel my own shoulders loosening, the knots of stress untangling bit by bit.

As we wander further through the lively streets, something inside me shifts. The vibrant energy of New Orleans seeps into my bones, and for the first time in what feels like forever, I allow myself to imagine a future that isn't clouded by the past. Maybe—just maybe—this trip is the start of something new. The beginning of a chapter where freedom and happiness aren't just fleeting, but possible.

As the night deepens, the vibrant energy of the city slowly fades, replaced by the rhythmic hum of cicadas and the distant murmur of voices winding down for the evening. I sit outside, the warm New Orleans breeze brushing my skin, and reflect on the past few days—the road trip, the laughter, the fleeting sense of freedom I haven't felt in what seems like a lifetime. It's a sharp contrast to the suffocating reality I've been trapped in with Adam.

Taylor breaks the silence, her voice soft but steady, like she's anchoring me back to solid ground. "You know, we've been through a lot, Callie. But we've always had each other. And we always will."

Her words settle over me like a comforting blanket, and suddenly, the tears I've been holding back spill over, hot and uninvited. I nod, my throat tight, struggling to find my voice. "Thank you, Taylor. For everything. I honestly don't know what I'd do without you." Each word feels heavy with the gratitude I've been carrying for her. Through every storm, she's been my constant—my anchor when everything else was slipping away.

She reaches over and gives my hand a firm squeeze, her grip grounding me even more. "You'll never have to find out. We're in this together, no matter what."

For a moment, we sit in that quiet understanding, and then Taylor breaks the silence again, her voice more reflective now. "I was scared too, you know. When I left Nick, I didn't know if I could make it on my own. But I did. And so will you."

I turn to her, meeting the fierce determination in her eyes. "It's just… sometimes it feels impossible to see the light at the end of the tunnel. Especially with everything that's happened."

She nods, her expression softening but still resolute. "I get that. But, Callie, you've got so much ahead of you. And you deserve to be happy. You deserve more than what you've been settling for."

I inhale deeply, feeling a shift inside, a small flicker of resolve rekindling. "You're right. It's time to stop dwelling on the past. It's time to start thinking about what's best for me."

Taylor smiles, her support unwavering. "Absolutely. And no matter what you decide, I'll be right there, cheering you on."

We sit together in a peaceful silence, the cool night air wrapping around us like a quiet reminder that things can change, that maybe, just maybe, everything will be okay. I feel lighter, like I can finally breathe, and for the first time in a long while, hope doesn't feel like such a foreign concept. Whether it's this city's magic or the warmth of being with family, I start to believe that things can get better.

Resting back in my chair, I pull out my phone, its familiar weight grounding me again. I start scrolling through social media, watching the endless parade of curated lives and picture-perfect moments, but none of it grabs my attention. Boredom sets in quickly, and my thoughts drift. Maybe I should check FlameFinder, just for a distraction. Anything to pull me away from the tangled mess of my own thoughts.

Taylor, as if reading my mind, glances over with a knowing look, casually leaning back in her chair but not-so-subtly trying to peek at my screen. "Have you checked your messages on the app since you updated your profile?" she asks, her tone both playful and teasing.

I chuckle, rolling my eyes. "Your timing is impeccable. Were your spidey senses tingling or something?"

Taylor grins, her excitement contagious. "Come on," she nudges. "Check your messages. Let's see if there's anything in there that isn't a disaster pickup line!"

With a deep breath, I open the app and navigate to my inbox. Sure enough, the messages have piled up. Most of them are cringeworthy at best, but as I scroll, one message catches my eye—different from the rest. I pause, intrigued, as a mix of curiosity and hesitation bubbles up inside me. Maybe this isn't such a bad idea after all.

fourteen

THE BAD TOUCH - BLOODHOUND GANG

OWEN - MAY 24, 2013

I get home from my disaster of a date with Heather and toss my keys on the counter, frustration coursing through me. Alright, maybe it wasn't a complete disaster, but it sure wasn't good either. No spark, no real connection—just a reminder of how complicated dating can be. I shrug off my jacket and slump onto the couch, pulling out my phone, the quiet of the apartment settling around me like a weight.

Out of boredom and curiosity, I decide to scroll through the dating app I had downloaded a while back. At this point, it can't get any worse, right? Faces blur together as I swipe, not expecting anything interesting—until I see her. Dark hair, striking green eyes, and a username that jumps out at me: ChaosCallie. Something about her stops me mid-swipe. She looks familiar, though I can't quite place why.

Intrigued, I click on her profile. Her headline makes me chuckle:

Not looking for another Baby Daddy. I already have one that I can't stand.

I smile. At least she's got a sense of humor. As I read further, I learn her name is Callie—figures, given her username—and that she's nine years younger than me. Normally, I'd steer clear of that much of an age gap, but there's something about her that feels different.

Her bio is refreshingly honest, filled with lighthearted sarcasm. She's a mom to a little girl, and she's pregnant. That part makes me huff out a laugh. I can already hear Luke in my head: Well, at least you can't get her more pregnant. Her mention of Maury and her baby daddy issues nearly has me in stitches. I keep scrolling, learning more about her. She's fun, she's real, and she loves coffee and reading—definite pluses in my book.

As I look at her profile picture again, her eyes draw me in. I swear I've met her before, or at least seen her somewhere. I can't shake the feeling, so I decide to send her a message, my curiosity getting the better of me.

> THATPIPEGUY3.14:
>
> What are your five favorite music artists? And yes, I will be judging you based on your answer.

I hit send and lean back, feeling a mix of excitement and nervousness. I can't seem to sit still so I wander into the kitchen, and pour myself a glass of whiskey. The apartment feels a little less lonely somehow. I go back to her profile and look at her pictures again. She is stunning, and I'm having a hell of a time placing where I've seen her before. Because I'm certain that I have.

I'm a little surprised when I receive a message back from

her relatively quickly. Especially because it's so late. I guess I'm not the only one in need of some entertainment.

> **CHAOSCALLIE:**
> That's a tough one!
> I guess I'll have to go with... Nirvana, Halestorm, Acceptance, Paramore, and Staind. Judge your pretty little heart out.

A smile spreads across my face. It's refreshing to see someone with some alt/rock taste instead of fucking country music which I cannot stand. I can only take so many versions of songs about someone's dog dying. Yes, I'm a hater. I know.

ThatPipeGuy3.14:

Aww! So, you think I'm pretty? Those are pretty solid choices. Nirvana though... were you even born yet when Kurt Cobain was still alive?

I take a sip of my drink, savoring the warmth it brings. Her response comes quickly, making me chuckle.

ChaosCallie:

Very funny, old timer! Yes, I was. Granted... I was just shy of four-years-old when he died but I mean... I was alive.

I grin, appreciating her quick wit. She's intriguing, I'll give her that.

ThatPipeGuy3.14:

Fair enough, young grasshopper. My name is Owen, by the way.

ChaosCallie:

I know, I read your profile, silly. But I appreciate the introduction. It's nice to meet you, Owen. I'm glad you feel my answer is worthy of being told your first name.

Oh, I definitely like this girl already. It's one thing to be able to have a conversation with people and not get bored to death but I love it when a woman can keep me on my toes and isn't afraid of a little friendly back and forth.

THATPIPEGUY3.14:

I have to say, based on your answers though, I'm guessing you're one of those former emo kids that hated very specific bands because they were "too mainstream," and/or "sold out."

CHAOSCALLIE:

First of all – there's no such thing as a "former emo kid." I've simply morphed into an Elder Emo.

And listen, you don't have to call me out. My hatred for The White Stripes and The Killers is warranted.

THATPIPEGUY3.14:

The White Stripes and The Killers are actually good though!

But you didn't say Nickelback was one of your favorites. So I'll give you a pass.

CHAOSCALLIE:

...

Lord, help me. If there's one thing that annoys me more than country music, it's Nickelback. I can't resist giving her shit for it at this point.

THATPIPEGUY3.14:

OMG! You like Nickelback?!

CHAOSCALLIE:

I plead the fifth.

THATPIPEGUY3.14:

Lying by omission! Forget my name. I'm revoking your right to know it!

> **CHAOSCALLIE:**
>
> Listen here, Gramps! You said you were going to judge me based on my Top 5. You can't bend the rules now.
>
> Besides, now it's your turn! Let me guess, Frank Sanatra, Elvis, The Beatles, and...?

I chuckle, enjoying the playful banter. I'm guessing that she hasn't heard of most of the music that I listen to. It's not even necessarily that she's younger than me either. My taste is a bit unconventional, but it's mine.

> **THATPIPEGUY3.14:**
>
> Hey! Put the claws away there, Calico Cat. I'm not that old. But if you want a lesson in good music, it's gotta be Cake, E-40, The Flaming Lips, Bloodhound Gang, and Dr. Dre.
>
> **CHAOSCALLIE:**
>
> Well... I honestly don't know because I've only heard songs by two of those artists but I will give you the benefit of the doubt.

I laugh, taking another sip of my whiskey. It's nice to talk to someone who has a different perspective on music instead of just hearing the same regurgitated bands mentioned over and over again.

> **THATPIPEGUY3.14:**
>
> I'm not surprised. I worked at a music store for a few years in Cedar Bluff so I got to listen to a lot of cool alternative stuff other people hadn't heard of.
>
> **CHAOSCALLIE:**
>
> And don't forget Bloodhound Gang. Haha! I don't think that I've ever met someone who has listed them as a favorite band. Let me guess, you also like to watch The Discovery Channel?

THATPIPEGUY3.14:

I mean... I don't dislike it. LOL! What are you up to tonight?

CHAOSCALLIE:

Sitting in New Orleans with my older sister. She insisted that I get on this freaking app just to see how many terrible pickup lines popped into my inbox.

I get up and stretch, feeling a bit restless. I head to the kitchen to refill my drink, the conversation with Callie making me feel more energized.

THATPIPEGUY3.14:

And... What's the verdict?

CHAOSCALLIE:

Out of 12 messages I looked at, I had six bad pickup lines, three "hey"/"hey girl", one "wanna fuck?" and an "I'll make you forget your Baby Daddy."

I wince at the thought of those messages. Even in my hoe-phase, I didn't see the point of talking to women like that. Dating apps can be brutal.

Sometimes, the women on the app are just as thirsty for attention as the men. Although, I'm certain that the women get bombarded way more frequently with unsolicited sexts than the men do. I only ran into that a couple of times.

THATPIPEGUY3.14:

YIKES.

CHAOSCALLIE:

Tell me about it! It's hard out here for a pimp.

THATPIPEGUY3.14:

Haha! Sounds like it. So why the trip to New Orleans? I've always wanted to go but never really had a reason to.

I sit back down on the couch, feeling more relaxed. Talking with her is already making the evening a lot more enjoyable than the date I had earlier tonight.

CHAOSCALLIE:

My step mom is from here. She and my dad moved down here from Iowa a few years ago. I needed a change of scenery so my sister and I came down for a visit.

THATPIPEGUY3.14:

Fair enough. So do you usually do the tourist stuff when you're down there or have you been to Cafe du Monde enough times that you don't get the hype for beignets anymore?

CHAOSCALLIE:

Excuse me, sir. But beignets will ALWAYS be worthy of the hype.

THATPIPEGUY3.14:

I guess you'll just have to bring me some.

CHAOSCALLIE:

Haha! I guess so. Or you need to take a vacation and come get some yourself.

THATPIPEGUY3.14:

Vacation time is hard to come by for me. I just finished my apprenticeship though so I'm hoping that I will be able to take my son on a fun trip soon.

I lean back and think about Barrett, smiling at the thought of taking him on a trip.

LOVE YOU MADLY

CHAOSCALLIE:
I bet he would love that. How old is your son?

THATPIPEGUY3.14:
He's three. Boys are a lot of fun. I saw on your profile that you have a little girl and another kiddo on the way. Do you know what you are having yet?

CHAOSCALLIE:
Not yet, I am supposed to find out after I get back from my trip next week.

THATPIPEGUY3.14:
Are you hoping for a boy or a girl?

CHAOSCALLIE:
Honestly, I'm not sure. I've gone through a lot in this pregnancy already so as bland of an answer as this is, I really just want the baby to be healthy.

THATPIPEGUY3.14:
I wouldn't say that is a bland answer. Seems pretty straightforward to me.

CHAOSCALLIE:
I guess for the sake of timing, I would say it would be easier for me to have a girl because I still have most of the things I need because my daughter Sara isn't quite a year old yet. If I'm having a boy, I do have some stuff that I could still use like a camouflage crib set.

THATPIPEGUY3.14:
You.... have a camo crib set...? That's...

CHAOSCALLIE:
AWFUL?! I know, but my soon-to-be ex-husband insisted.

THATPIPEGUY3.14:
He sounds like a real tool, if you don't mind me saying so.

> **CHAOSCALLIE:**
> Nope, you're spot on.

> Hey, I've got to get to bed. Sara is an early riser and this app is draining my phone battery for some reason.

I get up from the couch and wander over to the window, looking out at the quiet street below. The light of the streetlamps casts a soft glow, and I feel a pang of disappointment that our conversation is ending so soon. I take another sip of my whisky and glance around my empty apartment when my phone pings again.

> **CHAOSCALLIE:**
> If you're not a total creep, you can text me tomorrow.

I chuckle at her bluntness and head back to the kitchen to rinse my glass. It's been a while since I felt this kind of connection, even through a screen. I immediately add the phone number that she gave me into my contacts.

> **THATPIPEGUY3.14:**
> Sure, I can do that. Have a good night, Callie.

> **CHAOSCALLIE:**
> Sweet dreams, Owen.

I put my phone down, feeling an unexpected anticipation for tomorrow. There's something about Callie that makes me want to keep the conversation going. Her honesty, humor, and warmth have drawn me in like no one has in a long time. I glance at the clock, realizing how late it's gotten, but the excitement buzzing in my chest makes it hard to settle down.

I lay back on the couch, staring at the ceiling, reflecting on the evening. The date with Heather felt forced and uncomfortable. There were no real sparks, just the awkward politeness of two people trying too hard to find a connection that wasn't there. But with Callie... there was something genuine.

I pick up my phone again, reading back through our messages, smiling at her wit and openness. It's in reading back the messages that I realize we didn't even really get that "into the weeds," with our conversation. Yet, I feel like at the very least, there's potential for a friendship there.

Did I just fucking friendzone myself?

I look back at her profile one more time and realize that it would probably be difficult to find the time to meet her in person. Between Barrett and my job, I don't really have time for much else.

Now I'm getting way ahead of myself.

For now, I need to take it slow, one step at a time. I stand up, stretch, and head to my bedroom. As I close my eyes, I think about Callie and her smile from her pictures that I can only imagine is even more infectious in person. I hope she actually responds when I text her tomorrow. With that thought, I finally drift off to sleep, feeling lighter than I have in a long time.

fifteen
CALL ME MAYBE - CARLY RAE JEPSEN

CALLIE - MAY 25, 2013

The morning light filters through the curtains, casting a soft glow over the room. I reach for my phone, half-hoping there's a "good morning" text from Owen. Instead, my screen lights up with a name I wish I could erase from my life—Adam.

My stomach drops.

> **ADAM:**
> Callie, are you serious? You're on dating apps? You're fucking pregnant. What the hell is wrong with you?

A cold and relentless anxiety creeps its way in as I stare at the message. I know I shouldn't let him get to me but my now deep-rooted instinct to shrink and make myself smaller is still there. It's been there for so long now I'm not sure I'll ever fully be over my fear of him lashing out if I say the wrong thing.

His words cut straight through me, sharp and dripping

with judgment. *What if he's right? What if I'm wrong for wanting something more, something outside this mess with him? Does it make me a bad mom?*

My hand trembles as I set my phone back on the nightstand, desperately trying to push away the rising panic, but the room feels smaller and I swear my own heart is trying to beat out of my chest. *Just ignore him, Callie. Today is supposed to be a good day. Don't let him take that from you.* But that voice–his voice in my head–won't shut up. It never does, always reminding me how worthless I am in moments like this.

Another buzz, another message.

> ADAM:
> This is not okay. You're carrying my child and you're out whoring around? Unbelievable.

The knot in my stomach tightens then unravels on repeat as anger burns through my fear. My fingers itch to respond, to call him and scream at him through the screen.

But I can't.

As angry as his messages make me, my instinct to make myself smaller because of him infuriates me even more. I'm sick of my emotions being dictated by Adam.

Biting the inside of my cheek, tears fill my eyes. My fingers stay frozen over the keyboard while his words blur on the screen in front of me and memories of who he used to be flood back.

What the fuck happened to him that made him so hateful?

A part of me wonders if he's like this because of how I broke up with him when I was still in high school. Maybe that's exactly it. What else could it be?

There's a battle inside me between the familiar fear pulling me down and this new, fragile part of me that wants to fight back.

He doesn't own you anymore.

It's hard to remember that, especially when his words wrap around me, a suffocating hold I cannot break free from. He makes me doubt everything I thought I knew about myself. He makes me doubt my strength and my resolve.

I sit up in the bed, still staring at my phone and settle into a new position. When I look up from the screen, I catch my reflection in the mirror on the old vanity across the room. "He can't control you," I tell my reflection over and over again.

Taking a shaky breath, I straighten a little more, repeating a new mantra to myself silently. *He doesn't get to control you. You don't owe him anything.*

I finally type out a response.

ME:

> Adam, we've been over this. We're not together anymore. You don't get to control what I do anymore. You lost that right when you started looking elsewhere to get your dick wet.

I hit send before I second-guess myself, heart still pounding out of my chest. Or fall out of my ass.

The lingering fear gnaws at me, but there's something else now, too–something that feels like relief. Like I'm starting to break free, even if it's just a little.

His response unfortunately comes almost immediately.

ADAM:

> Go fuck yourself, Callie.

I let out a bitter laugh, feeling the anger bubbling up again, but this time, I don't feel the need to shrink. I'm tired of letting him win. I type out my response and realize I might be turning into a bit of a keyboard warrior but it feels good to stick up for myself for once.

> ME:
> Gladly. Someone's gotta do it right. Lord knows you didn't. How's Janelle?

Smug fucking prick.

I toss my phone onto the nightstand and climb out of bed, my skin still crawling with the need to wash away the control Adam still somehow holds over me. Just as I'm headed to the bathroom, Taylor bursts into the room, Sara following closely behind her.

"Hey! Ready for the crawfish boil?" she asks cheerily. "Sara's been up for a while but I figured I would let you sleep a little longer."

I force a smile, pushing aside my frustration with Adam. That was not the text I wanted to wake up to today. "Yeah, I just need to run through the shower. Give me thirty?"

My forced smile must not fool my sister because Taylor asks, "Is something wrong?" Guess I won't be playing poker with her any time soon.

I sigh, feeling tension creeping up my throat. "It's Adam. He's giving me a hard time. He must have seen my dating profile last night. And he's pissed," I admit, realization dawning that he has a girlfriend and is still checking Flame-Finder regularly.

At least that confirms that I wasn't the problem, I guess...

Taylor rolls her eyes. "Of course he's pissed. Janelle dumped him. He's just miserable and wants to drag you down with him."

My jaw drops open. "Wait–what?"

Taylor shrugs like it's no big deal, but there's a glint in her eyes. "Yep, I kept him on my friends list to keep an eye on him after you guys broke up. His relationship status changed to 'single' last night. Evidently, Janelle went back to her ex."

I blink, trying to process. A bitter laugh escapes my lips. She'd stayed with Adam long enough to get back at both of us, I'm sure of it. Adam dumped her for me all those years ago, and Janelle–vindictive as she is–probably planned this from the beginning. She wanted to see us both hurt. I have to say this news makes the fact that I ended my last text to him asking how Janelle was that much sweeter. No wonder why he shut up after that.

Taylor's eyes full with what I can only assume is concern as she meets my gaze. "Just promise me you won't take him back if he comes crawling to you again, okay?"

"I promise," I say without hesitation.

By the time I've showered and dressed, the weight of Adam's message has eased, replaced by a small sense of victory. I am finally learning to stand up to him. Leaving after I found him at Janelle's took every ounce of strength that I had. I'm glad to see I'm finally gaining more of that strength back. It feels empowering.

As I help my sister pack a cooler with drinks and snacks to take outside, I feel myself starting to relax. Today is about family, good food, and–hopefully–moving on.

We're just about to head outside when Taylor notices me staring off, silently wishing that the guy I met last night would just freaking text me already.

"You good?" she asks, a hint of worry in her voice. "Or is Adam still in your head?"

I shake my head, pulling my phone from my back pocket. Still no message from Owen, and I feel a flicker of disappointment. "It's not just Adam," I admit, my voice softer than I intended. "I was kind of hoping to get a text from someone else this morning."

Taylor raises an eyebrow, catching on immediately. "Wait —Owen? Did you give that guy your number?"

Shock is written all over her face, and I can't help but laugh. "Relax, Tay. If he turns out to be a creep, I'll just block him. It's not like I gave him my last name or anything. I just don't know if I'm going to keep my profile on FlameFinder and I liked talking to him. So I gave him my number instead."

"Just be careful, okay?" Taylor's voice softens, and I can see the worry etched in her eyes. She's always had this protective streak, and I get it—she's watched me crash and burn before.

"I know, I know," I say, though the weight of her concern is heavy. It's easier to deflect, to lighten the moment. I can't stand how she looks at me sometimes, like she's waiting for me to fall apart again. "But hey, don't worry too much. I gave him my address and social security number. He said he needed it to wire me some money. Oh, and did I mention he's a prince? From Nigeria. By this time next year, I'm going to be a queen!"

Her eyes narrow, but I can see the small twitch of a smile forming. "Okay, okay, I get it," she says, shaking her head. "But seriously, Callie, I just want you to be careful. Chaos Callie was... a little too reckless. I worry about you."

Chaos Callie. The way she says the nickname stings, though I know she doesn't mean for it to. I'm the one that said I was going to embrace the nickname again. Still, it's a reminder of who I was—wild, impulsive, always throwing myself into things without thinking. I can't decide if I miss her or resent her. Maybe a little of both.

"I know you mean well," I say, softer this time. Her worry pulls at something in me, and for a moment, I let myself feel the weight of it. "But don't worry, I'm not going to delete my profile just because of Adam. He doesn't get to win."

"It's not just about Adam though," I assure her. The truth sits heavy on my chest, and I hesitate before admitting it. "It's just... I don't know if FlameFinder is quite chaotic enough for me."

I wink, but the words sit heavier than I intended. There's something unsettling about not knowing who I am right now—caught between who I was and who I'm trying to become.

Taylor eyes me for a moment before grabbing a pillow off the sofa and chucking it at me. "You're impossible!" she huffs, clearly not amused by my teasing.

I catch the pillow, and we both burst into laughter, the tension finally breaking. It feels good to laugh, to let go, even if just for a second. But the undercurrent of uncertainty still lingers, threading through the laughter like a ghost I can't quite shake.

Sara tugs on my hand, her wide eyes filled with excitement over food I doubt she will actually eat. "Mud bugs, Mama! Mud bugs!"

I smile down at her, grateful for the distraction. For now, I'll focus on the moment, on her joy, and let the rest settle later. "We're coming, sweetheart. Auntie and I just needed to get a few things," I say, ruffling her hair.

Outside, the backyard is already buzzing with activity. Dad is manning the boiling pot, and the spicy scent of crawfish fills the air. Shelly is bustling around, setting up tables while my PawPaw supervises Dad, no doubt offering unsolicited advice.

I help Shelly set out utensils and drinks for everyone while her daughters Lana and Savannah hang back, catching up with Taylor. This is just the kind of day that I need right now–family and good food.

"I hope you're hungry!" Shelly calls out, setting down a tray. I hesitate, realizing I might need to avoid shellfish while pregnant, but Shelly reassures me with a wink. "Women in the

South have been eating crawfish while pregnant for years. You'll be fine."

Good. Crawfish is my favorite, and I'm not missing this. "I'm starving," I say as Taylor hands me a plate. We pile it high with crawfish, corn, and potatoes before settling at one of Dad's tables in the shade.

I glance over at Savannah's boyfriend, Brad, smoking a cigarette by the fence, an ankle monitor peeking out from under his jeans. *What the hell is that about?* I elbow Taylor, and when she notices, she mouths, "Oh my god," as we both stifle laughter.

That's one way to make a first impression.

Just as I suspected, Sara's not so lucky with her meal–after taking a big bite of lemon, her face scrunches up in disgust, and she chucks the whole thing to the ground. Taylor and I laugh as I clean it up, enjoying the lighthearted moment. I'd only attempted to give Sara one teensy bite of the crawfish because I didn't want her getting the spices on her hands but she quickly spit that out too. So, a peanut butter and jelly sandwich for her, it is!

Savannah makes her way over to say hello briefly but we don't exchange much in the way of conversation. Savannah is older than both Taylor and me. We grew up in two completely different worlds–us in the Midwest and Savannah and Lana in Louisiana. We didn't see each other often so sometimes it doesn't even feel like they are my sisters–especially with Savannah's cold demeanor.

Lana makes her way over too, more sociable and with a bubblier personality than our eldest sister. She sits down next to us and starts chatting about her plans, life, and how work has been. She's mentioned the same guy a couple times as she talks about work at the hardware store so I suspect there might be more to their relationship than she's willing to let on with so much of our family around.

As I make quick work of washing the spices off my fingers so I can clean the peanut butter and jelly off Sara, Shelly comes back to check on us. "Everything was delicious, Shelly," I say as she passes by with a pitcher of sweet tea. *God, I don't know how people drink that crap. No matter how much sugar you put in it, it's still dirt water.*

"Thank you, sweetie. Glad you could all be here," she replies with a warm smile. "It's been too long since I had all you girls in one place."

Dad joins us at the table, letting out a satisfied sigh. "Always good to have everyone together," he says, glancing around the bustling yard. I can't help but wonder how hard it is for him not to say anything about Brad's ankle bracelet. *Does he need special permission to be here? Are we going to have to worry about the police showing up?*

Later, as I grab a drink from the cooler, Taylor leans in. "So, have you heard from him yet?" She doesn't need to say who she's talking about–Owen.

I pull out my phone and shake my head. "Not yet. It's still early though." The disappointment seeps into my phone despite my best efforts to sound nonchalant.

When she asks what Owen looks like, I pull up his profile. "He's cute," she says after a quick glance at his deep brown eyes and neatly trimmed beard. I normally hate facial hair but his only adds further to how handsome he is. He looks rugged but his smile is playful and welcoming–honestly, it's fucking sexy.

After a semi-concerned look from Taylor, I assure her I'm not rushing into anything and remind her that the dating profile was her idea to begin with. Taylor smiles, reaching over to squeeze my hand, and tells me that she is proud of me for putting myself out there and just wants me to be careful. Her words make me feel a bit more grounded and supported, reminding me that I'm not navigating this new chapter of my life alone.

I slip my phone back into my pocket, feeling a lightness that wasn't there before. As I head back to the table, I catch Taylor's eye, and she gives me a small, knowing smile.

"Come on, girls!" Shelly calls, rallying everyone together. "We're getting a group picture before everyone leaves!"

We all huddle in close, arms slung over each other, and for a brief moment, the distance and differences fade. The camera clicks, capturing a snapshot of our perfectly imperfect family.

sixteen

PINCH ME - BARENAKED LADIES

OWEN - MAY 25, 2013

The sun glints off the water, casting a soft glow over the lake as I sit on the dock, Barrett beside me, his small hands gripping his fishing pole like it holds the key to the universe. The wind is calm, the world silent except for the occasional chirp of birds. Barrett's trying so hard not to wiggle, his little body practically vibrating with excitement. He thinks the stillness is what makes fishing serious—his child logic telling him that if we're quiet, we're doing it right.

A tug on his line snaps the silence, and Barrett's eyes light up, his whole face breaking into pure joy. He starts reeling it in, his breath hitching with effort. "Daddy, look! I caught one!" His voice cracks with excitement, and the thrill in his eyes hits me right in the chest.

I help him reel in the small fish—a carp, nothing special, but to Barrett, it's like he's just won the biggest prize. "Take a picture and send it to Mama!" His grin is infectious, and for a moment, *everything else fades into the background. Just me, Barrett, and this perfect moment.*

But as I kneel to unhook the fish and release it back into the water, a shadow shifts in the corner of my vision. I look up, and there she is. Standing at the edge of the clearing. My chest tightens. Her.

Barrett notices her too. "Who's that, Daddy?" His innocent curiosity laces with a hint of fear, picking up on my sudden tension.

I swallow hard, the hairs on the back of my neck rising. "I don't know, buddy." My voice comes out tight, barely above a whisper. She's never appeared when Barrett is with me.

I stand, my heart pounding as we move toward her. Each step feels heavy, a strange weight pulling me closer. Barrett's small hand tugs at mine, and for a moment, I consider turning back. But the magnetic pull—the same one I've felt in every dream—drags me forward.

When we're close enough to see her face, those familiar green eyes lock onto mine. They're softer today, almost gentle. But I've seen the pain behind them before, the haunted sorrow that always lingers just below the surface. What's different today?

"Hi," Barrett says, his small voice timid as he stares at her. He doesn't seem afraid—just... drawn in, the same way I am.

She kneels, her face level with Barrett's, and smiles. That smile —it tugs at something deep in my chest, something I can't explain. It's like coming home to a place I didn't know I was missing. Barrett steps closer, his curiosity getting the best of him.

"What's your name?" His question hangs in the air, but she doesn't answer. Instead, she lifts her hand—slowly, deliberately— and touches his cheek. Barrett giggles, the sound ringing through the clearing, and I can feel the warmth of it wrap around me like a blanket.

I take a step forward, my pulse quickening. "Who are you?" *The words spill out, rough and jagged.* "What do you want?"

She rises, her eyes meeting mine again. That warmth shifts into something else—something heavier. There's sadness there, deep and raw. She reaches out, and before I can stop her, her fingers brush my cheek. I freeze. The warmth of her touch sends a shockwave through me, familiar but electric, like I've been waiting for it all my life.

But why? Why does this feel like home?

Her touch lingers, and just as I'm about to speak, everything around us begins to blur. Her face, the dock, the lake—it all starts to dissolve, pulling away like sand slipping through my fingers. No. Don't go.

And then... she's gone.

I jolt awake, my heart slamming against my ribs. The early morning light filters through the curtains, the familiar surroundings of my apartment creeping back into focus. But the loss, the emptiness—that stays. I run my hands over my face, trying to shake the feeling that something—someone—is missing. Waking up from these dreams leaves me raw, vulnerable in a way that's starting to scare me.

Why her? Why now? Why is Barrett in these dreams? It's never been like this before. The thought of her with him—it unnerves me, the connection too deep, too real.

I get up, pacing the small apartment as the weight of the dream presses down on me. After a while, I make a cup of coffee, the strong, bitter taste doing nothing to ease the tightness in my chest. I need a distraction. Anything to pull me out of this.

Callie. I grab my phone and thumb through my contacts, pausing when I see her name. Maybe I should text her. But sending a "good morning, beautiful" text after just one conversation feels like the exact thing she warned me about—being too much, too soon. Just as I'm about to set the phone down, it begins buzzing with a call from Luke.

"Morning, sunshine," Luke's voice bursts through, too cheerful for how I feel. "How's it going?"

"Morning," I grunt, trying to shake the dream from my head. "What's up?"

"I'm calling to gloat. Heather texted me this morning, man. We're going out tonight. Thanks for the hookup." His voice drips with amusement, and I can picture the smirk on his face.

I force a laugh. "Glad I could help. Wasn't really feeling it anyway."

"Well, I was, so thanks for passing her along." There's a pause. "What's got you all quiet? Rough night?"

I hesitate, my fingers drumming against the counter. "Yeah. Weird dream again."

"Her?"

"Yeah. It was... different this time. Barrett was with me."

Luke's silence on the other end is heavy, like he's trying to figure out how to respond. "That's new. Maybe it means something?"

I shrug, even though he can't see it. "Or maybe it's just a dream, man. You know I don't buy into that cosmic soulmate crap."

"Hey, maybe you should. She keeps showing up for a reason." He laughs, but there's a seriousness there too.

I shake my head, trying to change the subject. "Speaking of cosmic bullshit—good luck on your date with Heather."

"Thanks, man," he says, clearly relieved by the shift. "I'll let you know how it goes."

After we hang up, I lace up my running shoes, deciding a

run might clear my head. As the familiar beats of "Big Poppa," by The Notorious B.I.G pump through my earbuds, I start my run, trying to outrun the lingering weight of the dream. But even as the music fills my ears and my legs burn from the effort, I can't shake the feeling that she's still there–just out of reach.

I step out of the shower a short time later after trying to scrub away the lingering unease from the dream, my phone buzzes again. I glance at the screen–Sabrina. Her voice comes through, apologetic and soft but ever-so-slightly panicked. Barrett forgot to pack his lion toys–or rather, I forgot to pack them–and he's been inconsolable without them. I can hear the guilt in her tone, like she hates having to ask for a favor. Before she even gets the chance to ask, I offer to make the drive to bring them to him. Anything for Barrett.

When I arrive in Cedar Bluff and Sabrina opens her front door, the exhaustion on her face is evident. She looks like she hasn't slept much, either. I feel bad knowing she probably had a long night with Barrett. I should have paid closer attention when we were gathering everything up as I brought him home.

"Thank you so much, Owen," she says, taking the toys from me. "He's been asking for them since last night but I didn't want to bother you while you were on your date."

I offer a small smile, trying to shake the weight of everything in my head coupled with knowing I was distracted when I brough him home and it's partially my fault that Sabrina didn't get any sleep last night. "Sab, it doesn't matter what I'm doing. If he needs me, I'll be here."

Sabrina nods in understanding and looks at me more

closely, concern etched on her face. "You look like you had a rough night. Did your date not go well?" she asks, then realization dawns on her and she corrects her train of thought. "Or maybe it went a little too well?" Her laugh is awkward, almost forced.

I laugh it off, shrugging. "It didn't go according to plan. But it's fine. Turns out, she's more Luke's type."

She frowns slightly; her worry etched on her face. "That sounds like a lot to unpack so I'm not even going to ask. But are you okay?" she asks.

I sigh, feeling terrible for burdening her. "I just haven't been sleeping well. My dreams are messing with me."

"You still see her, huh?"

Her question catches me off-guard and sends a jolt of guilt through me. I forgot I had told her about the recurring dreams when I was in a whiskey-drunken stupor the night our divorce was finalized. Thankfully, I wasn't drunk enough to tell her exactly when the dreams started.

Sabrina's expression softens. "It's okay, Owen. It's just a dream. Maybe the universe is telling you it's time to allow yourself to move on. It's possible that it's a message indicating your soul mate is somewhere out there, struggling to find you. Maybe she's stuck too."

Sabrina has always been the more spiritual person between the two of us. I'm too fact-based for religion. I have to see it and have tangible proof in order for things to make sense to me. Still, her words hit home, and I nod, feeling a bit more reassured. "Thanks, Sabrina. I needed that."

She gives me a supportive smile. "Anytime. You're doing great, Owen. Don't be too hard on yourself."

I stay for a while, spending some time with Barrett, though my mind never fully lets go of the dream or the weight of Sabrina's words. By the time I'm driving back home, the tension has eased a little, but not enough to keep Callie from creeping into my thoughts.

I've let enough of the day slip by already. When I get home, I'll definitely text her. Something light. Casual. No pressure.

But I can already feel the nerves kicking in.

seventeen

I WANNA DANCE WITH SOMEBODY - WHITNEY HOUSTON

CALLIE - MAY 25, 2013

Once Dad's guests leave, the house finally quiets, but my mind is still buzzing. I take a sleeping Sara out of her high chair and cradle her against me. She nestles in, her tiny thumb finding its way to her mouth, and I watch as she drifts deeper into sleep. My heart squeezes, a familiar ache that mixes love and fear. How am I going to juggle this—being a mom to her and another baby on the way, all while my world feels like it's barely holding together?

After laying her down in the portable crib, I head out to the porch, baby monitor in hand, and try to distract myself with a new Robyn Carr novel. I settle into the worn porch chair, letting the evening sun bathe me in a warmth I barely feel inside. As I flip the pages, the story barely registers. My mind is on Owen. I haven't heard from him all day, and it's ridiculous how much I've been hoping for a message.

Just as I'm about to force myself to focus on the book, my

phone pings. My heart leaps, irrationally, and I fumble to pick it up.

> **UNKNOWN:**
> What's up, chick? How's your day going?

I stare at the screen, my pulse racing. It's him. I'm almost certain of it. But I'm not about to show how giddy I am. I quickly type back.

> **ME:**
> New phone. Who dis? 😜

The reply comes instantly, almost too fast.

> **UNKNOWN:**
> You're hilarious.
>
> I guess you must have responded to the guy who said he'd make you forget your Baby Daddy and gave him your phone number, too. Damn, that's too bad. I thought I was special.

I laugh out loud despite myself, the tension in my chest easing just a little. Yep, it's Owen. His humor is a refreshing contrast to the chaos that is in my life lately.

Green Flag #3.

> **ME:**
> You caught me. He made me forget my Baby Daddy and the name of the guy I talked to last night.

> **UNKNOWN:**
> Very funny, Callie... But just in case you're serious, it's Owen.

The flutter in my stomach deepens. I shouldn't be this excited. Should I? Before I can overthink it, I save his contact.

> ME:
>
> Ohhhhh! Owen! That's right!
>
> I'm joking, obviously. I don't give my number out to everyone, believe it or not.

> OWEN:
>
> I'm curious... Why did you give it to me?

His question makes me pause. Why did I? This shouldn't be serious, just a fun distraction. But there is something about him, the way we clicked last night, the way thoughts of him lingered in my mind all day. It feels like something I could lose myself in. And that's dangerous.

> ME:
>
> Idk... I'm thinking about deleting the app because it's really not my thing and you seem like a decent enough human and I liked talking to you last night.

> OWEN:
>
> Decent enough? I'll take it. Haha!

His easy humor calms me, but the question still lingers in my mind: *Why did I give him my number?* Maybe I'm lonelier than I realized.

> OWEN:
>
> So what did you do today?

I glance around at the remnants of the day—the smell of crawfish still lingers in the air, and the memory of laughter with family feels both distant and close.

> ME:
>
> My dad hosted a crawfish boil, so we had family over. It was good to see everyone.

> **OWEN:**
> That's awesome. What are you up to now?

> **ME:**
> Trying to read a book but failing miserably. I love reading, but sometimes I struggle with it. I think I'm more of an audio learner.

There it is again, that vulnerable side I hate showing. It feels stupid admitting something so simple, yet it's a piece of me I can't help sharing with him.

> **OWEN:**
> Do you want me to leave you alone so you can read?

> **ME:**
> No, that's okay. I'm sure you can think of another way to keep me entertained.

The second I hit send, I freeze. That sounded way more suggestive than I intended. Shit.

> **ME:**
> Woah. I meant, like, keep me distracted from the book. That sounded way worse than I meant it to.

> **OWEN:**
> Oh, did it now? So you admit there was some intention behind it?

I bite my lip, my face flushing. What am I doing? This is insane.

> **OWEN:**
> Relax, Callie. I'm just messing with you.

> **ME:**
> Don't tease me if you can't please me.

What the hell did I just send?! My heart races as I stare at the screen, waiting for him to react. I need to backtrack.

ME:
> Sorry, that was a lot. Can I get a do-over?

OWEN:
> Haha! Sure thing. Wanna play a game?

ME:
> That sounds dangerous.

OWEN:
> Only if you want it to be.

ME:
> Oh my god! OWEN! 😳

OWEN:
> Callie, you're making this way too easy. Especially screaming my name like that. I'm pretty sure I can see you blushing from here.

ME:
> You're a shameless flirt, you know that?

OWEN:
> Yeah, my ex-wife mentioned that once or twice.

That thought makes me cringe and I cannot help but hope that's something she said to him after they split up. Please don't start collecting red flags...

OWEN:
> And no, I didn't cheat on her.

Oh, thank God.

I exhale a breath, relief flooding through me like a tidal wave. But there's a knot in my stomach that won't quite untangle. My mind flashes to Adam—every lie, every broken promise. I swallow the familiar bitterness that threatens to rise. Owen doesn't deserve to be punished for my past. Yet, my guard comes up reflexively, an instinct I can't shake.

ME:
> Am I that transparent? Sorry, cheating is a sore subject for me. My husband was less than faithful throughout our entire marriage.

I hesitate, the weight of the truth heavy in my chest. Saying it out loud feels raw, exposing a wound that still hasn't healed.

ME:
> Sorry, ex-husband. Or soon-to-be. I don't really even know what to call him.

OWEN:
> Asshole? 😛

I let out a startled laugh, the tension breaking for just a second.

ME:
> That works!

OWEN:
> So... about that game... Wanna play? It would be like "Truth or Dare," without the dares.

ME:
> Good. I'm definitely not in the mood for dares anyway. Last thing I need is to end up having to run around the yard naked or something.

OWEN:
> Now, when you put it that way...

ME:
> Nice try but not a chance. Okay, I'll go first. Sticking with the music theme, I've gotta know... Do you sing in the shower?

> OWEN:
> I might, but only when the house is empty. My singing is a solo act for a reason.

I laugh out loud, picturing him—beard lathered up, belting out some Tupac or Biggie based on what he told me about his music taste. The mental image is both hilarious and oddly endearing.

Then, just like that, my mind takes a detour, and I realize my pregnancy hormones are heating up more than just my cheeks. I shake off the thought, trying to focus as his next message lights up my phone.

> OWEN:
> What song do you dance to most in your living room?

> ME:
> I Wanna Dance with Somebody by Whitney Houston, obviously.

> OWEN:
> Ahhhh so there's the "basic" side you've been hiding.

> ME:
> I am NOT basic! It's a classic. You're losing major brownie points for that one, Owen.

I grin at the screen, feeling a little silly over how easily this conversation is flowing. It's strange—comforting, even. With each message, there's a warmth spreading through me, something that feels almost... normal. As if, just for a moment, I can let my guard down.

eighteen
I WANNA KNOW - JOE

OWEN - MAY 25, 2013

Talking to Callie has quickly become the highlight of my day. Every text, every moment we talk feels like peeling back another layer, and it's been a long time since I felt this kind of excitement. Our conversation flows so effortlessly, like catching up with an old friend who gets my weird sense of humor and makes me laugh until my sides hurt. Tonight, I'm sprawled out on the couch, phone in hand, the TV playing reruns of *The Big Bang Theory* that I'm not even paying attention to. My focus is on Callie.

ME:
(So, what's your go-to comfort food?)

The question hangs in the air as I wait, my heart inexplicably pounding. It's ridiculous, really. She's just a woman I met online, but there's this pull, something that makes me want to keep this conversation going forever.

> **CALLIE:**
> That's easy! Mac and cheese. It's the ultimate comfort food. Pineapple on pizza: yes or no?

I chuckle, shaking my head. She's throwing some curveballs. Good.

> **ME:**
> Absolutely yes. 🍍

> **CALLIE:**
> That's so fucking disgusting. 🤮🤮🤮

> **ME:**
> Well, we'll just have to agree to disagree on that one until you admit you're wrong.

> **CALLIE:**
> Don't hold your breath.

I laugh out loud, feeling all the tension in my body fade away. It's so easy with her. She's playful and sarcastic, and I can't help but want to know everything about her. The conversation flows effortlessly, with no awkward pauses, no struggling for the next thing to say.

> **ME:**
> Haha! I won't. What's your favorite movie?

I pause, wondering if this conversation feels as easy for her as it does for me. There's this connection, and I find myself hoping it's not just in my head.

> **CALLIE:**
> The Princess Bride. It's got everything: adventure, romance, humor.

> **ME:**
> As you wish.

There's a beat, and I wonder if she's laughing on the other side. I wonder what her laugh sounds like. I imagine it in my head–soft, sweet. God, why does it feel like I've known her for years?

> **CALLIE:**
> Haha! Okay, serious question. What's your biggest fear?

My fingers freeze above the screen. At this point, I can either deflect or give her a real answer. My gut tells me to trust her.

> **ME:**
> I'm afraid of failing my son. When his mom and I split, I left because I didn't want him growing up seeing two people who didn't love each other. But sometimes I wonder if I could have done more, or if I made the right choice.

The silence after I hit send feels heavy like I've exposed too much. But then her message comes through, and it's like she's right here with me, offering reassurance without even trying.

> **CALLIE:**
> That says a lot about what a great dad you really are. Bad parents don't worry about whether or not they are bad parents.

I blink at her words, feeling the warmth of them settle into my chest. I breathe easier, releasing some of the tension that started to build back up inside me. She doesn't just get it–she gets *me*.

> ME:
> I hope you're right.

> CALLIE:
> I am.

I smile, feeling a warmth spread through me at her words. I stretch out, shifting to get more comfortable, my feet propped up on the coffee table.

> ME:
> Alright, enough of the heavy stuff! What's something you've always wanted to learn?

I don't have to wait long for her answer.

> CALLIE:
> I've always wanted to learn guitar, but being left-handed made it tough. My boyfriend got frustrated teaching me, as I had to do everything backward, and my hands cramped awkwardly. I learned "Smoke on the Water," but ultimately, I gave up.

> ME:
> Well, your ex sounds like a real turd. I'm a leftie too, by the way. So I feel your pain. Sketching was always a pain in the ass because my hand always smeared what I was working on.

> CALLIE:
> Haha! So true! That was the worst part about art class. So frustrating! Do you have any siblings?

I walk to the kitchen, grabbing a soda from the fridge. The cool fizz feels good against my throat as I sit back down and type out my response.

ME: Just my stepbrother, Luke. We didn't grow up together, but we knew each other from school. Our parents got married after we graduated from college. But he's been one of my best friends over the last ten years or so.

CALLIE: Hold on...

You have a brother named Luke?

ME: Yes... why?

CALLIE: You are brothers named Owen and Luke?

ME: Yes...

CALLIE: Like Owen and Luke Wilson?! That's hilarious. 🌀

I burst out laughing, shaking my head.

ME: If you think that's great, you're going to really lose it when I tell you that my best friend's name is Will and my cousin's name is Vince.

CALLIE: Haha! That's awesome. You have the whole funny bunch.

Her response makes me wonder what her laugh sounds like.

CALLIE:

Must be nice to have a best friend as a brother. My sister and I get along now but she and I used to fight like cats and dogs.

I toss my phone onto the couch for a second, stretching again. I think about how easy it is to talk to her—how we've been texting for hours now, and it never feels like I'm struggling to find the next thing to say. It's just... natural.

ME:

Yeah, he's a great guy for sure.

I saw that you have some tattoos when I looked at the pictures on your profile. How many tattoos do you have and which one is your favorite?

CALLIE:

That's a double-up question. But I'll allow it. I have seven. And my favorite one is the cherry blossom tree on my right arm. I got it after I had my daughter.

ME:

SEVEN?! Damn, girl! 🔥 I only have one.

CALLIE:

Haha! I like getting tattooed. It's like therapy for me.

Seven tattoos. I can't help but smile. There's something undeniably sexy about a woman with tattoos—like every piece of ink tells a story. And the fact that she's got one dedicated to her daughter? That hits different. It's not just a tattoo. It's part of her, part of who she is.

My mind wanders, picturing the cherry blossom tree flowing along her arm, imagining how it looks, how it feels. God, I really can't get enough of this girl. It's like every little thing I learn about her makes me want to know more.

> **CALLIE:**
> So, what year did you graduate high school?

> **ME:**
> 1999.

> **CALLIE:**
> Wait a second…
>
> You are from Cedar Bluff originally, right? Did you play football?

> **ME:**
> I grew up in a small town in the Midwest. Do you even have to ask that? And what happened to no double-up questions? Because you just asked me three in a row.

> **CALLIE:**
> Fair point. Oh my god, you're not going to believe this…
>
> My mom was the cheerleading coach in Hawkridge back then. When I was a kid, we had a home game against Cedar Bluff and a bunch of the football players stole the cheerleading shirts from the girls' locker room because that's the locker room guest teams used!

I sit up, the memory coming back to me. Holy shit. That was us. I type back quickly, laughing.

> **ME:**
> No way! That was me and my buddies! We thought it would be hilarious. Was she pissed?

> **CALLIE:**
> Yes! She was irate! The next day, she called the Cedar Bluff superintendent and everything. He swore to her that you guys were going to be in huge trouble, possibly even suspended from the football team.

> **ME:**
> Haha! That's hilarious. Especially because no one ever said anything to us about it. Apparently, that superintendent was full of shit and didn't want his football players getting in trouble when we were headed for a state championship.

> **CALLIE:**
> Wow, what a small world. I'll have to tell her I met one of the culprits.

> **ME:**
> Is there a statute of limitations in Iowa for stealing cheerleading t-shirts?

This conversation feels like a ride I didn't even know I'd gotten on, each twist drawing me closer to her, each turn revealing something new. It's unpredictable, but in the best way—like there's no telling where we'll end up, and I'm not ready to let go. Not when every moment with her feels like something I've been searching for without even realizing it.

I stretch again, feeling a pleasant ache from laughing so much. I walk over to the window, looking out at the quiet street below, feeling a sense of peace I haven't felt in a while.

We move on to other topics, and I tell her about my love for fishing and cooking. When she confesses she's a terrible cook, I can't resist offering to cook for her someday. It's a small thing, but it makes the idea of meeting her in person seem all the more real.

When I ask her what the most embarrassing thing that has ever happened to her is, she starts telling me a story about how she slipped and fell down a flight of stairs when she was coming out of the band room in high school. Apparently, she had been wearing a long skirt that got caught under her heel and ended up slipping and landing on her butt before bumping down every step until she hit the floor.

> ME:
> Ouch, that sounds rough. Did you get hurt?

> CALLIE:
> Just my pride.

> ME:
> So you were a band geek in high school, huh?

> CALLIE:
> It's not your turn to ask a question. But yes, I sure was.

> ME:
> What did you play? The flute? Oh my god! Do you have a "This one time, at band camp..." story?!

I can't help myself; I hit send on the text without giving it much thought.

> CALLIE:
> Omg! No. I didn't even go to band camp. And I was on the drumline. I was the Captain my Junior and Senior year, actually.

> ME:
> Drumline has a Captain?

I already know the answer to that. The high school I went to in Cedar Bluff always did really well at band competitions. But I can't resist teasing her a bit.

> **CALLIE:**
> Yes! I was a cheerleader too, so most of the time I was marching, I was in my cheerleading uniform. Now, quit with the follow-up questions. You keep skipping my turns!

> **ME:**
> You're killing me here. You were a cheerleader too? Christ Almighty. Do you still have the uniform? And will you let me steal one of your old t-shirts? 😊

I wait for the conversation to continue but she doesn't respond. Wondering if I crossed the line with my cheerleader comment, I replay the conversation in my mind, searching for anything else that I might have said to upset her.

In a moment of panic, I send another quick message.

> **ME:**
> Hey, did I say something to upset you? You went silent on me, and now I'm imagining you plotting my demise with a drumstick... one of those big ones they use for the timpani drums.

I wait, hoping for a response, my mind racing with all the possible scenarios. Did I come on too strong? I tap my fingers nervously on my leg, silently pleading for her to reply and put my mind at ease.

nineteen

SO CONTAGIOUS - ACCEPTANCE

CALLIE - MAY 25, 2013

Once I hear Sara stirring awake, it snaps me out of the warm, easy conversation with Owen. The two hours since I laid her down have flown by, but now it's time to return to reality. I glance at my phone and feel a tug of disappointment. Talking to Owen has been a brief escape from the mess of everything else.

"Back to the chaos," I mumble, setting my phone down and heading inside to get Sara. She's blinking awake, her tiny arms stretching as she murmurs, "Mama." Her soft, warm body curls into mine as I lift her from the crib, and for a moment, the stress of everything else melts away. Her thumb finds its way to her mouth, and she rests her head on my shoulder.

I carry her into the living room and grab my phone from the porch, noticing another message from Owen:

OWEN:

Listen, it's not my fault, it's science. There's just something about a cheerleading uniform that is programmed in straight men's DNA.

A laugh escapes me. He's still hung up on the cheerleader comment. As if on cue, another message pops up:

OWEN:

Hey, Callie... I'm really sorry if I made you uncomfortable. I didn't mean anything by it. I was just messing around.

I quickly type back, feeling a twinge of guilt that I left him hanging.

ME:

You're okay! Sorry, Sara woke up from her nap and I left my phone on the porch.

OWEN:

Okay, good deal. I was worried that my cheerleader comment made it weird.

ME:

Nah, it's going to take more than that to scare me off. It's sweet that you were worried about it though.

OWEN:

I can be a bit sweet from time to time. Just don't tell anyone. It's bad for my image.

I smirk, still amazed at how easy it is to talk to him.

OWEN:

I had a really nice time talking to you today. Let's do it again soon?

ME:

Definitely. Have a good rest of your night, Owen. I'm going to go see what my dad and stepmom are planning for dinner tonight and offer to help them out.

OWEN:

You sure that's a good idea? A little birdie told me that you're a terrible cook.

ME:

Fair point. I'll talk to you tomorrow.

OWEN:

Looking forward to it.

A warmth settles over me as I put my phone down, but there's also an unexpected edge of sadness. The easy banter with Owen has been refreshing, something I didn't realize I needed. And the fact that he's hot as sin doesn't hurt either.

The rest of the New Orleans trip flies by in a blur of laughter and family moments. We squeeze in a steamboat cruise on the Mississippi, soaking in the jazz music, and by the time we return to Dad's, we're all exhausted but happy.

The car ride back to Iowa is long but uneventful. Taylor and I take turns driving while Sara naps in the backseat. As the familiar sight of Hawkridge comes into view, I can feel the weight of real life creeping back in. My ultrasound appointment looms ahead.

The sterile clinic air hits me as I lie back on the exam table. Adam insisted on coming, and I was too tired to argue. When the tech announces we're having another girl, Adam's face twists in frustration.

"Seriously?" He mutters, red creeping up his neck. His outburst in the small, quiet room is embarrassing, but it's also a reminder—a painfully clear one—of why I'm fighting so hard to end this marriage.

By the time Thursday rolls around, I'm sitting in my attorney's office, surrounded by paperwork. The proof of Adam's infidelity sits in a neat pile in front of me. The lawyer's confirmation that we can expedite the divorce feels like a lifeline.

Later, Brooke helps me navigate setting up with DHHS. As we stand in line, I feel a wave of gratitude and shame all at once. There's a stigma that lingers around state aid, but I push the guilt aside. My kids deserve everything I can give them, and I won't let pride get in the way.

Friday has arrived, and I find myself back at the coffee shop for another shift. The steady stream of customers and the aroma of freshly brewed coffee helps keep my mind occupied. Throughout the week, I've continued to chat with Owen. Our conversations have been a bright spot amid the chaos, his words offering a sense of normalcy and comfort. Each message from him brings a smile to my face, and I've realized how much I look forward to our talks.

Just as I'm leaving work, my phone buzzes with a text message.

> OWEN:
> Hey Callie, I hope you're having a good day at work! I'm headed to pick up Barrett so I might not have much chance to talk to you tonight.

> ME:
> I'm actually just about to clock out. Thanks for letting me know so I didn't think you'd gotten sick of me already if you don't reply. I hope you and Barrett have a fantastic night. Drive safe.

> OWEN:
> Thanks, I'm really looking forward to it.

> ME:
> I think it's admirable you don't let your phone get in the way of spending time with your son.

> OWEN:
> Just doing my job… Also, there's something I've been thinking about…

Oh boy. The ellipses are never a good thing. I hope I haven't been coming on too strong. When he and I started talking just under a week ago, I was really only looking for friendship, if anything.

But as much as we've gotten to know each other, I can't deny that I'm really drawn to him. There's just something about Owen that pulls me in and I smile every time I hear from him. He makes me laugh and having a sense of humor is something that I find so attractive.

I've only seen a couple of pictures of him but there's no denying that he's incredibly attractive. What I find so strange is that I have always said that I hate facial hair. Every time Adam would go a few days without shaving, I was constantly nagging him about it. But something about Owen and that full beard just does things to me and I cannot help but wonder what his beard would feel like between my legs.

Oh my God. Yep, I just went there.

Blaming it on pregnancy hormones, I try to shake it off and focus my attention back on what those three little dots are going to lead to.

> ME:
> Sure, what's up? Also – you're not texting and driving are you?

OWEN:

Nope, haven't left quite yet.

I know things have been getting a bit more intense in our conversations lately. I would be lying if I said I didn't find you incredibly attractive.

More fucking ellipses. That means there's a really big 'but' coming.

OWEN:

But, I think given the distance between us, it probably makes the most sense that we remain friendly instead of trying to pursue anything further. I work so much and already have a lot of drive time with picking up Barrett and dropping him off.

Reading his message, a pang of disappointment hits me. But I get it.

ME:

Plus, I'm in the opposite direction... I get it. It makes sense. Mighty presumptuous of you to think I needed this talk though. 😊

OWEN:

Honestly, I think I felt I had to lay it out there because well... I like you, Callie. I just don't see how it could be anything more when we haven't even been able to steal ten minutes to FaceTime.

ME:

I like you too, Owen. And I'm glad to call you a friend. Besides, I was getting tired of all those swoon-worthy texts anyway. Too much sweetness is bad for my teeth. 😁

OWEN:

Swoon-worthy, huh? 🤭

> I'm really glad too. You're an amazing person, Callie. And I love our chats. I just think this is what's best for now.

ME:
> I appreciate your honesty. Really. Have a great time with Barrett. Talk soon?

OWEN:
> Definitely. Take care, Callie.

Putting down my phone, I feel a wave of emotion wash over me. The disappointment is hard to shake, even if Owen is right. The distance between us makes things a bit more complicated. And I know I have enough on my plate without adding a long-distance relationship to the mix, especially with someone I have never met in person.

This just feels like the first of many rejections I'm likely to face in the future as a single mom with too much baggage. I take a deep breath and try to center myself before leaving the coffee shop.

This week, I have also been focused on planning Sara's first birthday party for this Sunday. Emotions well up as I think about it more. This isn't something I ever imagined doing without her dad. Adam wanted to have a joint party for her, but after his outburst at the ultrasound appointment, I told him there was no way that was happening. I was the only one who had been putting any effort into planning it anyway. I am determined to make it a special day for Sara, despite everything. And he's not going to ruin it for her.

Sara's first birthday party is a colorful burst of joy, set against the backdrop of a warm June day at the local park. The grassy area is alive with the laughter of children playing on the nearby playground, their excited squeals blending with the soft rustling of leaves in the breeze. A large pavilion, shaded by tall, ancient trees, serves as the gathering spot for family and friends. The picnic tables are draped in pastel-colored tablecloths, and bright balloons bob in the air, tied to the corners of the tables. Streamers in pink, yellow, and blue sway gently in the breeze, adding to the festive atmosphere.

The centerpiece of the decorations is a whimsical, two-tiered cake adorned with delicate sugar flowers and a fondant topper in the shape of a tiny tiara, perfect for the little princess of the day. Nearby, a table is laden with food and drinks, offering everything from finger sandwiches to fresh fruit and lemonade. It's simple but sweet, just like I imagined.

Guests start to arrive, filling the pavilion with chatter and warmth. Taylor is here, her blonde hair pulled back into a casual ponytail, chatting animatedly with Brooke, who is fussing over Sara's outfit—a cute, ruffled dress in soft pink that complements the theme. My mom stands off to the side, her eyes scanning the surroundings, a mixture of pride and worry etched on her face. Things like this always make her so high-strung. Beside her is Wayne, my step-dad, his arm casually draped over her shoulder as they watch the kids play. It's a picture of familial comfort.

Ava, my niece, is here too, bouncing around with the kind of energy that makes me jealous of the spunky little four-year-old. She's got a balloon in one hand and a cupcake in the other, her face smeared with frosting. I can't help but smile at the sight of her, so full of innocence.

I want everything to be perfect for Sara, for this day to be about her and the incredible year we've shared since she made me a mommy. But when Adam shows up uninvited, my heart sinks. His presence is like a dark cloud over the sun, casting a shadow on what is supposed to be a bright, happy occasion.

I catch sight of him approaching, a grin plastered on his face as if he belongs here, as if he has been a part of planning this party all along. He strolls up with a couple of large, wrapped presents in hand, the kind that scream 'I spend a lot of money on this' rather than 'I know what my daughter would love.' It's infuriating, the way he manages to insert himself into the day without a second thought.

Wayne sees him and sends me a look that silently asks if I want him to get rid of him. But I give him a subtle shake of my head when I see Sara running toward him, so excited to see her dad. She grabs him around the ankles and I cannot help but smile when she plops her little butt down on his shoe and wraps her leg around his tattooed calf forcing him to carry her on his leg as he walks.

The party carries on around us, the kids laughing as they chase each other on the grass, the adults mingling and catching up. But all I can see is Adam, moving through the gathering like he owns the place, acting like the doting father he hasn't been lately. He laughs and jokes with everyone, pretending as if nothing is wrong.

I stand by the food table, gripping a cup of lemonade so tightly that the plastic starts to crumple in my hand. Taylor notices and gives me a sympathetic look, but there's nothing she can say that will make this better. This was supposed to be a day about Sara, about celebrating her first year of life, but now it feels tainted.

Adam finally chooses to acknowledge my existence and starts walking over, that same smug grin on his face. "Hey, Callie," he says, as if we're old friends rather than two people waiting for our divorce to be finalized.

"Adam," I reply, forcing a tight smile. "I didn't expect to see you here."

"I couldn't miss my daughter's first birthday," he says, like it's the most obvious thing in the world. "And I brought some gifts. She's going to love them."

"Today is about spending time with her, not about how much money you spent."

He shrugs, unfazed by my tone. "I just want to make sure she has everything she needs."

I want to scream. But I bite my tongue, knowing that causing a scene won't do anyone any good.

Adam lingers for a while, talking to some of the other guests, showing off the gifts he bought like he's some kind of hero. All but one of the toys he bought are things she won't be able to use for years because they are too old for her. But I don't say anything. I try to focus on Sara, who is blissfully unaware of the tension around her. She's sitting in her high chair, giggling as Brooke hands her the top tier of the birthday cake which serves as her "smash cake."

Adam gets ready to leave as soon as Sara is done with her cake–leaving me to clean up the mess, like always. I hear him make a comment to my mom about how it's his new girlfriend Katie's birthday too so he has dinner plans.

Yep, it's only been a couple days since Janelle dumped him and Adam already has a new girlfriend. I would bet my left kidney that he was already talking to Katie while he was dating Janelle. He always seems to have a backup plan when it comes to relationships.

By the time the party winds down, I'm exhausted. I pack up the leftover food and the mountain of gifts, making a mental note to sort through everything later. Taylor and Brooke help me clean up, while my mom and Wayne take Sara and Ava to the playground for a bit longer.

Once everything is packed up, I stand in the now-empty pavilion, taking a deep breath. The day didn't go exactly as planned, but as I watch Sara toddle over to me, her face still smeared with cake and her eyes shining with happiness, I know that it was still a success. The day was for her, and in the end, that's all that matters.

twenty
USE SOMEBODY - KINGS OF LEON

OWEN - JUNE 2, 2013

The soft hum of the apartment's air conditioning fills the space as Barrett pushes his toy cars across the living room floor, his quiet giggles cutting through the otherwise still afternoon. I watch him from the couch, eyes lingering on the small smile stretching across his face. These moments should feel like a blessing. They do—usually. But today, even as Barrett plays, I can't help feeling distracted, like my mind is walking a tightrope between being present here and drifting somewhere else entirely.

Callie's face swims into my thoughts again. I replay our conversation from Friday—how I told her we needed to just be friends. She took it well. Almost too well, and that bothers me. Maybe I thought... hell, maybe I wanted her to fight me on it. To show that she felt the instant connection that I felt. But she didn't.

I glance over at Barrett, who's making little engine sounds

as he pushes his cars in circles. His world is simple. I wish mine still was.

The apartment feels heavy, despite the cool air. Barrett's laughter pulls me back for a moment, and I smile at him. It's a bittersweet reminder—no matter what's going on in my head, he's always right here, grounding me. But even that thought feels fragile today.

After tucking Barrett into bed that evening, I collapse onto the couch, exhaustion pressing down on me. The stillness of the apartment, once comforting, now feels oppressive. My phone buzzes, and I instinctively reach for it, grateful for the distraction.

CALLIE:

> I'm so sorry for bothering you, I know you have Barrett. I just need to vent. So if you have fifteen texts by the time you see this, forgive me.

I can't help but smile at her message, the familiar warmth stirring in my chest. There's something in the way she always apologizes for things even though she doesn't need to. As much as I would like to believe it's her way of being polite, I cannot help but feel like her constant need to apologize is because others have made her feel like a burden.

ME:

> It's okay, you have good timing, actually. I just put Barrett to bed for the night.

Her response comes quickly, and I can almost hear the exasperation in her voice as I read the text.

CALLIE:

> You won't believe what happened at Sara's birthday party today.

ME:

> What's up? Are you okay?

I lean back against the couch, feeling a twinge of concern.

CALLIE:

> My ex showed up with a mountain of expensive gifts for Sara. He wasn't even invited.

I frown, anger simmering beneath the surface. I've never met the guy, but from everything Callie's told me, he has a knack for making things difficult.

ME:

> Seriously? That's messed up.

CALLIE:

> Yeah, it was. Everyone was staring. It was so awkward.

ME:

> I can imagine. How did Sara react?

CALLIE:

> She loved the gifts, of course. But it felt like he was trying to show off or something.

I can practically hear the frustration in her voice through the text. My heart aches for her, knowing how much she wanted this day to be special for Sara without any drama. Knowing Callie's ex purposefully threw her off like that makes my blood boil a little.

> **ME:**
> Sounds like he's trying to one-up you. What a douchebag.

> **CALLIE:**
> Exactly. I just wanted a simple party for her at the park without drama and the Adam show.

I wish I could do more than send a few words over a screen. I want to be there, to take some of the weight off her shoulders and offer more than just a distant kind of support. Even if it's just as a friend—the very thing I asked her to be for me. But now, that feels like such a contradiction.

> **ME:**
> I'm sorry, Callie. You didn't deserve that.

> **CALLIE:**
> Thanks, I just needed to vent. I can let you go if you want to head to bed.

I hesitate, my thumb hovering over the screen. I should probably get some rest, but the thought of leaving Callie alone with her thoughts doesn't sit well with me.

> **ME:**
> No, that's okay. I'll probably be up for a while.

> **CALLIE:**
> How's your weekend been?

> **ME:**
> It's been good. Spending time with Barrett always helps me unwind.

> **CALLIE:**
> That's great to hear. You're a great dad, Owen.

A mix of emotions swirls inside me—pride, doubt, a flicker of something deeper I can't quite name. Her words mean more than I want to admit—especially because we haven't known each other long and I know we can't be something more.

ME:
Merely average.

CALLIE:
Something tells me there's nothing average about you.

ME:
Thanks, that means a lot.

CALLIE:
I should probably get to bed. It's been a long day. Sweet dreams, Owen.

ME:
You too, Callie.

I stare at her last message, feeling a mix of warmth and sadness. The distance and our complicated lives make it hard to see a clear path forward. Before I head to bed, I realize it's been a bit since I've seen the girl who used to visit me much more frequently in my dreams.

As I drift off to sleep, I realize... I am starting to miss my Dream Girl. Maybe I will see her tonight... *This is so not healthy.*

The next morning, I wake up from a dreamless sleep feeling a bit empty. I get ready for work and get Barrett his breakfast. When I glance at the clock, I realize Mom should be here any minute. She's a godsend watching Barrett while I go to work. On Tuesdays and Thursdays, Barrett goes to daycare at the hospital, which is convenient but still tugs at my heartstrings every time I drop him off. I want to be there for him as much as possible, but the reality of being a single parent with a demanding job makes it challenging. Thankfully, the more that I take Barrett to the daycare, the more comfortable he becomes in that environment and I know him being around kids his age is important for his development.

Callie crosses my mind more often than I'd like to admit. Our relationship has been intense, almost consuming, and I can't shake the feeling that I'm losing myself in it. I care about her deeply already, but something in me knows I need to pull back a bit. It's not just for my sake, but for hers too. It wouldn't be fair to pursue a relationship with her being so far away considering I already work so much and spend so much time on the road headed in the opposite direction when I get Barrett in Cedar Bluff.

The decision to take a step back from Callie isn't easy. I keep replaying our last conversation in my head. There's no doubt she feels the intensity too, but it's that same intensity that makes me wary. I've been down this road before, and I can't afford to make the same mistakes.

I head to work with a sense of determination. The day is filled with the usual hustle and bustle of maintaining the hospital's steam systems. Will and I are working on a tricky valve replacement in one of the older wings. It's hot, grimy work, but we've always made a good team.

As we wrestle with a particularly stubborn valve, I wipe my forehead and grin at Will. "You know, we should have our own TV show. 'Hospital Maintenance Heroes.' Fixing pipes and saving the day."

Will laughs, shaking his head. "More like laying pipe and

saving the day. 'Tune in next week to see if Owen and Will can conquer the boiler room crisis.'"

"Or, 'Will they survive the great cafeteria flood of 2013?'" I add, smirking.

He chuckles. "I'd watch that. Especially the episode where you get stuck in an air duct."

"Hey, that only happened once," I protest, laughing.

We both crack up, the laughter echoing through the empty hallway. It's moments like these that make the job more bearable, even enjoyable. Will has a way of lightening the mood, no matter how tough the day is.

During lunch, Will runs out to grab fast food while I head toward the cafeteria, still laughing about the air duct comment when I almost bump into someone rounding the corner.

"Whoa!" a female voice exclaims as I step back to avoid colliding.

"Sorry about that," I say, offering an apologetic smile.

She laughs, brushing it off easily. "No harm done."

I recognize her immediately—a new OB nurse. She's in her light pink scrubs, her warm hazel eyes matching the easy smile on her face. There's no denying she's pretty. *Not Callie-level pretty though.* I try to shake the thought and stay in the moment.

"I'm Owen," I offer, extending a hand.

"Karissa," she replies, shaking my hand. "You're in maintenance, right?"

"Sort of, I'm a steamfitter. My buddy Will and I work with the hospital's maintenance team, though," I explain.

She chuckles. "Well, thanks for keeping this place running. We'd be lost without you guys."

We fall into step together, heading toward the cafeteria.

"So, how are you liking it here so far?" I ask, glancing over at her.

"It's been great," she replies. "Everyone's been really welcoming, and OB is fast-paced, which I love. But it's a whirlwind for sure."

"I bet. Babies don't exactly come on a set schedule," I say, holding the door open for her as we enter the cafeteria.

"No, they don't," she laughs, grabbing a tray. "But that's part of the excitement. Every day is different."

We both scan the menu, and Karissa turns to me with a skeptical look. "Any recommendations?"

I smirk. "Avoid the meatloaf. Trust me."

She gives a mock-serious nod. "Duly noted. Salad it is, then."

As we move down the line, our conversation flows easily. There's something refreshing about the way she talks, no pretenses or awkwardness, just casual conversation. But in the back of my mind, I can't shake the thoughts of Callie. I try to stay in the moment with Karissa, but it's hard to ignore the tug I still feel toward someone else.

We find a table by the window, the sunlight casting a warm glow over the room as we sit down.

"So, do you enjoy your work?" Karissa asks, taking a bite of her salad.

"I do," I say honestly. "I like fixing things and problem solving. Plus, you never know what's going to come up. It keeps things interesting."

"That's what I love about nursing, too," Karissa says. "Every day is a puzzle to figure out. It's so rewarding when things come together."

We sit in comfortable silence for a moment, and I realize I may have made a new friend at work today. She's kind, quick to smile, and genuinely interested in the conversation. It would be so much easier to have conversations like this with her over lunch each day rather than pining for someone who lives over an hour away, someone I can't have.

The conversation sticks to lighter topics—upcoming hospital events, places to check out around town—but my thoughts keep drifting. I force myself back into the moment, noticing how Karissa's presence makes the day feel lighter, even if just a little.

As we finish our meals, I glance down and notice that she doesn't have a ring on her finger. Not that it means much, but it's something I can't help but take in.

"It was great meeting you, Karissa," I say, offering her a warm smile. "Maybe we can do this again sometime. How about lunch tomorrow?"

She smiles back, her eyes brightening. "Yeah, I'd like that."

We both stand, and as we head out of the cafeteria, I can't help but feel a flicker of something—maybe not the deep connection I have with Callie, but it's enough to leave me wondering. For now, at least, it's a start.

twenty-one
BACK TO DECEMBER - TAYLOR SWIFT

CALLIE - JUNE 5, 2013

The familiar scent of freshly brewed coffee fills the air as I step into *Brooked & Brewed*, the cozy warmth offering a small reprieve from the emotional chaos of the weekend. The rhythmic hum of the espresso machine and the quiet clink of cups ground me. For a moment, I can almost forget the mess that is my life.

I'm wiping down the counter for the third time when the door chimes. I glance up, expecting a regular, but instead, I see Matt.

My stomach flips.

There he stands, the same blue eyes, the same crooked grin, like no time has passed at all. He's dressed casually in a green Teenage Mutant Ninja Turtles shirt, looking older but still somehow exactly the same.

"Callie?" His voice is a wave of familiarity, one that crashes into me, stirring memories I thought I'd buried. Sneaking around. Stolen kisses. The way it all ended.

"I... Matt. Hey." My heart races, and I can't tell if it's from excitement or fear, or some twisted mix of both.

"How've you been?" he asks, leaning casually against the counter as if we're picking up where we left off. His gaze brings with it a flood of memories I've tried hard to leave behind.

The past is right here in front of me. But I'm not that girl anymore.

Matt had all of my firsts. Every single one.

"I've been... okay," I lie, trying to sound steady. "It's been a long time."

"Yeah, it really has." He glances around the shop, then back at me, his gaze warm but unsettling. "You look good, Callie. Happy, even. Heard you got married. And kids?"

I force a laugh that feels too hollow. "Married and divorced. I have a little girl. Sara. She just turned one. And, uh... I'm pregnant with my second."

His eyes widen, and for a moment, I think I see something flicker in his gaze—surprise? Regret? He's silent for just a beat too long, and I shift uncomfortably under the weight of his stare.

"Wow. That's... a lot," he finally says, and I can tell he's scrambling to find the right words. "But you look happy."

I give a half-hearted nod, knowing that "happy" is a stretch. "Yeah, I'm managing. Moving into my own place this week."

It feels like an out-of-body experience, talking to him after all this time. Memories of my mom's harsh lectures and the shame of losing my virginity so young flood back. It's like I'm being pulled into a past I worked so hard to bury.

Matt's gaze softens, and for a moment, it feels like we're both standing at the edge of something we used to know but can't quite grasp anymore. "So, are you... seeing anyone?" His voice is casual, but the question hangs between us, heavy with the weight of what-ifs.

"I'm figuring things out," I say, thinking of Owen. God, why am I thinking about Owen right now? *We're just friends.*

Matt chuckles, but there's an edge to it. "Well, it's good to see you, Callie. Maybe we can catch up properly sometime?"

The invitation lingers, and I hesitate. Seeing him has stirred up things I wasn't ready to feel again. But those days are long gone. I'm not that girl anymore.

"Maybe," I reply, not committing to anything.

He leans in for a hug, and I freeze for a second, unsure of how to feel. His scent—clean, grown-up, a far cry from the Axe body spray he used to wear—fills my lungs as his arms wrap around me. For a moment, it feels like old times, a brief flash of nostalgia that makes my heart clench. But as quickly as it happens, it's over, and he's pulling away, flashing that same playful grin that used to make me melt.

"I'll see you around, pretty girl," he says with a wink, before walking out the door, leaving me standing there like a ghost of my former self. That old nickname hits me harder than I would have expected.

As the door swings shut behind him, I feel like I've been hit by a truck. Everything feels too loud—the hiss of the espresso machine, the chatter of customers—and I can't shake the feeling that the ground has shifted beneath me. Memories and emotions crash over me in waves, and I find myself gripping the counter for stability.

I turn back to the task at hand, wiping down the counter with more force than necessary, trying to push it all down. But I can't. Seeing Matt again has stirred something in me, something I thought I'd buried long ago. The ache of missed opportunities, the question of what could have been if things had gone differently.

The door chimes again, and I take a deep breath, forcing myself to focus on the present. I can't live in the past. Not anymore.

twenty-two
IMPOSSIBLE - JAMES ARTHUR

OWEN - JUNE 6, 2013

By Wednesday, I'm restless, caught between the pull of two worlds.

On one hand, there's Callie—always at the back of my mind, her smile a ghost I can't shake. On the other, there's Karissa, whose flirtatious glances and casual conversations have become a tempting distraction. I'm telling myself the only way to shake off Callie is to explore other possibilities. It's a lie I desperately want to believe.

"So, Karissa," I say, trying to sound more confident than I feel, "how about we grab coffee after work sometime?"

She smiles, her lips curling up in a way that makes my stomach twist. "I'd like that, Owen. Friday sound good?"

I nod, feeling a tight knot in my chest. I should be excited, right? But as I walk back to the mechanical room, the buzz of it all fades when I think about Callie. Why is it always her?

Back at work, Will's leaning against a pipe, a smirk plastered on his face. "So, did you ask her out yet?" He's been teasing me about Karissa for days, his eyes glinting with amusement every time we're in the same room together.

"Yeah," I say, forcing a grin, "just coffee. Nothing big."

"Just coffee, huh?" Will waggles his eyebrows. "Remember, chicks dig guys with a sense of humor. Tell her about our TV show idea—'Hospital Maintenance Heroes.'"

I laugh, trying to bury the unease clawing at me. "You're impossible, man."

As we head to our next task, I send Mom a text to ask if she would mind running Barrett back to Cedar Bluff Friday night for me so that I can grab coffee with a friend after work, promising to pay for the gas.

Will starts humming a dramatic tune. "Next time on 'Hospital Maintenance Heroes'–Will Owen and his date ignite a fire that sets off the sprinkler systems?"

The rest of the day is a blur of tools clanking, steam hissing, and my mind wanders to Callie. Even though we've talked less, I can't help but think about her. Hell, maybe that's why I asked Karissa out. To push Callie out of my mind.

On Thursday, I text her—just to check in, just to hear from her. But I'm careful. I keep it casual. She's been giving me space, and maybe I should let that be enough.

ME:
Hey Callie, how's your week going?

Her reply is quick, but there's something... off.

CALLIE:
Busy but good. You?

ME:
Same. Work's been nuts... But I wanted to tell you something.

I hesitate, staring at the screen. What am I doing? I don't

owe her anything—we're just friends, right? But something about keeping this from her feels wrong.

ME:
We're friends, yeah?

CALLIE:
I'd like to think so. Why?

ME:
Well, there's a new nurse at work and I decided to ask her out for coffee tomorrow.

The bubbles pop in and out of view. What is she thinking? When her reply comes, it's casual. Too breezy. After seeing the bubbles appear, disappear, and reappear so many times, I expected something more. Something stronger than the lukewarm response now staring back at me from the screen.

CALLIE:
Oh, that's great! I hope it goes well. Need any dating advice?

I try to shake it off. She's being cool about this. So why does it feel like I'm fucking this up? And why do I feel a bit disappointed and brushed off? It's good that she's not mad about it... right? Because we're friends. Just friends. Like I wanted. *Wanted.*

ME:
Thanks! I might take you up on that. Any tips?

CALLIE:
Just be yourself. You're pretty great, Owen.

ME:
Appreciate it. How about you? Any plans for the weekend?

Another pause. Then—

CALLIE:

Maybe. One of my exes came by the coffee shop. Asked me to hang out sometime. I'm considering it.

The words hit me harder than I expected. It shouldn't matter—we're just friends. But it does. Jealousy claws its way up my chest, irrational and angry.

ME:

In my experience, exes are exes for a reason.

CALLIE:

True. But people change, right? Maybe he's different now. We were kids when we dated.

ME:

Just... be careful.

CALLIE:

Always. 😇

My stomach twists, and suddenly I'm not sure if I want this coffee date with Karissa after all.

Friday comes with the promise of the weekend and feels a little less hectic. Will and I are tasked with fixing a pressure issue in the basement boiler room. The dimly lit, cavernous space always feels like a different world, filled with the constant noises of machinery and the occasional hiss of steam.

As we work, Will looks over at me, a mischievous glint in his eye. "So, big date tonight, huh?"

I shrug, trying to play it cool. "Just coffee."

"Yeah, sure. Coffee," he says with a smirk. "Don't be a fool, wrap your tool."

"Jesus Christ. I can't take you anywhere," I say, shaking my head. "I don't give my cinnamon away on the first date."

Will looks at me, his head tilted slightly. "You don't give what?"

"My cinnamon. My spice. You know."

"What, are you a fucking Powerpuff Girl now, man? What the fuck are you talking about?" he asks, completely baffled.

"I don't plan on trying to get in her pants. That's all I'm saying," I explain.

He shakes his head and we go back to working in comfortable silence for a while, the rhythmic clanking of our tools almost soothing. The boiler room is sweltering, and the sweat trickles down my back, but the physical labor feels good, grounding.

We finish up our work just as our shift ends. I head back home to say goodbye to Barrett for the week and get ready for my date with Karissa. Back home, Barrett greets me with a big hug. His brown hair is tousled from his nap, and his dark brown eyes light up with excitement. "Daddy!"

"Hey, buddy," I say, lifting him up. "Did you have a good day with Nana?"

He nods enthusiastically. "We played with my cars and watched cartoons!"

Mom smiles from the kitchen, where she's finishing up dinner. "He's been a little angel."

I put Barrett down and walk over to her, giving her a quick hug. "Thanks for helping out, Mom."

"Of course, dear," she says, patting my arm. "You deserve a night out and there's a new little shop that opened in Cedar Bluff I've been dying to check out. I'll take Barrett to Sabrina's and then go take a look."

Mom finishes dinner while I take a shower and we all eat together before she leaves with Barrett.

I arrive at the coffee shop a few minutes early, my nerves starting to build. I laugh when I see the name of the place: *Cool Beans*. The small, cozy shop is filled with the rich aroma of coffee and the soft murmur of conversations. I spot Karissa at a corner table, her auburn hair catching the light.

She smiles as I approach, her eyes bright, "Hey, Owen!" she says, waving me over to the table.

We order our drinks and settle into a comfortable conversation. Karissa is easy to talk to, and I find myself laughing more than I expected. She tells me about her travels as a nurse, and I share stories from the hospital maintenance adventures. As we get to know each other more, I find out that she has two little girls, both older than Barrett. She reveals that she's been married before and her kids live with their dad full time because she travels for work.

As she talks about her experiences, I can't help but compare her to Callie. Karissa seems nice enough – kind, funny, and attentive – but my mind keeps drifting back to Callie's smile and I wonder what her laugh sounds like.

Karissa notices my distraction. "You okay, Owen?"

I snap back to the present. "Yeah, sorry. Just a lot on my mind."

She nods, understanding. "I get it. It's not easy juggling everything."

I appreciate her empathy and try to focus more on our conversation. We talk about lighter things–favorite movies, places we'd like to travel, funny stories from our respective jobs. Despite my wandering thoughts, I genuinely enjoy her company.

After an hour, the coffee shop starts to quiet down. We finish our drinks, and Karissa looks at me with a gentle smile. "This was nice, Owen. We should do it again sometime."

I smile back, feeling a bit conflicted. "Yeah, I'd like that."

We walk out of the coffee shop together, the night air cool and refreshing. As we reach our vehicles, Karissa turns to me. "Thanks for tonight. I had a great time."

"Me too," I say sincerely. "Drive safe."

"You too," she replies before getting into her car.

As I drive home, my thoughts are a tangled mess. Karissa is great, but the evening has made me realize how much Callie is still on my mind. I pull into the parking lot for my apartment complex and sit in the truck for a moment, trying to sort through my feelings. When I finally head to bed, my mind is still spinning with thoughts of Callie and Karissa.

The next morning, the house is quiet without Barrett's playful energy. It's strange not having him here, and I already miss his laughter. I get up and make myself a cup of coffee, staring out the kitchen window as I try to process everything. Needing advice, I decide to text the guys. I open up the group chat with Will, Luke, and Vince.

ME:
Hey guys, need some advice.

The responses come almost instantly.

WILL:
Oh boy, what did you do now?

LUKE:
This should be good. 😏

VINCE:
Did you accidentally set the hospital on fire?

I roll my eyes, chuckling despite myself. Leave it to Vince to throw out the most off-the-wall scenario.

I lean back against the counter, staring at my phone before typing out a response.

> ME:
> No, no fires. Went on a date with Karissa last night.

There's a pause. I take another sip of my coffee and brace myself for their inevitable teasing.

> WILL:
> And you survived without her stealing your cinnamon? Impressive.

I nearly spit out my coffee.

> VINCE:
> His what?
>
> LUKE:
> Was she wearing safety goggles?
>
> VINCE:
> Did you tell her about your adventures in the air duct?
>
> ME:
> THAT WAS ONE TIME!
>
> Okay, guys, seriously. I need help.
>
> WILL:
> We know this. But I don't think you're going to find the kind of help you need in this group chat.

ME:

> Haha, very funny. 😊 It went well, but I couldn't stop thinking about this girl I met online a couple of weeks ago.

WILL:

> Ah, the plot thickens.

LUKE:

> The chick from Hawkridge?

ME:

> Yeah, it's complicated. I care about Callie, but the distance is too much. It wouldn't be fair to her if I try to pursue a relationship with her because I wouldn't be able to actually spend very much time with her.

The silence stretches out this time. I pace the kitchen, waiting for a reply. I stop by the window, looking out at the parking lot. It feels too still, too empty without Barrett here.

WILL:

> Dude, if she's on your mind that much, it's worth figuring out.

I sigh, scratching my beard. Maybe he's right. But how do I figure this out without screwing things up more than I think I might have already?

LUKE:

> You're also single, man. There's nothing wrong with dating more than one person as long as you're clear with both of them that you're not interested in anything exclusive yet.

VINCE:

> Or you could start a reality show. 'The Bachelor: Blue Collar' 🔨 👕

> ME:
> What is it with you guys and reality shows? That's the last fucking thing I need right now.

I shake my head, imagining myself standing there with a bunch of women, handing out pipe wrenches instead of roses.

> LUKE:
> Maybe consider talking to Callie about it again. At least you'll know where you stand.
>
> VINCE:
> Plus, you can always call us for more terrible advice.

I chuckle again, but my thoughts are already spinning. Maybe I should talk to Callie. I lean against the counter, staring at my phone, debating. Not today. I'm not ready yet.

Deciding to put off reaching out to her a little while longer, I open the FlameFinder app, hoping that seeing her profile picture will help ease my mind a bit. I scroll through, searching for her. But nothing comes up.

Frowning, I search again. Still nothing.

Maybe she changed her username? I check my messages, but where her name used to be, it now says, "User Not Found." My heart sinks. She deleted it? Or blocked me? My stomach tightens, a pit forming in my gut.

I quickly type out a message to the group.

> ME:
> Callie deleted her FlameFinder profile. Should I be worried?
>
> VINCE:
> Are you sure she didn't just block you? 😊

LUKE:

Hang on, what's her username? I will see if I can find her profile.

ME:

ChaosCallie. If you find her and message her, I'll end you.

I hold my breath, waiting for their responses. It was one thing to have Luke hooking up with Heather. Callie is off-limits.

WILL:

Oh boy! 😬

ME:

What?

VINCE:

That's a hell of a username. 😼

WILL:

Exactly.

I let out a frustrated sigh. They are not helping.

LUKE:

User Not Found

I close my eyes, the reality settling in.

WILL:

Maybe she found someone she likes?

LUKE:

Or she's just done with online dating. It happens.

VINCE:

Find out next time on 'The Bachelor: Blue Collar.'

I sigh, closing my messages and exiting out of the Flame-Finder app. Callie is clearly moving on, and I need to figure out what I want before it's too late.

twenty-three
BREATHE (2 AM) - ANNA NALICK

CALLIE - JUNE 12, 2013

The soft buzz of my phone pulls me from sleep, the early morning light slicing through the cheap curtains like a knife. I groan, squinting against the brightness. These damn curtains. I fumble for my phone, barely awake, when Owen's name flashes on the screen, a small smile creeping onto my lips.

We've been texting constantly for weeks now. He's become my emotional lifeline, always there with a kind word or a sarcastic joke to make me laugh. It's frustrating how much I've started to rely on him, but here we are. If he were closer, I'd do more than just text him. It's that kind of friendship—the kind that could easily tip into something more, if only.

> **OWEN:**
> Good morning, sunshine! How's your day so far?

I stretch, feeling the warmth of the sun on my face. Owen's

sweet, respectful, and... a little oblivious sometimes–like a golden retriever. There's a flirty tone in most of our messages, and while I know he wants to stay just friends, I can't help testing the waters sometimes.

Still lying in bed, I snap a quick photo, letting the sun highlight my newly noticeable baby bump. It's a full-body shot, and I notice—oh yeah, there's a lot of cleavage there. Whoops.

ME:
> Still in bed, so I can't complain yet.

His reply comes almost instantly.

OWEN:
> Aww! You're actually glowing!

Glowing? Seriously? I send a picture with my boobs nearly falling out and I get "aww"?! That's it? I can't help but laugh, but a tiny sting of disappointment slips in. Maybe it's time to push him a little more.

ME:
> Sorry for the boob shot. These freaking things are always getting in the way now.

I wait, my heart picking up pace. My phone goes off with the text tone I set for him–the sound of a better bottle cap being popped. The sound plays two more times in rapid succession, and I smirk. Hook, line, and sinker.

OWEN:
> Haha! No need to be sorry. It was a nice picture.
>
> And I'm a boob guy so whether we're just friends or not, you won't get a complaint from me.

> I was just trying to be respectful and not draw attention to it.

Bingo. I bite my lip, knowing I've hooked him just enough. My mind churns. Why not take it up a notch? After all, he did admit he's a boob guy. I strip off my pajamas, leaving only my red lace panties on. The baby bump is there, sure, but I know I still look good.

Standing in front of the mirror, I snap another picture, this time strategically covering my breasts with one arm, letting just enough skin show to keep it fun. Damn, I look hot!

> ME:
> Sixteen weeks tomorrow! 🤰

I hit send, adrenaline surging. What was I thinking? I hop into the shower, waiting for the inevitable sound of my phone. Surely, he'll respond… right?

Fucking Chaos Callie making herself known again. Maybe this wasn't such a good idea.

As the hot water beats down on me, doubt starts to creep in. I finish my shower in record time, anxiety clawing at me. Still no response. Oh no. I wonder if I've crossed a line. I throw on some clothes, try to distract myself by getting Sara from her crib, but it gnaws at me. Should I text him and pretend the picture was meant for someone else? Would that be better or worse?

Maybe not since he knows that I've been talking to Matt again. But that's also thirsty as fuck so I quickly talk myself out of it and decide to just face the music later.

I have more important things to stress about at the moment.

Maybe that's why I was a little unhinged and sent that

thirsty-ass picture to my *friend* Owen this morning. Yeah, let's go with that. I obviously wasn't thinking clearly.

The morning rush begins to blur as I drop Sara off at my mom's, bag packed, ready for Adam to pick her up later. I'm a wreck, juggling my emotions—Adam having Sara for the weekend, the panic of sending that damn picture, and the crushing silence from Owen.

What the fuck was I thinking?

When I get to work, I'm practically vibrating with tension. Barely an hour into my shift at *Brooked & Brewed,* the door chimes, and my stomach drops. Matt walks in—flowers in hand.

Now I really feel like a dick for sending that picture to Owen this morning. I remind myself that I shouldn't feel bad because I have zero commitments to Matt or any other man for that matter. He looks around, spots me, and walks over with a grin.

"Hey, Callie," he says, eyes soft and kind. "Thought these might brighten your day."

Before I can even respond, the door slams open again, and there's Adam, looking murderous, Sara clinging to his arm with tear-streaked cheeks.

"Where's the giraffe, Callie?" His voice is sharp, cutting through the air like a blade.

I blink, scrambling to remember if I packed it. "If it's not in the bag, it's probably in my car. She was playing with it earlier," I mumble, already feeling the tension coil.

Adam's eyes narrow. "Give me the keys. I'll get it."

I dig into my pocket and toss him the keys, my heart

hammering. His eyes flick between me and Matt, who's standing awkwardly nearby.

Adam leans in, his voice dripping with malice. "Nice flowers, Callie. Guess you couldn't wait to move on. You're really a piece of work, huh?"

Matt's fists clench, but Adam towers over him. I shoot Matt a warning look—this is not the time to play hero.

"Good luck, man," Adam sneers, turning toward the door. "Enjoy my leftovers."

Matt, ever the calm one, just grins. "Pretty sure it's you who got my seconds, bud." He even winks.

Adam freezes mid-step, his face darkening. For a split second, I think we're about to have a full-on fight in the middle of my workplace. But he just storms out, slamming the door behind him.

I stand there, pulse racing, barely able to breathe.

"I'm really sorry about that," I say to Matt, trying to shake off the tremor in my voice. "Exes, right?"

Matt smirks, but I can tell he's shaken too. "No worries. Let's, uh, talk later?"

I nod, watching him leave. Adam returns moments later, practically throwing my keys at the counter before snatching Sara and muttering, "Maybe next time, focus on your daughter."

Fuck you, I think, watching him leave.

The rest of my shift drags, every moment punctuated by a growing sense of dread. When I finally get off work, I check my phone. Still no response from Owen. What the hell was I thinking sending that picture?

I drive home, flowers from Matt sitting awkwardly in the passenger seat, feeling more confused and alone than ever. The silence in the apartment is deafening.

twenty-four
WONDERWALL - OASIS

OWEN - JUNE 12, 2013

When I texted Callie early this morning before my shift, I expected the usual banter or a light-hearted message in return. What I didn't expect was the picture she sent back—a shot of her in bed, the camera angled in such a way that the first thing I notice is the hint of cleavage. My heart races for a second, a grin pulling at my lips. I don't know if she meant to show that much, but damn, I'm not complaining. It's the kind of thing that makes me second-guess every choice I've made about keeping things friendly between us.

I shake it off, trying to focus on the job. But as the day drags on, one problem after another, my thoughts keep drifting back to that picture. I tried to play it off when she apologized for the picture and a part of me wonders if she did it on purpose just to toy with me.

Just as I send off my response admitting that I am, in fact, a boob guy, Will shouts my name, needing help with a valve that's giving him trouble. The day spirals into one problem after another from there, with no time to catch my breath, let alone check my phone. We even worked through our lunch break.

Now, eight hours later, I pull out my phone as I head to the break room to grab my lunch box full of food I didn't have time to eat today, and there's another message waiting for me—this time, a photo that's even more daring. My breath catches. She's really pushing the boundaries now, and I can't help but wonder if I've been reading this all wrong.

"Damn, Callie," I mutter, shaking my head but not able to suppress the rush of excitement. She's bold. Bolder than I expected. I type out a quick message, trying to keep it light:

ME:
You sure know how to get a guy's attention.

After I hit send, I feel a tug of unease. Callie's playing with fire, and it's making things complicated. I'm still seeing Karissa, and while we're not exclusive, it feels like I'm stuck between two very different situations. As much as I've tried to keep things platonic with Callie, the lines are blurring fast.

My phone buzzes, and her message pops up, instantly pulling me back into the tension of it all.

CALLIE:
Well hey, stranger! Is that why it took you like eight hours to respond? 😊

I chuckle, but the pit in my stomach grows. I type back:

ME:
Sorry about that, work's been a beast today.

Before I can finish the conversation, Will claps me on the shoulder and I quickly exit the text thread. Callie's pictures are still burned into my mind, and I hope to God he didn't see anything. "You heading out?" he asks, his usual smirk plastered on his face. I really hope he didn't see her–because if he did, I might actually have to gouge his eyes out.

Callie may not be "mine," but the thought of anyone else seeing her like that sends a flare of primal possession through me. I push the thought aside, shaking off the ridiculous idea of threatening one of my best friends over a girl I'm not even dating.

"Yeah, man. Just wrapping up," I say, slipping my phone into my pocket, feeling like I've just dodged a bullet.

As soon as I'm out of the hospital and safely in my truck, I pull my phone back out. This thing with her is spinning out of control, and I need to reel it in before I end up doing something I'll regret.

> CALLIE:
> It's all good. Just forget I sent those pictures this morning. Obviously my brain fell out when I was sleeping last night.

Forget? As if I could.

> CALLIE:
> So, any plans tonight? Or just the usual unwind after a long day?

She's giving me an out, and I should take it. But instead, I go for the safer middle ground.

> ME:
> Probably just the usual. Need to recharge. How about you?

I hit send, but my mind's already racing. Just friends, I remind myself. But those pictures, that teasing—it's making me second-guess everything. I grip the steering wheel harder than necessary and start the truck, my thoughts a jumble of conflicting emotions.

I roll the windows down, knowing I'm going to need some fresh air on the way home. Just as I'm about to put the truck in reverse and pull out of the parking lot, my phone buzzes in the cup holder where I'd set it.

> CALLIE:
> Same here. Maybe we can chat later? I could use a distraction. Today was rough.

A distraction. Is that what I am to her? It feels like there's more going on here than either of us wants to admit.

> ME:
> Sounds good. I'll text you once I'm home.

I set my phone back down and look out the window just in time to see Karissa walking towards me in the parking lot. She waves and continues walking over.

"Hey, Owen," she says with a smile, oblivious to my internal conflict. "I was wondering if you'd like to go out again tomorrow night? Some of the nurses are getting together to go to Black N' Gold."

I nod, feeling a mix of excitement and uncertainty. "Yeah, that sounds good. I'll text you later to confirm?"

"Perfect," she replies, her smile widening. "I'll see you then."

When I'm about halfway home, I decide to give Sabrina a call so I can talk to Barrett. I miss him. The apartment is too quiet without him and I'm not looking forward to going home alone. Sab picks up after a couple of rings.

"Hey," she says, sounding distracted.

"I just wanted to see if I could talk to the little turkey for a sec. Is he around?" I ask. I need to hear his little voice.

"Yeah, just a sec." There's some shuffling before I hear his excited voice come through.

"Daddy!"

I can't help but grin. "Hey, buddy! What's going on?"

We talk for a few minutes and he tells me all about his day. No major events but sometimes, it's just good to hear him ramble and forget about the rest of the chaos in my life. By the time we hang up, I feel like I can breathe easier.

I pull into my parking spot and just sit there for a minute. My phone buzzes—it's another text from Callie, checking to see if I made it home okay since I had such a long day at work. Her thoughtfulness makes me smile.

ME:
Hey, just got home. Got some time to chat?

Her reply is instant, and I swear I can almost hear the relief in her words:

CALLIE:
Yeah, definitely. It's my first night in a while without Sara and I hate the quiet. Thanks for keeping me company. How was your day?

I could keep it simple. I could avoid the elephant in the room. But the guilt from her earlier photos still gnaws at me. I owe her honesty, at least.

ME:
Crazy busy. Barely had time to breathe. But... I feel like I should be upfront with you. I'm going out with Karissa again tomorrow. I didn't want to hide that from you.

There's a pause. Long enough that my chest tightens with dread.

CALLIE:
> Oh. Well that's great, Owen. Really. I hope it goes well for you.

I can't tell if she's being genuine or just putting on a brave face. Either way, the tension is thick now, and I can feel the distance creeping in.

CALLIE:
> I feel like I owe you an apology for the pictures this morning. I shouldn't have sent them, especially since you made it clear you just want to be friends.

Right. Just friends. I sit back on the couch, staring at my phone, debating whether I should delete the pictures. I really should.

ME:
> It's okay, I promise. I don't want to lose our friendship. You're important to me, Callie. I don't want to hurt you.

I toss the phone down on the coffee table, rubbing my hand over my beard. The apartment is too quiet—the quiet makes my thoughts seem louder. I get up, walking to the kitchen to grab a glass of water, hoping to wash away the tension.

CALLIE:
> I know. It get it, really. It's just been a day.

ME:
> What happened? Are you okay?

Her next message is longer, explaining how Adam showed up at the coffee shop where she works and started issues with her. Apparently Matt was there when it happened, bringing her flowers and asking her to go out with him. A pang of jealousy hits me although I know it shouldn't.

I can feel my jaw tighten. This guy better treat her right if he's going to keep showing up. My sense of possessiveness from earlier returns and I can feel the jealousy burning beneath my skin.

Thankfully, her next message makes me chuckle:

CALLIE:
Is today over yet?

I wish.

ME:
Not quite.

CALLIE:
Hey, you're handy, right? Think you can build me a time machine and get this day over with?

ME:
Let me grab the Delorean and I'll be right there.

CALLIE:
The what?

ME:
Oh my God. Callie! Have you never seen the cinematic masterpiece that is Back to the Future?!

CALLIE:
I mean... I've seen parts of it. I'm assuming the Delorean is that ugly silver car?

> **ME:**
> I don't think I've ever met someone who hasn't seen Back to the Future.

I shift, grabbing the remote and turning on the TV to avoid the silence in my apartment without Barrett here.

> **CALLIE:**
> Listen, I have a good reason. I watched Dennis the Menace when I was a kid and Christopher Lloyd is terrifying in that movie. I don't think I can handle him as some sort of spastic Doc!

> **ME:**
> You wound me!

> **CALLIE:**
> Good thing you've got that nurse to take care of you now...

Ouch.

> **CALLIE:**
> I'm just teasing. Thanks for listening, Owen. I appreciate you.

I glance at the screen for a second, then type out my reply.

> **ME:**
> Ditto.

I set the phone down, feeling a heaviness settle in my chest. The weight of the day, the uncertainty, and the mess I've created with Callie—it all presses down on me. I close my eyes, knowing that no matter how I spin it, someone's going to get hurt.

twenty-five

SAY SOMETHING - A GREAT BIG WORLD FEAT. CHRISTINA AGUILERA

CALLIE - JUNE 14, 2013

As I slip into my little black dress, a tingle of excitement rushes through me, mixing with the nervous flutter in my stomach. The early summer evening bathes my room in golden light, warming everything it touches, but my thoughts feel anything but calm. I pair the dress with my gray Chuck Taylors—casual but comfortable, a reminder that I'm keeping things light. At least that's what I'm telling myself. Tonight is going to be good. Right? It has to be. But the truth is, I'm not sure I'm ready for this—ready to be vulnerable with him all over again.

Matt arrives right on time, his familiar smile instantly soothing my nerves. But it's also unsettling. I can't ignore the years between us, the weight of history, the questions still lingering in the back of my mind. We share a hug—warm, easy, like falling back into something we both know too well. I want to trust this moment, trust him. But is it really that simple?

The drive to the restaurant is filled with easy conversation, a little too easy. We laugh about the old days, as if the time apart hadn't left cracks in our story, as if the past was nothing but teenage rebellion and first loves. But beneath the laughter, I feel the pressure building, the unspoken questions—can this really work again?

The restaurant is buzzing with activity, the clinking of glasses and low hum of conversation surrounding us. The scent of freshly baked bread fills the air, creating a cozy ambiance, but I'm not sure if I'm really here, really present. The flickering candles on the table feel too intimate, too romantic for the emotional rollercoaster spinning inside me.

As we reminisce over dinner, everything feels perfect on the surface. Matt's smile, his laugh—they're just as I remember, but something's changed. Or maybe I've changed. I can't help but think about the past—how we tore each other apart and how much harder I had to fight to put myself back together. He brings up stories of concerts we barely made it to, nights we spent wrapped in teenage dreams, but I find myself drifting, wondering if I'm setting myself up to relive old heartbreak.

By the time dessert arrives, I feel like I'm teetering on the edge of something dangerous. The way Matt looks at me—it's almost too familiar, too comfortable. His eyes linger on mine, and I can feel the pull, the temptation to fall back into him, into what we once had. But can I trust it?

After dinner, we walk through the park where we used to spend hours together, our hands brushing against each other's. The moonlight reflects off the pond, casting shadows across the path, and I feel the weight of every step. My heart races as Matt turns to me, his voice soft, vulnerable.

"I've missed this, pretty girl," he says, his eyes searching mine. "I know things were complicated back then, and I get why your mom hated me. But I've always wondered... What if?"

His words hit me like a tidal wave. I've asked myself that same question a million times. But as he leans in, our lips meeting in a slow, lingering kiss, I'm torn. It feels familiar, almost too familiar. Like a trap disguised as comfort. My body responds, but my mind won't stop screaming at me to slow down.

Back at my apartment, the pull to invite him inside gnaws at me, but I resist. I need to figure out what the hell I'm doing before I let things spiral. I'm not ready to fall back into old patterns, not ready to tear myself apart again for the sake of an almost love.

The next day, I'm dying to tell Brooke and Taylor everything, to pick apart the night and see if they can help me make sense of this chaos. We meet at *Brooked & Brewed* after closing, and the second the door locks behind the last customer, I feel a wave of relief. This is my safe space.

Brooke, always the instigator, comes back with a bottle of wine, some cider and three coffee mugs, setting the tone for the night. "Alright, spill," she says, her eyes lighting up with curiosity as she hands me a mug. "What happened with Matt?"

"It was great," I start, but my voice betrays me. The words sound hollow, unsure. "We had dinner, a walk around the pond, and... we kissed."

Brooke's face lights up, but Taylor catches the hesitation in my voice. "And?"

I sigh, staring into my mug of sparkling cider. "And... I

don't know. It felt good. Too good, maybe. But is it real, or am I just falling back into something because it's easy?"

They both exchange glances, and I know they get it. Matt is familiar, but the past is messy. Taylor leans back, sipping her wine. "You need to be sure, Callie. Old flames burn the hottest, but they can also burn you out."

I nod, but the uncertainty gnaws at me.

Despite having rekindled feelings for Matt, I've continued to talk to Owen almost every day. Our conversations have shifted, becoming more about supporting each other and even offering dating advice. It's been nice, but there is an underlying tension I can't ignore. I often find myself smiling at my phone, waiting for his next message, even though I know this is all a bit complicated.

As I sit on my couch Sunday evening with a cup of tea, my phone buzzes with a message from Owen.

> **OWEN:**
> Hey, Callie. Need some advice. Second date with Karissa on Thursday night didn't go well.

> **ME:**
> Oh no! What happened?

> **OWEN:**
> She got really jealous. Found out I once took the bartender, Heather, on a date. Heather's with my brother Luke now, but Karissa couldn't let it go.

> **ME:**
> That's tough. Jealousy can be a real turnoff.

Good thing this entire situation doesn't make me remotely jealous at all...

> **OWEN:**
> It definitely was. Made me rethink things with her. 🫠

> **ME:**
> I'm sure the alcohol was flowing and probably didn't help the situation. Have you talked to her since your date on Thursday?

> **OWEN:**
> Yeah, we have but it's been awkward.

> **ME:**
> Have you talked to her specifically about the jealousy stuff? Is that a dealbreaker for you? 🫠

> **OWEN:**
> It's not a dealbreaker but I definitely need to talk to her about it. It's unfortunate because she's really nice aside from that. I just don't know if I want to deal with the drama.

> **ME:**
> I don't blame you. That's tough.

> **OWEN:**
> Sorry for dumping on you, I just needed to run it by an objective third-party.

> **ME:**
> Of course. That's what friends are for, right?

Ugh. Sometimes calling myself his friend feels like an insult.

As the month ends, Owen's texts become less frequent. At first, I don't think much of it—he's busy, I'm busy. Life happens. But when days go by without a word, the silence becomes unbearable. I send a casual message, trying to keep it light, but the anxiety creeps in.

ME:
> Hey, Owen… Haven't heard from you in a bit. Hope everything's okay. Miss talking to you. Could really use a friend right now. 😔

No response.
After three days of not hearing from him, I'm pissed.

ME:
> I wish you would at least have the decency to tell me what's going on. If you're with Karissa now and can't talk, I get it. But just say that. 🥺

Still nothing. It hurts more than I expect, but I try to push the feelings aside. Maybe it is for the best. Owen is far away, and I need to focus on what is in front of me. Annoyed as I am by his silence, I still find myself checking my phone more often than I care to admit.

What the fuck, Owen?

twenty-six

PAYPHONE - MAROON 5 FEAT. WHIZ KHALIFA

OWEN - JUNE 17, 2013

As I walk through the front door, I kick off my boots and drop my keys onto the table, the clink of metal echoing through the apartment like a dull reminder of how empty the place feels without Barrett here. The day has been long—too long—and all I can think about is a hot shower to wash away the grime, followed by a cold beer. I pat my pockets, expecting to find my phone, but come up empty.

"Damn it," I mutter, my mind already spinning. I check the counter where I usually toss it, then my tool bag, even though I've never put it there before. No luck. My phone is missing, and the knot in my stomach tightens as I realize I probably left it at the hospital. We spent the day chasing down steam leaks all over the place, and who knows where it could've fallen.

I head downstairs to my mom's apartment, hoping she's home. A sinking feeling settles in when there's no answer at her door. The frustration I've been holding in all day bubbles up, and I scribble a note asking to borrow her phone when she gets back. "I'll just deal with it tomorrow," I tell myself, but the nagging thoughts won't quit.

I send Sabrina an email from my laptop, explaining the situation as best I can, feeling the frustration mount. No phone until payday means she'll have to get a hold of my mom if she or Barrett need anything. It's a small issue, but it eats at me.

The next morning, my mom knocks at my door, concern written across her face as she hands me her phone. "Everything okay, Owen?" she asks, her worry tugging at the edges of her voice.

"Yeah, just lost my phone at work," I say, trying to act like I'm not as bothered as I am. "I need to check in with Sabrina."

After calling to let her know what's going on, I hand the phone back. The drive to the hospital is silent, the usual light banter between Mom and me replaced by the heavy weight of losing pictures that are irreplaceable–two years of pictures of Barrett, precious moments I hadn't thought to back up.

The hospital offers no solution either. I scour every corner, check the lost and found, even leave a note in the staff room. Nothing. It's like the damn thing vanished. Running into Karissa in the cafeteria only adds salt to the wound when she makes a snide comment about me apparently ghosting her. After I explain the situation, she apologizes, but I can see the disappointment in her eyes.

The worst part, though, is Callie. Without my phone, I've lost the only way to contact her. I didn't even think to get her last name before she deleted her FlameFinder profile. Her absence bothers me in ways I didn't expect. It's only been a few days, but I already miss the easy conversation, her laugh, and the way she seemed to make everything feel lighter.

By Friday, I've saved enough for a new phone. The excitement of getting it quickly fades when I realize none of my old text messages come through. It's like I'm starting my life over without half of it. I input the phone numbers I can remember—Mom, Dad, Sabrina, Will. As I pull out the napkin with Karissa's number, I feel a twinge of guilt. I've been seeing her, but my thoughts are still stuck on Callie.

Even though Karissa's right here, physically present, something about this feels like I'm settling. The realization hits hard—Callie's not even an option anymore, and I missed my chance.

Sabrina and Mom try to help by sending me pictures of Barrett from their phones, but it's not the same. Those aren't my moments. They're not the memories I had captured—the ones that meant something to me. It's a bitter pill to swallow, knowing they're gone for good.

That evening, Karissa suggests a camping trip with her friends. The idea of getting away—unplugging from everything—sounds like a perfect escape. Maybe I need this. Maybe I need to throw myself into something else and let go of the things I can't control.

The drive out to the campsite is filled with the excited chatter of Karissa and her friends, the anticipation of a weekend in the great outdoors making the miles fly by. When we finally arrive, the beauty of the place takes my breath away. The campsite is nestled in a clearing surrounded by tall pine trees, their needles forming a soft carpet underfoot. The air is crisp and clean, and I feel a sense of peace that has been missing for a while.

Karissa's group of friends is large and lively, making the campsite buzz with energy. There's Josh and his girlfriend, Emily, who are inseparable and always seem to be laughing at some inside joke. Tyler and Bayleigh are the on-again, off-again couple who seem to thrive on the drama of their relationship. Then there's Jenna, who's single and more interested in her phone than the people around her. Rounding out the group are Nate and Derek. Derek's laid back attitude makes him easy to get along with but I have a feeling Nate is a different story. He's the kind of guy who seems to think he's the life of the party, but his constant side-glances at Karissa and his smug grin start to rub me the wrong way.

At first, all is well. Karissa is in high spirits, laughing and joking with her friends as we pass around beer and roast marshmallows over the fire. The light from the flames dances in her eyes, and for a moment, I start to believe that maybe this could work. Maybe I can let go of the past and focus on what's right in front of me.

We spend the evening swapping stories and laughing as the flames flicker and crackle in the darkness. Josh and Emily are cuddled up together, whispering and giggling, while Tyler and Bayleigh are deep in some sort of trivial debate about whether it's pronounced "s'mores" or "schmores." Bayleigh's insistence on the latter has Tyler in stitches, and their playful bickering adds to the lighthearted mood.

Jenna sits on the edge of the circle, scrolling through her phone, occasionally chiming in with a sarcastic comment that makes everyone laugh. At one point, she looks up and deadpans, "So, who's ready for a frolic in the woods?" There's a pause before everyone bursts out laughing, especially when she follows up with, "Seriously, though, I'm staying in the tent after dark. You guys can get eaten by bears or ghosts or serial killers or whatever."

Derek shakes his head with a chuckle, "No bears, Jenna. Just mosquitoes. Lots and lots of mosquitoes."

"Probably a good chance you can get eaten by a mountain

lion though," Nate adds with a nasty grin. He has positioned himself on the other side of Karissa, and I can't help but notice the way he keeps eyeing her, especially when she laughs a little too loudly at one of his jokes. He's one of those guys with a face you just want to punch. Nate is also one of those guys who seems to think that every woman is interested in him, and his overconfidence is starting to grate on my nerves. I find myself exchanging looks with Josh, who seems to be on the same wavelength as me.

We both get up and walk over to the table where we have food and mixers set out. "Do you think he practices that smirk in the mirror?" I whisper to Josh, nodding toward Nate, who's now showing off some "hilarious" video on his phone that's clearly not that funny.

Josh snorts into his beer, barely containing his laughter. "Oh, for sure. Probably spends hours perfecting it. And that hair…it's like he's in a constant shampoo commercial."

I chuckle, feeling a little better knowing I'm not the only one who finds Nate's antics a bit much. "Guess I don't have to worry about that," I say, removing my *Chicago Bears* hat and running my hand over my head that is clean-shaven. "But if he flips his hair one more time, I'm going to start calling him Bieber."

As the night wears on, I start to notice Karissa getting more and more drunk. She's taking shots with Tyler, who seems determined to outdo her, but Bayleigh and Emily exchange knowing glances, as if they've seen this all before. Josh tries to suggest that they all slow down, but his words fall on deaf ears.

"Karissa, maybe you should pace yourself," Josh says, his tone carrying a note of concern.

She just laughs, waving him off as she takes another shot. "I'm fine, Josh! Just having fun with my friends and my new boyfriend!" Her last sentence is followed by a hiccup that sounds more painful than funny, and Josh raises an eyebrow at me as if to say, "Good luck with that."

Nate, still watching Karissa with a bit too much interest, chimes in, "Yeah, Karissa's just here to have a good time. You don't have to babysit her, man." He winks at her, and I feel my jaw tighten.

Josh must sense my irritation because he quickly changes the subject, leaning over to me and saying, "You know, I hear there's a fishing spot nearby. Maybe we should check it out tomorrow before Nate tries to show us all up with his expert skills."

I laugh, grateful for the distraction. "Yeah, let's do that. Maybe we'll actually catch something... other than a headache."

Bayleigh suddenly jumps up, declaring it's time to go skinny-dipping before taking off running toward the lake, stripping off her clothes and throwing them behind her as she does and Tyler runs behind her picking them all up so she doesn't lose anything while also trying to take his own clothes off to follow suit. Josh looks at Emily who gives him a wink before taking off running behind her friend.

He turns to me with a sympathetic look and I can't help but laugh, understanding that he doesn't want to be rude by bailing on me mid-conversation but also that his girlfriend just ran off with the intention of getting naked and jumping in the lake. Derek asks Jenna if she wants to join him, but she is still glued to her phone. She finally looks up and declines the invitation with a quick shake of her head, staying behind while everyone else heads toward the water.

Nate seems to look at Karissa, contemplating making a pass at her right in front of me, but he decides against it. Likely only because we can all see how trashed she is. I watch them disappear into the darkness, leaving me alone with Karissa, who is anything but fine and Jenna, who is oblivious to the world around her.

Karissa stumbles over to me and hangs her arms around my neck. Her breath reeks of alcohol as she tries to kiss me and convince me that I should sleep with her, her words sloppy and insistent. I do my best to gently refuse her advances.

Her drunken cheer has turned to woozy confusion, and before I know it, she's stumbling toward the edge of the campsite, heaving up everything she drank. I'm right behind her, holding her hair back and trying to keep her from falling over. The smell of vomit and alcohol hangs heavy in the air, a stark contrast to the clean, pine-scented breeze I enjoyed when we first got here.

"Karissa, I think it's time to call it a night," I say, trying to keep my tone calm even as my frustration grows. "Let's get you back to the tent."

She gives me a sloppy smile and leans heavily against me, muttering something incoherent about how much she loves me for taking care of her. It's then that I notice Nate must have decided to come back to the campsite after not having a woman to skinny-dip with. I catch his smirk out of the corner of my eye, but I'm too focused on getting Karissa to a safe spot to care about whatever he's thinking.

After what feels like an eternity, I get her settled in the tent, where she mumbles incoherently before finally passing out. I sit outside for a while, staring into the dying embers of the campfire, trying to process the night's events. The distant laughter of the others echoes back from the lake, but I'm too exhausted to care. As Josh and Emily come back, he wanders over and takes a seat next to me, offering a sympathetic smile.

"Rough night, huh?"

I nod, letting out a long breath. "Yeah. This wasn't exactly what I had in mind when she invited me out here."

Josh claps me on the shoulder. "Welcome to the club, man. But hey, at least we've got fishing tomorrow, right? Just us, the water, and no Nate."

I chuckle, feeling a bit of the tension ease. "Yeah, I'm looking forward to it."

After heading back to the tent and discovering Karissa passed on top of both of our sleeping bags, I opt to grab some extra blankets from the truck and sleep in my truckbed instead. Looking up at the stars, I can't help but think about Callie. If she were here, she'd probably laugh at the absurdity of it all, making some smartass comment that would take the edge off my frustration. But she's not here, and I have to face the fact that I'm in this mess alone.

The next morning, Josh and I escape for the fishing trip we've joked about. The air is crisp, the kind of fresh morning air that makes you feel like you're getting a new start. The sun is just starting to break through the morning mist as we head down to the lake, its golden light filtering through the trees and casting long shadows on the ground. The peacefulness of the scene is a stark contrast to the messiness of the night before.

We find a quiet spot along the bank, the river gently flowing by, its surface sparkling under the early morning sun. I take a deep breath, the calm of the moment sinking in. As we cast our lines into the water, the rhythmic sound of the reels and the occasional splash as the lures hit the surface create a soothing background to our thoughts.

After a while, Josh starts talking, his voice low and

thoughtful, almost as if he's been waiting for the right moment to speak.

"Karissa's not usually like that, by the way," he says, glancing over at me, his brow furrowed. "She's been through some stuff. Her ex was... well, he was a real piece of work. Wouldn't let her hang out with us, kept her on a short leash. When they broke up, it was like she just wanted to let loose, you know? Make up for lost time."

I nod, feeling a bit more sympathy for her, a tightness in my chest that wasn't there before. "That explains a lot. I wondered if there was something more to it."

Josh casts his line out again, the water rippling where it lands. "Yeah," he says, staring out at the river. "She's a good person, but sometimes she goes a little overboard. I think she's just trying to find herself again."

I don't know what to say to that, so I just focus on the water, watching the ripples as they move downstream, feeling a heavy weight settle over me. Josh's words stick with me, though, making me see Karissa in a different light. Maybe she's not just a party girl. Maybe there's more to her story than I realized, and that realization makes me feel a mix of emotions. I'm not quite sure how to process—empathy, frustration, and a strange kind of guilt because maybe I judged her too quickly when we are still getting to know each other.

When we get back to the campsite around noon, Karissa is acting strange. The lively, confident woman I've gotten to know seems to have shrunk into herself, her shoulders hunched as she stares at the ground. She's quiet, avoiding eye contact, and there's a kind of heaviness about her like she's carrying something she doesn't know how to put down. I assume she's just hungover and feeling guilty about how she acted the night before. The way her eyes dart away when I try to talk to her, the nervous way she fiddles with the hem of her shirt, it all makes me feel like there's something she's not telling me... maybe because she's just not ready to. I don't push it, figuring she needs space to process whatever's happening in her head.

The rest of the day is uneventful, filled with mundane tasks of packing up and heading back home. As we drive, the silence between us is thick, uncomfortable. Karissa is still distant, her gaze fixed out the window, lost in thought. I try to shrug it off, telling myself that she just needs time to sort through her emotions... and probably her hangover.

twenty-seven
WHO KNEW - P!NK

CALLIE - JUNE 24, 2013

It's been over a week since I last heard from Owen. Each day, the silence stretches longer, like a wound that refuses to heal. I stare at my phone more than I'd like to admit, checking for a message that never comes. Every vibration sends my heart into overdrive, only to face the same disappointment. Nothing. Not even a "Hey."

I should have added him on social media, but I never thought it'd come to this. I don't even know his last name.

I need to let him go. I know this. But knowing doesn't make it any easier. And with everything else going on, maybe it's for the best.

Sara grips my hand tightly as we walk into my mom's house. She waddles along, her tiny feet pattering against the floor, making my heart swell with warmth. Lately, life feels like a blur. Work, exhaustion, and being pregnant with another child while trying to raise Sara on my own—it's a lot.

"Mom, we're here!" I call, releasing Sara's hand as she toddles toward her grandma with a burst of giggles.

"Thanks for watching her," I say as I bend down to kiss Sara's cheek. "I've got my OB/GYN appointment, and well, I don't think Sara's going to be a fan of that."

Mom smiles at me, concern written in the lines of her face. "Take your time, sweetie. You look like you could use a breather."

I nod, grateful for the small reprieve. The weight of everything is getting heavier, but hearing that steady heartbeat in the doctor's office—it brings it all back into focus. I'm going to be okay. We're going to be okay.

Later that evening, I'm at Matt's place, cuddled up on his couch while we watch *Sweet Home Alabama*. The movie feels oddly nostalgic, like it's mirroring our own story—two people who drifted apart, only to circle back again.

Matt leans in a little closer, his breath warm against my ear. "You know, this movie always reminds me of us."

I smile, a flicker of uncertainty creeping in. "Yeah. Do you think we could be like them?"

He grins, fingers brushing against mine. "Maybe we already are."

It's a sweet sentiment, but there's a nagging feeling deep in my gut. Despite the chemistry, something feels off. But I let it slide as one kiss leads to another, and we end up in bed. It's comforting, being with Matt again, but after he falls asleep, I stare at the ceiling, my thoughts swirling.

I slip out of bed quietly, my heart pounding with doubt. Was this a mistake? As I leave his place and drive back home, the weight of uncertainty presses down on me. It felt right in the moment, but now... now I'm not so sure.

The next day, Matt's behavior sets my instincts on high alert. He's distant, dodging my questions, his attention glued to his phone. When I try to talk to him about it over coffee at *Brooked & Brewed*, he brushes me off with some weak excuse about work.

Matty Red Flag #1.

"Is everything okay?" I ask, trying to keep my voice steady.

"Yeah, just busy," he says, barely meeting my gaze. The smile he gives me is hollow, a mask, and I know something's wrong.

The sinking feeling in my chest deepens.

That night, Matt comes over to my apartment. I try to shake off the doubts. He's been good to me, right? But as things heat up between us, just when we're lost in the moment, his phone rings. He doesn't just ignore it—he answers it.

"What the hell?" I mutter under my breath as he rolls over, turning his back to me, murmuring something to the person on the other end. My heart thuds in my chest, but I force myself to stay quiet. He's acting strange, and I don't like it.

When he finally hangs up, I ask, "Who was that?"

"A friend," he says, avoiding my eyes.

Red Flag #2.

It's not the first time he's dodged my questions, and now my patience is wearing thin. I don't push it, but that nagging feeling is back, stronger this time. He gets dressed, mumbles something about needing to go, and leaves.

I lay there, staring at the ceiling, feeling more alone than ever. He bailed and I'm not getting any answers tonight.

Red Flag #3.

Two days later, the truth unravels. His phone buzzes incessantly as we try to pick out a movie. I glance over at him, watching him silence the calls over and over, his face tight with guilt.

"Matt, who's calling you?" I finally ask, unable to take the tension any longer.

He sighs, his face pale. "There's something I need to tell you."

Red Flag #4.

And then it all comes spilling out. Not only does he have a girlfriend, but she's not just any girlfriend—she's his fiancée. And she's moving back to town soon, expecting to move in with him.

I feel like I've been punched in the gut. How could I have been so blind?

"I'll make this simple for you, Matt," I say, my voice colder than I feel. "We're done. I'm not going to be anyone's side piece. Get the hell out of my life."

His eyes widen, but I don't wait for him to respond. I get dressed, grab my keys, and leave without looking back.

As I sit on my back porch, watching Sara play with her toys, a sense of calm washes over me. The sun is setting, casting a soft glow over the yard. I may not have all the answers, but I know one thing for sure—I'm done letting men treat me like I'm disposable. No more distractions, no more heartache. I'm stronger than this, and I deserve better.

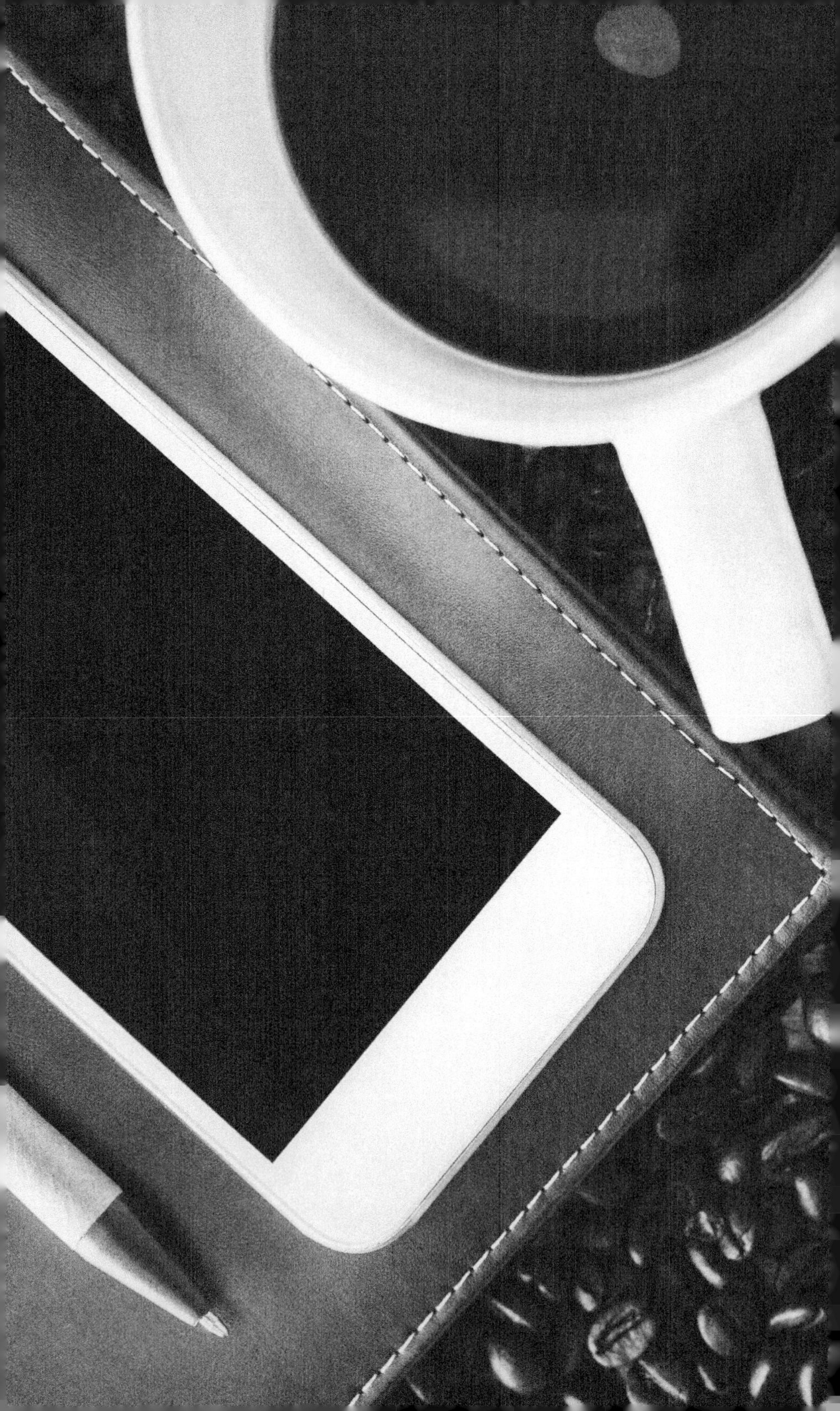

part two

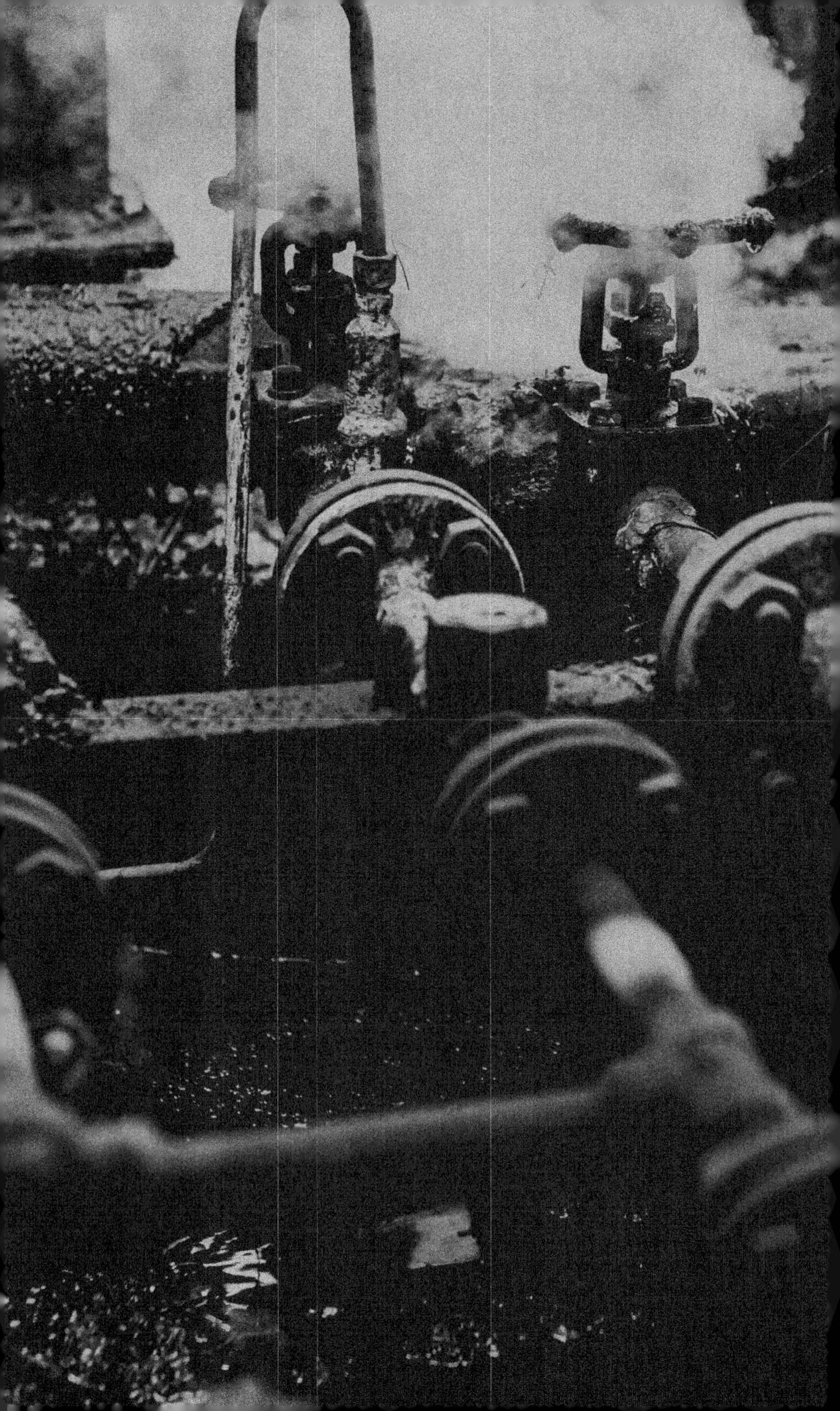

twenty-eight

AIN'T NO REST FOR THE WICKED - CAGE THE ELEPHANT

OWEN - JULY 4, 2013

In the days that follow the camping trip, things with Karissa seem to settle into a pleasant rhythm. The tension from the camping trip dissolves, replaced by a sense of normalcy that's almost unsettling in its simplicity. We have had no issues since then, and she's been a lot more laid-back, the initial spark I saw with her slowly returning. But we have spent little time together, either.

I've been stretched pretty thin between spending time with Barrett and work, so we've had trouble getting our schedules aligned. Karissa has been working some odd shifts here and there for extra cash too and I can't say I blame her, especially since it sounds like her ex doesn't help with her kids. Most of our communication since the camping trip has been through texts and the occasional lunch date in the hospital cafeteria. She wanted to spend today together, but I'd already made plans with Barrett and I am not comfortable introducing them yet. I don't think that sat well with her, and I should probably be thinking about how to make it up to her.

The sun is just beginning to dip below the horizon as I buckle Barrett into his car seat. He's clutching his new stuffed dinosaur, a bright green T-Rex he's dubbed "Mr. Chompers," like it's his lifeline, his little legs swinging with excitement. Barrett grins and makes sure Mr. Chompers is safely buckled in too, because apparently, that's going to be what keeps him from going extinct according to my three-year-old son.

Satisfied, Barrett goes back to making Mr. Chompers roar in a way that's more cute than terrifying. I climb into the driver's seat, mentally ticking off a checklist: Blanket? Check. Snacks? Check. Backpack with spare clothes and enough toy cars to start a dealership? Check. We're all set.

As I pull out of the parking lot of my apartment building, Barrett starts narrating an epic adventure involving Mr. Chompers battling other dinosaurs, saving the world from meteors, and possibly getting lemon ice cream afterwards. I can't help but laugh at some of the plot twists that his mind has come up with as I listen to him while we head toward Cedar Bluff.

"Daddy, Mr. Chompers says we need to go faster so we don't miss the fireworks!"

I glance back at him in the rearview mirror, his eyes wide with innocent urgency. "Well, you tell Mr. Chompers that I have a squeaky clean driving record and we're already going as fast as we can. Don't want to get pulled over by the police, do we?"

Barrett gasps dramatically. "No! Mr. Chompers doesn't want to go to jail!"

I bite back a laugh. "Good, because I don't think they allow dinosaurs in jail anyway." Barrett giggles, then turns serious as he directs Mr. Chompers to keep an eye out for cops.

We hit a bit of holiday traffic as we get closer to Cedar

Bluff, and I can feel Barrett's patience deteriorating. He starts to ask the predictable, "Are we there yet?" on repeat, and after the fifth time, I tell him, "We'll go faster if Mr. Chompers takes a nap."

Barrett frowns, holding Mr. Chompers up at eye level as if considering this very serious suggestion. "Mr. Chompers says he's not tired."

"Well, maybe he could just close his eyes for a little bit," I suggest, trying to keep a straight face.

Barrett thinks about this for a second, then nods. "Okay, but only for a little bit. Mr. Chompers wants to see the fireworks too."

Barrett fills the rest of the drive making fake snoring noises for Mr. Chompers, which has me bursting with laughter. By the time we roll into Cedar Bluff, the sun has dipped low, casting a warm, golden glow over the town. The park is filling up with people who are preparing for a fun evening with blankets, lawn chairs, and kids playing with sparklers.

I find a parking spot not too far from the park, and before I can even shut off the engine, Barrett's already trying to unbuckle himself, gripping Mr. Chompers tightly in one hand.

"Easy there, buddy," I say, laughing as I lean over to help him out of his seat. "Let's grab your stuff, and then we'll head over."

We walk into the park, and it isn't long before I spot Vince. I take a few minutes to catch up with him before Barrett and I continue on our way to find a spot to sit. Vince is with his fiancée, Zoe, and their daughter, Ainsley. While part of me would like to sit with them—given how close Vince and I were growing up—I just don't have it in me tonight. Zoe's an energy vampire, and after about two minutes of her complaining about Vince choosing the fireworks over picking up some extra holiday pay at the prison, I'm reminded of exactly why we don't hang out more often.

I use snow cones as a convenient excuse to bail, but before I leave, Vince mentions that he and Malcolm are organizing a cousin's weekend in a few weeks. Sabrina will have Barrett on vacation that week, so it'll be nice to have some adult time with family. I just hope Zoe's attitude during cousin's weekend is better than the way she's acting today.

The first firework bursts overhead, painting the sky in a cascade of bright purples and greens. Barrett's his face lights up and he lets out delighted giggles with every explosion, making my stress melt away. This is what it's all about—just being here, in this moment, with my son.

A part of me keeps circling back to Vince. I can't shake the worry that he's stuck in something that's only going to drag him down further. I've been there before, and I know how it ends—how it eats away at you until there's nothing left but resentment and regret.

As the fireworks finale comes to a close, a series of loud, dazzling explosions light up the entire sky. Barrett is clapping and cheering, completely absorbed in the spectacle. I pull Barrett close, savoring the simple joy of his happiness, but I know that our night isn't over just yet. I still need to drop him off at Sabrina's before I can head home.

When the last firework fades and the crowd begins to disperse, I start gathering up our things. Barrett's eyelids are already drooping as I pick up Mr. Chompers and his blanket, his energy finally winding down after the excitement of the evening.

"Come on, buddy," I say softly, helping him up. "Time to get you to Mom's."

Barrett nods sleepily, rubbing his eyes as he clutches Mr. Chompers to his chest. I carry him back to the car, his little head resting on my shoulder. He's half-asleep by the time I buckle him into his seat, his fingers still curled around his dinosaur.

The drive to Sabrina's is quiet, the only sound being the soft hum of the engine and Barrett's gentle snores from the backseat. My mind drifts, wondering what Callie's doing right now. I know it should be Karissa that I'm thinking about. But instead, Callie has been on my mind. I miss talking to her. I'm sure she'd enjoy a night like this, relaxed under the stars, with Sara probably asleep next to her.

We arrive at Sabrina's house, and I park in the driveway, careful not to wake Barrett as I unbuckle him and gently lift him out of the car. Sabrina's porch light is on, and I can see her silhouette in the doorway as she waits for us.

"Hey," she says softly as I approach, her eyes flicking to Barrett, who's still fast asleep in my arms.

"Hey," I reply, my voice low. "He had a big night. He's out like a light."

Sabrina smiles, reaching out to brush a strand of hair from Barrett's forehead. "He always has the best time with you."

"Yeah, we had fun," I say, feeling a pang of something I can't quite identify—maybe it's just the bittersweet reality of co-parenting, of knowing these moments are fleeting.

I carry Barrett to his room, tucking him into bed. He stirs a little but doesn't wake, his tiny hand still gripping Mr. Chompers. I pull the blanket over him, making sure he's comfortable before stepping back.

"Thanks for bringing him in for me," Sabrina says, her voice full of warmth.

"Of course," I reply, glancing at her. There's a familiarity between us, a shared understanding that comes from years of navigating this complicated relationship. We've had our ups and downs, but when it comes to Barrett, we're always on the same page.

"If you want to stick around for a bit, you can," she offers, her tone casual but her eyes searching mine.

I consider it for a moment, but the weight of the evening's events is pressing down on me, and I know I need some time to decompress. "Thanks, but I should probably head home. It's been a long day."

She nods, not pressing the issue. "Alright. Drive safe, okay?"

"Always," I say with a small smile, giving Barrett one last look before heading back to the door. As I step outside into the cool night air, my thoughts go to Callie again. I wonder if she's had as full of a day as I have. Maybe she's putting Sara to bed or enjoying a quiet evening. Either way, I wish I could talk to her.

twenty-nine
ALMOST LOVER - A FINE FRENZY

CALLIE - JULY 4, 2013

I swear, it's like the universe is punishing me for something I haven't even done yet—or maybe something I did years ago and forgot about. Either way, it's like I'm destined to take the hit. No reprieve, no mercy.

I thought, after everything that's happened recently, that I could at least take Sara to the fireworks and enjoy a normal evening. But of course, life had other plans. Wrong move, Callie.

Hawkridge was never going to be easy. I knew that. Coming back here, where every corner holds memories I'd rather forget, was bound to bring some tension. But I wasn't prepared for this—seeing ghosts from my past in broad daylight, before I've even had time to sit down on the blanket I spread out for Sara.

It's been years since I left this place behind, thinking I'd never look back. I spent so much time convincing myself I'd changed, that I'd grown beyond the mistakes I made as a reckless teenager. But karma? She's got a long memory, and it seems like everyone in Hawkridge does too.

We've only been here for five minutes before I spot him. Matt. Of course. And he's not alone.

There's a girl hanging off his arm, laughing at something he said. She's younger, and I vaguely recognize her. I think she used to go to the same summer day camp where Matt and I first met. Small world, right? Too small, apparently.

Seeing them together feels like a punch to the gut, but I hold it together. I can't let Sara see me upset, not when she's sitting on the blanket with her tiny hands playing with her toys, giggling like this is the best day of her life. For her, I have to hold it together.

Just as I'm trying to calm the jealousy rising in my chest, like some kind of sick joke, I spot another face from the past. Austin.

Damn.

It is as if the universe is trying to twist the knife. He's standing with a group of friends, looking as handsome as ever. Among them are familiar faces—the same guys he used to wrestle with in high school. Our eyes meet, and for a moment, I'm pulled back in time.

Austin and I had an on-and-off relationship for years. When we weren't together, my choices earned me a reputation that followed me like a shadow. When Austin finally ended things for good—by quietly changing his Facebook relationship status without even telling me—it felt like a mercy, more than I probably deserved. Yet, it also stripped away a part of my identity. Austin had been my anchor during those chaotic teenage years. No matter how badly I messed up, he always forgave me, and I did the same for him. Losing him sent me spiraling. The guilt, the confusion—it all consumed me. But the fleeting sense of being wanted, even when it was destructive, had been an addiction I couldn't easily shake.

Austin is about my height, incredibly fit, and carries himself with a confidence that never quite crosses the line into arrogance. That self-assurance was what first drew me to him when we met at a Homecoming bonfire my junior year. And he was just as smooth on the dance floor as he was on the wrestling mat.

He grins, and I feel my stomach twist. Even worse—he winks.

I immediately look away, heart pounding. Nope. Nope. Nope. Exes are exes for a reason, Callie. And Austin? His good looks were never enough to make up for the awkward, fumbling mess he was in bed.

I shake my head, focusing on Sara. The fireworks start, bright bursts of color lighting up the sky. I pull Sara close and settle the noise-canceling headphones over her little ears. She's mesmerized, her tiny hands clapping with excitement as she points at the sky. In this moment, everything else fades away. This is why I'm here—for her.

Not for Matt, not for Austin. For Sara.

After the show, I start gathering our things, trying not to think about how Matt and his new girl are strolling off, hand in hand. Austin is thankfully nowhere to be seen. Good riddance.

As I tuck Sara into her crib that night, my phone buzzes. I pick it up, curious.

Austin West has sent you a friend request.
I snort out loud. Not today, Satan.

The next few days pass in a blur of work, Sara, and trying not to let the past creep up on me. When Brooke texts to invite me to a girls' night at the coffee shop after closing, I jump at the chance. I need a break, and I need my girls.

We lock up after the last customer leaves, spread out snacks on the floor, and laugh like we're teenagers again. It's perfect—no guys, no drama, just us.

I tell Brooke about running into Matt and Austin at the park, and she shakes her head. "Matt's an idiot. You're way better off without him."

Taylor grins, nudging me. "And Austin? Ancient history. You've got too much ahead of you to look back."

Her words remind me of the tattoo on my back—the Chinese symbol for "past." I got it years ago, thinking it was so clever. Put it on my back so I'm always leaving the past behind me. Genius, right?

Their support is what I need, more than anything. We laugh until our sides hurt, and Brooke—always the instigator—chimes in with, "You don't need a man, Callie. You just need better toys."

I choke on my soda, cheeks flaming. Taylor, to my surprise, mutters under her breath, "So do I."

We clean up later, and as I hug my girls goodbye, I feel lighter. For the first time in a while, I feel like maybe, just maybe, things are going to be okay.

thirty
NOT OVER YOU - GAVIN DEGRAW

OWEN - JULY 10, 2013

The thought lingers, gnawing at me every time I glance at my phone—something is missing. Despite the smooth surface of my relationship with Karissa, it's as if there's this deep, unshakable void. A pang of regret tugs at me, sharper than I'd ever want to admit. It's not just the friendship I miss, though that's a big part of it. It's the connection. The ease. The way we just clicked.

Callie could send me a single text, some random teasing comment, and it would brighten my day in a way that nothing with Karissa ever has. With Karissa... everything feels dull, like we're just going through the motions. I know I shouldn't compare the two because they're so different, but the truth is, I can't stop myself. I keep wondering if I rushed into this thing with Karissa, trying to fill a space that maybe she was never meant to fill.

And the worst part? I'm still hung up on Callie. It's been eating at me every day. And there are so many reasons I keep telling myself it shouldn't. Especially because I'm the one that said we should just be friends rather than pursue anything further.

The days blur together, one after the other, each one feeling more like I'm drifting farther from who I used to be. I've been trying to keep things going with Karissa, hoping that maybe something would reignite between us if we spent more time together. But every time I'm with her, it's like my mind drifts back to Callie, replaying every moment we shared, every laugh, every smile. I can't stop comparing and I feel fucking terrible about it.

Sunday night, we went to this new restaurant in town, one of those trendy places with dim lighting, overpriced cocktails, and tiny portions that are supposed to be gourmet. I wanted to believe that a change of scenery might bring us closer. But even as we sat across from each other, talking about our days, about work, about her friends, I found myself tuning her out more than I care to admit. All I could think about was how Callie would probably laugh at the pretentious menu, making some sarcastic comment that would instantly lighten the mood.

It's not just the conversations that feel off; it's everything. We've spent time together, sure, but we haven't really been intimate. It's not that Karissa isn't attractive—she's beautiful, no doubt—but there's a nagging sense in the back of my mind that something's fundamentally wrong. The spark just isn't there. I keep thinking back to Callie's smile, wishing I had a picture of her... or had gotten her fucking last name.

It's not Karissa's fault that there's this emptiness she can't seem to fill. I can't bring myself to just rip off the bandaid and end it. But I need to. There have been moments when she's asked me if everything's okay.

She asked it softly one night as we sat on her couch, the glow of the TV casting shadows across her face. We watched

The Notebook–yes; she tried to *Notebook* me–and I spotted her more than once during the film looking over at me to see if I was having any kind of emotional reaction. When the movie was over, she asked me if everything was okay and I tried to play it off.

But even as I nodded, I could feel the weight of my own lies. How could I tell her that every love story just reminds me of the girl that I stuck in the friendzone without giving us a fair shot because of the windshield time?

By Wednesday, I had replayed that conversation in my head a thousand times, wondering if she could tell that I'm struggling to see the point to move forward in our relationship. We haven't been together that long and might as well have a clean break now.

Then, out of the blue, I get the call that could change everything for me.

I'm elbow-deep in pipe dope adhesive, trying to fix a busted valve, when my phone rings. The number's unfamiliar, and I almost let it go to voicemail. I'm not in the mood for telemarketers, but something makes me answer it.

"Hello?"

"Hi, is this Owen?"

"Yeah, who's this?"

"This is Sandra from the Verizon store in the Iowa City Mall. Someone turned in a phone and according to the serial numbers, it belongs to you. They said they found it in the drop ceiling above the hospital lab."

You've got to be fucking kidding me.

I stand there, my phone pressed to my ear, stunned. I can't believe it. "You found my phone? That's amazing! I'll be there as soon as I can."

I hang up, still in shock. After all this time, my phone—the one with all the photos and texts from Callie—has been found.

I should feel relieved, maybe even excited. I'll finally have Barrett's pictures back, along with all the memories attached to them. But it hits me that this is about more than just a phone. It's about everything I've been avoiding.

I stand there, wiping my hands, the weight of the moment sinking in. I've been pushing down feelings, trying to move forward, but no matter how hard I try, Callie is always there, just beneath the surface.

The thought of having Barrett's pictures again chokes me up, but it's not just the photos—it's everything tied to them. All the little moments I've tried to forget, every conversation with Callie, every laugh, every text. It feels like I'm being handed a second chance, not just with the phone, but to finally confront what I've been running from.

I let out a long breath, the wrench heavy in my hand. Maybe it's time to stop avoiding the truth and face what I really want—and who I really want it with.

thirty-one
I TOUCH MYSELF - DIVINYLS

CALLIE - JULY 10, 2013

By Wednesday, I have never been more thankful for Amazon Prime in my life. I took Brooke's advice and splurged on a few new toys. My sex drive is already incredibly high and when I am pregnant, it's even worse.

As soon as I get the notification that packages have been delivered, I rush out the door to grab them like a kid excited to see what Santa brought on Christmas morning.

I open the package and wipe down my new rabbit vibrator before slipping back into bed. I close my eyes and search back through my mental spank bank, struggling to create a scene in my mind to help get me in the mood.

It's been too long since I've had mind blowing sex and I try thinking of different scenarios but nothing seems to get me there. I grab some of my new lube off the nightstand and just let the toy do its job, trying to clear my head completely.

The setting I selected has a low speed pulse on the shaft and a quicker pulsing vibration on the rabbit. I slide the tip of the toy between the lips of my pussy allowing the lower vibration on the head of the toy to hover on my clit for a moment before sliding it lower and pushing it inside me.

With the toy fully inside me, the rabbit vibrates against my clit and the sensation almost tickles. It quickly becomes overwhelming. I click the button on the bottom of the toy twice to slow down the pulse on the rabbit, allowing myself to ease into the new sensation. Usually when I take care of myself, I focus on my clit only so this combination of being filled while the toy vibrates against my clit is more than I'm used to. And I don't hate it. *I should have gotten one of these a long time ago.*

My mind drifts to thoughts of having a man's head between my legs, wishing his tongue would slowly massage my clit in the way that the toy isn't able to. The picture in my mind becomes more clear as my mind drifts to Owen. Since I've never met him in person and I don't know what he's actually like in bed, I'm able to mold the images in my mind to what would make me feel good.

I remember his beard and fantasize about what it would feel like to have him between my legs. Wondering if the hair above his top lip would tickle in the same way the rabbit toy does. I imagine him tasting me, worshiping me... sliding two fingers inside me slowly while he sucks on my clit and I swallow hard. The thought of him tasting me quickly turns to me wondering what I would taste like on his tongue.

I've always thought that was so fucking sexy. When a man is willing to take his time to please a woman and then makes her taste herself on his lips when he's done. A few guys I have been with have tried this but no one actually lives up to the heat of it in my mind. I picture Owen kissing me roughly while he ravages the rest of my body, demanding and unable to get enough... *Yes, please!*

I let my imagination run wild for a little longer, thinking

about what his hands would feel like on my skin. A man like Owen isn't going to have soft hands. He's going to have calluses and I guarantee his hands are strong, not even remotely soft to the touch. Thoughts of the way his firm grip would feel on my neck send a wave of pleasure through me.

His upper body strength must be pretty impressive too... Strong shoulders and arms... *Fuck, I bet he could throw me around like a rag doll.*

Thoughts of him picking me up and wrapping my legs around him as he pushes my back against a wall, slamming into me over and over play on repeat. My mind starts to go hazy as I pick up the pace pulling the vibrator out slowly and plunging it back in as images race through my mind of what being thrown around by a man like him would be like. My chest heaves and I bite my bottom lip as heat washes over my entire body and I come harder than I probably have in years.

After a few minutes, my breath levels out and I head to the bathroom to clean the toy. I come back into my room and open up my nightstand to put everything away. Definitely going to need that close by from now on. I toss the lube into the drawer and close it. Better keep that on standby too because the toy is not small by any means.

I'm going to need more batteries too.

I chuckle at myself and my insatiable pregnancy hormones, turning away from the nightstand when I hear a sound that makes me freeze where I stand.

My phone goes off with the sound of a beer bottle cap being popped. I slowly turn around to face my desk where my phone currently sits on the charger. I swear I do that slow blinking thing that happens in cartoons where you can hear the little "plink plink" noise as the characters eyes go wide.

Yep, that has to be exactly what I look like right now. As I pick my jaw up off the floor, I walk toward my phone as if it's going to bite me when I pick it up.

No. Fucking. Way.

My cheeks still feel hot from my orgasm and I try to take a deep breath before I can bring myself to actually pick up the phone to read the message.

thirty-two
OVER MY HEAD (CABLE CAR) - THE FRAY

OWEN - JULY 10, 2013

I stare blankly at my phone, the call with Sandra replaying in my mind. My old phone has been found, and all the messages and pictures I thought were lost forever are within reach. At this point, I'm just thankful that I didn't leave it on top of a boiler where it would have melted and I really would have been screwed.

Relief mingles with dread as I consider what this means for my conversations with Callie. The weight of unspoken words hangs heavy in the air, my chest tightening with the uncertainty of it all. My stomach churns with anxiety and hope, the duality of wanting to reconnect with Callie and fearing what her response might be if I reach out.

If there even is one.

"Hey, Earth to Owen," Will's voice snaps me out of my trance. I look up to see him grinning at me, the fluorescent lights of the mechanical room casting a harsh glare on his face.

The familiar metallic smell of steam permeates the air, grounding me back to the present. "What's going on?"

"They found my phone," I say, my voice still tinged with disbelief. "Someone turned it in at the Verizon kiosk at the mall in Iowa City."

"No shit?" Will's eyebrows shoot up. "Only you would leave a cell phone in the fucking ceiling."

"Maybe if you weren't a giant with a bum knee, you'd be the one climbing up into the ceiling instead of me," I retort, shaking my head. The clang of tools and the hum of machinery creates a symphony of background noise.

"Fair point. But you're still an idiot," Will laughs, clapping me on the back. His laughter echoes through the room, momentarily lifting the tension. "So, are you going to try reaching out to that Callie girl you were talking to before you lost it?"

I sigh, running a hand through my hair. "I don't know, man. I haven't figured that out yet."

Will's expression turns serious. "You need to make sure you don't cross any lines you can't come back from. Having inappropriate conversations with another woman, especially now that you're dating Karissa, is still cheating. Even if you're thinking about breaking up with her, it doesn't give you a free pass to mess around."

His words hit me harder than I expect them to. I feel a pang of guilt deep in my chest. "I know, man. I'm not going to, I'm not like that," I assure him. "It was different when I talked to Callie and Karissa and I weren't exclusive yet. I just... I hate the idea of hurting anyone. I need to figure out what the hell I'm doing."

Will nods, his expression softening a bit. "Just be honest with yourself and with them."

"Thanks, man," I say, appreciating his straightforwardness.

Will has always been no bullshit and I value that in our friendship. "I'll figure it out."

We get back to work and after a bit, he asks me if I've seen his channel locks. He's always losing them. I really am surprised that it wasn't Will that lost his phone somewhere random as fuck. I look around for a moment before I spot his channel locks and laugh.

"Nope, haven't seen them anywhere, bud. But you can always use the one sitting on top of the cart right behind you," I say, smiling because they are his channel locks that would have been directly in his line of sight if he had just turned around. He shakes his head, telling me to shut up and get back to work.

After finishing up work around 4 p.m, I grab my stuff and head straight to the parking lot. The drive from Mount Vernon to Iowa City takes about thirty minutes, but it feels like an eternity. My mind races with thoughts about the messages I might find on my old phone. The familiar scenery passes by in a blur as I speed down the highway, my heart pounding with anticipation.

As I pull into the mall parking lot, I take a deep breath, trying to steady my nerves. The walk to the Verizon store feels surreal. I spot a woman behind the counter and her name tag confirms she's Sandra, exactly who I was hoping to see. She greets me with a warm smile.

"We charged it for you," she says, handing me the phone. "It should be good to go. Obviously you won't be able to make calls or texts from it anymore since you got a new device already but you should be able to recover your photos and everything."

"Thank you so much," I say, relief washing over me. I hurry out of the store and find a bench in the mall where I can sit and turn on my phone. The moment it powers up, I hold my breath, hoping everything is still there. When the home screen finally appears with my favorite picture of me and Barrett, relief floods through me.

I will never not back up pictures again. There they are. Every single one of them. Thank fucking God.

The phone starts to ping with messages that were sent before it was turned off. There are several from the group chat with the guys, but I don't pay much attention to those. My eyes are drawn to Callie's messages. My heart sinks as I read them.

> CALLIE:
> Hey, Owen... Haven't heard from you in a bit. Hope everything's okay. Miss talking to you. Could really use a friend right now. 😔

Shit... I hope she's okay.

> CALLIE:
> I wish you would at least have the decency to tell me what's going on. If you're with Karissa now and can't talk, I get it. But just say that. 😢

Yikes...

I'm really going to need to think before I send her a text... I'm not sure how this is going to go.

I don't know if she's even going to respond.

What if she's already moved on?

I have, I think to myself.

Fuck.

No, I haven't. Not really.

I make the drive back home and ponder what I'm going to say to her. The ride back to Mount Vernon feels even longer. The sun is setting, casting a warm orange glow over the fields. I keep rehearsing different messages in my head, none of them feeling right.

By the time I pull into my driveway, the sky is a deep blue, and the first stars are starting to appear. I head into my apartment, kicking off my shoes and dropping my keys on the table again. The familiar scent of home does little to calm my nerves. I sit down at the kitchen table, staring at my phone.

I type out what feels like fifty different messages and delete them all. Finally, I decide to just go for it.

> ME:
> What's up, chick?

Fucking brilliant.

thirty-three
CLUMSY - FERGIE

CALLIE - JULY 10, 2013

OWEN:
> What's up, chick?

I blink, staring at my phone as if the words will rearrange themselves into something that makes more sense. It's been three weeks. Three. Whole. Weeks. And that's all he has to say? No apology, no explanation—just a casual, "What's up, chick?" like he didn't completely vanish for nearly a month.

My grip tightens around the phone. I want to yell, scream, throw the damn thing across the room. After all the texts I sent, practically begging for a reason, some kind of closure... and this is what I get?

He ghosted me. And he thinks he can just walk back into my life like nothing happened.

I take a deep breath, steadying the flood of emotions that rush through me. Anger, hurt, confusion... they all blend together in a messy swirl that makes my chest ache.

Then it hits me—I'm standing in my room without any bottoms on, fresh off an orgasm I conjured up by thinking about Owen. And now he's texting me.

Universe, you have a sick sense of humor.

For a second, I consider not replying. Let him sweat it out. Let him send another dozen texts without a response, see how it feels. But that's not who I am.

Instead, I pull on a pair of jeans, and in my most mature, composed fashion, I type:

> ME:
> New phone, who dis?

There's a slight satisfaction as I hit send, the perfect balance of sass and sarcasm. Maybe it's childish, but I don't care.

> OWEN:
> You used that line already, Callie.

> ME:
> Oh, did I? Must have forgotten just like you "forgot" to text me back for three fucking weeks.

> OWEN:
> I deserved that. But I can explain.

Oh, this should be good. I sit on the edge of my bed, arms crossed, waiting for whatever excuse he's about to dish out.

> ME:
> I'm listening…

> OWEN:
> I lost my phone at the hospital. I couldn't replace it right away, and I hadn't backed up anything. I didn't just lose your number, Callie. I also lost two years of photos of Barrett.

I pause, my anger flickering. Losing pictures of his son... that's a punch to the gut. The typing bubble appears again, and I hesitate, waiting to see what else he has to say.

OWEN:

> I get that this looks bad, and I know you're pissed, but I swear I didn't ghost you on purpose. I just got my old phone back today. Someone found it and turned it into the Verizon store.

> You've been on my mind, though. I missed you.

I bite my lip, reading his words. Damn it. It's hard to stay mad when he says stuff like that.

ME:

> To be fair... I wasn't sure I was going to respond either. It's kind of crazy, though–I was just thinking about you.

OWEN:

> You were?

ME:

> Yeah.

There's a long pause, and I can practically feel the weight of his next question.

OWEN:

> I'm okay, I guess. Things have been hectic. How are you? How's the baby? And Sara? Are you guys doing okay?

ME:

> We are alright... It's been a long couple of weeks.

OWEN:

> Wanna talk about it?

LOVE YOU MADLY

The offer catches me off guard. Before I know it, I'm spilling everything—about how stressful the last few weeks have been, about Matt, and about feeling completely overwhelmed. Owen listens, really listens, offering quiet support without judgment. Somehow, talking to him feels like coming up for air.

OWEN:
> You're been through a lot. I'm glad you're doing okay, though.

ME:
> I'm getting there. How about you?

OWEN:
> I've been seeing Karissa exclusively, but I'm not sure if it's going to work out. It's... complicated.

ME:
> Complicated seems to be the word of the year.

Just as I'm about to respond further, my phone buzzes with a call from Mr. Parker, my landlord. The conversation is brief but life-changing—he's offering me a bigger place, and he's cutting me a huge break on the rent if I help clean it up. I feel a weight lift off my shoulders. A new place, more space for Sara, and a fresh start.

ME:
> Oh my God! Guess what?! 😊

OWEN:
> Chicken butt?

ME:
> Cute. No, My landlord offered me a three-bedroom house at a discounted rate!

OWEN:

That's amazing, Callie! You definitely deserve some good news.

ME:

Don't jinx me!

OWEN:

No jinxes, I promise. You've got this.

I glance around my tiny, cluttered apartment, feeling the weight of exhaustion settle over me. The thin walls and constant noise have made it impossible to really get any rest. Nights filled with loud music and early mornings with Sara's cries have left me drained.

More often than not, she and I have fallen asleep in the older rocker recliner that Mom gave me watching *Strawberry Shortcake* and *Tinkerbell* DVDs on my computer monitor because I haven't been able to buy a TV yet.

ME:

I hope so. I guess I'm kind of glad you got your phone back.

OWEN:

I'm glad I got it back too, Callie. So glad.

I smile, feeling lighter than I have in weeks. Owen and I text for a little while longer, but for the first time in a while, I feel like things might be looking up. Sure, I still have a lot to figure out, but for tonight, I'll let myself feel good about this tiny victory.

thirty-four
JUST A DREAM - NELLY

OWEN - JULY 10, 2013

I lie back on the bed, staring at the ceiling, the conversation with Callie replaying in my mind. Reconnecting with her has been a comfort in a sea of uncertainty. Her news about moving into a new place brings a smile to my face. She deserves a break after everything she's been through. I just hope this is the beginning of something better for her. Maybe I shouldn't be so emotionally invested in her but there's a force there I cannot deny for much longer.

I close my eyes, trying to shake the feeling that's gnawing at me. Exhaustion from the day seeps into my bones and when I drift off to sleep, thoughts of Callie mix with memories from my past until they all blur together, pulling me under.

Trees loom overhead, their branches forming a canopy as I stand among the towering timbers. The cool air smells of the pine trees that surround me. A wave of déjà vu washes over me, but everything feels much more vivid somehow.

As I walk deeper into the trees, the path becomes clearer, lined with small, delicate flowers that seem to glow in the dim light. I follow the path, my heart pounding with anticipation and fear of the unknown. The sound of a flowing stream reaches my ears, and I feel drawn to it.

I enter a clearing where a small, crystal-clear stream cuts through the farmland. I find my Dream Girl standing near the water's edge, her dark hair cascading down her back. Her skin glows in the evening sun, making her look like an angel. She turns slowly, and her green eyes lock onto mine as the now familiar hints of purple shimmer in the dim light.

She holds a small red box in her hands. It is intricately decorated with symbols I can't quite make out. She looks at me with sadness and determination, like she's frustrated that I haven't figured out what she's trying to tell me.

"Who are you?" I ask, my voice echoing in the stillness.

She still doesn't speak, but her eyes convey a depth of emotion that takes my breath away. She steps forward, holding out the box to me. I reach out, my hands trembling, and take it from her. The moment our hands touch, a warmth spreads through me, and the symbols on the box begin to glow faintly.

I open it and find a single, worn paragraph inside. My pulse quickens as I carefully pull it out. The photo is of a family standing in front of a house that feels familiar although I'm certain I've never seen it before. The man in the picture looks like an older version of me–almost identical to how my dad looks now. Beside him is an older version of what I can only assume must be her. Both people in the picture are smiling, happiness radiating off of them.

My head is spinning when I look back at her, "Is this us?"

It could be. I feel a surge of emotions–hope, confusion, longing–hit me hard. Somehow, I know the choices I make will shape what comes next for me.

Before I can ask anything else, the dream starts to fade. The timbers and the stream dissolve into a blur of earthy colors, leaving me with only the image of the photograph as everything else slips away.

On Thursday morning, I jolt upright in bed, my heart racing. I try to center myself in the moment and grapple with the fact that it was just a dream. I try to recall as many of the little details about the photo as possible, but aside from the woman's hair and eye color, the details escape me. The dream felt more vivid, more real, like a force I can't explain. But somehow, I can never fully picture her face when I am awake. So why did it feel so real?

I scroll back through my conversation with Callie last night and am reminded of a few pictures that should still be in my old phone. With Callie back in my life, the need to end things with Karissa feels more urgent. Regardless of what happens next, I know my feelings for Callie are stronger than they should be for someone in a relationship, and I cannot keep avoiding the inevitable.

I drag myself out of bed to get ready for work, attempting to shake off the lingering thoughts of everything that is going on in my life. I decide I'll reach out to Karissa at some point today so we can finally have the conversation I've been trying to avoid because I don't want to hurt her feelings.

As I settle into my usual routine at work, my phone pings. Instantly, I find myself hoping it's a message from Callie. But when I see it isn't, a wave of disappointment washes over me. Instead, it's Karissa saying that she needs to talk to me about something and I agree to meet her in the cafeteria for lunch.

When I reach the cafeteria, I find Karissa dressed in her usual pink scrubs–a requirement for the OB department where she works. She sits at our usual table with a bright smile that tells me we may not be on the same page like I had hoped when she texted me with "We need to talk," vibes earlier.

The hospital cafeteria buzzes with the usual chatter and a part of me hopes it will mask the uneasy conversation I may be on the verge of having with her.

"Hey, babe," she greets me with a kiss on the cheek as I sit down. The term of endearment catches me off guard–she's never called me that before.

"Hey," I reply, trying to shake off lingering thoughts from last night's dream and Callie. My mind scrambles to keep up, and I can't help but feel my chest tightening and I pray I can keep my panic at bay. For a moment, I was convinced she was going to end things. But now, I'm not so sure.

Fuck.

Karissa must notice my distraction and gives me a concerned look. I explain I have a lot on my mind, trying to figure out how to handle this. The panic creeps its way up further and I realize I'm not going to be able to do this in the middle of the hospital cafeteria. When she tells me that she wants to take the next step in our relationship, it throws me a bit. We've only been dating for a month or so.

"I want to meet your son," she says, her voice gentle yet firm. "And I'd like you to meet my daughters. We could get them together for a play date if you want."

I take a deep breath, my mind racing. "Karissa, that's not where I'm at right now."

Her smile fades, replaced by a frown. "What do you mean?"

"I'm not ready for you to meet Barrett yet. It's too soon," I say, trying to be as gentle as possible. I want to end things with her completely but I can't bring myself to do it here at work.

Her expression hardens, anger flashing in her eyes. "Too soon? We've been dating for a month, Owen. How much longer do you need?"

She's joking, right?

The knot in my stomach tightens. "I just need to be sure before introducing Barrett to someone new."

Karissa pushes her chair back abruptly and the harsh screech of the chair legs against the tile floor cuts through the air. "You know what? I've got enough on my plate myself and I don't need to deal with your commitment issues right now."

"Karissa, wait," I say, reaching out to her, but she's already storming off, leaving me sitting there, stunned.

Well, fuck.

I'm not looking forward to cleaning that mess up later.

After work, I meet the guys at the bar and I'm grateful that even Vince is able to come tonight. The familiar environment of Black N' Gold and the laughter of friends provide a much-needed distraction. We talk about work, sports, and everything in between, the conversation flowing easily.

I'm in the middle of a story about a particularly tricky repair job when my phone buzzes. I glance at the screen and see a text from Callie.

> CALLIE:
> Hey, you drive a truck, right? You wanna help a pregnant bitch move this weekend?

I chuckle at her crassness. Callie sure has a way with words. Excusing myself, I step out onto the patio. Without giving it much thought, I dial her number. It's time we actually spoke on the phone.

The fact that I've had a few beers is probably giving me a little liquid courage.

The phone rings a few times before she picks up. "Hello?"

"Hey, Callie," I say, a smile spreading across my face. "So, you need help moving, huh?"

There's a pause, and then I hear her laugh. "Yeah, I do. Didn't expect you to call, though."

"Figured it was about time we talked," I reply. "Plus, I couldn't resist the chance to hear your voice."

Shit. I shouldn't have said that.

"Well, here it is," she says, a hint of amusement in her tone. "So, are you free this weekend?"

"I can make some time," I say, wondering why I didn't offer yesterday when we spoke. "I'd be happy to help."

"Great," she says. "I really appreciate it, Owen."

"No problem at all," I assure her. "So, what's the plan?"

We spend the next few minutes discussing the logistics of the move. It feels good to hear her voice, to connect on a level beyond texts. By the time we hang up, I'm looking forward to the weekend.

I head back inside the bar, rejoining Will, Luke, and Vince at our table. The noise of the bar and the laughter of my friends providing a comforting backdrop as I slide back into my seat.

"Who was that?" Will asks, raising an eyebrow.

"Callie," I say, taking a sip of my beer as if my heart isn't pounding in my chest. "She needs help moving this weekend, so I'm going to head up to Hawkridge after work tomorrow to give her a hand."

"Hawkridge? That's a bit of a drive," Luke remarks, leaning back in his chair. "You must really like this girl."

"You sure it's just a hand you're going to give her," Vince chimes, taking a pull from his beer and trying to hide his smile.

"She's a friend," I say, shooting a glare Vince's way. "Plus, she's pregnant and doesn't have anyone else to help her out. It's not a big deal."

Vince smirks, nudging Luke. "Yeah, just a friend. Sure."

I roll my eyes but can't help the small smile that forms on my lips. "Seriously, guys. She's a good friend, and she needs help."

Will nods, giving me a more serious look. "Well, it's good of you to help her out."

"How much help does she need?" Luke asks with a wink. "I know a few good men that could also help her, if you know what I mean."

"Luke," I say through gritted teeth, "Not. Fucking. Cool."

Luke throws his hands up in mock innocence. "I'm kidding!"

Will attempts to relieve the sudden tension between Luke and me. "Just make sure you don't overdo it. Moving is a pain in the ass."

"I know," I say. "But it's worth it to see her settled in a new place. She's had a rough time lately, and she deserves a fresh start."

Luke clinks his beer bottle against mine. "To fresh starts, then. And to good friends."

We raise our drinks, the mood lightening again. As we talk and laugh, I can't help but feel a sense of anticipation for the weekend. Helping Callie move might just be the start of something new for both of us.

"So, how did you end up reconnecting with Callie?" Vince asks, leaning forward with interest. "Last I knew, you hadn't talked to her in a while and started dating Karissa. I'm so out of the loop, man."

"Pulling double shifts constantly will do that to you," I remind him.

I take another sip of my beer, stalling as I gather my thoughts. My mind is racing, trying to find a way to answer Will's question without overcomplicating things. "I lost my phone a few weeks ago," I finally say, my voice steady, "and just got it back. She was one of the first people I reached out to when I got it back. We've been texting since."

Will raises an eyebrow, clearly not buying my casual tone. "Did you ever actually get her last name?"

The question hits me like a punch to the gut. Fuck. My stomach drops. How the hell did I never think to ask her that? We've been talking non-stop, like old friends who've known each other for years. But somehow, the basics got lost in all of it. "No..." I admit, dragging the word out as if speaking slowly will lessen the sting of the realization. How could I have been so careless?

I pull my phone out of my pocket, feeling an unsettling mix of embarrassment and disbelief. I've been so caught up in everything else—our conversations, the ease of falling back into talking to her—that I missed something this obvious. My fingers hover over the screen as I notice a new notification. It's from Callie, with the address of her new house. Perfect timing.

I force myself to focus. I can't let this slip through the cracks again. Time to ask the awkward question.

ME:
So, I have an awkward question...

As soon as I hit send, my nerves spike. Is this really awkward? Or am I making it weird? I glance around the bar, trying to distract myself from the sudden anxious feeling in my chest. Maybe she won't even care. It's not like I've known her for years... except it kind of feels like I have.

The screen lights up almost immediately, and her reply pops up.

CALLIE:
Oh God.

> **ME:**
> Callie... What's your last name? You never told me.

Why does this feel so big? It's not like knowing her last name changes anything. But at the same time, it kind of does. It's another step. Something deeper. Something about getting this answer feels like the next level—like I'm finally closing the gap between the girl I used to text and the real person she is now.

Her response comes with a playful edge, and I can't help but smile. She's always been quick with the jokes.

> **CALLIE:**
> Oh my god! You're right! I guess that should have been one of your questions early on. LOL!

> **ME:**
> So...?

> **CALLIE:**
> I'll show you mine if you show me yours. 😼

> **ME:**
> Klein. Your turn.

My thumb hovers over the send button, and for a split second, I wonder what she's thinking on the other side of the phone. Does she feel this same pull? Or is it just me? God, maybe I'm reading too much into everything.

The text bubbles pop up, and the anticipation makes my chest tighten. Here it is.

> **CALLIE:**
> It's Madden.

> Well, it will be Madden again. Legally, it's Graham right now. But it won't be once my divorce is finalized.

ME:
> It's nice to meet you, Callie Madden.

As I send the last message, a smile tugs at my lips. The name suits her. And while this whole conversation might seem small, it feels like another brick in the foundation of something I can't quite define yet. But I want to find out.

As I drive to Hawkridge, every mile feels longer than the last, anticipation building with every turn. It's like the universe decided to make this trip twice as long just for shits and giggles. Thanks, universe.

Today is a fresh start for Callie and I cannot help but wish it was a fresh start for me too. I want to be there for her in any way I can. I tell myself that it's just about helping a friend, but I know I'm lying to myself. There's this nagging feeling that maybe, just maybe, I'm not ready for what this weekend might mean.

I try to focus on the road, but my thoughts keep drifting back to Karissa. Why didn't I end things with her before I left? Maybe the hospital cafeteria wasn't the right place but I could have done it after work before meeting up with the guys. I'm just delaying the inevitable but I don't want to be the asshole who breaks up over text.

I should've gone to see Karissa first, cleared the air before driving out here. But no, that's too reasonable, Owen. Good job. Now I'm heading to Callie's like I don't have another loose end trailing behind me, waiting to turn into a disaster.

The irony's not lost on me. Here I am, heading to help a woman who's moving on from her past, while I can't even properly disentangle myself from my present.

As I finally pull into her driveway, I cut the engine and just sit there for a second. The sound of silence fills the truck, broken only by the low hum of the cooling engine. This is it. I take a deep breath, but it gets caught halfway down, nerves tightening my chest. It's excitement laced with uncertainty, like I'm standing on the edge of something big, and I don't know if I'm about to step forward or fall flat on my face.

As I step out of the truck, the cool air hits me, and for a moment, I stand there, taking it all in. The house, the driveway, the yard—everything feels so... still. Like the calm before a storm. Maybe it is.

I'm about to take a step toward the house when I see it— the door on the side of the house starts to open. I freeze, caught mid-step like a deer in headlights. My heart skips a beat, my mind running a thousand miles an hour. Is it Callie? What the hell do I even say when I see her?

It's been so easy to talk over text, but seeing her face-to-face? That's something else entirely. And part of me, the part I've been trying to ignore, wonders what happens after this. What does this mean for us? For me?

The door creaks open a little further, and I feel like time has slowed down again. I take a deep breath, nerves twisting in my gut. This is it. I just hope I don't fuck it up somehow. Whether we eventually become more than friends or not, I just know I can't lose her again.

thirty-five

WAITING FOR SUPERMAN - DAUGHTRY

CALLIE - JULY 12, 2013

My heart is racing as I wipe down the counters in my new kitchen, trying to keep myself busy and calm the nerves fluttering in my stomach. I've been looking forward to seeing Owen, but the anticipation is almost too much to handle. The past few days have been a whirlwind, and now, he's on his way to help me move into my new place. We've talked so much, shared so much, but this will be the first time I've ever seen him in person.

I glance at the clock, knowing he'll be here any minute. I try to focus on the task at hand, but my mind keeps wandering back to our conversations and the connection we've shared. It's strange how someone can become so important in such a short amount of time.

Every word we've exchanged, every laugh shared—it all comes rushing back, making me realize how deeply he's impacted me. It feels surreal that he's about to step into my world, making the transition from virtual to reality. I wonder if he feels the same anticipation, the same nervous excitement.

The sound of tires crunching on the gravel driveway pulls me out of my thoughts. I peek out the window and see a truck pulling in. I swear my heart falls out of my ass. His truck looks so much like my first vehicle–a '98 green Chevy S-10. Thanks to a crazy request that I made to my dad when I was little though, my S-10 had flames on it. I try to talk myself out of thinking that this must be some sort of sign.

What are the odds, right? It's like the universe is playing some kind of joke on me, or maybe it's just a coincidence. Either way, my heart feels like it's trying to beat its way out of my chest. What will he think of me in person?

I take a deep breath, wiping my hands on a dish towel before heading toward the door. Butterflies fill my stomach as I turn the knob and step outside. It feels like a scene from a movie, where the whole world stops and focuses on one moment.

Owen steps out of the truck, and for a second, time stands still. He looks just as I imagined, maybe even better. His presence fills the space around him, and I can't help but feel drawn to him. He's here. He's really here.

Holy. Fucking. Shit.

We start to walk toward each other, and with each step, the anticipation builds. I have to force myself to stay calm when all I want to do is shriek with excitement and hurdle myself into his arms.

Stay calm.

When we finally reach each other, he wraps me in a huge hug, lifting me slightly off the ground, careful not to squeeze me too tight because of my growing belly.

I close my eyes, savoring the feeling of his arms around me, the warmth of his embrace. And he smells so fucking good –

like citrus, sea salt and eucalyptus. It's overwhelming, and I have to remind myself to behave. No matter how strong my feelings undeniably are for him, he has a girlfriend and I will not be the other woman.

"Hey, Callie," he says softly, his voice sending shivers down my spine as he rests his chin on the top of my head.

"Hi," I reply, pulling back slightly to look at him. Our eyes meet, and for a moment, those corny montages in the movies make so much more sense to me.

I suddenly feel self-conscious about my outfit–pink capri sweatpants and a gray cami. I wish I had worn something cuter, but I needed to be comfortable. My hair is probably greasy and I should have thrown on a hat. Being pregnant in July is bad enough without adding moving into the mix. His gaze is warm and reassuring, though, and I can tell he probably doesn't notice I look like a hot mess.

We stand there for a moment, just taking each other in. The connection between us is palpable, and I can't help but feel hopeful for what's to come. I take a deep breath and remind myself to keep my feelings in check. Owen is with someone else, and I need to respect that.

But I don't want to.

"It is so great to finally see you, Callie," he says, taking off his aviator sunglasses to rest them on top of the bill of his Chicago Bears hat. His eyes are a deep and soulful brown, dark as freshly brewed coffee.

There's so much that I want to say to him. However, "Ditto," is all that comes out.

We stand there like that for a little longer than we probably should. But I feel like I've waited so long for this moment. Why did he have to go and get a girlfriend?

For the same reason why you were fucking Matt, I remind myself. *Because we aren't together.*

When we finally break apart from the hug, I can't help but smile up at him. He's not extremely tall but it doesn't take much to be substantially taller than me at five-foot-three-inches. And I have to shake off the thought that we fit together like this so perfectly. "Ready to get started?"

"Absolutely," he replies, returning my smile. "Let's get you moved in."

As I climb into the truck and buckle my seatbelt, Owen starts the engine. I notice him glancing around the cab with a slightly panicked look on his face. The inside of the truck is a bit messy–wrappers, receipts, and a few random items scattered around. He scrambles to gather everything up, trying to clean as quickly as possible. He obviously wants to make a good impression too. It's endearing and makes me like him even more, if that's even possible.

We make the short drive to my apartment and head inside. I show him the boxes and furniture that still need to be moved to the house. Owen immediately gets to work, lifting a heavy box with ease. I follow his lead, grabbing a smaller box and heading toward the truck.

He makes everything look so effortless. His strength, his charm–it's intoxicating.

I quickly realize that moving my dresser is going to be the hardest part of this and I'm honestly not sure I will be much help. Just as he sees me staring at the piece of furniture trying to figure out how in the hell we are going to get it out of here, he runs back out to his truck and comes back with a freaking dolly he must have had in the truck bed.

This man is more than prepared and it makes me chuckle. I never would have thought to use a dolly. And I'm wondering how he even has one. I can barely plan what I'm going to have for breakfast on a daily basis, much less plan ahead for things that I *might* need.

It's then that I notice his shirt has a logo on it for a moving company. I assume that he worked there and that's why he knows exactly what to do. However, when I ask him about the shirt, he tells me that he actually bought it from Goodwill and wore it today because he thought it would be funny and that the furniture dolly came from an estate sale.

As we load up the truck, I can't help but admire how effortlessly he handles everything. It's like he's done this a million times before. Meanwhile, I should be the one with moving expertise. Moving into this little house marks the fifth time that I've moved in the last year. I'm desperately trying to find stability for me and my girls and hoping this is the last time I will have to move for a very long time.

We only have to take a couple of trips back and forth, and before long, the apartment is empty.

"All set?" he asks, wiping a bead of sweat from his forehead.

"Yep," I say, trying to ignore the flutter in my chest every time our eyes meet. "Let's blow this popsicle stand."

He laughs as we climb into the truck.

As we drive back to my new house, the song "Cups" by Anna Kendrick from the movie Pitch Perfect comes on the radio. "Oh, I love this song! Can I turn it up?"

"Sure," Owen replies, smiling.

I enthusiastically turn the volume knob, not paying attention much as it lands on level twenty-nine. We drive for a moment before Owen quickly reaches over and turns it up one more notch to level thirty.

I glance at him, puzzled. "Twenty-nine not quite loud enough for you?"

He chuckles. "I don't like odd numbers. I'm a numbers guy—everything has to be even."

I laugh, shaking my head. "That's kind of adorable."

He shrugs, still smiling. "We all have our quirks."

As the music plays, I start singing along, tapping the dashboard to the beat. I'm giving an impromptu concert that Owen didn't know he was in for today.

When the song ends, I turn to him and say, "I want this song played at my funeral." He gives me a bewildered look. "What?! It's a great song!"

"For a funeral?" he asks, raising an eyebrow.

"Yep! It's perfect."

He laughs and shakes his head. "If you say so."

"I do say so! Besides," I tease, "we all have our quirks, right?" I add with a playful wink.

Once at the new house, Owen helps me unpack and put things away. We work together seamlessly, with Owen easily lifting heavy items and me directing where things should go.

As we move boxes, I notice Owen pause, looking around like we're missing something. "Hey, where's Sara's crib? I assumed it was already here when I didn't see it at the apartment. I was going to put it together for you."

I sigh, feeling a bit embarrassed. "I gave the old crib to Adam. I'm planning to pick up a new one tomorrow. For tonight, Sara can just sleep with me."

He nods, understanding. "Got it. If you need any help with that, let me know."

"That's sweet, Owen. But I don't expect you to come back here again tomorrow. That's a long drive."

He shrugs and we continue unpacking. The atmosphere becomes more relaxed as we finish up and I am grateful that he has been here to help. This would have taken me forever to do alone. We joke and tease each other, the playful and flirty banter making the work feel less like a chore.

As I put away the last of the dishes in the kitchen, a thought occurs to me and I turn to Owen. "Is your girlfriend going to be mad that you're helping a damsel in distress like me?" I ask, only half-joking.

He looks at me, a serious but soft expression on his face. "I don't know, and I don't really care if she is. You're my friend, Callie. I'm going to be here for you, even if she doesn't like it. And besides," he adds more to himself than to me, "we aren't doing anything wrong."

"I suppose that's true," I say feeling a warm blush spreading across my cheeks because I know I would do all the wrong things with him if I could. God, these pregnancy hormones need to simmer down. But there's something so magnetic about this pull that I feel toward him.

As the night winds down and I get the last of my things put away in the bathroom, Owen prepares to head home. I walk him to the door, feeling a pang of sadness that he's leaving.

"Thank you so much for all your help today," I say, giving him a hug goodbye. "Don't be a stranger, okay?"

He wraps his arms around me, holding me close. "I won't be. I promise."

Inside, I wish he would kiss me. *Why does he have to have a stupid girlfriend?* The thought lingers as we hug, and I swear I feel him placing a soft kiss on the top of my head. My heart flutters, but I keep my feelings in check.

"I'll see you again soon," he says, pulling back slightly to look at me.

I nod, smiling. "I'll hold you to that."

As he drives away, I lean against the back of my new front door and rest my head back with a thunk. *Ouch.* I wrap my arms around myself, already missing his touch and wondering when I will see him again. I slowly slide my back down the door until I'm sitting on the floor staring up at the ceiling.

I can see my reflection in a mirror that we hung on the wall across from the front door and I feel ashamed of myself.

"He's got a girlfriend, Callie. A fucking girlfriend. What are you doing?! You cannot catch feelings for this guy," I reprimand my reflection aloud like a lunatic. "You're just rebounding because of everything that's happened lately with Adam and Matt. It's nothing. Don't try to make it something."

But it's not nothing.

In fact, it's just the opposite.

Part of me wonders if I just want him so badly because I know I can't have him. Because he can't be mine. But that cannot be the case because I wanted him before he had a girlfriend. Before he lost his stupid phone.

He had told me that there was no way it would work out because we live so far from one another. But if that's the case, then what the hell was today?

It seemed like the timing worked out just fine and he was able to get here when he wanted to be.

Why is the universe so cruel that it would send me the right guy at the wrong time?

And why did he show up now?

Why didn't he show up months ago when we first met online before he wrote me off so quickly and shoved me into the friend zone?

What changed?

God, I must look so pathetic. I guess he just couldn't help feeling sorry for me since I was desperate enough to ask for his help.

I guess chivalry isn't dead though. So there's that.

thirty-six

BLURRED LINES - ROBIN THICKE, T.I, & PHARRELL WILLIAMS

OWEN - JULY 12, 2013

Driving away from Callie's house, my mind is spinning. I grip the steering wheel tighter, my knuckles turning white. Leaving her tonight might just be one of the hardest things I've ever done.

Not kissing her took every ounce of restraint that I have. But it is important to me that I don't cross that line. I've already bent the rules more than I should have when it comes to Callie.

I need to end things with Karissa.

I need to end them before I see Callie again because I don't think I will be able to resist kissing her when I see her again. Not unless she tells me I can't, anyway.

Being with Callie was so easy. I think I always knew it would be. But I convinced myself that the distance was going to be a barrier I wouldn't be able to work through. Fuck, I'm still not sure how I would work that out or if she would even want to.

She wants to, though. She has to want to. It couldn't have been just me who felt the connection between us today.

I know I'm not the only person that felt that tonight. There's no fucking way she missed that. How bad I wanted her—needed to be around her.

And fuck, her laugh is intoxicating. She is crass and beautiful and sweet and she smells so fucking good. Like roses and warm sugar.

And she has such a potty mouth.

Makes me wonder what other things she can do with that filthy mouth of hers...

Fuck.

Okay, what I mean is, she swears a lot. Like... A LOT. She was throwing F-bombs into our conversation like it was confetti or glitter or sprinkles or some shit.

I mean, I swear a lot in my mind but usually I don't curse out loud all that much. I've gotten so used to watching my mouth around Barrett that keeping all the *fucks* inside my head has become second nature.

She is *so* not the kind of girl you take home to mom. Well, not the kind of girl most moms would love anyway. Except mine. I can't help but think of how well she would get along with my mom because this girl is no bullshit.

Now I'm getting ahead of myself and I have no doubt that I'm spiraling. My chest tightens, and I struggle to catch my breath. The familiar signs of a panic attack are creeping in. I pull over just outside of Hawkridge, the truck coming to a stop on the gravel shoulder. The image hums softly as I rest my head against the steering wheel, trying to steady my breathing.

My palms are starting to sweat on the steering wheel and I know myself well enough to know that I need to get a handle on my anxiety before I drive any further. I just need to gather my thoughts and make a plan. Times like this make me wish Uncle Teddy was still here. He would know what to do.

These last several months without him have been brutal. Honestly, I think that is why Vince has thrown himself into working so much. Not only does he have a child to provide for but he doesn't want to cope with the loss either. And Vince won't listen when I try to remind him that his dad just had a heart attack and maybe he should think about slowing down instead of ramping up his stress levels because working at the prison cannot possibly be a low-stress job on its own.

Uncle Teddy always knew how to help me untangle the mess in my head. But he's gone now. I'm on my own with this one. When he died, I was in the middle of weaning myself off tranquilizers I'd been taking for years due to the severe panic disorder I was diagnosed with in college because I felt entirely too numb. Teddy was the one who encouraged me to get help for my panic attacks when I didn't think Dad would understand because he'd always compartmentalized things and avoided talking about feelings.

The week that Teddy died was my second week without the medication. I didn't realize it then, but coming off that anti-anxiety medication was notoriously tough. I had been reckless about stopping it because I was just so tired of feeling numb. I didn't want to be that way anymore, especially not when I had Barrett. So, I quit cold turkey.

The emotions I'd suppressed with medication flooded back all at once, overwhelming me. About a month after Teddy died, my doctor reached out, concerned about why I hadn't been refilling my prescription. She was incredibly worried when I told her I'd stopped taking them and said I was lucky I didn't have a seizure during the withdrawal period.

Teddy's death hit me like a freight train, and I've been struggling to regain my footing ever since. I know I should probably get on something again but I just need to feel for a while. Maybe not feel THAT much, but at least feel something.

My breathing slows, but the ache in my chest remains. First thing's first, I need to end things with Karissa. Regardless of whether or not things with Callie develop into more than friendship, I know that Karissa isn't someone I can see myself with long term. The thought of breaking up with her knots my stomach, but it's something I have to do.

I glance at my phone, contemplating calling Vince, but I know he's probably at work. Instead, I sit in the darkness, the occasional car passing by, headlights briefly illuminating the interior of my car. I need to focus. I need to find a way to handle all of this. But I need to take it one step at a time.

Taking a deep breath, I decide instead to send Karissa a text message asking her to meet me for brunch in the morning. I need to rip off the band-aid as soon as possible. I slip my phone back into my pocket and put the truck into drive again, determined to face this so I can move on.

Standing in my kitchen the next morning, the smell of freshly cooked bacon and eggs fills the air. I have set the table with care, the brunch spread looking almost too perfect for what I'm about to do. The sunlight streaming through the window feels mocking, too bright for the weight of this moment. My stomach churns with nerves as I hear Karissa's car pull up outside. I take a deep breath, trying to steady myself.

This needs to happen.

The doorbell rings, and I quickly wipe my hands on a towel before heading to the door. I open it to find Karissa standing there, her face lighting up with a smile that makes what I am about to do even harder.

"Hey, Owen!" she greets cheerfully, stepping inside. "This smells amazing."

"Hey, Karissa," I reply, trying to keep my voice steady. "Come on in. I figured we could have brunch here. More private."

"That sounds perfect," she says, slipping off her shoes and following me into the dining area. She looks around, taking in the effort I've put into the meal. "You've outdone yourself."

"Thanks," I say, forcing a smile. *Fuck. She must think this is my way of apologizing to her for upsetting her Thursday when she wanted to meet Barrett.* "Let's sit."

We take our seats, and I serve the food, my mind racing with how to start the conversation. The silence stretches between us, thick and suffocating. We eat in silence for a few awkward moments before I finally gather the courage to speak.

"Karissa, we need to talk," I begin, setting my fork down and looking her in the eyes.

Her expression shifts, concern flickering in her gaze. "What's going on, Owen?"

I take a deep breath, feeling the weight of my words. "I think we both know that things aren't really working here. And after a lot of thinking, I've realized that we're just not what I'm looking for long-term. It's not fair to either of us to keep this going when I don't see a future here."

Karissa's face falls, her eyes widening in shock. "You're breaking up with me?"

"Yes," I say, my voice soft but firm. "I'm sorry, Karissa. I just don't think this is working."

Karissa's eyes are wet with unshed tears, her lip quivering. She fumbles in her bag, hands shaking. I brace myself for what's coming. "You... you can't do this," she whispers, pulling something from her purse with trembling fingers.

Before I can react, a small white object lands in the middle of my plate. My stomach lurches.

A pregnancy test.

"I'm pregnant," she says, her voice cracking under the weight of the words.

"Okay," I say slowly. "And you're throwing the test in my breakfast because?"

"Because you're trying to break up with me and I'm fucking pregnant."

For a split second, the room tilts. My vision narrows, and for just that one heartbeat, I doubt myself. I rack my brain, searching for a gap, a drunken blur where I could have missed something—but no. No, I was sober. I was there. We didn't... we couldn't have.

"Karissa," I say, forcing calm into my voice. "That's impossible. We didn't—"

She guffaws. "We slept together the night we all went camping. You must have been too drunk to remember."

I can't believe she's actually trying to gaslight me into thinking we slept together. "Karissa," I say, trying to be gentle even though I'm so pissed I can feel my skin starting to heat. "That's not possible. I didn't drink much that night because you were so sloppy drunk and I wanted to make sure that you were taken care of. We didn't sleep together. I don't know who you're thinking of but it wasn't me."

Karissa's tears turn to anger. "How can you say that to me? You must be getting your days mixed up. You were drunk."

"No, Karissa." This woman is really starting to test my patience. "*I* was not drunk. *You* were." My voice is low, trying to stay calm. "I remember everything from that night, and I know for a fact we didn't sleep together. If you're pregnant, it's not mine. I won't even try to unpack the fact that you got pregnant while we were dating because maybe you were already pregnant and didn't know it yet but fuck. There's no way the baby you're having is mine."

She glares at me, her face flushed with anger. "I can't believe you're doing this. You're just trying to get out of taking responsibility!"

"I'm telling you the truth," I insist. "That," I say, pointing to her stomach, "is not my kid." I then point to a picture of Barrett nearby. "*THAT,*" I continue, "is my kid. And I do just fine taking responsibility for him. If you and I had slept together and if that child were mine, I would take responsibility for them too. But you," I take a deep breath and let it out slowly to avoid calling her something that I shouldn't, "are wrong."

Karissa stands up abruptly, her chair scraping against the floor. "You're a bastard, Owen. I can't believe I trusted you."

"I think it's time for you to go," I say, standing up slowly and pointing her toward the door.

She storms out, slamming the door behind her. I stand there, the sound of her car starting and driving away echoing in my ears. My shoulders slump as I sink back into my chair, my appetite gone.

I slump into the chair, head in my hands. It's over. The weight of the confrontation crashes into me all at once. The anger, the disbelief... it's all there, simmering just beneath the surface. I should feel relieved. But instead, all I feel is the empty silence she left behind.

What the actual fuck?

thirty-seven
LEGO HOUSE - ED SHEERAN

CALLIE - JULY 13, 2013

I thought that I would have slept better last night considering Sara wasn't here to keep me up but I had no such luck. It was like my brain wouldn't shut off. The memories of finally meeting Owen had my mind racing. I never actually expected him to show up when I sent him the text asking him to help me move. And even though him coming to help me was unexpected, I'm incredibly glad he did.

Having the chance to finally see him meant more to me than I care to admit. Part of me is glad that he didn't make a pass at me while he was here because he's in a relationship with someone else. And I refuse to let myself fall back into the old patterns I'm just starting to pull away from. But my chaotic side wanted to throw all of that out the window and kiss him like I've been wanting too for so long now.

I just wish things weren't so complicated.

To add insult to injury, I have to make the drive to Burlington to pick Sara up from Adam's this morning. I am dreading seeing the man that has made my life hell for the last couple of years. Of course, I'm looking forward to seeing Sara but interacting with Adam is the last thing I want to do today.

When I pull up to the house we were supposed to share, I take a deep breath before walking up to the door. Adam opens it before I can even knock with Sara toddling around his legs. My heart swells at the sight of her, and she runs to me, wrapping her tiny arms around my legs.

"Hi, sweetie," I say, bending down to scoop her up. "Did you have fun with Daddy?"

She gives me a nod and Adam informs me that she didn't sleep very well last night. That makes two of us. Just as I am about to leave, Adam looks a bit awkward, scratching the back of his neck. "Callie, uh, Katie stayed over last night. I thought you should know."

My initial reaction is a flash of anger and hurt. He has his new girlfriend spending the night while my daughter is here? I want to lash out, but I bite my tongue and refuse to give him the satisfaction of knowing it bothers me.

"Okay," I say finally, my voice steady. "Thanks for letting me know." I force a smile, not wanting to upset Sara.

My phone buzzes in my pocket as I buckle Sara into her carseat. I see there's a text from Owen, and I can't help but smile. I'm fairly certain my head is still spinning from my first time meeting him yesterday.

OWEN:
Hey, how's it going?

I sigh, fingers tapping out a reply as I finish buckling Sara in.

> ME:
>
> It's been a rough morning. I just picked Sara up from Adam's. I'm already exhausted and tempted to lay down and take a nap with her when I get home, but I still need to buy her crib today.

I slide into the driver's seat and start the car, my phone buzzing again before I pull away from the curb.

> OWEN:
>
> Sounds like you need some rest. Don't push yourself too hard. Yesterday was a long day. The crib can wait. Just take it easy.

> ME:
>
> You're probably right.

> OWEN:
>
> Usually am. 😊
>
> Text me when you get home, okay? Be careful.

> ME:
>
> Always.

A small smile tugs at my lips as I put the car in drive and head home. It's comforting to know someone cares.

Once home, I send Owen a quick text to let him know I made it back safely. His words from earlier echo in my mind and I decide he's right. I'll get the crib tomorrow. Today is for rest. And laundry. I need to get some laundry done. Sara can just sleep in my bed tonight.

When I lay Sara down in the *Pack N Play* for her afternoon nap a couple hours later, her little face looks so peaceful. Once she drifts off to sleep, I take a moment to look for my phone because I lost track of it sometime after I got back to the house. I find it on top of a laundry basket full of clothes I was supposed to fold just before Sara started getting cranky and see a couple texts from Owen waiting for me.

> OWEN:
> Glad you made it home okay.
>
> I hope your afternoon with Sara turns out to be better than your morning was.

> ME:
> Sorry, lost track of my phone. Just laid Sara down for her afternoon nap.

I decide to start folding the laundry I started earlier while I wait to hear back from him. A short time later, I hear the crunch of gravel outside. Curious, I look out the large picture window in the living room that overlooks the driveway and my heart skips a beat as I watch the now familiar green truck pull up to the front of the house.

Owen gets out of his truck, a grin on his face as he reaches for his phone, reading the text message I sent him a few minutes ago while he must have been driving.

"Good thing you told me that you laid Sara down for a nap or I would have been that asshole that rang the doorbell and accidentally woke up your kiddo," he says with a wink.

I can't help but laugh in disbelief, feeling warmth spread through me. Before I can get my wits about me enough to ask him what he's doing here, he walks to the bed of his truck, pulls down the tailgate and lifts out a large box.

"Owen, you didn't..." I start, feeling overwhelmed.

He brings the box to the porch, setting it down gently. "I figured you could use a hand since you were too tired to go anywhere else today."

Tears prick at the corners of my eyes as I stare at the box. "Owen..."

"Is it too different from what you planned on getting? I just got white because I noticed the dresser you have for her was white so I just got something that matched," he says, almost frantically.

I wipe away the tears that are now falling from my eyes. This man... I don't even know what to say. I slowly shake my head as the tears continue to fall trying to let me know that it's not that I don't love the gift. "This is too much, Owen. I.... we.... Why would you do this?"

He looks at me, his expression softening as he leans the box against one of the porch columns and steps closer to me. "Callie... I did this because you're my friend and you needed some help."

Ouch. I'm immediately reminded that I'm in the friend zone with this man. This incredible man that just bought me a crib for my daughter because I was too tired to go get one. This man that just drove here yesterday and helped me move out of my shitty apartment. This man who... isn't mine.

"Owen," I say softly, "please know that I'm not at all trying to sound ungrateful but I cannot accept this. It's too much." *And I'm pretty sure your girlfriend will be pretty pissed about it.*

"Callie, please accept this. I want to make sure you're taken care of."

And before I can stop myself, I blurt out "I'm not going to be anyone's side chick, Owen. This gift is not a gift that you give a friend. And those things are not the things that you say to just a friend. You have a fucking girlfriend!"

His eyes go wide and I clap my hand to my mouth to shut myself up and take a deep breath.

"What I mean," I say, trying to keep my voice steady, "is that you shouldn't do these grand gestures for people when you have a girlfriend."

"Not anymore," he says simply, his eyes never leaving mine.

My breath catches in my throat, and I feel a rush of emotions. *Holy. Fucking. Shit.* "What did you say?" I ask, dumbfounded.

"I said," – he steps closer to me and takes my hands in his – "not anymore."

"You better not be fucking with me," I say, my voice trembling with a mix of hope and fear. He's so close now that I can feel his breath when he lets out a low chuckle.

Owen's dark eyes sparkle with a hint of mischief as he reaches up and turns his hat around backwards. *Why is that simple move so fucking hot?*

"Callie," he says, gently lifting my chin so I'm forced to look at him, "I assure you, this is not what I have in mind when it comes to fucking," he pauses, letting the word hang in the air before adding with a teasing smile, "*with* you."

I don't miss the innuendo in his tone or the fact that the grip he still has on my right hand has become more firm and… possessive as his left hand lets go of my chin.

I look up at him, really taking in his features. His deep brown eyes hold mine with an intensity that makes my knees feel weak. He's wearing a fitted gray t-shirt that shows off his broad shoulders and strong arms, and his jeans hang just right on his hips. He looks rugged and handsome, every bit the man who has invaded so many of my thoughts since we started talking two months ago.

"I mean it, Owen," I say, stomping my foot in frustration like a protesting teenage girl.

"Oh, I have no doubt," he assures me. And he fucking winks at me, that damn playful glint in his eyes making my heart race even more.

God, he's so close now the pull my heart feels toward him almost hurts. I can't help but smile through the tears.

I take a deep breath, my heart pounding in my chest. "So, what now?"

"Well, first, I'm going to need you to put the claws away," he says, giving my hand three soft squeezes before letting go, and I feel the loss of his touch in my whole body. "And then, I'm going to need you to invite me inside so I can get this crib put together for you unless you want me to build it on the front porch."

Owen smiles, a look of pure sincerity in his eyes. His smile transforms his face, making him look more handsome, if that's possible. I can see the genuine care and affection in his eyes, and it sets my heart ablaze.

"Okay," I whisper, my voice barely audible as I step aside and gesture toward the door. "Come on in."

As he picks up the box and walks inside, I follow as the butterflies in my stomach rage around like they are trying to find a way out.

thirty-eight
COUNT ON ME - BRUNO MARS

OWEN - JULY 13, 2013

Carrying the box into Callie's house, I start to feel a level of unease settling in my chest. I should have thought this through a bit more. Springing this on her, especially with Sara here, wasn't my smartest move. I just wanted to do something nice for her and make life a little easier. But I didn't think about the major boundary I'm potentially crossing by asking to be here when she has her daughter.

As I set the box down in the living room, I glance at Callie. She's watching me, a soft smile playing on her lips. Despite my worries, she seems to be okay with it. Still, guilt gnaws at me. What was I thinking, just showing up like this?

"Callie..." I say, rubbing the back of my neck. "I didn't think about the fact that Sara would be here when I just showed up like this. If you need me to go, I can. I just wanted to help since you were so worn out. I should never have assumed that you'd be okay with me coming here like this when your daughter is here."

Callie shakes her head, her smile widening, her eyes filled with understanding. "Owen, you have nothing to apologize for. This is the nicest thing that anyone has ever done for me. I appreciate it more than you know. It just caught me off guard. I'm not usually a big fan of surprise visits. But I know your heart is in the right place. And I think it's really sweet that you did this for me. For us," she says, tipping her head in the direction of where Sara must be sleeping in Callie's bedroom.

I nod, my eyes meeting hers. Her deep green eyes draw me in, brimming with appreciation and something I can't quite place. "I get it. I just wanted to make things easier for you. But I should have asked you first."

She steps closer, placing her hand on my arm. Her touch is warm, comforting. "You're sweet, Owen. And thoughtful. It's just going to get some getting used to... someone caring like this."

Her touch sends a warmth through me, but it also makes me a bit sad knowing that she clearly hasn't been cared for in the way she deserves in the past. "How about I hang out for a while while Sara is asleep? We can wait to put the crib together so we don't wake her up."

Callie's face lights up with excitement. "Sure! We can watch a movie while we wait. I was finally able to get a little TV for the house, so I don't have to watch movies on my computer anymore."

"That sounds great," I say, genuinely relieved that she's okay with me sticking around. "What do you want to watch?"

Callie walks over to where the new TV sits proudly on a small stand. She grabs a stack of DVDs and starts flipping through them. "I have a few favorites here. How about *The Notebook*?" she suggests with a wink.

I cringe involuntarily, and Callie laughs, the sound light

and melodic. "Okay, clearly, that's a no. How about *Juno* instead?"

I grin, deciding to tease her a bit. "We could always watch *Dennis the Menace?*"

Callie's eyes widen in horror, and she shakes her head vehemently. "Absolutely not! I told you that movie scares the crap out of me!"

We decide on *Juno*, but I make her promise to watch *Back to the Future* with me someday. As we settle on the couch and the movie starts, I can't help but steal glances at Callie. There's something about being here, in her space, sharing this simple moment that feels right.

As the movie plays, my phone starts buzzing repeatedly. I glance at the screen and see Karissa's name flashing. I send it to voicemail and shove it back in my pocket, but a few minutes later, it buzzes again.

Callie notices and frowns. "Is everything okay?"

"It's Karissa," I admit, feeling a bit frustrated. "She keeps calling, but I'm sending her to voicemail. I'm not dealing with her drama right now.

Callie looks unconvinced. "Owen, if you're not together, why is she calling you so much?"

"She's not thrilled that I broke up with her this morning."

"Weren't you guys only together for like a month?" she asks, curiosity piqued.

I nod and pull out my phone, typing a quick text message to Karissa to remind her we aren't together anymore and to please stop calling me. I hit send and then turn the screen to show Callie. "Here, see? I'm not lying to you."

Callie glances at the message briefly before handing the phone back to me. "You didn't have to show me that. I'm sorry. I shouldn't have gotten snippy about it. I just can't deal with cheating and drama."

"I just want you to know that I would never lie to you about something like that," I say, meeting her gaze earnestly. The sincerity in my voice is palpable, and I hope she feels it too. She's obviously overwhelmed, though so I don't want to go down the rabbit hole of telling her of the bullshit Karissa said to me about being pregnant and stress her out further.

She nods, and we turn our attention back to the movie. Just as it's getting to one of the more emotional parts, we hear a small cry from the other room. I guess that means Sara is awake.

Callie pauses the movie and gets up. "I'll be right back."

I watch as she heads to her bedroom to get Sara, and I cannot help but miss what it was like when Barrett was that age. He was always so snuggly after his naps. It's way too soon to think about it but my mind starts to wonder what it would be like to be a family with them anyway.

Callie comes out of the bedroom holding Sara, who looks sleepy, her light brown hair is disheveled from her nap. Her big blue eyes are wide with curiosity and she has a pacifier in her mouth that makes me chuckle as I read the words "Mute Button" on it. She's clutching a well-loved stuffed giraffe, its faded spots and frayed ears indicating how much it's been cherished. She rubs her eyes with her tiny fists, making her that much more adorable. My heart melts at the sight.

Callie approaches me with a nervous smile. "Owen, this is Sara," she says softly, setting her daughter down on the floor.

I crouch down to Sara's level, giving her a gentle smile. "Hi, Sara. It's nice to meet you."

Sara looks at me with wide eyes, clutching her stuffed giraffe tighter. Callie gently nudges her and then reaches to remove the pacifier from her mouth, causing a loud comical pop as it releases. "Sara, can you say hi to Owen?"

Sara's little voice is barely audible as she whispers, "Hi."

She is so precious. I reach out slowly, not wanting to startle her. "Is that your giraffe? He's very cute."

Sara nods, her grip on her giraffe loosening slightly. "Jeffer-y," she says, her voice a bit stronger now.

"Jeffrey is a great name," I say, giving her a reassuring smile. "Do you like giraffes?"

Sara nods again, a small smile forming on her lips. I glance up at Callie, and our eyes meet. There's a look of gratitude in her eyes, mixed with something deeper, something that makes my chest tighten. She's letting me into this part of her life, and I completely understand the significance.

"I'm going to hang out with her in the living room while you work on the crib if you don't mind," Callie says, heading over to the small play area she's set up with toys and books. She sets Sara down and Sara pops her pacifier back in her mouth and immediately starts playing with her toys. Her pacifier bobs up and down as she babbles softly to herself.

"Of course. Whatever you need," I reply, my voice a little hoarse from the wave of emotions.

As I carry the crib box to Sara's room, I can't help but think about how natural this feels, being here with them. I open the box and start setting out the pieces and tools, my mind racing. The quiet gives me a moment to process everything. I can hear Callie and Sara playing in the other room, their laughter filling the house. It's a comforting sound, one that makes me feel at home. I've never felt like this before, and it's both exhilarating and terrifying.

While I work, my thoughts drift back to Barrett. How would he fit into this dynamic? Could he bond with Sara? Would he feel comfortable here, with Callie and me? The thought of Barrett and Sara playing together brings a smile to my face.

The crazy thing is I had zero interest in allowing Karissa to meet Barrett. But with Callie... it just feels different. It feels like we would all fit together seamlessly. I need to pump the brakes before my mind goes too far. *One day at a time, Owen.*

As I start assembling the crib, my mind drifts to the future. What will happen between Callie and me? Can we make this work? Does she want to make a go of this? I want to be there for her as more than just her friend. The thought of being a part of her life with Sara, of building something real and lasting, fills me with a sense of purpose I haven't felt in a long time. I imagine Barrett being here, playing with Sara, us all spending time together as a blended family. The idea warms my heart and makes me hope for a future where we can all be happy together.

By the time the crib is halfway assembled, I hear footsteps behind me. Callie peeks into the room, holding Sara in her arms. "How's it going in here?"

I smile, wiping some sweat from my forehead. "Making progress. It's going to look great once it's done."

She steps closer, looking at the pieces starting to come together. "Thank you, Owen. For everything."

I look at her and Sara, feeling that same warmth and determination. "It's my pleasure Callie. Really."

After I finish assembling the crib, Callie insists on making me dinner, which I am admittedly a little hesitant to eat, considering she's told me on numerous occasions that she is a terrible cook. But it's tacos, and I figured those couldn't be screwed up too much. They actually weren't that bad. Far from authentic, but still slightly less likely to make me shit my brains out than a certain fast food "Mexican" restaurant. I can't help but smirk to myself as I eat; she's sitting across from me, nervously watching for my reaction like she's expecting me to spit it out or something. This girl... she cares so much, even about the little things, and it's fucking adorable.

After dinner, Callie puts Sara to bed in her room where the crib is ready to go. She's put on new elephant crib sheets and mutters something under her breath that sounds like, "At least it's not fucking camo," as she fights to get the fitted sheet on the crib mattress. I can't help but chuckle at that—she's got this fierce independence about her that I can't get enough of. She doesn't take shit from anyone, not even inanimate objects like crib sheets, and I love that about her.

This girl is something else.

Once Sara falls asleep, we settle back on the couch. There's a comfortable silence between us as we watch another movie. This time, I'm choosing the movie. I shuffle through her DVD collection and cannot believe that she doesn't own a single Will Ferrell movie. Not a single one. I let her know that this makes me question our friendship, and she has the audacity to say he's "not that funny." I pretend to be outraged, but I'm mostly amused by her blatant disregard for what I consider comedy gold.

We opt for *Pineapple Express* – fucking classic. Apparently she bought it in one of the cheap DVD bins at the store and hasn't watched it yet because it's still wrapped in plastic. As the movie starts, we sit close, our shoulders almost touching. Callie's legs are curled up underneath her, and she keeps shifting, trying to get more comfortable. It's a small thing, but every little move she makes pulls me in closer, like she's got some invisible force field I can't escape. And truthfully, I don't want to. Her laugh as the movie plays—loud, unapologetic, even as she claims the movie is idiotic—sends warmth spreading through my chest. I catch myself just watching her, the way her eyes light up even when she's rolling them at the dumb jokes. It's one of those moments that feels almost surreal, like how did I get here, sitting on this couch with this incredible woman who has no idea how much she's starting to mean to me?

Callie turns to me as the movie ends, her eyes searching mine. Without a word, she leans in, and our lips meet in a soft, tentative kiss. The world seems to pause, and all I can focus on is the feeling of her soft pink lips against mine. It's like all those months of holding back, all those what-ifs and almosts, have culminated into this one moment. And damn, it feels right.

The kiss deepens, and I can feel Callie's hands sliding up my chest. Her touch is electric, sending shivers down my spine. She moves closer, her body pressing against mine as she leans into the kiss. One of her hands moves to the back of my neck, her fingers slowly tickling my scalp as she runs her hand over my short hair. I swear, the sensation alone is enough to undo me.

Her kiss is driving me crazy and I don't ever want it to stop. I reach my hand over to pull her on top of me so that she's straddling me on the sofa. I'm certain that the little whimpers and moans that escape her lips are going to drive me mad. I've never enjoyed kissing as much as I do in this moment.

Every part of me wants to lose myself in her, to just let go and finally have what I've been craving since the first time we spoke. But somewhere in the back of my mind, a voice reminds me to slow down. I've heard that women get more worked up when they are pregnant, but something tells me that's not what's going on right now. This is three months of wishing we could be together crashing into us all at once, and it's taking everything in me not to just give in. But I can't. I can't let myself get carried away because this girl... she matters. So fucking much.

She reaches down to my belt and I grab her wrists to stop her, trying desperately not to squeeze too tight. I pull back slowly from our kiss and she tugs on my bottom lip slightly with her teeth as a low growl escapes me. *Fuck.*

She looks at me with confusion and a hint of hurt flashing across her face. "Did I do something wrong?" she asks, her voice barely above a whisper.

"No, Callie, you didn't do anything wrong. It's just... I don't want to rush this," I tell her as I move my hands from her wrists and take her hands in mine, squeezing them gently. I can feel the tension in her, the way she's trying to hold it together, and it kills me to think that she might be doubting herself right now.

She looks down at our hands intertwining and I can tell she's upset that I stopped her. "Hey... look at me," I say gently. When she lifts her gaze to meet mine, I can see tears welling up. "Hey, hey... Please don't cry. I just don't move quite this fast."

She blinks, clearly surprised. "So now I'm fast?" she asks, defensively.

"Hey, don't be like that. I am not saying that there's anything wrong with you so don't put words in my mouth." She bites her bottom lip and starts fidgeting with her hands in mine nervously, and fuck, if it isn't the cutest thing I've ever seen in my life. She looks so vulnerable, and all I want to do is protect her from whatever doubts are swirling in her head.

"I mean," I say, lifting her chin so she'll look at me again as tears fall from her eyes and I brush them away with my thumbs and hold her face steady, "I don't want to rush this. I don't rush into sex. I have a three date minimum before I get into bed with someone. And I want to do things right with you." I'm terrified that saying this will make her push me away, but she needs to know I'm not going anywhere. Not now, not ever.

Her expression softens, and she gives me a small, understanding smile. "I'm sorry. I didn't think we were rushing. We've been talking for what feels like forever and now that I finally have you here with me... I just don't want to lose you."

"Callie, you don't have to be physical with me in order to keep me coming back." I hope she believes me because every word is true. It's not about the sex. It's about her.

"I'm sorry if I overstepped." I can see the sincerity in her eyes and feel the weight of her words.

"Baby, don't cry. It's okay," I hesitate, realizing I probably shouldn't have called her that.

She cries into my chest and sniffles when she's finally able to stop her tears. She reaches up at the same time I do to wipe away her tears. "I just thought you didn't want me," she finally admits.

God, if she only knew how badly I want her. I pull her face to mine and kiss her deeply, wrapping my arms around her in a hug, holding her close. "I do want you, Callie—more than you know. But I respect you too much to rush this. I want to make sure we do it right."

She nods, and I can feel her relaxing in my arms. "Thank you for being honest with me."

"Always," I whisper, pressing a kiss to the top of her head. "I promise."

As the night grows later, I know it's time to leave. I walk to the door and Callie follows. Before I step outside, I turn to her, taking in her face one last time. I lean in, kissing her goodbye. As I pull away, I notice the hint of amethyst in her eyes and my breath catches.

Wait a minute...

"Goodnight, Owen," she says softly as I stand dumbfounded as the realization hits me that I've seen those eyes before.

This is fucking intense.

"Goodnight, Callie."

As I walk to my truck, my mind races with thoughts of what this all means. Callie is literally the girl of my fucking dreams.

And I'm so fucking gone for her.

thirty-nine
STAY - RIHANNA FEAT. MIKKY EKKO

CALLIE - JULY 19, 2013

Despite the distance and our hectic schedules, Owen and I have continued to talk every day. I'm still in disbelief over the fact that he bought a crib for my daughter, put it together, and refused to let me pay him back for it. There's something so sincere about the way he cares for me. I feel like I don't deserve it.

I am still so mortified over my behavior that night and the fact that I tried to give him a blowjob as a thank you for everything he's done for me. I've apologized to him about it on multiple occasions and he has been so sweet about it, assuring me he just didn't want to rush it. And he didn't want me to think that he expected things like that from me.

Tonight, Owen is taking me out for our first official date and I couldn't be more excited. We haven't put a label on things but I know I'm not interested in being with anyone else.

With Sara at Adam's for the weekend, I can't help but wonder if Adam is going to pull some shit just because he knows I have a date tonight. Even though he has a girlfriend of his own to worry about, I wouldn't put it past him.

As I get ready, my mind races with thoughts of Owen. I'm filled with anticipation as I ponder what tonight has in store. I rummage through my closet, trying to find the perfect outfit. Something classy but also a bit sexy. Normally, I wouldn't put this much pressure on myself when getting ready for a date but I want tonight to be perfect.

After struggling to fit into numerous dresses that no longer accommodate my expanding belly, the panic sets in. I grab my phone, frantically calling Brooke.

She senses my distress right away when I give her a shaky hello.

"None of my fucking clothes fit!" I exclaim, my voice filled with frustration and anxiety. "I can't go on my first date with Owen looking like a whale!"

A soft chuckle escapes my best friend. "Excuse me? A whale? Don't you dare talk about my bestie like that. And even if you were, you'd be the cutest whale in existence! Like Baby Beluga!"

I manage a smile, though my nerves are still bubbling to the surface. "Thanks, Brooke... I'm just having a total meltdown right now. I want things to go right tonight. It's really important to me."

"I know, honey," she says, her laughter light but genuine. "Don't stress. We're going to find you something perfect. Have I ever steered you wrong?"

True to her word, Brooke arrives a short time later with an armful of sundresses. We lay them out on my bed, and I try them on one by one. After a few misses, I slip into a simple white sundress with black and red flowers. It flatters my body's new shape without feeling too restrictive. And it makes my tits look amazing. So that's a definite win, right?

My best friend smiles at me. "That's the one! You look beautiful, Callie."

I glance at my reflection in the mirror, feeling a surge of confidence. "Thank you, Brooke. You're a lifesaver."

"Anytime, girl. I suggest putting a handkerchief in your purse before you leave."

"Who the fuck carries handkerchiefs anymore?" I ask, confused.

"I'm just saying you're going to have that poor man drooling. Take him something to clean up with," she suggests with a wink. I immediately burst into laughter as she walks out the door.

I hope she's right. I've been growing increasingly self-conscious, and I want to look my best for our date.

With my outfit sorted, I add a touch of makeup, just enough to highlight my features, and pull my hair into a loose braid that drapes over my right shoulder. I glance at the clock and realize I need to get going or I'm going to be late meeting Owen in Iowa City for our date.

When I arrive at the seafood restaurant we agreed on, I take a moment to steady my nerves.

This is it.

I step out of the car and walk towards the entrance, smoothing my dress one last time. When I see Owen waiting outside, my heart skips a beat. He's sporting a light gray V-neck shirt that exposes a bit of his chest hair. I'm not a fan of facial or body hair, but here I am, trying to avoid jumping the bones of the man in front of me, who also has a full beard.

I'm certain I've never been so attracted to a man before. His deep brown eyes lock onto mine, and for a moment, it feels like the world stops turning.

"Hello, beautiful," he says, his voice warm and inviting.

I reply, feeling breathless, "Hey, you."

"You look great."

"So do you," he says, stepping closer and leaning in to give me a soft kiss on the cheek. His familiar eucalyptus and citrus scent fills my senses, and makes me second guess not bringing a handkerchief.

Owen takes my hand, and we head into the restaurant. As the hostess leads us to our table, I take a moment to soak it all in. The ambiance is perfect, and the company is exceptional. Owen reaches across the table, taking my hand in his. "I've been looking forward to this all week," he says, his dark eyes meeting mine.

"Me too," I reply, feeling our connection deepen. His touch sends a warm, comforting sensation through me, and I can't help but squeeze my thighs together a bit.

The hostess hands us our menus, and I can't help but chuckle. "So, any recommendations for a seafood restaurant in the middle of Iowa?" I tease, raising an eyebrow.

Owen laughs. "I know, right? But trust me, their lobster mac and cheese is amazing."

"Alright, I'll take your word for it," I say, grinning.

After placing our orders, I take a moment to survey the surroundings. The restaurant is cozy and inviting, with warm lighting that casts a soft glow over everything. There's a gentle hum of conversation around us, creating a pleasant background noise. Owen weaves his fingers with mine, and the simple gesture fills me with a deep sense of comfort.

The conversation flows easily, filled with laughter and light teasing. Owen's stories are so funny, they make me laugh until my sides hurt. He has a way of making me feel completely at ease, like we've known each other forever.

As our food arrives, I'm struck by how delicious everything looks. The lobster mac and cheese is rich and seasoned. The explosion of flavor with each bite leads me to moan in appreciation. Owen grins at me, clearly amused by my reaction.

"Told you it was good," he says, winking.

"This might be the best thing I've ever tasted," I reply, taking another bite. "It's better than sex!"

"I wouldn't go that far."

"I would," I insist.

"It seems like you're not experiencing the proper type of sexual activity," he remarks, his smile widening.

It's been a long time since I've felt this relaxed and happy. Something about being with Owen feels right. We share stories from our childhoods, dreams for the future, and everything in between. I feel increasingly connected to him, certain of a special bond between us.

"So, if you could travel anywhere in the world, where would you go?" Owen asks, leaning forward with genuine interest.

"London," I say without hesitation. "I've wanted to go since I read the first book in the *Harry Potter* series."

"I never really got into those. I think I was a senior in high school when they came out," he says.

I tuck my lips inward and bite back a giggle that's trying to escape. "I'm pretty sure I was eight...," I say, unable to hide my laugh any longer.

"I forget that you're nine years younger than me."

"It must be because I'm so mature for my age," I reply sarcastically.

Owen chuckles, shaking his head. "You definitely keep me on my toes. But seriously, London sounds amazing. We should go someday."

I laugh, feeling a flutter of excitement at the thought. "That would be incredible. What about you? Where would you go?"

"Jamaica," he replies with a smile. "I've been before, and

it's beautiful. The beaches, the culture, the music. I'd love to go back."

I smirk, remembering the story he told me about his cousin getting into trouble there. "Hopefully, your cousin doesn't get us into any sketchy situations while we're out."

Owen chuckles, shaking his head. "Yeah, I'll leave him at home this time."

We continue to share our dreams and aspirations, the conversation flowing effortlessly. I feel a deep connection with him, and I'm grateful for this moment.

"Callie, I need you to know how much you mean to me," he says quietly, his eyes locking onto mine with an intensity that makes my heart race. "Talking these last few months has been incredible, and finally meeting you has been even better. I'm so glad we're more than just friends now."

My chest tightens with emotion. "I feel the same way, Owen. You've brought so much joy into my life, and I'm so glad you didn't keep me in the friend zone."

He smiles, squeezing my hand gently. "Me too."

As we finish our meal, we step outside into the crisp night air. The walk to our vehicles is filled with charged silence. Owen stops suddenly, cups my face in his hands, and kisses me with an intensity that sends shivers down my spine. His kiss is hungry and passionate, and I respond with equal fervor. When we break apart, we are both breathing hard.

"I don't want this night to end," I confess.

Owen smiles, his dark eyes pouring into mine. "Would you like to come see my apartment?" he inquires.

I stare at him for a moment in stunned silence. "What about your three-date rule?"

"Oh, that still applies. Coming back to my place doesn't mean I expect sex."

"Fair point."

"I don't give away my cinnamon that easily," he says.

"Your what?!"

"My cinnamon," he shrugs.

I cannot help but laugh. This man is ridiculous. But I am here for it. "Sounds tasty," I say with a wink.

"Easy there, tiger."

"Oh, come on, it's not my fault. Don't expect me not to get worked up when you kiss me like that," I tease innocently.

"You're right," he says, leaning in to kiss my cheek softly, his warm breath tickling my ear. "Besides, something tells me you're more of a 'Kitty' than a tiger."

Oh, my God.

forty

GIRL, I WANNA LAY YOU DOWN - ALO FEAT. JACK JOHNSON

OWEN - JULY 19, 2013

After dinner, we drive separately to my apartment so she doesn't have to leave her car in Iowa City overnight. I spend the entire drive home trying to tame the growing bulge against my zipper thanks to the way she kissed me. And I didn't miss the heat in her gaze at my little "Kitty" comment.

Noted.

Fuck, this girl is going to give me a run for my money, but neither of us was ready for the night to end at the restaurant.

Unlocking the door to my apartment, I feel excitement and nerves thrumming through me. As I push open the door, I gesture for Callie to step inside first. Her eyes widen with curiosity as she takes in the minor details of my apartment. It's a modest space, but seeing her here makes it feel special. I follow her in, the weight of the night's emotions settling around us like a cozy blanket.

It feels right having her here in my space.

"Make yourself at home," I say, trying to keep my voice steady. As I watch her walk into the living room, I am certain that I have never seen a more beautiful pregnant woman in my life. I also cannot help but notice how amazing her ass looks, even in the flowing sundress. I'm trying to remember why the hell I have that three-date rule. It might be time to revise the rulebook on that one.

Callie turns to me with a smile that reaches her eyes. Her fucking dimples will be my undoing; I'm sure of it. The hint of amethyst in her eyes catches the dim light, and this really feels like a dream.

"Your place is really nice," she says.

I chuckle, rubbing the back of my neck. "It's nothing fancy, but it's home for now. I'm planning to move out once the landlord finds a new tenant. I hope to move back to Cedar Bluff before Barrett enters kindergarten."

Her eyes light up at this news. "Really? That's great news! It'll be nice for you to be closer to your son. I cannot imagine how hard it must be not living there with him."

I nod, but inside, I am conflicted. Moving back to Cedar Bluff will put me even further away from Callie, and I wonder what that will mean for our new relationship. But I have to do it for Barrett. He needs stability, and I need to be closer to him as he starts school, or I won't be able to keep my current visitation schedule with him.

We settle on the couch, and I can feel the tension crackling between us. I want to reach out, pull her close, and lose myself. Everything about us is unconventional–she's dealing with a divorce and her pregnancy–yet I can't shake the feeling that this is exactly where I belong.

God, I want nothing more right now than to feel her against me.

"Do you want something to drink?" I offer, standing up

quickly, maybe too quickly. "I have water or Diet Coke from my mom babysitting Barrett."

"Water is fine," she says, her voice soft–almost like she's becoming shy. I head to the kitchen, taking a moment to collect myself as I fill two glasses with ice and water. When I return, she's looking at the photos on the wall–pictures of my family, some of Uncle Teddy. Her fingers trace the frame of one photo, her expression unreadable.

"That's my Uncle Teddy," I say, handing her a glass. "He was... well, he meant a lot to me."

She takes the glass, her eyes meeting mine with understanding. "You've mentioned him before. He sounds like a great man."

"He really was." I sit back down, closer this time. "I miss him every day."

"I'm happy we did this tonight," she says, her voice barely above a whisper. "I've been looking forward to it all week."

"Me too." I reach out, taking her hand in mine. Her fingers are soft, her touch grounding me in the moment. "I've wanted this for a long time, Callie. I'm sorry I ever thought that we wouldn't work because of the distance. But I am really glad that it gave us the opportunity to get to know each other without the pressure of dating."

"I completely agree. I think everything worked out exactly like it was supposed to." She smiles, a blush creeping up her cheeks. "I'm really sorry about the other day. I know we need to take things slow, but... it's hard."

"That's what she said." I laugh, the sound easing the tension. "Tell me about it. But I think we're doing okay. One step at a time, right?"

"Right," she agrees, squeezing my hand. We sit like that for a while, just holding hands and talking. Everything feels so natural between us.

She snuggles closer to me and we decide to watch reruns of That 70's Show. We sit there cuddled together, and I swear I can feel all the tension in my body melting away.

Midway through an episode, Callie chuckles. "You know, I'm pretty sure if I were a sitcom mom, I'd be Kitty Forman," she laughs. "Minus the cooking."

"Guess that makes me the grumpy old man of the relationship, huh?"

"Yep! Right down to the ugly green recliner," she says, nodding in the direction of the old La-Z-Boy recliner Mom bought for me as a teenager that I can't seem to let go of.

"Fine by me." I laugh, remembering my comment outside the restaurant earlier. "Guess that little nickname is going to come in handy after all."

"You're something else, Owen." She giggles, her cheeks turning pink.

As the episode plays, I find myself more focused on her than on the show. I love the way she laughs and the way her body fits perfectly against mine. My thoughts drift, but I can't ignore the electricity between us, the way her hands feel in mine, and the warmth of her body pressed close.

During the third episode, I feel her breathing slow and her body relax completely. A soft whimper escapes her lips, and I realize she's fallen asleep. I gently shift her so she's more comfortable, careful not to wake her.

Watching her sleep, I feel a sense of peace and contentment wash over me. I lean down, brushing a kiss to her forehead, and decide I'm going to stay here a while longer. As she sleeps, her lips curl into a faint smile, and I wonder what she's dreaming about.

After a few more episodes play, Callie stirs, her eyes fluttering open. She looks up at me with a sleepy smile. "Did I fall asleep?"

"Sure did," I whisper, stroking her hair gently. "Come on, let's get you to bed."

She nods, too tired to protest. I help her to her feet and lead her to the bedroom. She climbs into bed and looks up at me with those captivating eyes. "Will you stay with me?"

I hesitate for a moment, then nod. "Of course. But first, let me get you something more comfortable to sleep in."

I grab one of my Darling Ridge Farms t-shirts from the dresser and hand it to her, letting her know she can change in the bathroom and where to find the extra toothbrushes.

She takes the shirt with a grateful smile and chews on her bottom lip for a moment. "Owen, can you help me with this?" She turns, presenting her back to me, and I see the zipper of her dress.

I step closer, gently pulling the zipper down, probably going slower than necessary. My fingers brush her soft skin and I bend down to kiss the spot where her shoulder and neck meet. Her breath catches as my warm breath tickles her skin.

"There you go," I say, my voice huskier than I intended.

"Thank you," she murmurs, holding the dress against her chest as she heads to the bathroom. I wait, trying to calm the anticipation building inside me. When she steps out wearing my t-shirt, I'm stunned.

Somehow, she looks even more beautiful in my clothes. The shirt falls high on her thighs, clinging softly to her curves, highlighting her growing belly. Her slightly tousled hair looks so sexy, and the fact that she's not wearing a bra makes my dick jump.

Fuckkkkk.

"You look... amazing."

"Thank you," she whispers before walking over to the bed and slipping under the covers and rolling over onto her left side. It makes me smile because she chooses the side of the bed that I don't sleep on. She then declares my bed is the most comfortable bed ever. She's perfect.

After slipping off my shoes, I slide into bed behind her. As soon as I'm under the covers, she snuggles close, her body fitting perfectly against mine.

I wrap my arms around her, holding her close and she fucking wiggles her ass against my cock. "You are not playing fair, Kitty," I whisper into her ear.

She looks over her shoulder at me in mock innocence. "I couldn't possibly know what you mean. I'm just getting comfy," she teases.

We lie there in darkness, the only sound being our continued breathing as I slide my hand up and down her leg. I can feel the heat between her thighs warm against my dick and kiss her softly behind her ear.

I bring my left hand back up her thigh, over her hips. As my hand stills on the top of her ribcage, I give her ribs a gentle but possessive squeeze and a whimper escapes her.

"Oh, you are going to be so much fun to play with," I tease, pressing a kiss to the spot between her neck and shoulder that spurred a reaction from her just a few minutes ago.

She struggles to control her breathing as my name escapes her trembling lips.

"Good night, Callie." I can't help but chuckle as she lets out a frustrated huff.

"That's so mean!" With a pout on her face, she grabs my arm and pulls it around herself, seeking my embrace again.

forty-one

WHY CAN'T I? - LIZ PHAIR

CALLIE - JULY 20, 2013

As I wake up, the soft morning light filters through the curtains, bathing the room in a warm, golden glow. Owen's body curls protectively around mine, his arm draped across my waist, and I feel the steady rise and fall of his chest against my back. For a moment, I just lie there, savoring the quiet stillness of the morning, cocooned in the warmth of his embrace. It's a peace I haven't felt in a long time —a sense of belonging, like everything is exactly as it should be.

The weight of his arm resting against my pregnant belly makes me a bit self-conscious, all too aware of the unusual situation we're in. The baby's been kicking more often, and I worry she might kick now, startling him or breaking this perfect moment.

Last night replays in my mind, and a small smile tugs at my lips. It was perfect—everything I hoped for and more. But as the morning light settles in, so do the doubts. Can this really work? With everything we both have going on?

I shift slightly, trying not to wake him, and am met with the unmistakable press of his hardness against my back. Jesus. He stirs, his arm tightening around me as his lips brush softly against the back of my neck, sending a shiver down my spine.

"Morning, Kitty," he practically purrs in my ear, his voice still thick with sleep and amusement.

God... why does that nickname make my pussy clench?

"Morning," I whisper back, feeling the heat rise in my cheeks. My mind spins, both from the warmth of his touch and the nagging voice in my head wondering what happens next.

He starts to kiss a slow, deliberate trail down my neck, rolling me gently onto my back. His lips are warm, sending goosebumps across my skin as his fingers lightly brush up and down my arm. I laugh, the self-consciousness creeping in. "Owen, wait. I have morning breath."

He chuckles against my skin, undeterred, as his lips travel lower, lifting my shirt just enough to expose the lace thong beneath. A low growl escapes him when he notices the lace, and I feel a surge of heat flood through me.

He meets my gaze with a mischievous glint. "Your mouth isn't the only place I plan to kiss you this morning." His voice is low, filled with promise, as his hand trails upward, cupping my breast and teasing my nipple with his lips.

"Really?" I manage to ask, trying to sound casual but failing miserably.

"Mmmhmm," he murmurs, his thumb brushing over my nipple before he pulls back just enough to smirk at me. "I'm starving. Breakfast is the most important meal of the day, you know."

His grin is wicked, and I can't help the flush that creeps up my neck. "Breakfast, huh?"

He nods, leaning in to kiss me lower. "Though, I wasn't exactly thinking of pancakes." He pauses, his lips hovering dangerously close to my belly button. "Unless that's what you want...?"

"After," I say quickly, my breath hitching as his mouth makes contact with my skin again.

He slowly pulls down my panties and tosses them aside as I whimper. As he lowers himself to kiss me again, he brings his hand from its place on my hips to gently brush over the lips of my pussy, making me squirm. I gasp as he slides a finger inside me and quickly adds a second and moves them in and out of me excruciatingly slow.

Owen continues his pace and places soft kisses against my hip joints on each side of my inner thigh. He teases me by exhaling as he moves from one side to the next without allowing his lips to touch my slickening arousal. As my toes curl with anticipation, he slides the pad of his thumb between my sex and moves it in small circles against my clit.

I have never been so close to orgasm this quickly before in my life. And I am certain that this time, it isn't just the pregnancy hormones that have me worked up like this. This man is taking his time to explore my body. He is attentive and every time he does something that gets a reaction out of me, I swear I can see the spark in his eyes.

He brings his mouth close to my clit and makes contact in the same instant that he moves his thumb away. He nips and sucks my most sensitive bundle of nerves, and I swear, I stop breathing. Nothing has ever felt this fucking good. I don't think it's possible that anything will ever feel this good again... That is, until he starts working his fingers at a faster pace, curling them up to hit the perfect spot. I feel an intense hot wave rolling over me as he sucks my bundle of nerves harder. His name is on repeat coming from my lips like the most beautifully broken record and I cannot hold back any longer.

"I'm going to–"

He hums into me, the vibration sending me over the edge, and I come hard, my body trembling beneath his touch. It's like nothing I've ever experienced before, and as I ride the wave, I feel myself let go completely, no longer holding anything back.

Owen pulls away slowly, his eyes dark with satisfaction as he kisses his way back up my body. His beard glistens, and I'm desperate to taste myself on his lips. He knows it too.

He hovers above me, his mouth tantalizingly close. And when he finally kisses me, I lose myself all over again, the intensity of it sending another wave of heat through my body.

But then he pulls back, his breath coming fast as he looks down at me, a teasing smile playing on his lips. "You're making it hard to stick to my three-date rule, Kitty."

I groan, rolling my eyes. "You and that rule..."

"Hey," he says, kissing my forehead. "It's not easy for me either. But I want this to be right."

I smile, though frustration simmers beneath the surface. He's right, of course. I don't want to rush things either, not with him. But God, it's hard to resist.

"Trust me," he says in a low, gravely tone that might make me orgasm all on its own. "I'm torturing myself more than I am you, I can assure you."

"Somehow, I doubt that," I say with a grin, reaching for my panties and sliding them back on, the cool fabric brushing against my skin. I catch his eyes lingering on me, a playful smile tugging at his lips as he leans back, relaxed but still watching.

"So," he says, his voice warm and easy, "how do you like your eggs?"

forty-two
EVERYTHING YOU WANT - VERTICAL HORIZON

OWEN - JULY 20, 2013

I lean over Callie and my fingers brush a stray strand of hair from her face. The taste of her still lingers on my lips, the sweetness of her skin and the way she responded to my touch etched into my memory. I'm not ready to leave this moment, but if I don't stop now, I'm never going to stop and I don't want to fuck this up with her. I don't want to be just another fuck for her. Because she's not just another fuck for me.

She looks up at me with a lazy, satisfied smile, her eyes still sparkling from our time together. "So, how do you like your eggs?" I ask as if I didn't just have my head buried between her legs moments ago.

"Surprise me," she teases, slipping her black panties back on her voice a bit raspier than normal.

"Surprise you, huh?" I reply, raising an eyebrow. "I think I can manage that."

I kiss her forehead quickly before heading to the kitchen,

my mind still reeling from everything we shared. The taste of her, the way she responded to me, it's all still fresh in my mind, making it hard to focus on anything else.

Stepping into the kitchen, I realize how bare it is. Not much to work with, but I'll make it work—eggs, some leftover veggies, and bread for peanut butter toast. Simple, but it'll have to do.

The eggs sizzle as they hit the pan, and I start chopping veggies, letting my thoughts wander. Last night and this morning–it's more than I ever expected. I can't help but wish I'd given her a chance sooner, instead of letting distance be my excuse. I didn't consider the fact that it could work with the right person. For the right person–I could make the effort.

The way she tasted, the way we connected, it's more than I ever could have hoped for. But as perfect as it all feels, there's still a part of me that's a little nervous. I want this to work so badly, and I know there's a lot riding on how we navigate the next steps.

I should've offered to take her out for breakfast, but selfishly, I wanted to keep her here, in my bed, for as long as I could.

As I finish cooking, I hear the soft padding of her footsteps behind me. I turn, and there she is, walking into the kitchen with a sleepy smile, her hair still tousled from bed and my Darling Ridge Farms t-shirt back on.

"It smells too good in here. I couldn't stay in bed–I had to see what you were up to," she says, taking a seat at the counter, her eyes bright with curiosity.

I chuckle, turning back to the stove. "Just whipping up something simple. It's not much, I'm sorry. I really need to get to the grocery store. But I've been so busy and just eating out lately."

"Yeah, you have," she teases, winking. The blush creeping

up her neck says enough—she definitely enjoyed herself this morning.

I spread a generous layer of peanut butter on the toast and it melts slightly, creating the perfect creamy texture. I plate the food, adding a few fresh strawberries for a touch of sweetness, and set everything in front of her.

"This looks amazing," she says, eyeing the plate full of food.

"I could say the same about you," I reply, setting a napkin and silverware next to the plate in front of her.

After a few bites, Callie pauses, looking over at me with a grin. "Hey, do you have any cinnamon sugar?"

I raise an eyebrow, a slow smile spreading across my face. "I thought I told you I don't give my cinnamon away for free."

Callie laughs, leaning in a little closer. "I know you said that, but I was wondering if I could steal some? I bet it tastes so good, Owen." She winks at me again, and I can't help but chuckle at the level of pure sex in her voice.

This. Fucking. Girl.

"Well, since you asked so nicely," I say, reaching over to the small spice rack on the counter. I hand it to her with a grin. "I suppose I can make an exception this time."

She takes the cinnamon sugar, sprinkling a little over her toast before taking another bite. "Mmm, you were right," she says, licking a bit of sugar from her lips. "It really does taste amazing."

The way she says it, the way she looks at me–it sends a rush of warmth through me, and I realize how much I want this, how much I want her to be part of my life. And how much I hope to be a part of hers.

As we finish eating, I set my plate aside, feeling a slight nervousness creep in. I take a deep breath, knowing it's time to ask her about meeting my family this weekend while some of my cousins are in town for the county fair.

"So, Callie," I start, trying to keep my tone casual, "there's something I wanted to talk to you about."

She looks up at me, curiosity and mild concern in her eyes. "What's up?"

"Well, some of my cousins are going to be in town this weekend and they are going out on Friday night. I was wondering if you'd like to come with me. It's a big family thing, and I'd really like you to be there."

Her eyes widen in surprise, but then she smiles, that warm, genuine smile that always makes my heart beat a little faster. "A good ol' family reunion, huh? I would love to go. It means a lot that you want me to be there."

Relief washes over me, and I squeeze her hand, feeling a weight lift off my shoulders. "That's great. I'm really glad you're up for it. Sabrina asked if she could have Barrett for an extra week to take him to Gulf Shores for vacation, so he'll be gone this week and next. I need plenty of stuff to keep myself busy. When he returns, I will have him for two weeks, and I was hoping maybe we could get the kids together then."

"That sounds perfect," she says, her eyes excitedly bright. Then she hesitates for a moment, her fingers idly playing with the edge of the napkin. "But... I have one condition."

I raise an eyebrow, intrigued. "Oh? And what's that?"

"If I go to see your cousins in Cedar Bluff on Friday, you have to come to Hawkridge for the Halestorm concert Saturday night."

I blink in surprise, then laugh softly. "The Halestorm concert?"

"Yep," she nods, her eyes sparkling. "I've been dying to go, and I think it'd be even more fun with you there. Besides, it's only fair–family time for you, and a concert for me."

I can't help but grin. "So, if I agree to go to a concert with you, you'll come to a bar with me on Friday night and deal with my drunk cousins while you're sober?"

She shrugs, her expression playful. "That's the deal."

"Deal," I say, reaching out to shake her hand, though I can't resist pulling her closer for a quick kiss instead. "I think I'm getting the better end of this bargain, though."

"Oh, trust me," she whispers against my lips, her eyes twinkling, "I think we both win."

"Oh yeah? Why's that?"

"Because after the concert... that'll be our third date," she teases, giving me a knowing wink.

I lean in and kiss her again, feeling the truth of her words in the way she holds me close. This is a big step for us, but it feels right–like we're moving in the direction we're meant to go.

When the kiss breaks, we stay close, foreheads touching as we both take a moment to catch our breath. Her fingers trace lazy patterns on the back of my neck, sending a shiver down my spine.

"You know," I murmur, brushing my lips against her temple, "if this third date goes the way I'm hoping, we might need to find a way to sneak out of that concert early."

I capture her lips with mine again, the kiss deepening as she wraps her arms around my neck, pulling me closer. The warmth of her body pressed against mine is intoxicating, and for a moment, I lose myself completely in her–her taste, her scent, the way she feels in my arms. It's like everything else fades away, leaving just us in this perfect moment. Her taste is so deliciously sweet it makes me delirious.

When we finally pull apart, both of us are breathless, our foreheads still touching. I can see the same mix of desire and contentment in her eyes that I'm feeling, and it makes my heart swell.

"Maybe we should finish breakfast before we get too carried away," she whispers, her lips brushing mine as she speaks.

"Probably a good idea," I agree, though my body protests the idea of pulling away from her. I reluctantly step back, giving us both a moment to catch our breath.

We fall into an easy rhythm as we finish our breakfast, the conversation flowing naturally between us. It's like all the barriers that once stood between us have finally crumbled, leaving us free to explore whatever this is–whatever we're becoming.

After we finish eating, I clear the plates and start rinsing them off in the sink. Callie joins me, drying each dish as I hand it to her. It's a simple, domestic moment, but it feels like something more–like a glimpse of what our lives could be like together.

As we work side by side, I can't help but imagine more mornings like this. More shared breakfasts, more laughter, more kisses that leave us both breathless. It's a future that I never dared to hope for, but now that it's within reach, I want it more than anything.

When the last dish is put away, Callie turns to me, her eyes soft and full of emotion. "Owen, I... I really appreciate this. Everything. I know it's still new, and there's a lot to figure out, but... I'm really glad we're doing this."

I reach out, tucking a strand of hair behind her ear. "I'm glad too, Callie. And we'll figure it out. Together."

She nods, a small hopeful smile playing on her lips. "Together," she echoes.

The sun sinks low in the sky, casting long shadows over the fields. The farm is quiet, the soft rustle of corn in the breeze and the steady hum of crickets the only sounds. I've been here before. It's the same dream—the one that slips through my fingers every time I try to grasp it.

I stand at the edge of the field, the air heavy with anticipation. The old barn looms ahead, bathed in the fading glow of dusk, and beyond it, Uncle Teddy's farmhouse—a place that once felt like home, now distant, unreachable. Since his death, I've never made it to the house in these dreams. Every time I get close, I wake up.

But tonight, something is different. There's a pull, a sense of urgency I've never felt before, drawing me deeper into the field. The sky darkens, purple and blue washing over the landscape, and my heartbeat quickens as the barn comes into sharper focus. My gaze sweeps the horizon, searching for her—the girl with the emerald and amethyst eyes. The one who's always just out of reach, her face blurred by the waking world.

Then, I see her.

Standing near the barn, her back to me, her dark hair catching the last of the light. My chest tightens. I quicken my pace, desperate to reach her, to finally see her face. I call out, my voice raw with need, and she turns, slow and deliberate, her movements like a ripple in time.

Her eyes meet mine, and everything else fades away. The farm, the barn, the world—all of it dissolves into the background.

It's Callie.

A wave of recognition crashes over me, knocking the breath from my lungs. How could I not have known? All this time, she's been here—in my dreams, haunting me with those eyes. But it's not just recognition. It's deeper. It's always been her.

She steps forward, her gaze locked on mine, her voice soft, almost like a whisper carried on the wind. "Owen." There's relief in her tone, but something else, too. Longing, maybe. As if she's been waiting for me, just as I've been searching for her.

"You found me."

Her words hit me like a punch to the gut, and the realization settles deep in my chest. This girl, the one I've been chasing for so long—it's always been Callie. My heart pounds, a mix of disbelief and certainty filling the space between us.

I move toward her, faster now, drawn to her like gravity. She smiles—warm and genuine, the kind of smile that makes everything else fall away. "I've been waiting for you," she says, her voice carrying the weight of something unspoken.

She's holding the small, ornate box. Its intricate symbols shimmer faintly in the dim light, just beyond my understanding. She extends it to me, and as our fingers brush, warmth radiates through me, grounding me in the moment. The connection between us hums, stronger than ever.

I open the box, knowing what I'll find inside—the photograph. But this time, the image is clearer. It's a family—a man, a woman, and their children, standing together in front of a house. The man is an older version of me, and the woman is Callie, unmistakably her. We're smiling, a sense of peace and happiness written across our faces.

I stare at the picture, my throat tightening as I take in the sight of two little girls and a boy. The boy looks just like me when I was younger, but I know it isn't me. "Barrett," I whisper. My heart lurches as I recognize the older girl—Sara. And the tiny blonde, barely standing on her own... she's ours.

A tear slips from my eye and falls onto the photograph, blur-

ring the image for a moment. When I look back at Callie, I know. This is the answer I've been waiting for.

It's always been her.

When I wake up Thursday morning, my chest feels heavy with the weight of the dream. Callie is miles away in Hawkridge, and the distance feels unbearable. I want to call her, to tell her everything, but how do you explain something like that? How do you put into words a dream that feels like fate?

Instead, I send a simple text:

> ME:
>
> Good morning, dollface. I can't wait to see you tomorrow. 😊

As I set the phone down, the memory of the dream lingers, refusing to fade. This isn't just a connection. It's something bigger—something that's been pulling us together long before we even met. And now that I know... now that I'm sure... I know I'll never be able to let her go.

forty-three
A THOUSAND MILES - VANESSA CARLTON

CALLIE - JULY 25, 2013

My phone buzzes softly on the nightstand, nudging me from sleep. I blink groggily, fingers brushing over the cool surface as I bring it closer. Owen's name lights up the screen, making my chest flutter with warmth.

> **OWEN:**
> Good morning, dollface. I can't wait to see you tomorrow. 😊

A smile tugs at my lips. Even in the stillness of early morning, his text chases away the quiet of the room, flooding me with a sense of anticipation. I linger on the message, savoring the moment before instinctively pressing the call button. I need to hear his voice.

He picks up after the second ring, his voice a mix of grogginess and warmth. "Morning, dollface. Didn't expect you to call this early."

"I could say the same to you," I tease, leaning back against the pillows. "Why are you up so early?"

He hesitates, as if searching for the right words. "I couldn't sleep," he admits, his tone soft. "Had a lot on my mind."

"Anything you want to talk about?" I ask, hoping he'll open up.

He pauses, and I can almost picture him rubbing the back of his neck, contemplating. "I had this dream... about us," he finally says, his voice quieter. "It felt different, though. Like it was trying to tell me something."

His words send a shiver down my spine. I had a similar dream last night too—something that felt bigger than just a regular dream. "Good different, I hope?" I ask, keeping my voice light.

"I think so," he says. "It just made me realize how long I've been waiting for something like this."

His confession hits me like a gentle wave, wrapping me in warmth. I swallow, finding my voice. "Owen..."

"I know it sounds crazy," he cuts in, his voice steady but vulnerable. "But it's like I've known you forever, longer than a few months. Like my soul is drawn to you, and that doesn't make any sense because I'm not someone who believes in stuff like that. But with you... I don't need proof. I just know it's real."

His words send my heart racing, the truth of them resonating deep within me. "It doesn't sound crazy," I whisper. "I feel it too."

There's a silence between us, not empty but full of everything unsaid. Finally, he breaks it, his voice softer, more certain. "I can't wait to see you tomorrow."

"I can't wait either," I reply, my heart light. "It's all I've been thinking about."

We stay on the phone for a while longer as I get things

ready to take Sara with me to work. When we finally hang up, I'm left with a sense of certainty I haven't felt in a long time. Owen has this way of making me feel cherished in a way I've never experienced.

The memories from last weekend linger—a mix of laughter, shared glances, and quiet moments. Tomorrow feels like a promise, and I'm ready for it. But more than that, there's something deeper—an undeniable pull, a connection that seems to have been there all along, drawing us into each other's orbit. I wonder if Owen feels it too.

I run my fingers along the edge of the phone, grounding myself in the coolness of the metal, trying to hold onto this feeling, like I could bottle it and carry it with me through the day.

I take a deep breath, smiling softly. This feels different from anything before. With Owen, it's not just going through the motions—it's real. And I'm ready for whatever comes next.

I glance at the clock on the wall, noting the hands inching closer to my shift's start time. Sara stirs slightly in my arms, her small body fitting perfectly against mine, her soft breath warm on my shoulder. I kiss the top of her head, savoring this quiet moment before the day begins.

"It's going to be a busy morning, baby girl," I whisper. "But Grammy and Poppy Wayne will be here soon to pick you up."

She sighs softly, snuggling closer, and I can't help but smile. Even though juggling work and motherhood has been overwhelming, these small moments make it all worth it. I gather her diaper bag and my purse, balancing everything as we step out into the crisp morning air.

When we arrive at Brooked & Brewed, Sara is more awake, her big, curious eyes taking in the shop. I set her up in one of the cushioned chairs near the back, pulling out her favorite toys, including her beloved plush giraffe.

"Okay, let's get you settled," I say, placing a few more toys in front of her. She immediately grabs the giraffe, babbling happily to it.

I start setting up for the morning rush, grateful that Brooke has been so flexible, letting me bring Sara in for these early shifts. It's a juggling act, but seeing Sara here with me feels right. She's part of everything I do now.

The rhythmic hum of the coffee machines fills the air, and I lose myself in the motions of the morning routine. As I glance at Sara, who is happily playing with her giraffe, a wave of contentment washes over me. Despite the craziness, I wouldn't have it any other way.

A couple of hours later, the door chimes, and I smile as Mom and Wayne walk in, their faces lighting up when they see Sara. My mom swoops in, planting kisses all over Sara's cheeks.

"There's my sweet girl!" she coos, as Wayne gives me a warm smile, always the quiet one.

"Thanks for picking her up," I say, stepping out from behind the counter. "She's been a little fussy this morning, so just keep an eye on her."

Wayne nods, his hand resting on my shoulder. "We've got her covered. Make sure you rest your feet when you can, honey. They look a little swollen."

I laugh softly, appreciating his concern. "I'll try, I promise."

After they leave with Sara, the shop falls into a comfortable rhythm. The morning rush keeps me on my toes, but there's a lightness in my chest knowing I'll see Owen tomorrow. As I catch my breath between customers, I pull out my phone and see a text from Owen, along with a link to a song.

> OWEN:
> Made me think of you.

My heart flutters, and a small smile tugs at my lips. I quickly type out a response:

> ME:
> Sorry, I've been swamped! I'll listen to it as soon as I get the chance. Can't wait to see you tomorrow!

The steady stream of customers keeps me busy, and the usual hum of chatter fills the space. It's not until a lull in the morning rush that I finally have a moment to take a break just as my sister Taylor's name pops up with an incoming call on my phone.

"Hey, Tay," I say, wiping my hands on my apron as I lean against the counter.

"Hey, Callie! How's my favorite niece doing?" Taylor's voice is bright, the kind of cheerful that instantly makes you feel lighter.

"She's good, went with Mom and Wayne this morning. What's up?"

There's a brief pause on the other end, then a playful sigh. "Okay, I'm just going to come out and say it: I have baby fever. Like, seriously considered calling Nick to ask if he will procreate with me again. It's that bad!"

I double over with laughter. "Procreate? Really, Tay?"

"Yes! I need my fix. Can I steal Sara for a few days so I can remember what it's like to have a smaller child and talk myself out of it?"

I can't help but laugh at the way she says it, imagining the exaggerated pout on her face. "Steal her, huh? You really want to take her for a few days?" I tease, already knowing Taylor's answer.

"Yes! Besides, it'll give you a little break. You've been running yourself ragged lately, and you deserve some downtime."

I hesitate for a moment and feel a bit guilty for considering taking her up on this offer because Sara was just with Adam last weekend and I don't want to pawn my daughter off on other people.

"Listen, Callie. I'm the one asking you if I can take her so stop feeling some type of way about it and let me take care of my niece for a couple days," she says, as if she can see directly into my mind. "You were already going to have me watching her for the Halestorm concert since Mom and Wayne can't do it. What's a couple more days? I can even pick her up tonight. Before too long, you're not going to have time for yourself at all. Please let me do this."

"Okay," I finally say with a grin. "You can have her for a couple days. But if she gives you any trouble, don't hesitate to call me. When would you like to pick her up?"

We decide Taylor will meet me at Mom's tonight after my shift so we could all go out for ice cream. I'm looking forward to seeing Ava, and the girls are going to have a little movie night. They will probably stay up watching Sara's favorite *Strawberry Shortcake* movies while my niece and sister treat Sara like their real-life babydoll.

"Thank you for letting me take her for a couple days. Ava is going to be so excited. And you need to take some time for yourself. You deserve it."

Her words are sincere, and I feel so grateful to have her. "I appreciate you, Tay."

We say our goodbyes, and I hang up, feeling lighter than I have in days. Knowing that I get to spend tomorrow and Saturday with Owen sounds like exactly what I need.

forty-four
LOVE YOU MADLY - CAKE

OWEN - JULY 25, 2013

The day has been a restless blur, a mix of nervous energy and anticipation I can't shake. No matter how hard I try to focus at work, my mind keeps drifting back to Callie—her voice from this morning, soft and sleepy, still clings to me like a warm, comforting echo.

During my break, I stumble across a song I haven't heard in years: Love You Madly by Cake. The upbeat rhythm, the playful lyrics—it fits how I feel when I think of Callie. Without overthinking it, I send her the link. It's not a grand gesture, but it says what I can't put into words right now.

ME:
Made me think of you.

As my shift drags on, I find myself checking my phone more often than I'd like to admit, waiting for a reply that doesn't come. That nagging doubt creeps in—did I overstep? Maybe she didn't like the song, or worse, maybe I'm reading too much into this.

Just as my nerves are about to get the best of me, my phone buzzes with a message from her. It's like she could feel me spiraling, right when I needed her most. The timing is uncanny, as if she knew I couldn't stop thinking about her, even from miles away.

> CALLIE:
> Sorry, I've been swamped! I'll listen to it as soon as I get the chance. Can't wait to see you tomorrow!

I head home and settle onto the couch, trying to distract myself with some mindless TV. But the restlessness won't let up, so I shoot a text to the group chat, hoping the guys will pull me out of my head for a while.

> ME:
> We need to plan something soon.

> WILL:
> Down. Been too long.

> LUKE:
> As long as it doesn't involve Vince's terrible idea of karaoke night again, I'm in.

> VINCE:
> You say that like you didn't have a blast. My rendition of Livin' on a Prayer was fucking legendary.

I chuckle, shaking my head as I picture Vince, microphone in hand, belting out the lyrics with all the enthusiasm in the world and none of the talent. The memory makes me smile, the tension easing a bit.

> **ME:**
> Legendary? More like nightmare fuel.

WILL:
Still trying to scrub it from my brain, man.

> **ME:**
> The trauma is real.

I laugh out loud, the sound filling the quiet room. These guys always know how to lift my spirits, even when I don't realize I need it.

LUKE:
Speaking of things to forget, Heather wants to drag me to one of those paint-and-sip things this weekend. Wine, painting, and her friends–send help.

WILL:
Dude, it's not that bad. You get to drink, and the painting is just part of the background noise.

VINCE:
Plus, if it makes Heather happy, that's all that matters, right? I would much rather do something like that with Zoe than some of the other shit she insists on–specifically anything that will be a giant pain in the ass.

LUKE:
Yeah, yeah. I know. She's into it, so I'll suffer through it. But seriously, if you don't hear from me after Saturday, send a search party. Because I might go insane.

> **ME:**
> Are you honestly saying you're going to go insane surrounded by the number of women that are bound to be at that thing?

> VINCE:
> Ha! He's gotcha there, bro.
> LUKE:
> Point taken.

I grin, knowing Luke's just putting on a show. At this point, I'm pretty sure he'd do anything for Heather, even if it means pretending to enjoy an evening of wine and awkward painting. And it's in that moment, hearing Luke talk about his plans with Heather, that I realize I've been holding back with the guys.

> ME:
> I get it, man. I'd do the same for Callie if she asked me to. Honestly, I've been falling hard for her. Like, harder than I ever thought I would.
> VINCE:
> I'm looking forward to meeting her tomorrow.
> WILL:
> Wait... Have you told anyone in the family that you're dating a pregnant woman?
> LUKE:
> God, I would pay to be a fly on the wall at that little get-together. Wrong side of the family, though. 😬
> ME:
> Honestly, I hadn't thought about it. But at this point, I kind of can't wait to see the look on everyone's face. And I mean... It is a public place. If you guys want to go to Cedar Bluff tomorrow and meet my girlfriend, then I'm not stopping you.

In response, Vince sends a *Celebrate good times, come on!* GIF and I nearly howl with laughter.

WILL:

About time you found someone who makes you feel that way. Just don't screw it up by singing to her.

I laugh again, feeling a weight lift off my chest. Their jokes are exactly what I need, but their support means even more.

ME:

Yeah, she's amazing. I just don't want to mess this up.

VINCE:

Or, you know, don't. Seriously man, you got this.

As the conversation peters out, I set my phone down, trying to focus on the TV again. But nothing holds my interest. The anticipation of seeing Callie tomorrow is like a current running through me, impossible to ignore, and every time I close my eyes, I see her smile, hear the softness in her voice.

By the time the late afternoon sun starts casting long shadows across the room, my phone buzzes again. I glance down, half expecting more nonsense from the guys when I see Callie's name on the screen.

CALLIE:

Hey, handsome! I'm finally off work. What are you up to?

A slow grin spreads across my face, the kind that starts in my chest and works its way up, warming me from the inside out. I quickly type out a response, my fingers moving faster than my thoughts.

ME:

Not much, just hanging out. Why, what's up?

> **CALLIE:**
> Just curious. I can't wait to see you. I've been thinking about it all day.
>
> That was a great song, by the way. I had never heard it before.

> **ME:**
> I'm glad you liked it.

> **CALLIE:**
> Love it. 🩶

> **ME:**
> Oh yeah?

There's something about waiting for her reply that fills me with sweet, almost unbearable anticipation. The seconds tick by, each stretching out, making the silence between us feel tantalizing and torturous. I keep my phone in hand, the screen lighting up briefly before fading back into darkness, mirroring the way my thoughts flicker between excitement and uncertainty.

She doesn't reply right away, and I try to convince myself that it's because she's busy—probably picking up Sara from her mom's or maybe caught up in some last-minute task. Still, that little seed of doubt lingers, gnawing at the edges of my thoughts. I try to shake it off, reminding myself that she has a life too, and it doesn't revolve around our every text.

To distract myself, I decide to order a ham and pineapple pizza. I pull up the app, my fingers moving automatically through the motions of placing the order, but my mind is still on Callie. The thought of seeing her tomorrow both excites and unsettles me in a way I haven't felt in years.

The doorbell rings earlier than expected. I glance at my watch—definitely too fast for the pizza. Shrugging, I grab some cash and head to the door, my mind still half-occupied with thoughts of tomorrow and Callie. But as soon as I swing it open, the air catches in my lungs.

It's not the pizza guy.

forty-five

KISS ME - SIXPENCE NONE THE RICHER

CALLIE - JULY 25, 2013

As I approach Owen's apartment, a flutter of nervous excitement rushes through me, making my steps lighter. I've never done anything like this before. This feels like one of those grand gestures from the romantic comedies I used to love—spontaneous, maybe even a little reckless, but I couldn't wait until tomorrow to see him. I smooth down my dress, a simple black cotton one that clings in all the right places.

I knock lightly on the door, feeling my heart pound with anticipation. The door swings open, and Owen's expression—equal parts surprise and delight—makes my pulse quicken.

"Love it," I say softly, echoing my text from earlier, and step forward, wrapping my arms around him. The familiar scent of him, warm and comforting, envelopes me as I press my lips to his.

The kiss starts soft, but quickly deepens, full of the longing that's been building for days. His hands slide up my back, pulling me closer. I can feel his smile against my lips, a shared warmth that has my heart skipping a beat. Time seems to slow, the world outside fading away as we get lost in the moment.

When we finally pull apart, Owen's eyes meet mine with an intensity that sends a shiver down my spine. "Surprise," I whisper, feeling a little breathless.

His grin widens. "You have no idea." He leans in to steal another quick kiss. "What are you doing here?"

"I couldn't wait till tomorrow," I admit, my voice soft. "Taylor wanted a couple of days with Sara, so I thought I'd surprise you."

"I'm glad you did." His voice drops lower, like he's speaking some hidden truth, and the sound of it makes my heart race. "I've missed you, Kitty."

Before I can say anything, he captures my lips again, this time with a kiss that's deeper, more urgent. The heat between us builds quickly, hands exploring, hearts racing. I lose track of where we are, completely caught up in him.

"Ahem."

We jerk apart, breathless, as reality snaps back into focus. Standing just a few feet away is a kid in a red uniform, eyes glued to the pizza box in his hands like it's the only thing keeping him grounded. His face is beet red, clearly having caught us mid-makeout.

"Pizza's here," Owen says, chuckling as he straightens up, smoothing a hand over my hair.

"Perfect timing," I manage to say, cheeks burning with embarrassment.

"Clearly," the kid mutters under his breath, but Owen just laughs, letting the kid off the hook as he hands him some cash.

Once the door shuts behind him, Owen carries the pizza

box to the counter, flashing me a grin. "I'm starving," he says, popping open the lid with more excitement than necessary. The scent of melted cheese and—oh God—pineapple fills the air.

"Please tell me you didn't get pineapple," I groan, crossing my arms and eyeing the box.

He shrugs, grabbing a couple of plates. "I did, and you're going to try it."

I take the plate he offers, narrowing my eyes at the offending fruit on my pizza. "Your taste in pizza is making me question your judgement."

Owen laughs, biting into his slice like it's gourmet. "I don't know. I think my judgement is pretty solid. I mean, I picked you, didn't I?"

I roll my eyes but can't help the smile that tugs at my lips. "Fair point. But if this sucks, we're going to have to reevaluate everything."

Owen steps closer, his voice dropping to a low murmur. "Nah, you're like pineapple—sweet, a little tangy, and addictive. The kind of thing I could devour forever."

I laugh, pushing him playfully. "Okay, smooth talker. But if this pizza is gross, I'm blaming you."

He grins, watching me expectantly as I take a tentative bite. To my surprise, it's... not terrible. I narrow my eyes at him, trying to hide my amusement. "Okay, fine. It's not bad, but I'm blaming weird pregnancy hormones."

"See? Told you I had good taste." He winks, taking another bite, and I can't help but feel completely at home with him.

After eating half my weight in pineapple pizza, Owen sits beside me, his arm draped across the back of the couch, his fingers occasionally brushing against my shoulder. Each touch sends a little spark through me, a reminder of the connection we share. I lean into him, letting my head rest against his chest, listening to the steady rhythm of his heartbeat. It's a sound that grounds me, that makes everything else seem distant and unimportant.

"This feels nice," I murmur, my voice barely above a whisper. "Being here with you like this."

He tightens his arm around me, pulling me a little closer. "Yeah, it does," he replies softly, his breath warm against my hair. "I could get used to this."

I smile, closing my eyes as I soak in the warmth of his embrace. There's something about being here with him, in this quiet, peaceful moment, that feels so right. It's like all the worries and uncertainties of the day have melted away, leaving just the two of us, wrapped up in each other.

We stay like that for a while, just enjoying the simple pleasure of being close. But eventually, Owen shifts slightly, his hand coming up to gently tilt my chin so that I'm looking into his eyes. There's something in his gaze, something tender and affectionate that makes my heart skip a beat.

"Callie," he begins, his voice low and sincere, "I'm really glad you came over tonight. I know it was a spur-of-the-moment thing, but... it means a lot to me."

I can see the emotion in his eyes, the way he's searching for the right words to express what he's feeling. I reach up, my fingers lightly tracing the line of his jaw beneath his beard, and give him a reassuring smile.

"I'm glad I came too," I say, my voice soft but steady. "I needed to see you. I... I couldn't stop thinking about you all day. And now that I'm here, I just... I feel like this is where I'm supposed to be."

His expression softens, a gentle smile tugging at the corners of his mouth. "I feel the same way," he admits, his voice barely above a whisper. "It's like everything just falls into place when I'm with you."

I lean in, pressing a soft kiss to his lips, a silent affirmation of everything we've just said. The kiss, gentle at first, quickly deepens as the unspoken emotions between us surge to the surface. I can feel the intensity of his feelings in the way his lips move against mine, in the way his hands slide up to cradle my face, his thumbs brushing lightly against my cheeks.

A soft sigh escapes me as I melt into the kiss, letting myself get lost in the sensation of being so close to him. His touch is both tender and possessive, like he's trying to memorize the feel of me in his arms. The warmth of his body seeps into mine, and I can feel my pulse quicken, the heat between us building with each passing second.

He pulls back just enough to look into my eyes, his gaze burning with intensity. There's a raw vulnerability there, something that makes my heart clench even as my body hums with need.

"I don't want to let you go," he murmurs, his voice rough and filled with emotion.

"Then don't," I reply, my fingers threading through his hair, pulling him back to me.

Our lips crash together again, the kiss even more heated than before. His hands are everywhere, exploring, caressing, claiming, and I can feel my control slipping, the desire overwhelming me. I let myself get lost in him, in the way he feels, the way he tastes, the way he makes everything else fade into the background.

The kiss intensifies, our breaths and tongues mingling in a

frenzy, the world around us fading away until it's just the two of us, lost in the heat of the moment. It's like everything we've been holding back, all the unsaid words, are pouring into this embrace, and I can't get enough.

When we finally pull back, our breaths are mingling in the small space between us, our foreheads resting against each other. His eyes are dark with emotion, and I can see the vulnerability there, the raw intensity of his feelings laid bare.

"I've missed you," he whispers, his hands coming up to cradle my face, his thumbs brushing lightly against my cheeks. "More than I realized."

"I've missed you too," I reply, my voice catching slightly with the weight of the emotions swirling inside me.

For a moment, we just sit there, lost in each other's gaze, the rest of the world fading away. It's one of those rare moments where everything feels perfect, where nothing else matters but the two of us and the connection we share.

Then, as if he can't help himself, Owen pulls me back in for another kiss. This one is slow and lingering, filled with all the emotions we haven't put into words. His hands slide down my back, pulling me closer until there's no space left between us. I can feel his adoration, his affection, in every touch, and it makes my heart swell with a warmth that I've never felt before.

I can't help but respond, my own hands roaming over his chest, feeling the solid warmth of him beneath my fingertips. The kiss deepens, becomes more urgent, as the need to be closer to him overwhelms me. His hands slide up to tangle in my hair, and I can feel the desperation in the way he holds me, like he's afraid to let go.

When we finally pull back, we're both breathing heavily, our hearts racing in tandem. He presses a soft kiss to the top of my head, his lips lingering there for a moment as if to reassure himself that I'm really here.

"I could stay like this forever," I whisper, my eyes drifting closed as the exhaustion of the day finally starts to catch up with me.

"So could I," he murmurs, his voice soft and filled with affection. "But we've got all the time in the world."

His words wrap around me like a promise, and as I snuggle back into his embrace, I feel a sense of peace settle over me. And I've never been more certain this is where I belong.

forty-six
SUFFOCATE - J. HOLIDAY

OWEN - JULY 26, 2013

The warmth of her body pressed against mine last night was a comfort I didn't know I was missing until it was there. Lying here, wrapped in each other felt like the world had narrowed down to just the two of us, a safe haven where nothing else mattered. I hadn't realized how deeply I craved that connection until it happened—the soft sound of our breathing fell into sync, filling the silence between us. It was more than just physical closeness—it was a deep, unspoken understanding, a wordless promise that we were exactly where we were meant to be.

Despite the temptation, I resisted burying myself in her last night. The way she looked at me, her eyes full of lust and longing, was almost too much. I could feel the heat between us, the way her body responded to mine, and it took all of my self-control to prevent things from going any further. However, knowing how much she desires me—seeing the arousal mirrored in her green eyes—only intensifies the heat. I have never experienced such a powerful connection with a woman as I do with Callie.

Curled up with her this morning, I remind myself why I set this ridiculous three-date rule in the first place—because I'm looking for something real. But I already know the connection with Callie is real, and the temptation to break my own rule is at an all-time high. I know to some, three dates might not seem like that long to wait, but when I am with Callie, something almost primal stirs in me, and I am not sure how much longer I can hold back.

Callie is still asleep when she rolls over to face me, and I adjust myself quickly, praying I don't wake her up before wrapping my arms around her and pulling her close. I lay like that with her for a bit, taking in her beauty and wishing we could stay like this forever. She is absolutely breathtaking. I can't help it when a small chuckle escapes after I feel a small kick from her belly hit my stomach. I felt the baby kick for the first time last night when my arm was wrapped around her as she slept. I won't bring it up because I don't want her to feel self-conscious. For now, this is just a moment for me and the baby, whose life I can only hope to be a part of.

It's insane, really. We've only just started dating but I cannot help thinking about my future with her and what having a family with her would be like.

Callie wakes a short time later and tells me that she's going to give her mom a call to let her know she will be staying with me, cracking a joke about possibly sending her mom a picture of my driver's license "just in case." When she tells me not to panic if I overhear her calling me her boyfriend, I can't help but smile. We haven't put a label on things yet, but I think it's safe to say after everything that's happened recently, I am hers, and I certainly hope she is mine.

I can tell she is nervous about how I'd react to her labeling me as her boyfriend—like she expects me to bolt. But the truth is, I'd be fine with her calling me just about anything at this point. Hell, she could call me "Daddy," and I probably wouldn't bat an eye.

Now there's a thought...

And with that, I think now might be a good time to take a cold shower and give her some privacy so she can talk to her mother.

Callie and I head to a small cafe for lunch, and her silence makes me a bit nervous. I wonder if I did something that could have upset her or if something happened when she was on the phone with her mother earlier. She is picking at her Caesar salad, barely touching the grilled chicken on top. She's never been distant like this with me. I reach over, touching her hand to get her attention. "Hey, what's on your mind?"

She looks up at me with a faint smile. "Just a little anxious about tonight."

I let out a sigh of relief, selfishly grateful that she isn't upset over something that I did or said. "Meeting my family?" I guess. She nods, and I give her hand a reassuring squeeze. "They're going to love you."

"What if they don't?" she says, a nervous laugh escaping her as she jabs at a crouton with her fork. "I mean, meeting them for the first time while I'm six months pregnant? It's a lot. What if they think—"

"First of all, it doesn't matter what they think. Second, you are beautiful and smart and snarky and perfect."

"Far from it," she mumbles, her voice soft. She's avoiding my eyes and looking down at her plate.

"Perfect for me," I say softly, reaching out to tip her chin up to meet my eyes. "And yes, you happen to be pregnant. But that's just part of your story, not the whole of who you are. They will see that you're so much more than that—how funny you are, how strong," I pause, wanting her to see the truth in my words. "If it would make you more comfortable, I can call my cousin Vince and ask him to let everyone know ahead of time. Just say the word."

She shakes her head quickly. "No, don't do that. I still think seeing their reactions and trying to figure everything out will be funny. You know me: ChaosCallie and all that. I'm just still worried about what they will think."

I want to do whatever I can to make this easier for her, but I also want to respect her choice. I lean over the table to kiss her forehead to remind her I'm here for her—no matter what.

As we step into the pub, I can feel the tension in my shoulders melt away. This place feels like a portal to another time, with its rich, dark wood paneling that seems to deepen the warmth of the space, and the ornate tin ceiling tiles that gleam softly above us. The centerpiece of it all is the back bar—a towering, intricately carved masterpiece that commands attention the moment you walk in. Originally crafted in Belgium and brought over a century ago, the bar has a history as rich as its design.

The low light makes the bottles on the glass shelves shimmer like precious gems, casting a warm amber hue. The ambiance here is both high-end and inviting, exuding sophistication without being pretentious. It's a place where you can relax in a luxurious leather seat, enjoy a perfectly made cocktail, and feel you're treating yourself with no pretense. The atmosphere embraces you like a comforting, intimate gesture, urging you to unwind and relish the moment. For those seeking a more formal setting, there's a room tucked away from the ornate bar area, where elegant seating and a quieter, more refined atmosphere invite deeper conversation and a touch of privacy.

Callie walks beside me, her hand resting in mine, and I can't help but notice how well she fits with me. She moves with a quiet confidence that I find incredibly attractive. Her dark brown hair cascades in loose curls pulled over her left shoulder, and she's wearing a black-and-white striped maxi dress that shows off her ample chest in the best possible way. It hugs her curves in all the right places, making her look even more effortlessly beautiful. I feel a surge of pride just having her on my arm, and the realization hits me:

She's mine now.

As we make our way through the crowd, I spot Vince near the end of the bar. He's leaning against the counter with a beer in hand, talking to his brother Malcolm and Malcolm's wife, Valerie. Zoe's there too, perched on a barstool. I wasn't sure she'd be here tonight considering the attitude she typically gives Vince about these things, but it looks like she might be in a good mood tonight. When Vince catches sight of us, his face lights up.

"There they are!" he calls out, raising his glass in greeting.

We head over, and the introductions start. I can feel the curious eyes on us–more specifically, on Callie. Vince pinches his lips together, trying to bite back a smile. Looks like he didn't even tell Zoe. This is almost too much fun. Callie seems to be getting a kick out of it, too.

A bit further down, more of my cousins huddle together, including Vicki and her brother Joel, along with his wife Julia.

My cousin Bruce sits alone at a video gambling machine, oblivious to anything happening around him. Pretty sure he only showed up because he's hoping someone will cover his bar tab.

Aside from Bruce, it's apparent that everyone is trying to figure out what's going on without coming right out and asking. For now, everyone's being polite, holding back their questions, but I can sense the anticipation building. I can't help but relish in the chaos. I know it's only a matter of time before someone brings up the obvious. Especially since they are all drinking already.

Vince gives Callie a warm handshake, Zoe pulls her into a quick, awkward hug, and Malcolm offers a nod of approval. Valerie is sweet, complimenting Callie's dress, and I can see Callie relax a little more with each interaction. It's going well. Better than I expected, honestly.

The evening unfolds with the usual banter and catching up. The place fills with the sound of laughter and clinking glasses, and Callie seems to blend right in. She's talking with Valerie and even Zoe like they're old friends, and I catch Malcolm giving me a subtle thumbs-up when she's not looking. It's all going great, but I can still feel the uncertainty from the surrounding people continuing to dance around the question.

Will and Luke arrive later, with Heather in tow, and the dynamic within the group shifts instantly. Luke's presence is like a spark, igniting the atmosphere with his infectious energy. Within seconds, he's cracking jokes, his voice carrying a playful edge that draws everyone in. Heather, bless her, does her best to keep up with Luke's rapid-fire humor. She laughs along, her smile genuine, even when it's clear she's not entirely sure she gets the joke. It's clear she wants to belong, and in her own way, she's already becoming a part of our little circle, her presence softening the edges of Luke's wild humor.

Just as I think we might make it through the night without anyone asking, Vicki orders a shot of tequila, downs it with a quick gulp, and turns back to face Callie and me. She's a spitfire–petite, with white-blonde curls that barely brush her shoulders, and a personality that's about ten times her size. I'm honestly shocked she hasn't already inquired about the baby, considering her lack of subtlety. But I know we're in for it now because Vicki and tequila are a hell of a combination.

"So," she says, her voice cutting through the noise like a knife through butter. "Are we going to ignore the baby in the bar, or are you going to fill us in?"

And there it is.

Callie freezes, her eyes wide with surprise and amusement, before we both erupt into uncontrollable laughter. It's the kind of laughter that doubles you over, making it hard to catch your breath. Vince, Will, and Luke join in as if on cue, their laughter filling the room and bouncing off the walls. The sound of a sharp *thwap* cuts through the chaos as the back of Zoe's hand smacks against Vince's chest, followed by a whispered but clearly exasperated, "You knew about this?!" Her incredulous tone only fuels the hilarity, and we all dissolve into another round of laughter, my sides aching as tears fill my eyes.

The tension from earlier vanishes, replaced by a shared moment of pure, unfiltered joy that draws us all closer together. I slide my arm around Callie and pull her close, a reassuring gesture to ease her tension. She leans into me, and I press a soft kiss to her temple, letting my lips linger there for a moment as I start to rub soothing circles on her lower back.

"We met when she was already pregnant," I say with an easy smile, trying to keep things simple. But there's a part of me that wants to say more, to tell Vicki that Callie's piece-of-shit ex cheated on her when she was still early in her pregnancy, leaving her to navigate everything on her own. The thought burns me up inside, but I remind myself that it's not my story to tell, not here, not now. Instead, I add a playful twist, trying to steer the conversation toward lighter ground. "But I'm taking full credit for all the dad jokes in this kid's future." The playful remark earns a few chuckles, and I can feel Callie relax a little more against me, the tension slowly melting away as the moment passes.

For a split second, everyone just stares. Well, everyone except the guys who still can't stop snickering. Then Joel, who's been quiet all night, starts to laugh. It's a big, booming laugh that seems to break the tension like a dam bursting. "Well, that clears things up!" he says, lifting his beer in a toast. The rest of the group follows suit, laughter erupting around us, and just like that, the awkward moment is gone.

"Leave it to you, Owen, to keep us all guessing," Malcolm says with a grin, shaking his head in mock exasperation. "You've always been the prankster of the family, but I gotta say, this one takes the cake."

I can't help but chuckle, especially with the sound of Callie's laughter bubbling up beside me. She's trying to stifle her giggles, but it's a losing battle, and the way her eyes light up with amusement makes my heart do a little flip. "Hey, someone's gotta keep things interesting," I reply with a playful wink, tightening my arm around her and giving her upper ribs a gentle squeeze. "Besides, what's life without a little suspense?"

Malcolm shakes his head, still grinning. "Suspense? More like you just like watching us all scramble to keep up with whatever twist you're throwing our way."

I laugh, leaning in closer to Callie, who's practically doubled over at this point. "What can I say? I like to keep you guys on your toes. Gotta make sure the family gatherings are never boring, right?"

Callie's pregnancy quickly becomes just another topic of conversation, woven seamlessly into the night's banter. It's amazing how quickly my family has shifted gears, treating Callie like she's been a part of the group forever. I watch her as she chats with Valerie, Zoe, and Vicki, her hand occasionally drifting to rest on her belly by instinct every time she talks about the baby. It's a small gesture, but one that makes me feel a surge of protectiveness and pride.

At one point, Luke starts in on a completely ridiculous debate about who is going to teach the baby how to fish.

I can't help but laugh. "Luke, the last time we went fishing at Darling, you damn near threw your pole into the lake."

"That was an off day," he insists, waving me off.

Heather, who's been giggling beside him, finally speaks up. "The only thing you caught that day was a cold."

Luke groans, but the rest of us are falling over ourselves with laughter. "Fine, fine," he concedes, throwing his hands up in mock surrender. "I'll let Owen handle the fishing lessons. But I still get to be the cool uncle."

I can't help but wonder if all this is making Callie feel like things are moving too fast, but she doesn't miss a beat. "The very coolest," she promises.

I realize that hearing Luke welcome Callie into the family is promising. I'm hoping that he will put in a good word for us with Beverly and Dad when I eventually introduce Callie to them as well.

The night continues with more of the same–laughter, teasing, and stories being passed around like we're all old friends. And as I watch Callie laugh and joke with my family, I can't shake the feeling that she's always belonged here.

As we step into my apartment, the air seems to shift, like the space itself has been waiting for us. Callie pauses just inside, her hand lingering on the wall as she takes in the room, removing her shoes after the long day we've had together. There's a softness in her green eyes, a quietness that matches the gentle lighting.

"Your place feels...different tonight," she says after a moment, her voice low and thoughtful, almost as if she's speaking to herself.

I watch her as she moves deeper into the room, her fingers brushing lightly over the back of the couch, trailing along the edge of the kitchen counter. She stops and turns to look at me, and there's something different in her expression—something tender, almost reverent.

"How so?" I ask, curious about what she's thinking, my gaze never leaving her.

She turns to me, a gentle smile touching her lips. "I'm not sure what it is exactly. But being with you just feels like home," she says simply. There's a depth to her words that tugs at something inside me. Callie walks back toward me, her bare feet padding softly across the floor, and reaches out to touch my arm, her fingers light but reassuring.

That one simple touch sends warmth through me, and I can't help but smile back at her. I feel a sense of peace settle over me that I didn't know I needed.

I walk over to my computer and turn the music on. I reach out, taking her hand in mine, and without a word, we sway to the music, her head resting on my chest.

The first notes of "Suffocate" by J. Holiday fill the room, the sultry, slow rhythm wrapping around us like a warm embrace. Callie's eyes light up, and she steps closer, her hands finding their way to my shoulders.

"You know," she says with a teasing smile, "my great-grandmother always used to say, 'Life's too short to dance with ugly men.'"

I chuckle, resting my hands on her hips and pulling her closer. "Good thing you don't have to worry about that tonight," I tease, leaning in just enough that our noses brush.

She laughs, the sound low and soft, sending a shiver down my spine. "No, I don't," she agrees, her voice dropping to a whisper.

"Dance with me?" I ask as her hand brushes across the back of my head just above my neck, my recently buzzed hair tickling her fingertips. She smiles, pulling me closer to her until the only space between us is the area just above her belly.

As we dance to the rhythm, her head lies against my chest, her breath warming my neck, her soft body gently pressing against mine. Every touch, every small movement feels like a promise, an unspoken declaration of everything we've been feeling but haven't yet put into words. It's a simple thing, dancing like this, but it's filled with a depth that makes my heart ache in the best possible way.

The music swells around us, the lyrics and melody creating a cocoon that makes the world outside disappear. I close my eyes, letting myself get lost in the moment, in the feel of her in my arms, in the way our bodies move together. It's like everything else fades away, leaving just us here, in this perfect, shared space.

As I hold her close, her heartbeat steady against my chest, a realization settles deep within me, like a truth that's been waiting to be acknowledged. The thought comes so naturally, so effortlessly, that I wonder if it's been there all along, just waiting for me to notice.

There is no doubt in my mind.

I am madly in love with this woman.

As if she can sense my thoughts, she pulls me down for a kiss. I hold her a little tighter, my heart torn between wanting to tell her and wanting to protect this perfect moment we're sharing. I don't know when or how I'll say it, but one thing is certain: Tonight, I'm going to show her exactly how much she means to me.

We continue to dance, the tension between us simmering just beneath the surface, building with every step, every brush of our bodies. There's a heat between us, a connection that feels almost tangible, and I know we're both feeling it—the pull, the need that's been growing stronger all night.

The song ends, fading into the background, but we don't stop moving. I pull back just enough to look into her eyes, and the intensity there nearly takes my breath away. There's desire in her gaze, yes, but also something deeper, something that makes my heart pound in my chest.

"I need you, Callie," I say, my voice rough with the weight of everything I'm feeling.

Her eyes soften, and she reaches up to cup my face in her hands, her touch gentle but sure. "Then take me, Owen," she whispers, her voice steady despite the tremble in her hands. "I want this, I want you. So fucking bad."

I wrap my arms around her waist, capturing her lips in a slow but intense kiss, pouring all the emotions into that one connection.

Electric. Addictive. Consuming.

Without breaking our kiss, I slide my hands down lower, wrapping them behind her thighs and picking her up quickly before she has the opportunity to object. As I settle my hands on her ass while she holds onto me a bit tighter, I can sense the hesitancy in her grasp. I pull back from our kiss with a silent check-in, trying to determine the cause of her hesitation.

Is she self conscious or is she having second thoughts? Her grip tightens around the back of my neck and I can see now that she's scared I'm going to drop her. "Don't worry, Kitty. I've got you."

With Callie secure in my arms, our lips find each other again, the kiss deepening with every step I take toward my bedroom. The room around us fades into a blur, the only thing that matters is the feeling of her mouth on mine, the way our bodies press together. The gentle sway of our movements only heightens the intensity between us, each kiss a promise, each touch a reassurance.

When we reach the bed, I lay her down gently, and for a moment, I just look at her. The way her hair fans out across the pillow, the way her chest rises and falls with each breath, the way she looks up at me with those eyes that seem to see right through to my soul—it's almost too much. But I don't look away. I can't. She's mesmerizing, and I want to memorize every inch of her, every curve, every detail.

I help her slip out of her dress, revealing the white thong and–FUCK–no bra.

This. Fucking. Girl.

"You just had to go and make the temptation that much harder to resist, huh?" I tease. She smiles and nods slowly as I lower myself onto the bed beside her, my dick pulses with desire.

Callie's eyes lock on mine, filled with a trust and longing that makes my pulse race. Every part of me yearns to touch her, to show her how much she means to me. I'm acutely aware of the need to be gentle and careful of the life growing within her.

In this moment, she is the embodiment of a goddess, a vision of strength and beauty that has me in awe.

"What can I say?" she taunts. "I'm in the mood for some of that cinnamon you've been hiding from me."

I let my hands roam over her, mapping out every curve, feeling the warmth of her skin under my fingertips. But I'm mindful, cautious, as I move closer. My touch lingers just above her belly, my palm brushing lightly against the curve, and I pause meeting her gaze and making sure that me touching her belly in such an intimate way isn't too much for her. The last thing that I want to do right now is make her uncomfortable.

"You are so stunning, Callie."

She lets out a soft hum as I trail kisses down her stomach and run my hand up her leg from her knee to the apex of her thigh. I want to show her with every moment just how much I want this–want her. Need her. Love her.

Even though it feels like this is all happening really fast, I don't care. At this moment, I know what I want. And it's her. It will always be her.

"I cannot believe you're finally mine," I say as I reach my hand to cup her face and place a soft kiss on her lips. She doesn't say anything for a long moment but she doesn't have to. Her sharp intake of breath tells me that she feels the connection too. She must know this is something far beyond anything either of us has ever felt before.

I don't rush. Each touch lingers, her body responding to me in ways that nearly undo my control. A soft gasp escapes her lips as I tease her, bringing her to the brink, where even I am struggling to maintain control. I slip her thong to the side and glide my fingers over her clit, eliciting a soft moan from her as I prop myself up just enough to turn her toward me. The moment our eyes meet, I lower my mouth to her breast, pulling her nipple between my lips, savoring the way she arches into me.

Every moment feels like a careful dance between caution and desire, an exquisite tension building between us. My cock throbs against her leg, the ache nearly unbearable, but I focus on her, on the way her hands clutch my shoulders, her nails digging in slightly as I quicken the rhythm of my hand. I slip two fingers inside her, feeling her warmth envelop me, and it takes everything in me not to lose myself completely.

I pause for a brief moment, just to breathe her in. The scent of her skin, the intoxicating fragrance of her arousal—it pulls something primal and raw from deep within me, something that demands to be unleashed.

I crave her.

She is perfection.

And so fucking mine.

forty-seven
DOIN' IT - LL COOL J

CALLIE - JULY 26, 2013

It doesn't take long before the first orgasm courses through my body as Owen makes me cry out in pleasure, making me want him even more. I know I've been more pushy than I should have about the boundaries he set but the way he toys with me, the way he worships my body... I think even the most innocent of women would be wanting for more of him.

I want to make him feel good in the same way he does for me. I want him to need me the way I need him. I want him to make love to me while also taking everything my body can give him.

I kiss him passionately, proving how much I've been yearning for this moment with him. Before my nerves take over and I begin to worry about my weight or how my body looks, I boldly urge him to lay on his back as I straddle him. Our kiss is passionate and leisurely.

Owen lifts his upper body slightly, pulling his shirt off

over his head in one swift movement before laying back down on the bed. As he looks up at me, my mostly naked body on full display to him, the words "fucking Goddess" escape his lips. I bend down to kiss his neck, the salty taste of his skin sparking more desire from me. As I trail my lips further down his skin, I put my hands on his belt, starting to pull to undo it before glancing up into his eyes, awaiting permission.

He gives me a single nod and I finish undoing his belt and begin unzipping his jeans, desperate to get his cock free. I need to taste him. Need to feel him everywhere. Thankfully, he doesn't stop me as I pull his jeans down, finally exposing his hard length. I'm immediately made aware that this man is well above average in every possible way. And God help me, it's going to hurt in the best fucking way imaginable.

The tip is already wet with pre-cum and I am immediately overtaken by the urge to flatten my tongue and lick it off the head of his perfect dick. So, that's exactly what I do.

A throaty growl comes from his lips and drives me to continue. I take him into my mouth slowly, determined to tease him just as he has done to me. As I open my mouth wider to take in more of him, I can feel my panties getting more and more wet, the urge to touch myself while I suck his cock taking over. When I fit his full length into my mouth, I reward myself by slipping my right hand into my panties, using two fingers to make small circles over my clit.

"Fuck yes," he says, his voice fueled with pure lust. "I would love to watch you fuck yourself, Kitty. Will you do that for me? Will you show me?"

I nod in agreement while I continue to suck his length, growing more eager with every bob of my head.

"Good girl," he says. And his praise makes me completely feral. I wrap my free hand around his dick and move it in rhythm with my mouth, my movements drawing out more and more moans from him.

He reaches down, sliding his hand along the side of my neck before his fingers weave into the hair on the back of my head. And God damn, if it isn't the hottest fucking thing I've ever felt in my life. His grip tightens on the roots of my hair as he slowly thrusts himself into my mouth.

I continue rubbing my clit as he demands I go faster. I remove my hand from his shaft and suck with more vigor just as a second orgasm makes its way to the surface. "That's it. Come for me, Kitty. Give me all of it. You look so beautiful when you fall apart for me."

With his cock still deep in my throat, my body begins to tremble, and I feel a warm wave wash over me, a somewhat unfamiliar rush deep within my core. As if he can sense that I'm holding back due to the unfamiliar sensation, he tightens his grip on my hair and I peer up at him, locking my eyes to his as I continue working over my clit. "I said, give me all of it, Kitty. I'm not going to tell you again."

And that's all it takes. Those demanding words are my complete undoing, and the floodgates open as hot liquid pours from me, dripping down my hand while I use his cock to massage the back of my throat.

I've never been so fucking turned on in my life and I haven't even fucked him yet.

Praying that he doesn't stop me, I remove my now soaked panties and toss them aside before climbing back up his body to straddle him. But I don't try to slide him inside me. Instead, with his cock laying flat on his stomach, I slide it between my slit and begin grinding on him, making sure I don't go at an angle where he might slip inside me.

He must enjoy the sensation as much as I do because he grabs ahold of my hips, his tight grip sure to leave fingertip-size bruises on me. The tighter he squeezes, the more I feel myself growing wet as the head of his cock teases my clit every time I slide up and down. I can tell by the "FUCKKKK" that escapes his lips that this is becoming almost unbearable for him.

Good.

He's made me wait for it. Now, it's his turn to wait. I use him in the best possible way, determined to make him beg to slip inside of me. Reaching my hand between us, I start stroking his length against my clit. This seems to drive him more mad and it only drives me on further. Lining him up with my entrance, I look at him, awaiting the permission I so desperately crave.

He nods slowly as the words, "Please, Kitty," leave his lips. I decide to toy with him a bit more before giving him what we both want. As I continue to tease him, his fingers to dig into my hips and a growl escapes his lips.

"I only ask nicely once," he tells me and a slow smirk plays on my lips.

"Is that so?" I ask, slowly allowing the tip of his thick cock to enter me.

"Mhmm," he purrs.

I pause for a moment, my eyes locking with his. "Are you sure you're ready for this?" I realize it's a little late to ask now, but I would also stop in a heartbeat if he asked me to—a sad heartbeat, but a heartbeat nonetheless.

"Ye–," he starts to answer but the first letter was all I needed to hear before I dropped myself down on him fully, taking in all of him as all the breath in my body leaves my lungs. He emits a low chuckle when he realizes I must have underestimated his size. That little move of mine backfired on me, considering I am the one who is left breathless.

"God, you are so fucking perfect, Callie," he whispers, his

voice rough, reverent, like he's memorizing this moment. His hands press into my hips, grounding me as I lose myself in the rhythm we've found together. The depth of his voice, the sincerity in his words—they wrap around me, soothing and igniting in equal measure, as if he's not just here with me, but utterly and completely mine.

Placing my hands on his chest to hold myself steady, I begin raising and lowering myself on him, my pace quickening as he seems to only be able to utter the word "fuck" every time I take him in again. With his hands still tight on my hips, he thrusts his hips upward as he pulls me down, making my full chest bounce more than it already was.

Before I know it, I've given up every ounce of control I thought I had. He takes me over and over, making me come completely undone. The noises that leave us both are primal. Guttural. Needy. I cannot get enough of this man.

Just as I feel my orgasm about to unravel me, he slows his movements and moves his right hand from my hip, and places his thumb on my clit. My whole body tenses, and the same warm rush from before washes over me, this time even more intense than when he watched me earlier.

"Good girl," he praises again as he continues to work his thumb over my clit, causing another wave to surge through my entire body.

This man just gave me back-to-back orgasms in a matter of seconds. I am so done for. I am officially convinced it could never get better than this.

In this moment, I am dying to admit to him how much he means to me. But I don't want to scare him away. Instead, I let the edges of my restraint soften just enough to allow a piece of my full truth to slip through.

"God, it feels so good to be yours," I whisper, praying that he understands the true meaning behind my words.

Owen's eyes darken, his focus on me unwavering. His hand slides up my side, slow and deliberate. It feels like a promise as much as it feels like he's claiming me too. He pulls me closer, his breath warm against my cheek, and the low timbre of his voice vibrates through me.

"Good," he says, the possessive tone filled with a depth that makes me weak. "Because you are all mine."

With that, he flips me quickly onto my back and lifts my legs in the air, holding them together at the ankles. He slides back inside me, gradually increasing the pace at which he fucks me as if to make sure that he's not going to break me. He sets both of my ankles on his right shoulder, and I'm convinced that if it weren't for my belly, he'd fold me in half and twist me like a fucking pretzel.

God, if this is what sex with him feels like when we have to be careful, I can only imagine what it must be like when he's not worried about hurting me.

I can feel the muscles in his body tighten, and he grips my ankles as hard as he'd been holding my hips earlier. And for the fourth time since we entered this room together, my body is completely overtaken with an orgasm that feels so good I never want it to end. As I come apart in his grasp, he quickens his pace, and I can feel his release fill me. We come together for what feels like an eternity. Our connection completely solidified now that he's marked me from the inside out.

I am addicted–a fiend for him already.

The way he worships my body is a drug that I never want to lose. I belong to him now.

Mind. Body. Soul.

forty-eight
GOLD DIGGER - KANYE WEST

OWEN - JULY 27, 2013

I've been up for hours, trying to keep busy, trying to distract myself from the thoughts that have been circling in my mind since Callie left for Hawkridge this morning. Last night was perfect and I feel a bit lost without her now.

I grab a coffee and lean against the kitchen counter, staring out the window at the faint blush of dawn. My thoughts are tangled, caught between the anticipation of tonight and the lingering shadows of yesterday. It's strange how quickly I've gotten used to having her around. I never thought I'd be the kind of guy who gets used to someone's presence so fast, but there it is.

With time to kill before I need to head out, I decide to get some cleaning done. It's more about keeping my hands busy than anything else—anything to keep my mind from spiraling. As I scrub the counter, I let my thoughts drift to Callie. The way her laugh fills the room, the way her eyes light up when she talks about the things she loves, the way she fits so perfectly into the space beside me, like she's always belonged there.

I think about how far we've come in such a short time. From that first conversation to where we are now, it feels like we've crossed a thousand miles together. But it's not just the distance we've covered—it's the way she's changed me, the way she's made me want more than I ever thought I deserved.

But then, as I'm wiping down the sink, my phone buzzes on the counter. I glance at it, expecting some mundane notification, but the name that flashes on the screen stops me cold.

Karissa.

I hesitate, my hand hovering over the phone, before I swipe the screen open. The image that greets me is an ultrasound, the grainy black-and-white picture unmistakable. But something's off. The details—the name, the date, everything that should be there—are blurred out, deliberately covered. A chill runs down my spine as I stare at the screen, my mind racing through all the possibilities. There's no way this baby is mine. We didn't even have sex.

This woman is fucking crazy. Level Expert.

I set the phone down, trying to push the image out of my mind. I'm not going to let her get to me, not today. I've got too much to look forward to, too much riding on tonight. I'm not going to let her mess that up.

But before I can push the thought away, the phone buzzes again. Another message. This time, it's a text.

> KARISSA:
> You think you're slick, don't you? I know about your little girlfriend. Saw the picture. You got her pregnant too, didn't you?

My heart skips a beat, and I feel a cold knot form in my stomach. What the hell is she talking about? I pick up the phone again, and as I reread the message, realization starts to dawn. She must have seen that photo—the one from last night when I was with my cousins. Vicki took a beautiful black-and-white shot of Callie, and while her belly isn't completely visible, anyone looking closely could probably guess.

But how did Karissa even see that? And why the hell is she trying to stir up trouble now?

The unease lingers, gnawing at the edges of my thoughts, refusing to be ignored. I try to focus on the cleaning again, but my hands are shaking, my mind spinning with a thousand what-ifs. After thirty minutes of trying to distract myself, my phone buzzes again. Another message.

This time, it's not from Karissa. It's from Josh, her friend—the one I went fishing with. The one who was there that night on the camping trip with us.

> JOSH:
> You're a piece of shit, Owen. You know that? A garbage human for not taking responsibility. You think you can just walk away? Pretend it never happened? Grow the fuck up.

The words hit me like a punch to the gut, but anger quickly follows, hot and sharp. I shouldn't be surprised. Karissa's always been good at playing the victim, at twisting the truth to make herself look like the innocent one. But this? This is a new low, even for her.

I don't hesitate before firing back a response, my fingers flying across the screen.

> ME:
> Josh, you were there that night. You know damn well what happened. Karissa was trashed, and nothing happened between us. Nothing. The only way I'd be a trash human is if I had actually slept with her when she was too drunk to give consent. But I didn't. So don't let her drag you into her bullshit.

I hit send, my heart pounding in my chest. I'm not proud of the way my hands are shaking, of the way my mind is racing with all the worst-case scenarios. But I know I'm right. I know what happened that night—or rather, what didn't happen. And I'm not going to let Karissa rewrite history just to fit her twisted narrative.

The phone stays silent after that, and I'm left standing in the middle of my kitchen, my thoughts a tangled mess of anger, frustration, and a creeping sense of dread. I rake a hand over my short, buzzed hair, trying to steady myself, trying to remember that I've got bigger things to focus on.

Callie. The concert. Tonight.

I've been looking forward to this, to the chance to just be with her, to lose ourselves in the music and forget about everything else, if only for a few hours. Especially after last night. And I'm not going to let Karissa or anyone else take that away from me.

But even as I try to push it out of my mind, the weight of it lingers, heavy and suffocating. I know I need to tell Sabrina about all of this—about Callie, about Karissa's latest stunt—but I've been putting it off, not wanting to ruin her vacation with more drama from my end. She's down in Gulf Shores with Alex and Barrett, and the last thing I want is to disrupt their peace with my problems.

But now? Now I'm starting to think I should have just gotten it over with. Because if there's one thing I've learned about Karissa, it's that she doesn't let things go. And the longer I wait, the worse this could get.

I glance at the clock, realizing I've still got a few hours before I need to pick up Callie. The apartment feels too quiet, too oppressive, like the walls are closing in around me. I need to get out, clear my head before the weight of it all crushes me.

Grabbing my keys, I head out the door, the morning light blinding after the dimness of the apartment. The cool breeze hits my face, and I take a deep breath, trying to shake off the tension that's settled in my chest. I start walking to my truck, letting the rhythm of my steps and the fresh air help me reset.

Tonight is about Callie. It's about us, about everything we're building together. And no matter what Karissa or anyone else throws at me, I'm not going to let it destroy what we have. I can't wait to see her, to feel her hand in mine, to lose ourselves in the music and the night.

I just got her. She's finally mine. And I'm not letting someone who is probably trying to chase a better child support paycheck fuck that up for me.

I take another deep breath and get into my truck, determined to focus on what matters, to hold on to the good things that are waiting for me. Tonight is going to be a good night. And I'm going to make damn sure of it.

forty-nine
IT'S NOT YOU - HALESTORM

CALLIE - JULY 27, 2013

Thanks to Taylor taking Sara for the weekend, I've been able to catch up on cleaning and even have all the laundry washed, dried, folded, *and* put away. I can't remember the last time that happened and it won't last long so I'll cherish it for the next day or so.

I've just finished getting ready for the concert and I am so excited. I've seen Halestorm in concert once before a couple of years ago and it was incredible. I went with my cousin and two of her friends. We had a blast except for getting lost on the way home.

I check myself one last time in the mirror, smoothing a hand over my black maternity tank top and adjusting my ponytail. My red Converse feel like the perfect touch—only lightly worn and showing off the signatures from the last time I attended a Halestorm concert. I think this is the first time I've worn them in two years because I've been too afraid the signatures would come off. Permanent marker is only so dependable, you know?

As I step out onto the front porch, the sticky evening air wraps around me and I'm grateful that I was smart enough to put my hair up in a ponytail instead of attempting to wear it down on this hot summer day. My naturally wavy hair would be a frizzy mess if I hadn't put it up. It feels like only a matter of seconds before I catch my reflection in the large picture window out front and see the baby hairs that frame my face and nape of my neck have already started to curl.

There's a nervous energy buzzing under my skin. Even though I saw him this morning, the hours apart from Owen feel like days. Last night was incredible. And I don't know if he feels the same way but it was easily the best sex of my life. And that's saying something because well... I was a trollop, remember?

The familiar rumble of Owen's green Chevy S10–who I know now he's named Trevor–pulls my attention to the end of the gravel driveway. The butterflies in my stomach must be hosting a frat party because they are most definitely drunk.

I know that I have a history of falling fast. I know that I might as well face it, I'm addicted to love–see what I did there? But seriously, there's something about this man that tells me I've known him so much longer than just a few short months. I can feel it in my bones.

Owen parks and steps out of the truck, his eyes immediately locking on mine as a smile spreads across his face. There's something so intense in his gaze, something that makes my breath catch in my throat and I actually have to remind myself to breathe.

"You look incredible," he murmurs, his voice low and full of heat as he strides toward me. He wraps his arms around me in a hug before resting his hands on my hips and pulling back a bit to look me over again. His eyes roam over me, taking in every detail from top to bottom. There's something in his expression that makes me feel cherished, like I'm the only thing in the world that matters to him in this moment.

Before I can say a word, he pulls me close again and his lips are on mine. It's a kiss that's as intense as it is passionate, a melding of emotions that words could never fully capture. His hands slide up my back, pulling me even closer until there's no space left between us. I slide my hand onto his chest and feel the steady beat of his heart against my palm, matching the rhythm of my own racing pulse.

When we finally pull apart, both of us are a little breathless, and I can see the playful glint in his eyes. "If you're not careful," he teases, his lips brushing against mine as he speaks, "we might miss the concert."

There's a lightness in his tone, but beneath it, I can feel the depth of his warning, the way last night shifted something between us. I laugh softly, the sound filled with a mix of relief and happiness. "Well, we wouldn't want that," I reply, my voice tinged with the same playful energy. "Although, if I was going to miss Halestorm for anyone, it would definitely be you."

Owen's smile widens, and he leans in for one more quick kiss, his lips warm and reassuring against mine. "Ditto," he says with a wink. "But I know how much you've been looking forward to this concert, so let's get you out of here before you end up ass up with your face in a pillow."

"Halestorm, who?" I tease, pretending to pull him toward the house.

His smile evolves into a soft chuckle. "As tempting as that sounds, dollface, I think we'd both regret missing tonight."

"Speak for yourself," I pout even though he's right. I've

been waiting a long time for this concert, and I love that I get to spend it with him.

"Tsk, tsk, my pretty Kitty. There's plenty of time for that later." He guides me toward the truck and reaches out to open the passenger door, and I can't help but admire his movements.

"Okay, okay," I say, lifting my hands in mock surrender. "Let's go to the fairgrounds before I change my mind."

As I slide into the seat, I catch a glimpse of the signatures on my red Converse and a smile tugs at my lips. The memories of the last concert rush back, and I can't help but feel a sense of excitement.

Owen rounds the truck, grinning as he gets into the driver's seat. He leans over to me to give me one more kiss before starting the engine. The truck roars to life, and soon, we're heading down the gravel driveway, the excitement between us growing with every mile. The evening sun dips lower in the sky, casting a warm glow over everything as we drive toward the fairgrounds, ready to lose ourselves in the music and in each other.

The fairgrounds are alive with the hum of conversation, the distant rumble of motorcycles, and the scent of grilled food mingling with the faint sweetness of hay and freshly cut grass. Overhead, the sky deepens into twilight, a canvas painted in rich hues of indigo and violet, as the day slowly gives way to the night.

Owen is beside me, a steady presence whose warmth seeps into me with every touch. His hand rests lightly on the small of my back, his fingers occasionally brushing against my skin, sending little sparks of warmth through my body. There's an intimacy between us now, something that wasn't there before last night—a connection that feels deeper, more profound. It's like the air between us is charged with something electric, something that makes me feel alive in a way I haven't felt in a long time.

I sneak a glance up at him, my heart doing little flips at the sight of his relaxed smile. His eyes catch mine, and there's something in them that makes me feel seen, truly seen, like he's looking at me and seeing everything that I am, everything that I've been through, and still choosing to stay. Last night changed things, not just the way we touch but the way we look at each other, like there's this unspoken understanding, a shared secret that binds us in ways words can't describe.

As we walk, I take in the crowd around us—leather jackets, band tees, and the occasional flash of brightly colored hair. It's a mixed group, people from all walks of life, drawn together by their love for the music that's about to fill the air. The ground beneath our feet is a mix of dirt and gravel, crunching underfoot as we move closer to the stage where the band will perform. The excitement is palpable, a collective anticipation that makes the air buzz.

Before we get too close, Owen suddenly veers off toward one of the merch booths. "Hold on a sec," he says, pulling me along with a playful grin.

"What are you up to?" I ask, curious as he sifts through a rack of t-shirts.

He picks one out, a black Halestorm tee with the cover art from the band's first album splashed across the front, and holds it up for me to see. "How about this one, babe?"

I laugh, touched by the gesture. "It's perfect."

Without another word, he hands the vendor some cash

and passes me the shirt. I pull it on over my tank top right then and there, grinning up at him as I adjust the fit.

With the new shirt clinging comfortably to me, we continue our way toward the stage. I can't help but feel a thrill of excitement, not just for the concert but for the fact that I'm here with Owen, sharing this moment with him. It's like everything that's happened between us has been leading to this—this night, this concert, this feeling of being completely in the moment with someone who makes me feel like I'm more than just the sum of my past mistakes.

But then, I see him.

Adam.

The sight of him hits me like a punch to the gut, making me stop dead in my tracks. He's standing near one of the food trucks, his arm casually draped around the waist of a tall, curvy brunette with glasses that I recognize from around town. She was a year ahead of Adam and Taylor in high school so we never went to school together–Katie. She's laughing at something he's said though I can't hear them from where we are standing. The sight of him leaves me feeling paralyzed because I know he's going to start problems as soon as he sees us.

Owen senses the shift in me and he presses his hand to the small of my back.

"What is it, babe? What's wrong?"

I swallow, trying to shake off the icy grip of the past that's creeping over me. "It's Adam," I mutter, nodding toward him, my voice barely above a whisper. Just saying his name feels like reopening a wound I thought I'd finally healed. "He's by the food trucks. The one in the black shirt standing next to the brunette with glasses."

Owen's dark eyes flick in the direction of the food trucks, his jaw tightening. There's a pause, and I can feel Owen turn his eyes back to me, protective and steady. He doesn't say anything more, just gives a slight nod, and I'm grateful for it. I don't want to talk about Adam right now. I don't want him to have any more space in my mind than he already does.

But of course, the universe has other plans.

As if on cue, Adam's eyes lock onto mine from across the fairgrounds. I see his expression shift–his jaw clenches, and the lighthearted conversation he was having with Katie and the people around him vanishes in an instant. My pulse quickens and I can feel the knots forming in my stomach. His gaze moves to Owen's hand on my back, and the calculating cold look I know all too well takes over his face. The look has always made me feel small.

Adam stalks toward us, dragging Katie along without a second thought. She has a confused expression on her face as he jerks her away from whatever conversation she'd been having. Owen squeezes my hand three times as he takes a small step forward, putting himself between Adam and me, tense and prepared.

"I've got you, dollface," Owen says, his voice low and calm, but there's an edge to it now.

Adam's stride is fast and purposeful–as if he's on a mission to destroy my night. "Callie!" Adam shouts, his voice clipped as he steps away from Katie. "What the fuck are you doing here? Where is Sara? You're supposed to be with her." Now that he's closer, I realize that he's wearing a security shirt which means he was hired to help at the event. *Fucking perfect.* Adam knows Halestorm is one of my favorite bands. I can't help but think he took the gig just to spite me.

Before I can respond, Owen takes a step forward, his presence commanding but calm. "You want to try that again, bud?" Owen asks, his voice steady and controlled, but there's no mistaking the warning behind his words. It's then I notice that we've gained an audience. God damn it, if we get kicked out of here, I'm going to be devastated. For so many reasons.

Adam's gaze flicks from Owen back to me, his nostrils flaring. He's taller, broader than Owen. But there's something in Owen's stance–solid and unyielding–that gives Adam pause. There's no intimidation in Owen's expression, just a quiet, protective resolve that makes it clear he won't back down.

"She's with Taylor," I finally manage to say, my voice steady despite the twisted anxiety making my chest feel tight. "I'm allowed to have a night out too, Adam."

Adam's eyes narrow, a sneer creeping across his face as he sizes up Owen. "This your new thing, Callie? Letting someone else handle your responsibilities?" he jabs.

Owen's voice cuts in again, cool and firm. "She doesn't owe you an explanation."

The tension is thick, and the air around us is heavy. Adam glares at Owen, his hands balling into fists at his sides, but Owen doesn't flinch. He stands unwavering, and I can feel the weight of his stance like a shield between me and everything Adam is trying to stir up.

Adam's eyes glance between Owen and me, and I can already feel the tension rising. Before things escalate further, Owen takes another small step forward, his posture relaxing but still protective. He extends his hand, the muscles in his forearm flexing as he makes the gesture. His jaw is clenched, and I can tell he's working to stay calm, yet there's a glimpse of something more sinister in his gaze—a possessiveness I definitely don't mind.

I never thought I could be more attracted to this man, but his protective nature is definitely intensifying my connection to him.

"Let's try this again," Owen says, his voice steady but firm, the unspoken edge of authority clear. "I'm Owen. Nice to meet you," he says, his tone laced with sarcasm.

Adam looks at Owen's hand for a beat too long, his expression hardening as if he's deciding whether to take the olive branch or twist it. He finally accepts the handshake, but there's nothing friendly about it. His eyes narrow as they land on the sunglasses Owen hasn't removed, despite the sun dipping below the horizon.

"A little late for shades, don't you think?" Adam's tone is pointed, a subtle challenge wrapped in casual words.

Owen doesn't flinch. "I wear my sunglasses at night," he shrugs, and the nod to the Corey Hart song has me fighting back a laugh. "Bright lights," he quips, his voice calm but tinged with a toughness, like steel encased in velvet. Owen's words carry no apology or respect for the man who is still technically my husband; instead, there's a quiet confidence that I have grown to admire immensely.

"Look," he continues, his voice steady but firm, "we don't have to make this difficult. Maybe we can find a way to get along. And maybe you can learn to check your tone while we're at it."

Adam's eyes flick toward me before slowly moving back to Owen. The sneer on his face grows. "Right," Adam says, "I'm sure we have so much in common." His gaze shifts toward me again, making the insinuation all too clear.

The implication hits like a slap, sending a rush of anger and disbelief surging through me. How dare he? The sheer arrogance of his words makes my blood boil. Adam's always known how to cut deep, to twist the knife in ways that make me question myself, but not tonight. Tonight, I won't let him have that power over me. Not with Owen here. Not anymore.

Heat rises in my chest as memories of all the times Adam made me feel small rush to the surface. My anger is right there, ready to spill over, but Owen's presence beside me pulls me back. He doesn't even blink at Adam's dig, doesn't let it get to him. Instead, he stays calm, so composed that I almost wonder how he's keeping it together. But I can feel the tension radiating off him, like he's a spring wound tight, ready to snap.

Owen draws in a sharp breath, and when he finally speaks, his voice is low and deliberate, each word clipped. "You treated her like garbage. I treat her like the goddess she is. We are not the same."

And now I'm officially a puddle for this man. No one has ever shown up for me like this.

The weight of his words hangs in the air, and for a moment, everything feels suspended. My heart pounds in my chest, each beat louder than the last. Adam's face twists as he processes the insult, his jaw working furiously as if he's trying to swallow the bitter pill Owen just handed him. It's like he can't quite believe someone would stand up to him like this—especially not in front of me.

I glance at Owen, feeling the deep sense of gratitude well up inside me. He's not just defending me; he's dismantling every lie Adam has ever told me about myself. Every cruel word, every time he made me feel like I wasn't enough–Owen's obliterating it all with a single sentence.

But Adam's silence only lasts for a heartbeat. I can see the fury building in him, the way his nostrils flare and his fists tighten at his sides. He's calculating his next move, gearing up for another hit.

Before Adam can get a word out, I step forward, my patience hanging by a thread. My voice comes out sharper than I meant. "Katie, may the odds be ever in your favor." The words slip out with more bite than I expected, but I don't regret them. She has no idea what she's getting into.

I turn to Owen, my hand slipping back into his as I force myself to breathe, trying to steady the storm of emotions churning inside me. "Owen, let's go. I want to check out the merch booth," I lie, my voice tight but determined. I need to put distance between us and Adam before the situation escalates further.

As we walk away, my heart is still racing, but Owen's hand in mine is a lifeline. He gives me a reassuring squeeze, his thumb gently brushing over my knuckles as if to remind me that I'm safe now—that Adam's words no longer hold the power they once did. And in that moment, I realize something important: I've finally broken free of the hold Adam had on me. Not because of Owen, but because I've chosen to be with someone who lifts me up instead of tearing me down.

I don't wait for a response, just turn on my heel and lead Owen away, my heart pounding in my ears. The tension in Owen's body is palpable, but I squeeze his hand, trying to ease some of it, trying to remind him—and myself—that Adam doesn't get to have any power over us. He squeezes mine back three times in response.

"That could've gone worse," I say, my voice light but laced with the remnants of adrenaline. I try to shake off the encounter, focusing instead on the steady rhythm of Owen's footsteps beside me, the way his thumb traces soothing circles on the back of my hand.

Owen chuckles, though it's a bit strained. "I didn't take him for the type to get worked up over sunglasses."

"Yeah, well, Adam has his own set of rules," I reply, rolling my eyes as the tension slowly starts to drain from my body. "But don't worry about it. He's just being territorial."

Owen slows down, pulling me gently to the side, out of the main flow of people. The crowd surges around us, a wave of noise and movement, but in this little bubble, it's just the two of us. He tilts my chin up, his eyes searching mine with an intensity that makes my breath catch. "You sure you're okay?" he asks, his voice soft but firm, like he's ready to fight my battles if I'd just let him.

I nod, this time more convincingly. "I'm fine, really. I just —" I pause, taking a deep breath, the cool evening air filling my lungs. "I just want to enjoy this night with you."

His expression softens, the edges of his mouth curling into that smile that makes my heart do funny things. He leans down, pressing a kiss to my forehead, the warmth of his lips lingering long after he pulls away. "Then let's do that."

We continue walking, the encounter with Adam fading into the background as the excitement of the concert starts to take over again. The energy in the air is infectious, a collective anticipation that makes the ground seem to pulse beneath our feet. By the time we reach the stage area, the sky has darkened completely, and the lights on the stage cast a glowing halo over the sea of heads in front of us.

The first chords of *Here's to Us* tear into the night, a raw, powerful sound that sends a thrill straight through me. The crowd erupts, and I lose myself in the music, in the pounding rhythm that seems to sync with the beat of my heart. Owen is beside me, his presence grounding me even as the music lifts me up, and for a moment, it's like the whole world falls away, leaving just the two of us and the music that fills the space between. The surge of the crowd, the lights flashing in time with the beat, the raw energy of Lzzy Hale's voice—it all wraps around us, creating a cocoon of sound and emotion.

The lyrics of the song resonate in my chest, each word striking a chord deep inside me. It's a song about survival, about celebrating the highs and lows, the moments that define us, and the ones we choose to leave behind. I glance at Owen, and I know he feels it too—the connection, the unspoken promise that no matter what happens, we'll face it together.

There's a moment during the chorus when Owen turns to me. In the dim, flickering light, I see something in his eyes that sends a shiver down my spine. It's like he's trying to tell me something without words, something that's been building between us since the night we first met. I reach for his hand, lacing my fingers with his, and he squeezes back, the warmth of his touch spreading through me like a promise.

As the song crescendos, the crowd sings along, voices rising in unison, and I feel like I'm part of something bigger, something more than just a concert. I'm part of this moment, this connection between me and Owen, and the thousands of people around us who are all here for the same reason—the love of music, the celebration of life, the shared experience that makes us feel alive.

When the song ends, the crowd roars its approval, and I find myself breathless, the adrenaline still coursing through my veins. I turn to Owen, laughing, my heart pounding in time with the fading beat. "That was amazing!"

A few songs later, *It's Not You* begins, and I can't help but laugh at how fitting it is. The opening riff tears through the crowd, and before I know it, I'm screaming the lyrics at the top of my lungs, letting the music and words fuel me. The song's energy surges through me, and I can't help but think of how perfect the lyrics are for tonight's run-in with Adam.

I glance at Owen and laugh, knowing he's watching me jam out with a smile on his face. It's cathartic, freeing even, to let go and belt the words with zero restraint, being exactly who I want to be, not worried about what Owen might think of my own little concert I'm throwing myself.

Between songs, Owen turns to me, his grin wide, eyes

sparkling with the same exhilaration that's coursing through me. His gaze lingers, warm and full of something deeper than just excitement. "Watching you let go is beautiful," he says, his voice soft but filled with admiration. "And I have to say, you look damn good in that shirt."

His words send a flutter through my chest. I glance down at the Halestorm tee he bought me earlier, feeling a sudden rush of warmth—not just from the memory of him picking it out, but from what it represents. It's such a simple thing, a band tee, but right now it feels like a symbol of this night, of us. Of everything that's beginning between us. Something new, something more than just surface-level attraction. I look back up at him, feeling my heart swell. "Thanks. I think I'll keep it."

"You better," he teases, his voice dipping just enough to make my pulse quicken as he pulls me closer. There's a moment, the world blurring around us, where it's just his warmth against me, the sound of the crowd fading as I lose myself in the weight of what's passing between us. His arm tightens around my waist, and I feel it again—that unspoken connection, as if every beat of the music is pulling us even closer together.

As the band transitions into their next song, we fall back into the energy of the crowd, the pulse of the music weaving around us like a spell. I let myself get lost in it, in the pounding rhythm and raw power of the performance, but even as I do, I'm aware of Owen beside me, anchoring me in a way that feels so right. It's not just about the music anymore; it's about this—us. It's a perfect night, the kind that fills you up and leaves you feeling like you're exactly where you're meant to be. A sense of fullness settles over me, and I know I'm not just experiencing the concert; I'm experiencing something bigger—this connection that hums between us, undeniable and strong.

The band takes a break, and as the crowd begins to disperse a bit, I notice a small line forming near the side of the stage. My heart skips a beat as realization hits. "Owen, they're signing stuff!"

The excitement in my voice pulls a grin from him, wide and genuine. He looks down at me, his eyes full of that same infectious energy, like he's ready to share in whatever makes me happy. "Let's go, then," he says, nodding toward the line.

His words are simple, but they mean more than that. It's the way he's always there, right beside me, ready to dive into whatever moment comes our way. And as we make our way toward the line, I can't help but think about how easy this is with him—how natural it feels to be with someone who sees me, who lifts me up and doesn't hesitate to be a part of my world. My heart flutters, and I know—this night isn't just about the music. It's about us, and this incredible thing that's building between us.

We join the queue, and I can barely contain my giddiness as we get closer to the front. When it's finally my turn, I am excited to see they have the gold *Sharpie* markers on the table and ask the band to sign my new shirt. The drummer notices my shoes and I'm thrilled to death when he says that he remembers signing those a couple years ago.

The band members smile, taking in the shoes and continuing to sign the shirt on my back. Lzzy Hale gives me a wink as she hands her bandmate the marker. "Rock on, girl."

When I turn back to Owen, he's watching me with this look—one that sends warmth flooding through me, making my heart flip. It's not just the admiration in his eyes, it's something deeper, like he's truly seeing me. All of me. The way he looks at me, it's as if I'm the only person in the world right now, like I'm worth more than I ever believed I could be.

No one has ever looked at me like this.

"Best weekend ever," I say, the words coming from somewhere deep inside, a place that feels full and complete. I mean every word. There's something about tonight, about us, that feels like it's all clicking into place. Like this is exactly where I'm meant to be.

"Definitely," he agrees, his voice soft but thick with meaning. He pulls me close, his arms wrapping around me in a way that makes me feel safe, cherished. His breath brushes my ear, sending a shiver down my spine as he leans in. "Now, let's get you home so I can worship that pretty little pussy and show you what a goddess you really are."

His words are raw, but they hit me in a way that makes my heart race, a thrill coursing through me. It's not just the heat in his voice, it's the way he says it—like he's been waiting all night for this, like I'm the only one who can make him feel this way. I can feel the tension between us, the kind that pulls tighter with every second we stand there, the weight of his words making my pulse quicken. A flush creeps up my neck, but there's no embarrassment in it—just anticipation. He makes me feel wanted, like I'm something to be adored, and it's a feeling that wraps around me, making my skin tingle.

This is more than just desire. It's connection, it's intimacy, it's the way he sees me, the way he makes me feel like no one else ever has.

The drive back home is filled with a quiet, electric anticipation. The memory of Owen's words lingers in the air between us, wrapping around me, heating my skin. Every glance he steals, every slight touch of his hand on my thigh as he drives sends my thoughts spiraling. I can feel the tension building with each passing mile, the promise of what's to come hanging in the space between us like a heavy, intoxicating cloud.

By the time we pull up to my house, my pulse is already racing. Owen cuts the engine, his eyes locking onto mine as if he's been waiting for this moment all night. The air between us shifts, charged and thick with desire. There's a silence that hangs for a beat, both of us knowing what's coming next.

Once we're inside, the door barely clicks shut before Owen's hands are on me, pulling me against him. His lips crash against mine, fierce and hungry, as if the tension has finally snapped. My back presses against the wall, his body heat surrounding me, every inch of him making my skin tingle. The kiss is full of promise, full of everything he said earlier, and it sends a rush of heat straight through me.

"I've been waiting all night for this," he murmurs, his breath hot against my ear as he trails kisses down my neck, each one sending a jolt of electricity through me. His hands slide over my hips, lifting me slightly as I instinctively wrap my legs around his waist.

"Owen..." My voice is a breathless whisper, barely holding back the anticipation that's been building all evening.

"I told you I'd worship you, didn't I?" His voice is low, a rumble that vibrates against my skin, full of that same possessiveness that makes my heart race. He carries me toward the bedroom, every step deliberate, as if he's savoring the control, knowing that he's about to make good on every word he promised.

We reach the bed, and he lays me down with such reverence, as if I'm something sacred. His hands glide over my skin, pushing up my shirt, exposing my belly, my chest. His touch is slow and deliberate, as if he's memorizing every inch of me.

"You're so beautiful," he breathes, his lips grazing over the swell of my belly, kissing every exposed inch of skin with a gentleness that makes me melt. He works his way down, his kisses trailing lower, leaving a path of heat in their wake. I can feel the anticipation building, my body responding to every brush of his lips, every glide of his fingers.

And then he's there, between my legs, pulling off my clothes with a deliberate slowness that has me nearly trembling. His eyes lock onto mine, and the intensity of his gaze holds me captive. His desire for me is plain as day. He presses a soft kiss to the inside of my thigh, his hands gripping my hips as he leans in, his breath hot against my skin.

He doesn't break eye contact as he murmurs, "Let me show you how a goddess is meant to be worshipped."

His mouth finds me, and the first touch of his tongue sends a shockwave through my body. I arch into him, my hands fisting the sheets as a moan escapes my lips. He begins slowly, teasing and taking his time, his tongue delivering deliberate strokes that leave me dizzy with pleasure. It's almost too much, the way he's lavishing attention on me, like he's determined to worship every inch of me the way he promised.

I'm lost in it, in him, the way he's making me feel like I'm the only thing that matters, the way every touch, every kiss, feels like he's pouring everything he has into me. My whole body is on fire, the tension winding tighter with every flick of his tongue, every gentle graze of his fingers against my skin.

"Owen," I gasp, the heat building to a point where I can barely stand it. My body is trembling, every nerve alight, my hands reaching for him, needing more, needing him.

And just when I think I can't take it anymore, he pushes me over the edge, the tension snapping as wave after wave of pleasure crashes through me. My body arches off the bed, his name a breathless cry on my lips as I come undone beneath him.

As I regain my senses, Owen hovers above me, eyes filled with desire and a satisfied grin playing at his lips. He bends down, placing a gentle kiss on my mouth, and I can taste myself on him, the lingering heat between us still palpable.

"You taste so fucking good," he whispers, his voice husky as he pulls me close, wrapping me in his arms. His breath is warm against my neck as he murmurs, "And I'm nowhere near finished with you yet."

fifty
BETTER TOGETHER - JACK JOHNSON

OWEN - AUGUST 2, 2013

It's been six days since that night with Callie, six days since I memorized every inch of her in a way that still leaves me breathless. The memory of her lingers—her warmth, the way she looked at me like I was her entire world. I can't stop thinking about it, constantly replaying each moment in my mind.

But life doesn't stop just because I can't get her out of my head.

As I step out of the hospital, the late afternoon sun casts long shadows across the parking lot, the warmth on my skin doing little to ease the tension coiled tight in my chest. Two weeks. It's been two long weeks since I last saw Barrett in person. FaceTime calls have been our lifeline, but they're nothing compared to the feeling of holding him, hearing his laugh in person, or seeing the way his eyes light up when he talks about dinosaurs or trains. It's the longest I've ever gone without being with him, and the hurt of missing him is a constant reminder of the downsides of co-parenting. Every day away from him feels like a day lost.

I drive toward Sabrina's house and the familiar route seems longer than usual. My mind keeps wandering to Callie. The memory of her, so vivid and warm, lingers with me. I haven't seen her since the night of the concert, and the hollow space inside me grows wider with every day that passes without her. I try to convince myself that this is just how things are right now—she's busy with Sara, and I've got Barrett. But the longing, the need to be near her, doesn't care about logistics. It gnaws at me, a constant, quiet hunger that I can't shake.

When I finally pull up in front of Sabrina's place, I take a deep breath, forcing myself to focus on the moment. I'm here for Barrett, and that's what matters right now. But as soon as Sabrina opens the door, I can tell something's off. The look in her eyes—a combination of curiosity, concern, and something else I can't quite place—throws me off balance.

"When were you going to tell me that Barrett was going to be a big brother?" Sabrina's voice is calm, but there's an edge to it that cuts right through me. It's a tone I've heard before, usually when something important is on the line.

My stomach drops. I knew this conversation was coming, but I thought I would be the one to bring it up, not the other way around. "He's not, Sabrina. Not biologically," I say, feeling the words lodge in my throat. "The woman I'm dating is pregnant, yes. But Callie was pregnant when I met her."

The words hang in the air between us. I consider telling Sabrina more details, trying to help her understand. But there are certain things about Callie's circumstances that aren't my story to tell. Frankly, it's not Sabrina's business to know what my girlfriend has gone through.

Sabrina's eyes narrow slightly, her posture shifting as she

crosses her arms over her chest. "Sounds messy, Owen. You need to be careful. Especially with Barrett involved."

I nod, her words weighing heavily on me. "I know," I say, trying not to sound defensive. "I'm going to introduce Barrett to her tomorrow. I swear I wouldn't do that if I weren't sure about her. I need you to trust my judgment like I trusted yours when you met Alex."

Sabrina's expression softens just a bit, and she sighs. "Okay, Owen. I trust you," she says finally, but I can tell from years of knowing her there is something else on her mind.

"Is there something else bothering you, Sabrina?" I pry.

She hesitates, and I feel anxiety start to creep in, wondering if something is wrong. "No, nothing bothering me," she says. "I do need to talk to you about something else, but it's good news. I got a call this morning that Barrett was accepted into the preschool program."

Preschool. The word hangs in the air, surreal. It feels like just yesterday I was holding his tiny hands as he took his first steps, and now he's already on the verge of classrooms and new friends. I'm so damn proud of him, but the thought of him growing up, of him needing me less, tugs at my heart.

"That's great news... but I suppose that means we will have to revisit our visitation if he's going to be attending preschool here, right? I won't be able to drive him to preschool every morning from Mount Vernon." My heart sinks further at the thought of losing time with my son. I knew this would happen eventually, but I'm not ready. I don't know if I ever will be.

She nods, a worried expression across her face. "I know it's hard. But we might need to figure out a different arrangement in a couple of months," she says, her tone more thoughtful now. "With preschool starting soon, we might have to adjust from the one week on, one week off schedule."

"We'll figure it out," I manage to say, my voice steady

despite the storm of emotions inside me. Another thought occurs to me and I decide I might as well put everything out in the open. "While we are on the subject of change, my landlord gave me the official thirty-day notice a couple of days ago. Someone decided to lease my apartment long-term, so I'll have to find another place to live."

Sabrina raises an eyebrow. "Preschool, a pregnant girlfriend, and house hunting? That's a lot to deal with all at once."

"Tell me about it," I say with a shrug. "But I'll figure it out. I always do."

The air between us is thick with unspoken words. I can feel the weight of everything hanging over us—our past, our son, the lives we're building separately now. I clear my throat, trying to break the tension. "How was your vacation?" I ask, hoping to shift the conversation to something lighter.

"It went well," she says, but there's a hint of something in her voice that makes me look at her more closely. "Alex and I... we're getting married." She holds up her hand, and the sunlight catches on the ring, making it sparkle.

My stomach tightens at her words, and for a moment, I'm thrown off. It's not that I didn't see it coming, but the swiftness of it catches me off guard. Yet, who am I to judge? Being with Callie is the clearest thing I've felt in years. And if Sabrina's found that with Alex, then I want that for her too.

"Congratulations, Sab. I'm glad you found someone that makes you happy. You deserve it."

Sabrina smiles, and for the first time since I got here, it feels genuine. "Thanks, Owen. I'm happy for you too. I just worry about you."

We stand there for a moment longer, the awkwardness slowly fading into something more familiar, more comfortable. Whatever's ahead, I know we'll figure it out—for Barrett's sake, if nothing else. And tomorrow, when I introduce him to Callie, I'll be one step closer to the future I'm starting to believe might actually work out.

Before the conversation can get any heavier, I hear the sound of small footsteps, and then I see Barrett. I crouch down just in time to catch him as he throws himself into my arms, almost knocking me over as the tightness in my chest finally loosens. All the stress, the worries about the future, melt away the second Barrett's tiny arms wrap around my neck. This right here—this is all I need. The steady rhythm of his little heartbeat against me drowns out every doubt I've had today.

"Daddy!" he squeals, his excitement bubbling over. His little hands grip the fabric of my shirt, and I hold him close, inhaling the familiar scent of his watermelon shampoo.

"Hey, buddy," I say, my voice rough with emotion. "I missed you so much." I stay there, crouched on the ground, holding onto him like he's my lifeline. Because, in so many ways, he is.

"I missed you too, Daddy!" he says, squeezing me as tight as he can.

After a few more minutes of hugs and a quick exchange with Sabrina about the essentials—extra clothes, snacks, Mr. Chompers, and his lions—I buckle Barrett into his car seat and start the drive home. But as I drive, the weight of everything that's happened in the last few weeks settles on me. There's so much up in the air right now—my living situation, navigating the distance and my relationship with Callie, and now, the need to adjust our co-parenting schedule.

I glance over at Barrett, snuggled up with his lions in his car seat. He's already dozing off, his head leaning to one side, and my heart squeezes with love and worry. I need to figure things out, not just for me, but for him too. I've got less than thirty days to find a new place to live, and the pressure is almost suffocating with everything else going on.

On a whim, I decide to stop by the new townhouse apartments being built on the edge of town. I've seen the construction site a few times on my way to and from Cedar Bluff, and something about it calls to me now. Maybe it's the need for a fresh start, or maybe it's just the hope that something new might bring a little more stability into our lives.

When I arrive, I speak with the leasing agent and put my name on the waiting list. The townhouses aren't scheduled to be completed until next year, but at least it's a step forward. Still, reality hits me hard—I'm going to need to find another option in the meantime. The clock is ticking, and I can't afford to be without a place for Barrett and me.

I drive away from the construction site as the sun begins to set, casting the world in shades of gold and orange. With Barrett snoozing peacefully beside me, I feel a fierce protectiveness settle in my chest. I'll make this work—for him, for Callie, for this new life that I'm determined to build.

When I pull into the parking lot at my apartment complex, Barrett is still sound asleep in his car seat, his small chest rising and falling with each peaceful breath. I just sit there for a moment, watching him, feeling that familiar combination of overwhelming love and the bittersweet ache of knowing he's growing up faster than I'd like.

I carefully unbuckle him, lifting him into my arms and trying not to wake him. As I carry him inside, his eyes flutter open, and he looks up at me with that sleepy, trusting gaze that never fails to melt my heart.

"Are we home, Daddy?" he murmurs, his voice thick with sleep.

"Yeah, buddy. We're home." I press a kiss to the top of his head, the scent of his watermelon-scented shampoo filling my senses. "How about we have some dinner, and I tell you a story before bedtime? I have a big day planned for us tomorrow."

Barrett's curiosity is piqued as I make one of his favorite dinners—grilled cheese and tomato soup. He watches me intently, his little legs swinging from the stool at the counter as I cook. I can see the little gears turning in his head.

"Where are we going tomorrow?" he asks as I place his dinner in front of him. He scoops the grilled cheese into the tomato soup and sloshes a bunch of it over the side of the bowl all over the counter, making me chuckle.

"Well," I start, grabbing a napkin to wipe up the mess, "I thought we'd go visit a friend of mine. Her name is Callie, and she has a little girl named Sara who's about a year and a half younger than you. They have a nice house with a backyard where you two can play."

As I wipe up the rest of the spilled soup, I notice the way Barrett's little hands try to mimic mine, his face scrunched in concentration as he uses his shirt sleeve to clean up a few new drops that landed in front of him. I chuckle as I give him a napkin, which he quickly tucks into his collar like a bib.

Barrett pauses mid-bite, looking up at me with wide, curious eyes. "Can we play on the swings?"

I grin, glad to see him so excited. "Maybe. We'll see if there's a park nearby. But I'm sure you'll have a lot of fun."

Barrett's questions continue one after another—this curiosity of his always reminds me of myself as a kid. Little moments like this hit me harder than he could ever know and remind me that I'll never truly be ready for him to grow up.

"Is Callie nice?" he asks, as if he's carefully weighing this new information.

"She's very nice," I say, nodding. "I think you'll really like her and Sara. They're fun to be around."

Barrett's face lights up with a smile, and he goes back to his dinner with renewed energy, as if the promise of tomorrow's adventure has given him a second wind. "I can't wait, Daddy! I'm gonna show Sara how fast I can run."

"I'm sure she'll be impressed," I say, watching him with a mix of pride and affection. This is what it's all about—seeing him excited, knowing that he's going to have a good time, and feeling like we're moving forward, step by step, toward something better.

As Barrett finishes up his dinner, I can tell his mind is already racing ahead to tomorrow. His little legs swing even faster from the stool, and he chatters on about all the things he wants to show Sara—how high he can jump, how he can make funny faces, and how he can do a somersault, which he promptly demonstrates right there in the kitchen, making me laugh.

"Careful, buddy," I say, still smiling as I help him back onto the stool. "Save some of that energy for tomorrow."

Barrett grins up at me, his eyes sparkling with excitement. "I will, Daddy. I promise."

As I put him to bed for the night, I can't shake the faint thread of nerves. Introducing Barrett to Callie represents a significant milestone in our relationship. I can only hope my instincts are correct and that this is the right move.

fifty-one
THE BOY IS MINE - BRANDY & MONICA

CALLIE - AUGUST 2, 2013

I pull into the restaurant parking lot to meet Mom, Taylor and my niece Ava for dinner. It's one of Mom's favorite places to eat and we are celebrating her birthday a couple of weeks late. It's been forever since we had a girl's night like this. Despite the chaos of getting Sara out the door, there's a warm and comfortable familiarity to the restaurant.

Inside, the restaurant is just as cozy as I remember. The familiar scent of garlic and fresh bread in the air. It's honestly surprising to me that my mother loves this restaurant as much as she scolds Taylor and I for overeating. We are greeted by the hostess who leads us to a booth near the back.

Mom takes the girls to the bathroom to wash up and Taylor and I have a seat at the table. As soon as she's out of earshot, Taylor turns to me with a serious look that instantly puts me on edge.

"Callie... How well do you really know Owen?" she asks, her voice low, almost hesitant.

I blink, caught off guard. "What do you mean? I know him pretty well. Why?"

Taylor reaches into her bag and pulls out her phone, her expression unreadable. "I got a message today from a woman named Karissa. She says she's Owen's ex."

A gnawing unease settles in the pit of my stomach, refusing to let go. *What the fuck? Why is this woman messaging my sister?*

"What did she say?" I ask, my chest tightening.

My sister hesitates before handing me her phone. "Read it for yourself."

I take the phone, my fingers trembling slightly as I scroll through the message:

> *Hi Taylor,*
>
> *I know this message is super random, but I didn't know who else to contact. I tried contacting Callie, but her privacy settings won't let me message her directly. I saw that you're her sister, and I'm really worried about her. This is going to be a lot, so please bear with me. She's dating my ex-boyfriend, Owen. We were together for a while, and I thought everything was going well, but he broke up with me out of the blue. And I just found out I'm pregnant with his child.*
>
> *I'm concerned that he might do the same thing to Callie, especially since she's pregnant with his baby, too. I know how hard it is to be left alone, and I don't want her to go through that. Owen has a tendency to ghost people, and I'm scared he'll hurt Callie like he hurt me. Please, just tell her to be careful.*
>
> *I really don't want to cause any drama, but I thought she should know what she might be getting into. I'm only reaching out because I care.*
>
> *Thanks, Karissa*

My hands tighten around the phone as I read the message

again, my mind racing. I glance up at Taylor, who's watching me closely. There's pity written all over her face, and my stomach sinks because I don't want this to be her impression of Owen. My gut is telling me that it's not true, and I'm afraid my sister will think I'm being naive.

"I don't believe it," I say, exasperated.

"I know," Taylor says, "It's crazy."

"No, Tay. I'm saying I literally do not believe it. I don't believe her. I think she's lying. Owen would have told me. This is just a woman scorned because her boyfriend dumped her. I'm telling you, there's no way this is true. He knows I don't have time for bullshit."

"Callie...," Taylor warns.

"Taylor, I'm telling you it's not true. I don't know how I know, but I just do. She doesn't even realize I'm not pregnant with Owen's baby," I say, my voice charged with anger. "She probably saw the picture his cousin took somehow and thought that he'd cheated on her with me or that he was cheating on me with her. Either way, I'm not buying it. This bitch has a fucking screw loose."

Taylor nods, expression softening. "I will admit, the timing feels pretty weird. I'm sorry for upsetting you. I just thought you should know."

I let my sister know that I appreciate her looking out for me as Mom and the girls return to the table. I take a deep breath, trying to steady the rush of emotions swirling inside me. "Karissa is the girl Owen broke up with the day after he helped me move," I tell Taylor. "He told me it was over between them before we started seeing each other. I don't believe her."

"What's going on?" Mom inquires.

"One of Owen's exes is off her rocker, apparently," Taylor says.

"Oh, you got that message too?" Mom asks. "I didn't read the whole thing. It sounded like a scam to me."

I think my eyes are going to actually pop out of my head. *She messaged MY MOTHER?! What the fuck?*

Before I can respond, Mom shrugs nonchalantly. "Oh, don't worry about it, sweetheart. I figured it was just some crazy person. I didn't give it a second thought."

"Still, she's got some nerve," Taylor adds, shaking her head.

I take a deep breath, trying to push the irritation down. "Yeah, she does. But I'm not going to let it ruin our night."

Mom smiles, reaching across the table to squeeze my hand. "Good. Now, let's enjoy this dinner."

I force myself to relax as the waitress comes by to take our orders. We spend the rest of the meal chatting about lighter topics—Mom's garden, Taylor's latest project at work, and Ava's obsession with dinosaurs. I try to focus on the conversation, but my mind keeps drifting back to that message. I can't help but feel a flicker of unease, despite how sure I am that Karissa's lying.

By the time dessert rolls around, Sara is getting fussy, and Ava is starting to nod off. I offer to take the girls outside while Taylor and Mom finish up inside. The cool evening air is a relief after the stuffy warmth of the restaurant, and I bounce Sara on my hip as we walk around the parking lot. Ava trails behind, dragging her stuffed dinosaur along the ground.

When Taylor and Mom finally join us, we say our goodbyes in the parking lot. I buckle Sara into her car seat, and Mom gives me a quick hug before getting into Taylor's car with Ava. I wave as they drive off, then slide into the driver's seat, exhaustion starting to creep in.

By the time I get home, Sara is fast asleep, her little chest rising and falling steadily. I carry her inside, careful not to wake her, and gently place her in her crib. After making sure she's settled, I head to my room, the weight of the day finally catching up with me.

I flop onto my bed, pulling out my phone. The urge to message Owen is overwhelming—I need to tell him about what happened tonight, to hear his voice and let him reassure me that this is all just a ridiculous misunderstanding. I scroll through my contacts until I find his name, then type out a quick message:

ME:

> Hey, I need to talk to you about something that happened tonight. Can you call me when you get a chance?

I hit send, my heart thudding in my chest. I know Owen wouldn't lie to me, but there's something about Karissa's message that's stuck with me, no matter how hard I try to shake it off.

As I lie back against the pillows, waiting for his reply, I tell myself that everything will be fine. Owen and I have something real, something solid. There's no way a message from his ex is going to change that. But as I close my eyes, I can't help but wonder what else Karissa might try next.

A few moments later, my phone buzzes, jolting me from my thoughts. It's a message from Owen.

OWEN:

> Hey, Dollface. I'm just getting Barrett down for bed. I'll call you as soon as he's asleep. Is everything okay?

I exhale, the tension in my shoulders easing just a bit at his quick response.

> ME:
> Yeah, everything is fine. Just need to talk to you about something. Take your time.

I send the message and toss my phone onto the bed, trying to distract myself by tidying up Sara's room. I pick up her little clothes, the soft fabric feeling like a lifeline in my hands. I fold them with more care than necessary, anything to keep my mind from spiraling. But it's no use. My thoughts keep drifting back to Karissa's message, to the unsettling feeling that someone is trying to wedge themselves into the safe space Owen and I have been building.

I've been in relationships where trust was fragile, where every little thing felt like it could shatter what we had. But this —what I have with Owen—is different. It's solid, real. So why does this feel so unsettling?

The soft hum of my phone pulls me from my thoughts. I grab it, seeing Owen's name on the screen, and I quickly swipe to answer.

"Hey," I say, my voice a little shakier than I'd like.

"Hey," Owen's voice is warm, familiar, instantly soothing in a way that makes my chest ache with relief. "Barrett's finally asleep. What's going on?"

I sit down on the edge of my bed, running a hand through my hair, trying to gather my thoughts. "So, something happened tonight. Taylor told me she got a message from your ex, Karissa."

There's a brief pause, just long enough for my heart to skip a beat. "What? Why would Karissa message Taylor?"

"She said she's pregnant with your baby and that she's worried you'll ghost me like you did to her." The words tumble out in a rush, like I'm trying to get rid of them as quickly as possible, as if speaking them faster will make them less real. I close my eyes, bracing myself for his response, for anything that might confirm or dispel this nagging doubt.

Owen sighs heavily on the other end, "Callie, I'm so sorry you even had to hear that. But she's lying. We never even slept together. I have no idea why she's saying this, but there's no way her baby is mine."

His words hit me like a wave, washing over the lingering anxiety, leaving in its place a growing sense of relief. "I figured as much," I say, my voice softer now, the irritation slowly falling away. "But I needed to hear it from you."

"I get it," Owen says, and there's a tenderness in his voice that makes my chest tighten. "Thank you for not assuming the worst or thinking I'd keep something like that from you. I'm really glad you told me. I'll talk to her, make sure she doesn't bother you or your family again. I'm really sorry you had to deal with this, Callie."

"It's not your fault," I reply, my fingers absentmindedly tracing the patterns on the bedspread. "I just... I hate that she's dragging you into this mess, and now my family too. It's just a lot."

"I know," Owen says, his tone gentle, filled with a quiet determination. "But we'll get through this. I'm here for you, okay? We'll figure it out together."

His words wrap around me like a protective shield, and I can't help the small smile that tugs at my lips. "Thanks, Owen. I appreciate that."

"Anytime, gorgeous," he replies, and I can almost hear the smile in his voice, that playful warmth that always manages to make me feel a little lighter. "Try not to worry about it too much. We're good, okay? And I'm really looking forward to tomorrow. The kids are going to have a blast."

"Me too," I say, the anticipation for tomorrow bubbling up,

pushing the remnants of worry aside. "I can't wait to meet Barrett. I think Sara's going to adore him."

"Same here. Barrett's going to love her," Owen replies, and there's a soft, tender note in his voice that makes my heart swell. "Get some rest, and I'll see you tomorrow."

"Okay," I whisper, the knot in my stomach finally starting to loosen. "Goodnight, Owen."

"Goodnight, Callie."

As I hang up, I let out a long breath I didn't realize I'd been holding. Owen's words echo in my mind as I curl up in bed, pulling the covers around me. We're good. And tomorrow is going to be a fresh start—just the four of us, enjoying a day together. I focus on that thought, letting it anchor me, letting it be the thing that carries me into sleep.

fifty-two
I LOVE YOU - THE BEES

OWEN - AUGUST 3, 2013

I pull into Callie's driveway, thinking that I should probably buy stock in a fuel company with all these long trips. As much as I know she's worth every mile, making this drive each week has become a real investment. But there's something about being here that just feels right, like the missing pieces of my life are finally fitting together. God, when did I get so sentimental?

I glance over at Barrett, who's quietly taking in the surroundings from his car seat. "Are you ready to meet some special girls, buddy?" I reach over and squeeze his hand three times—a small gesture we've adopted for "I love you." He squeezes back twice, our little way of reassuring each other.

After unbuckling him, I scoop him up, and he snuggles close. I grab his bag with my free hand and make my way to the door. Callie's little white house stands quietly before us, welcoming us in that way only a place that feels like home can. Before I even knock, the door swings open, and there's

Callie with Sara perched on her hip. Her smile, bright and welcoming, makes my heart do that familiar flip. Standing there in the soft afternoon sunlight, she's radiant. It all feels so seamless like we're slipping into a life that was always waiting for us.

"Hello, Dollface," I say, stepping inside, one of my favorite nicknames for her slipping out naturally.

"Hey, you," Callie replies, her voice as warm as a favorite song. She steps back to let us in, her familiar scent surrounding me. Part of me wants to lean in and kiss her right now, but with Barrett here, I hold off for the moment.

"This must be Barrett," she says, her face lighting up as she looks at him with an openness that makes my chest tighten. She shifts Sara slightly, balancing her on her hip as she reaches a hand out to Barrett, who's half-hiding behind my leg, peeking out at her with a mix of shyness and curiosity. "Hi, Barrett. It's nice to meet you. Your dad's told me so much about you."

Barrett, ever the cautious observer, studies her with those wide, curious eyes before turning his attention to Sara. I can see the uncertainty in his face, the way he's trying to process these new faces, this new environment. I reach behind me to rub his back gently, hoping to soothe any lingering nerves. "This is Callie," I say, keeping my tone light and easy. "And this is Sara. Can you say hi, buddy?"

He looks up at me, and I nod, letting him know it's okay.

"Hi, Buddy," Barrett parrots with a giggle.

Sara pops her favorite *Mute Button* pacifier out of her mouth and gives a soft hello with a shy smile. At only fourteen-months-old, Sara doesn't talk much yet. But I can tell that she's excited to have someone to play with.

Callie meets my gaze, and for a moment, everything else fades away. It's just us, standing here in this perfect little bubble, watching these two lives blend together in a monumental and simple way.

"So, what would you guys like to do today?" Callie asks, breaking the moment with a soft smile that sends a ripple of warmth through me as we all head inside.

"Well," I start, looking around the cozy, familiar space of her living room, "I thought we could let the kids play here for a bit. Maybe head outside if they get restless, then see where the day takes us."

"Sounds good to me," Callie replies, her eyes following the kids as they explore each other. "They seem happy enough for now."

Barrett walks over to Sara, his gaze curious and intent. Sara, a little unsteady on her feet, holds out one of her toys—a small, plush dinosaur. She offers it to Barrett with a quiet fascination, and after a moment's hesitation, he takes it. Watching them, something clicks into place inside me. This—seeing my son interact with Callie's daughter, watching them form a quiet connection—fills me with a sense of contentment I didn't know I needed.

The two of them seem perfectly in sync in their own small, silent way. I see in them the seeds of something special, something I'd love to watch grow. As I think of the future, a picture unfolds—these two growing up together, Callie and me by their side, creating a life filled with moments like this.

Callie steps a bit closer, and the warmth of her shoulder against mine grounds me in this perfect moment. I feel my phone buzz in my pocket, snapping me out of it. When I see Will's name on the screen, I give Callie an apologetic smile.

"Sorry, I should take this," I say.

"Go ahead," she replies, her smile reassuring me as I step into the hallway for a little privacy.

"Hey, Will. What's up?" I ask, keeping my voice steady.

"Owen, just a heads-up—we're done with the Iowa City job," Will says, his tone serious and straightforward. "So here's the deal. You've got a few options: take the layoff, find another contractor, or come with me on the next job. Some investors are opening up a ranch resort, West Haven, over in Columbus Junction. It's right by the Iowa River, about thirty-five miles east of Cedar Bluff. It's also an option for Cedar Rapids in a few weeks, but that's a bit farther."

I take a deep breath, trying to process it. The Iowa City job coming to an end feels both unsettling and like an opportunity. "Columbus Junction, huh?" I say, turning the idea over in my mind.

"Yeah, it's a good gig," Will says. "Could be a place to settle for a while. No rush; just wanted to give you all the info."

My thoughts immediately go to Barrett. Cutting down the distance would be a relief, making it easier to be in his life day-to-day. And then there's Callie. Columbus Junction would mean being close to her, seeing her and Sara without the constant planning around long drives.

"Will," I say, my voice steadier, "Columbus Junction sounds like it might be exactly what I need. Thanks, man. I'll figure things out, but this sounds promising."

"Take your time, but not too long," Will chuckles. "I need to give them a headcount soon. Just let me know."

We end the call, and I stand there for a moment, letting everything sink in. This decision is more than a job change—it's about where I want to build my life.

When I rejoin Callie in the living room, she's watching the kids, her expression soft and thoughtful. "Everything okay?" she asks gently.

"Yeah," I say, though there's a weight in my voice. "Will just called to let me know the Iowa City job is wrapping up. He's offering me a spot on his next project—a ranch resort in

Columbus Junction. It's close enough that I'd be near Barrett and even closer to you."

Her eyes light up as she considers the idea. "So that means we'd get to see a lot more of each other?"

I nod. "Yeah. But it also means making some decisions about my living situation. My landlord gave me a thirty-day notice since he found a long-term tenant. I need to figure out where to go."

Without missing a beat, Callie takes my hand, squeezing it gently. "What about staying with your mom?" she suggests thoughtfully.

I shake my head. "Mom's place is too small for Barrett and me. I want him to have his own space, a place that feels like home."

She's quiet for a moment, a pensive look crossing her face. "What if... you stayed here? I mean, it'd be temporary if that's what you need. You're here all the time anyway, and you'd be close to Barrett. And... close to us."

The suggestion is so unexpected, yet so perfect, that I'm momentarily at a loss for words. "Are you serious, Callie?"

She nods, her eyes softening as she looks at me, and I can tell that this isn't just an offhand comment. There's a vulnerability in her expression, a quiet hope that makes my chest tighten. "I know it's fast, Owen. I've always been the kind of person who falls quickly. I know that about myself," she admits, her voice steady but tinged with a hint of self-awareness. "But this... with you, it's different. It feels like we've known each other for so much longer, like everything just clicks. What we have... it's what I've been chasing after most of my life. And now that I have it, I don't want to spend time away from you if I don't have to. I've never felt this way before, not like this. We've been spending so much time together, and it feels right. I think it could be good for us. Plus, you're in a tough spot. No matter where you move, you're going to end up having to uproot Barrett. You might as well bring him to a place where you and I can help each other out. I could talk to Brooke and see if I can work around your schedule on weeks when you have him. I know this is fast, babe. But I want so much to be a part of your life. You moving in here, even if it's just for a little while, might be crazy, but it could also make a lot of sense for us if you think about it."

Her words wash over me, dissolving any lingering doubts I might have had. The thought of moving in with Callie, of being here with her and Sara every day, fills me with a sense of anticipation and contentment that I didn't realize I was craving. But it also breaks my heart a bit because it's reminding me of what Sabrina said to me yesterday about potentially losing time with Barrett now that he's been accepted into preschool.

I study her face, the way her eyes are searching mine for a sign, any indication of what I'm thinking. I can see she's nervous, even though she's trying to hide it. This is a big step, and we both know it. But there's something so natural about the idea, something that feels like it's always been part of the plan, even if we didn't realize it until now.

I reach out, taking her hand in mine. The touch is grounding and reassuring, and I give it a gentle squeeze, letting her know that I'm right here with her at this moment. "You're right," I say, my voice steady as I meet her beautiful green eyes. "It does make sense. And honestly? It feels right to me, too. I want to be here, with you and Sara. I want us to figure this out together."

Her lips curve into a smile, not the playful one from before, but a softer, more genuine smile that reaches her eyes and warms my heart. "I'm glad you feel that way," she whispers, and I can hear the relief in her voice, see the tension ease from her shoulders as she relaxes into the moment.

As we sit there, hands entwined, I reflect upon how far we've come in such a short time. It's been a whirlwind, but one that feels so right, so perfectly timed. There's something about Callie, about us, that's different from anything I've ever known. It's like we were always meant to find each other, to build this life together.

"Are you sure, Callie?" I ask, needing to hear it again, to make sure I'm not just imagining this. "I don't want to rush anything or make things more complicated for you. You already have a lot on your plate."

She nods, a small, reassuring smile tugging at her lips. The kind of smile that tells me she's not just saying this to be nice—she's saying it because she means it. "You have a lot going on too, babe. We can team up and help each other out. We'll figure out the details as we go, but I really think this could work. For all of us."

I let out a breath I didn't realize I was holding, feeling the weight of uncertainty lift off my shoulders. I can't stop the grin that spreads across my face, one of those genuine, can't-help-it kind of smiles. "Let's do it. I think you're right. It does make sense."

As the words settle between us, the sound of the kids' laughter bubbles up from the other side of the room, a sweet reminder of what's at stake. I glance over to see Barrett and Sara holding hands, making their way down the hallway toward Sara's room. The sight of them together, so natural, so easy, fills me with a kind of hope I haven't felt in years. Callie follows my gaze and smiles.

"Looks like they're off to explore," she says with a soft chuckle, and there's so much love in her voice that it tugs at something deep inside me. "Sara's probably showing Barrett her dinosaur collection."

I laugh, the sound light and carefree, something I haven't

felt in a long time. "What is it with kids and dinosaurs? Barrett loves them too."

"They're so sweet together," Callie says, her voice filled with that note of affection that always gets to me, makes me want to pull her closer and never let go.

"Yeah," I agree, my voice softer now, filled with something deeper. "They are."

As the kids disappear down the hallway, Callie leans into me, her head resting against my shoulder, and I wrap my arm around her, pulling her close. This—this moment, this connection–it's everything I've been searching for, everything I didn't know I needed. The warmth of her body against mine is so grounding. "We'll take it one step at a time," I murmur, pressing a kiss to the top of her head. "But I want to be here, Callie. With you, Barrett and Sara."

Her breath catches, and for a moment, she's silent, letting the weight of my words sink in. I can feel her heart beating against me, fast but steady, like mine. Then she pulls back just enough to look up at me, her eyes shining with emotion, with something that looks a lot like the beginning of forever. "I want that too, Owen."

There's a vulnerability in her voice, a raw honesty that makes my heart ache in the best way. I lean over, capturing her lips in a kiss that's slow and deep, a promise of everything we're building together. It's a kiss that says I'm all in. When we finally pull back, I rest my forehead against hers, savoring the quiet, intimate moment. The world outside may be chaotic, but in this bubble we've created, everything feels perfect.

Just as we're soaking in that closeness, there's a sudden burst of tiny footsteps. I barely have time to register them before Barrett bursts into the room, his little face scrunched up in a dramatic expression of disgust. "Eww!" he exclaims, pointing at us like he's just caught us doing something scandalous.

Callie and I both laugh, pulling apart slightly but still holding onto each other. I look down at Barrett, who's standing there with his hands on his hips, clearly unimpressed by our display of affection.

"Eww, Daddy!" Barrett repeats, his tone somewhere between serious and playful.

Callie chuckles, giving Barrett a teasing look. "What's wrong with kissing, Barrett?"

But Barrett isn't done. He furrows his brow, looking up at me with all the seriousness a toddler can muster. "Does that mean you're getting married now? Like Mommy and Alex?"

His words catch me off guard, and I glance at Callie, who's smiling but clearly as surprised as I am. I kneel down to Barrett's level, keeping my tone gentle. "Well, buddy, not exactly. Kissing doesn't always mean people are getting married. But it does mean we care about each other a lot."

Barrett seems to consider this, his little face thoughtful as he processes the information. "But you do love Callie, right?"

I hesitate for a moment, caught off guard by his question. And I can feel Callie's body tense up beside me. I've been trying to figure out for days how I was going to tell Callie how I really feel about her. And now that we've discussed the possibility of me moving into this house with her and Sara, I guess there's no time like the present. I smile, feeling a warmth spread through me. I guess now is as good of a time for her to find out as any. "Yes, I do, Barrett. Very much."

I look over at Callie to see that she has tears in her eyes—happy ones, I hope. She smiles at me and looks back at Barrett, reaching out to hold his hand. "And I love your daddy too," she adds softly.

Barrett looks between us, his expression softening as he

nods, seemingly satisfied with our answers. "Okay," he says finally, his tone accepting, like he's just made peace with the situation. Then, without warning, he turns and dashes back down the hallway. Before I can fully relax into the moment, he skids to a stop at the door, eyes wide with realization. "Wait!" he shouts, darting back into the room and making a beeline for his bag. He rummages through it with a determined focus until he triumphantly pulls out Mr. Chompers so he can show his very own stuffed dinosaur to Sara.

"Got it!" Barrett declares, clutching the toy to his chest like it's the most important thing in the world. He flashes us a grin, his earlier disgust completely forgotten, before springing out of the room again, his little footsteps fading into the distance.

Callie and I exchange a look, and then we're both laughing. "That was... something," Callie says, still chuckling as she stands up.

"Yeah, it was," I agree, standing with her. "Kids, huh?"

She nods, her eyes sparkling with amusement. "Kids. They keep you on your toes, that's for sure."

As we sit back down together on the couch, the laughter fading into a comfortable silence, I can't help but think that moments like this—unexpected, sweet, and more than a little chaotic—are exactly what I've been missing. And now, with Callie and our kids, I have everything I've ever wanted.

"I meant what I said, Callie. I love you madly. I've known it since before I met you. I think it was solidified when I lost that goddamn phone. My heart ached for you."

"Ditto," she says simply, leaning forward to place a soft kiss on my lips. She feels like home, like everything I've ever wanted and more than I ever could have hoped for.

"I never told you this before but when I was married to Sabrina, I started having these dreams about a woman that wasn't her." Explaining this to her is either going to make her think I'm insane, or it's going to solidify the fact that this—Callie and me—is meant to be.

Callie stares at me, unsure what to say, so I take a deep breath and continue explaining. "She had long brown hair and these brilliant green eyes." Callie's lips turn up in a smile. "She started showing up in my dreams the night before I married Sabrina. And I spent years dreaming about her until one day not too long ago, it all clicked. She was you, Callie. You are the literal girl of my dreams. When I say I knew I loved you before I met you, it's not just some cheesy lyric from a Savage Garden song. It's true."

She looks at me, nearly speechless and I don't think I've ever quite seen that from her. After a long moment, she speaks. "Owen, I love you too," she says, placing a soft kiss on my lips.

"I started falling for you from the moment you asked me what my five favorite bands were, and I haven't stopped falling since. I fall more in love with you every day, and I know that's never going to stop. You are everything that I've been chasing after my whole life. I always knew that there had to be something more out there for me. And it's you. It's you and it's Barrett. It's all of us together. I love this little family we're building. And I know it's fast. I know it's crazy. But I also know I've never felt this way before. I've always wanted to feel it but I never truly have."

"So," she continues, tears welling in her eyes, trying to break free, "if you'll have me—if you'll accept all of my crazy, all of my weird, all of me—then I can promise you that I will love you every second of every day. In this lifetime and the next. I'll choose you every time. I just need you to promise that I'll always be enough for you."

Her words almost hurt as I can feel the pain from her past breaking her within the last few words. "Baby, I promise. I will never stop. You are enough. You're it for me. Today. Tomorrow.

Every day from here on out. You're stuck with me," I say, grabbing her cheeks and placing a gentle kiss to her forehead. "I love you, Callie Madden. You will forever be my always."

As we share this moment, the weight of past struggles fades, replaced by a peace I hadn't known was possible. This is where I'm meant to be—with Callie, Barrett, and Sara, in a life we're building together, one small, perfect moment at a time.

fifty-three
NEVER AGAIN - KELLY CLARKSON

CALLIE - AUGUST 6, 2013

The day is finally here.

The courthouse looms ahead, a solid, imposing structure that seems to absorb the early morning light, casting long shadows across the cracked pavement. It's an old building with weathered stone steps that lead up to heavy double doors. I let out a slow, measured breath, feeling the moment's weight settle into my chest like an anchor. Today is the day I officially close the chapter on a part of my life that feels like it's been dragging on forever.

For a second, I just sit there, staring at the courthouse, letting the reality of it all sink in. This is the place where my marriage, the one that was supposed to last forever, will be officially declared over. It's strange how something so monumental can be reduced to a few pieces of paper and a couple of signatures.

Adam didn't put up a fight when my attorney sent over the paperwork; he just didn't want to pay for an attorney, so everything moved forward quickly. As much as I hate him, this divorce is still a reminder of everything he put me through and how little the life we shared seemed to matter to him.

But maybe that's a good thing. The quicker it's over, the quicker I can move on. Still, I can't help but feel the sting of it, the finality. I want this—I know I do. But that doesn't make it any easier. In this moment, I feel like a complete failure.

The air feels heavy as I finally step out of the car, my shoes making a dull thud against the pavement. I'm surprised by how calm I feel, like there's a sense of inevitability about this, as if it was always going to end this way. My heart beats steadily, almost in sync with the rhythmic sound of my footsteps as I approach the courthouse. Each step brings me closer to that final moment, to the release I've been waiting for, yet it also makes the weight of what I'm about to do more tangible, more real.

I reach for the metal door handle and pull it open, the sound of the courthouse door creaking in my ears, a somber reminder that this is it. There's no going back now. I'm about to walk into a room where my past and future will collide, where the life I thought I was going to have will officially end, and where the life I've been building can truly begin.

The courtroom is colder than I expected. The air conditioning hums quietly, a stark contrast to the tense silence that fills the room. I sit on the hard wooden bench, my back straight, hands folded tightly in my lap. The room is simple, almost sterile, with plain walls and a judge's bench that seems too large for the small space. A few empty chairs are scattered around, making the room feel even lonelier.

My eyes flicker to the clock on the wall. Five minutes past the scheduled time. There's no sign of Adam, not even a hint of his presence in the hallway outside. I swallow hard, trying to push down the anxiety gnawing at the edges of my composure.

I thought I'd be prepared for this, but sitting here, waiting, it all feels too real, too raw.

The door at the back of the courtroom swings open, and I turn my head, my breath catching in my throat. But it's not him. Just another attorney, shuffling papers as they make their way to the front. I exhale slowly, trying to keep my emotions in check. I don't know why I expected him to be here. Deep down, I knew he wouldn't show. It's easier for him this way—just disappearing, letting everything happen without having to face me or what we've become.

The judge, a stern-looking woman with sharp eyes and a no-nonsense demeanor, enters the room and takes her seat. She glances over her glasses at me, then at the empty space where Adam should be. The silence stretches, heavy and uncomfortable. My attorney leans in, whispering something I can barely register. It's procedural, just instructions on what will happen next. I nod mechanically, my focus drifting to the door one last time. Still nothing.

"Is the respondent present?" the judge asks, her voice carrying a note of finality.

My attorney stands, clearing his throat. "No, Your Honor. The respondent was notified of today's proceedings but has not appeared."

The judge nods, as if she expected this. "Very well. We will proceed in his absence."

Her words hit me harder than I anticipated. There's no more waiting, no more wondering. It's happening, and there's no stopping it. I feel a strange sense of abandonment wash over me, a mixture of relief and disappointment that he couldn't even be bothered to show up for this.

The judge reviews the documents, her pen scratching against the paper as she signs her name, sealing the end of my marriage with a few swift strokes. My attorney hands her another set of papers, and I catch a glimpse of the familiar text. My heart skips a beat as I see the line where Adam's name is printed next to mine, along with the words "and the unborn child, due November 2013." It's like a punch to the gut, a painful reminder of the tangled web I've found myself in.

My hand instinctively moves to my belly, resting protectively over the life growing inside me. It's strange to know that even though Adam has been absent most of my pregnancy, he's still attached to this child on paper. This feels like another step that solidifies my identity as a single mother exactly one week before what would have been Adam and my second wedding anniversary.

"The court hereby dissolves the marriage between Callie Graham and Adam Graham," the judge announces, her voice cutting through my thoughts. "In addition, the petitioner, Callie Graham is awarded custody of Sara Graham, with every other weekend visitation awarded to Adam Graham. Custody of the unborn child will be determined six weeks after the child is born. For now, the petitioner will retain full responsibility."

It's done. Just like that, the life I once knew is officially over. I should be happy, relieved, something... but all I feel is a quiet emptiness, a strange detachment as the judge speaks a few more formalities that barely register in my mind.

The judge gives me a small nod, and my attorney gathers the documents. I stand, my legs a little unsteady as I force myself to move. My heart pounds in my chest, and I can feel the weight of everything pressing down on me, but there's also a lightness, a tiny flicker of hope, that maybe—just maybe—this is the first step toward something better.

As I walk out of the courtroom, I don't look back. There's nothing left for me there. Through the window, I see the sun shining as if the world is oblivious to the monumental shift that just occurred. I pause for a moment and take a deep breath. It's over.

I push open the courthouse doors, stepping into the bright August sunlight. The sudden warmth feels almost jarring after the cool, sterile air inside. I pause at the top of the steps, my eyes squinting against the glare as I take in the world around me. Everything seems surreal, like I'm watching a scene unfold from someone else's life. The hum of passing cars and the chatter of people on the sidewalk feel distant, muted, like they're happening on the other side of a glass wall.

I run my fingers through my hair, feeling the soft breeze brush against my skin, and let out a long, shaky breath. It's done. The papers are signed, the words have been spoken, and the life I had with Adam is officially behind me. A part of me feels like I should be crying, or at least feel something more profound than this numbness that's settled in my chest. But instead, there's just this strange, quiet calm—a sense of closure that I wasn't sure I'd ever find.

I pull my phone out of my bag, my fingers trembling slightly as I swipe through my contacts. Owen's name stares back at me, and for a moment, I just stare at it, letting the familiar comfort of his name ground me. I tap the screen, bringing the phone to my ear as I descend the courthouse steps. It rings once, twice, and then his voice fills the silence.

"Hey, Dollface," Owen says, his voice warm and familiar. "How did it go?"

The sound of his voice feels like a lifeline, something solid to hold onto. I close my eyes, letting the relief wash over me. "It's done," I say, my voice steadier than I expected. "Adam didn't show up, so they went ahead without him."

There's a brief pause, not of hesitation but of Owen letting me set the pace. "And how do you feel?"

I stop at the bottom of the steps, looking out at the world

that continues to spin, completely unaware of the monumental shift that just took place in my life. I think about his question, letting it sit with me for a moment. "I feel... free," I finally say, the word tasting both strange and wonderful on my tongue. "It's weird and kind of sad, but mostly I just feel like I can finally breathe again," I tell him. It's as if I've been holding my breath for years, and now, with one simple act, the tension is starting to unwind.

I can hear the smile in his voice when he responds. "That's good, Callie. You deserve that."

I bite my lip, blinking back the sudden sting of tears. There's so much I want to say, so many emotions swirling inside me, but the words get tangled up in the quiet. Instead, I let the silence stretch, hoping he understands the gratitude that's too big to fit into a sentence. He's been my constant, my support when everything else felt unsteady, and I'm not sure I would've gotten through this without him.

"So, what's next?" Owen asks gently, as if sensing my thoughts.

"I'm going to pick up Sara from my mom's, and then I'm heading to Taylor's for a girls' night," I tell him, my voice softening at the thought of my daughter. Just the idea of seeing her, holding her close, feels like the final piece of this puzzle I've been trying to solve. "I need to see her, you know? Remind myself why I did all this." She's my why, the heartbeat of every difficult decision I've made.

"I get it," Owen says quietly. "And hey, if you need anything, just call me. I'm here."

"I know you are," I whisper, my heart swelling with the simple truth of it. Owen has been my constant through all of this, the steady presence I didn't know I needed until he was there.

"I love you, Callie," Owen says suddenly, his voice firm and sure, cutting through the noise like a beacon. "I just wanted you to know that."

I'm taken aback, not because I didn't expect him to say it, but because of how genuine it sounds and how deeply it resonates with me now. The words mean so much more to me now than they ever did in my marriage that is now over. "I love you too, Owen Klein. Thank you so much for being here for me through all of this."

"Anytime, Doll. There's nowhere else I'd rather be," he says.

"You know, I usually hate it when people say 'I love you' as they're hanging up," I admit, a small laugh escaping despite myself. "It always feels so obligatory, like something you say out of habit. But with you, it doesn't feel that way."

"I'm glad," he replies. "Now go enjoy your girls' night. You've earned it."

"Will do," I say, feeling lighter than I have in a long time. "Talk to you later."

"Later," he echoes, and with that, the call ends.

I tuck my phone back into my bag, taking one last look at the courthouse before turning toward my car. The weight that's been pressing down on me for so long feels like it's finally starting to lift. The path ahead might still be uncertain, but I know I'm moving in the right direction now.

A few months ago, while I was working a shift at the coffee shop, Taylor and Brooke came up with the idea of having a divorce party. They even wanted to do one of those "burn the dress" celebrations. However, they were sad to hear that I'd already thrown the dress and wedding album in a dumpster one day in a fit of rage when I still lived at the apartment. So, we settled on a girls' night at Taylor's house instead.

When I open the front door of my sister's house, I am met with the aroma of popcorn, nail polish, and baked goods I can only assume were made by my best friend, Brooke. The comforting scents pull me out of my post-courthouse haze and into my friends' warm, chaotic embrace. The living room is a colorful mess of snacks, a massive bowl of fruit punch with floating strawberries, and an impressive array of face masks laid out like war paint. It's the perfect setting for the kind of night where nothing matters but laughter and letting go.

"Welcome to the first official meeting of the Divorcees Who Hate Their Exes Club!" Taylor declares as I walk in, raising a cup of fruit punch in a mock toast. She's wearing a face mask that's supposed to be soothing green tea but has hardened into a shade of murky green that makes her look like she's trying to audition for a low-budget sci-fi movie.

With her long auburn hair piled into a messy bun and her hazel eyes sparkling with mischief, Taylor has a chaotic energy that always feels like home. She's the one who'll make you laugh until your sides hurt, even when you're knee-deep in life's messiest moments. It's comforting to know I can always depend on her.

My big sister wraps me in a hug that feels exactly right at this moment, and I can't help but laugh as I wipe my cheek, where some of her face mask has smudged when she held me tight. Looking around the room, I see the familiar faces of family and friends I haven't had the opportunity to see in a while.

Meredith, Wayne's daughter, lounges on the couch in oversized sweats and a faded basketball tee, her dark curls piled into a loose bun. With her effortless beauty, all she needs is a swipe of lip gloss and a confident smile. She's nearly six feet tall, towering over me as she stands to hug me. "Callie, I've been waiting for this day like it's the season finale of *One Tree Hill*," she says, squeezing me.

"It's not that exciting," I laugh. "But yeah, I miss that show way more than I'll ever miss Adam."

We share a hug before she settles back on the couch.

My cousin Olivia is setting up a mini nail salon on the coffee table, laying out every shade of nail polish imaginable, from classic reds to sparkly purples. With her dark curls and bright yellow sundress that pops against her tan, she waves a glittery nail file like a magic wand. "Tonight's all about you," she says with a wink. "No arguing—you're getting the full mani-pedi treatment, like it or not."

"Alright, if I must," I say with a hint of sarcasm, though the idea sounds fantastic. I can't even remember the last time I had any kind of spa treatment and my feet are killing me from being on them at the courthouse earlier today. "But I vote for black polish with silver on my ring finger—that's the only bling I'll ever need. I am *not* getting married again."

Meredith rolls her eyes at that. "Girl, never say never," she says, popping a bite-sized treat into her mouth. "Taylor tells us you're seeing someone, and it's gotten pretty serious."

I shoot a glare in Taylor's direction and she gives me a sorry expression. I guess everyone was bound to find out anyway. "Yes," I admit, "I am seeing someone and yes, I suppose you could say it's serious. But that doesn't mean I'm getting married again."

"I give it a year!" Brooke exclaims from the kitchen, and I cannot help but laugh.

After a moment, Brooke comes in with her arms full of baked goods that she sets down in a spread on the coffee table. Her hair is in her signature low-side ponytail, and she has a pink clay mask on that is cracking from her exaggerated expressions as she snorts at Taylor's smeared face mask. "Oh my god, Taylor, you look like Shrek if he had a spa day that went horribly wrong."

Taylor gasps, mock-offended, then bursts into laughter. "Says the one who looks like a Pepto-Bismol ad gone wrong."

"Hey, this is a luxury brand, thank you very much," Brooke retorts, pouring a glass of punch before handing it to me. "And besides, you can't put a price on self-care, even if it makes you look like a pink goblin."

I plop down between them, setting Sara on the floor with her toys. She immediately toddles over to the coffee table and grabs a handful of popcorn, stuffing it into her mouth, which makes me momentarily panic that she might choke. Lexi, Brooke's daughter who's a little older than Sara, sits beside her, carefully stacking blocks in a perfect little tower, her long blonde curls bouncing with every excited wiggle.

Brooke raises an eyebrow at me, her mask cracking even more with her smirk. "So, how does it feel to be a free woman?"

I think for a moment, trying to put words to the jumble of emotions swirling inside me. "Weirdly anticlimactic. I expected fireworks or at least some dramatic music, but nope. Just a judge with a coffee stain on her robe and a clerk who looked like he'd rather be anywhere else. It's like the world kept spinning, and I'm still here trying to catch my breath."

Taylor snorts, almost spilling her punch. "Classic. I always imagined my divorce would be some kind of dramatic movie moment, you know? Like, walking out with sunglasses on, flipping the bird. But it was mostly just me crying in the car while eating cold McDonald's fries."

Meredith nods sympathetically. "Yeah, divorce is never glamorous. It's more like, 'Here's your paperwork, good luck figuring out the rest.' But hey, at least you get a clean slate."

"And cake!" Brooke announces with a flourish as she disappears into the kitchen, only to re-emerge carrying a massive, eye-catching cake on a silver tray. It's decorated in bright pink frosting with neon green accents, covered in edible sparkles, and reads in bold, cheeky letters:

SINGLE AND READY TO MINGLE (OR NOT).

I burst into laughter, my hand flying to my mouth. "Oh my god, Brooke, you actually baked a divorce cake?"

Brooke beams with pride, setting the cake on the coffee table. "Of course I did! This is my finest work—both pastry and petty combined. Because nothing says 'moving on' like cake with a side of sass."

Olivia leans in closer, admiring the cake. "This is iconic—the perfect blend of 'celebrate' and 'screw you.'"

Sara, blissfully ignoring the gravity of the occasion, crawls over and smacks her tiny hands into the cake, grabbing a fistful of frosting and smearing it across her face. Lexi squeals in delight and joins in, swiping a bit of frosting herself. The room erupts in laughter as Sara giggles, her face now a sticky mess of pink frosting and toddler joy.

"Well, I guess Sara's officially blessed the cake," Taylor laughs, handing me a fork. "Go on, Callie. Take the first bite of your freedom."

I take the fork, digging into the part that says "MINGLE," and savor the absurdly sweet, slightly too-sugary frosting. It's ridiculous, over-the-top, and exactly what I need right now. "This is amazing, Brooke."

Brooke grins, clearly pleased. "It's what I do best—deliciously aggressive desserts. And hey, if anyone deserves a big ol' slice of 'screw you' cake, it's you, Callie."

Meredith raises her punch glass, her eyes glimmering with a mixture of mischief and genuine warmth. "To new beginnings, kicking exes to the curb, and the unpredictable chaos of whatever comes next!"

Taylor, Olivia, and Brooke all raise their glasses, and we clink them together, the sound echoing with joy and a hint of rebellion. Lexi and Sara clap their frosting-covered hands in unison, adding their own gleeful applause, and I can't help but laugh. Tonight isn't about pretending everything's perfect; it's about reveling in the mess, finding the joy in between the cracks, and knowing that no matter what comes next, I'm surrounded by the people who will laugh with me, cry with me, and always, always show up with cake.

As we dig into the cake, chatter fills the room, drowning out the noise of the day. And for the first time since I walked out of that courthouse, I feel truly free—not just from the past, but from the weight of it all. And that, I realize, is worth celebrating.

The night continues with a steady stream of laughter, snacks, and several questionable choices from Taylor's collection of random spa products. Thankfully, my niece, Ava, has done a wonderful job keeping Sara and Lexi entertained so we can have our "boring grown-up time," as she called it, before ushering the girls into the playroom to watch a movie.

"Okay, now that the kids are occupied and Ava won't be traumatized by my adult drama," Taylor says, glancing nervously toward the hallway to make sure the coast is clear, "I've got a confession to make."

The room falls silent as we all turn our attention to her. Taylor, who's usually the one doling out snarky comments and keeping things light, suddenly looks more serious, her expression wavering between nervous and hopeful. She pulls her face mask off in one quick swipe, tossing it aside like she's shedding a layer of pent-up stress.

Taylor chews her lip, fidgeting with the edge of her punch

cup. "Okay, so... I don't completely hate Nick." Her voice is barely a whisper, as if saying it louder might shatter whatever fragile truth she's holding onto. "Ava's dad, Nick. We've, um... kind of been talking again."

Brooke's eyes widen in surprise, nearly dropping the nail polish brush she's been using on Olivia's toes. "Oh my god, Tay, are you serious? Like... talking talking?"

Taylor nods, a little sheepishly. "Yeah. It started with co-parenting stuff, you know, for Ava. But then it kind of... evolved? We've been texting more, and he's been showing up to Ava's soccer games, and not just the ones he's scheduled to be at. And—don't freak out—but we went to dinner last week. Alone."

Olivia gasps, clutching her heart like she's watching a soap opera unfold. "Wait, are we talking 'dinner dinner' or like, 'we're still pretending to be mature co-parents dinner?'"

Taylor groans, burying her face in her hands for a moment before peeking through her fingers. "It was 'dinner dinner.' As in, no kids, actual adult conversation, and he paid."

I can't help but smile at Taylor's admission. I always loved Nick and was sad for both him and my sister when they split up. "How did it feel?" I ask gently, giving her space to sort through her tangled emotions.

Taylor sighs, the kind of deep, conflicted exhale that says more than words can. "It was... good. Really good, actually. But I don't know. Part of me feels like an idiot for even considering it, you know? Like, what if we just end up right back where we started, with him flaking out and me feeling like I'm holding the pieces together on my own?"

Meredith, ever the pragmatist, speaks up. "People can change, Tay. I mean, sometimes they don't, but sometimes they do. And if he's showing up and making an effort, that's not nothing."

Brooke nods, reaching out to squeeze Taylor's hand. "You've got to do what feels right for you and Ava. And hey, it's okay to not completely hate him. It doesn't mean you're committing to anything right now. Just take it one step at a time."

Taylor's eyes flicker with uncertainty, but there's also a glimmer of something else—maybe relief at finally saying it aloud. "I just don't want Ava to get her hopes up, you know? She's already been through enough. And I don't want to be that mom who gets caught up in some wishful thinking and drags her kid along for the ride."

Olivia sighs, a thoughtful expression crossing her face. "Look, you're an amazing mom. And you're also allowed to figure things out without having all the answers upfront. If Nick is stepping up and proving himself, that's worth paying attention to. And if it doesn't work out, Ava's got a mom who loves her more than anything."

Taylor nods slowly as if letting the words settle over her. "Yeah, I guess you're right. It's just... complicated."

I reach over and give her a gentle nudge. "And if it gets too complicated, we've got your back. We can scare him off with more of Brooke's divorce cakes or something equally passive-aggressive."

Everyone laughs, the tension breaking as Taylor wipes the last bit of mask residue from her cheeks. "Thanks, guys. Seriously. I needed this."

Meredith raises her punch glass again. "To messy lives, complicated feelings, and friends who are willing to make fools of themselves to keep you sane."

As laughter fills the room again, I realize I'm not just starting over; I am finally finding the strength to choose happiness—for Sara, for my friends, and for myself.

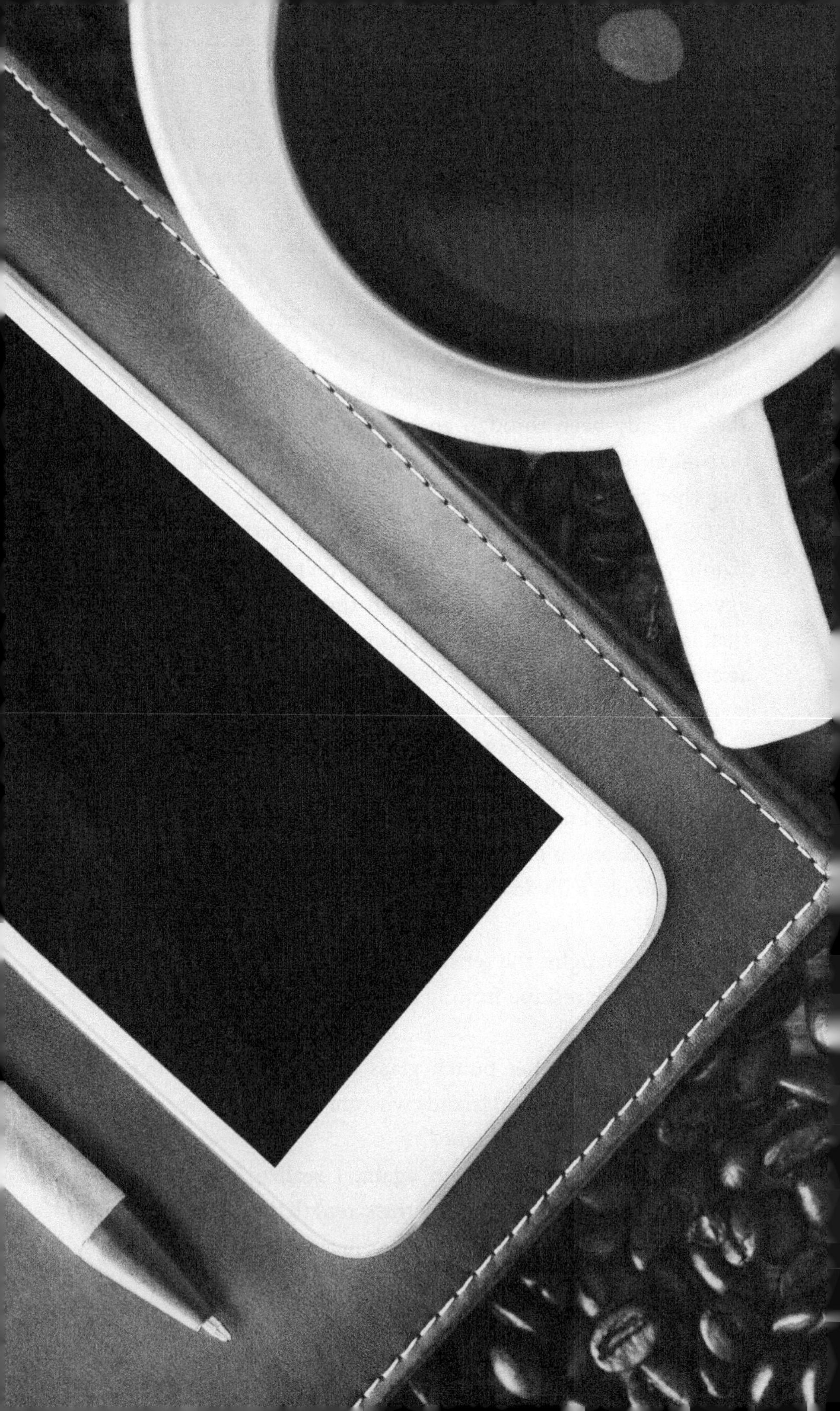

part three

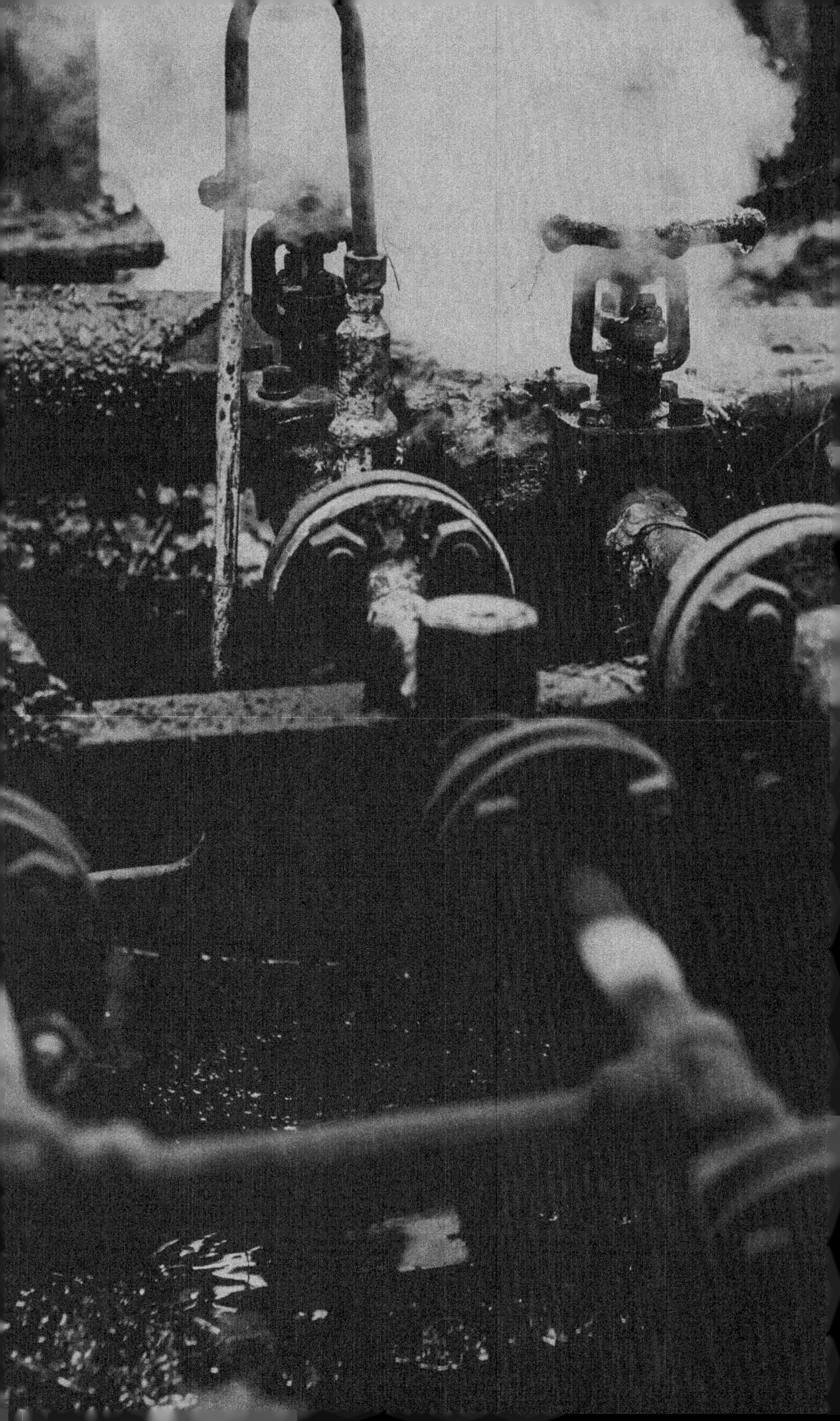

fifty-four
SLOW MOTION - TREY SONGZ

OWEN - AUGUST 22, 2013

A feeling of contentment washes over me as I pull into the driveway. Tonight marks my first official evening living with Callie and Sara. I linger in the truck for a moment, allowing the stress of a long workday to fade away.

When I step inside, I'm greeted with the comforting smell of the spiced apple candles Callie loves to burn mixed with something else, something sweeter. The scent lingers in the air, and I realize she must have been baking something earlier. Judging by the lack of baked goods on the counter, I'm going to guess things didn't go according to plan.

I can almost picture her here in the kitchen, fussing over every detail. She has always insisted she's a terrible cook, but lately, she's been trying to learn more—testing out new recipes as well as her patience. Sometimes, she will even text me pictures of her "experiments." It's charming, the way she wants to get things just right. No matter the outcome, each effort feels like a piece of her she's offering up, making me fall for her that much more.

As I round the corner to the living room, I find my beautiful girlfriend on the couch with Sara nestled beside her, the two of them bathed in the soft light from the TV. Callie looks up as I walk in, and there's a smile on her face that makes the long day worth it—a smile that feels like coming home.

"Hey," she whispers, careful not to wake Sara, who's teetering on the edge of sleep. She must not have napped today. Sara's tiny hand clutches the hem of Callie's shirt, her little body curled up against her like she never wants to let go.

"Hey," I reply, leaning down to kiss Callie's forehead. The warmth of her skin under my lips is familiar, grounding, and I can't help but press another kiss to Sara's forehead, inhaling the soft, sweet scent of baby shampoo. These little moments—the everyday moments that might otherwise seem unremarkable—remind me why all of this is worth it. They're not just Callie and Sara anymore; they're my family.

"How was work?" Callie asks as she shifts slightly, making room for me on the couch.

"Long," I say, sinking into the cushion beside her with a sigh. "But it's good. We're making progress on the steam lines, and Will's been a big help. We've got a good system going." I glance over at her, catching the way her eyes soften, and I know she understands. She always does.

We move through the rest of the evening in a comfortable rhythm that's quickly becoming familiar. I help Callie with dinner, our movements synchronizing in the kitchen as we prepare a quick meal. Sara chatters sleepily, her words slurring as her eyes grow heavier, and by the time we finish eating, she's almost out again. I scoop her up, feeling her tiny arms wrap around my neck as I carry her upstairs.

I take Sara to her room and tuck her in, smoothing the soft, faded pink blanket over her tiny body. I stand there momentarily, watching as her breaths even out, her small chest rising and falling in the rhythm of deepening sleep. She's so peaceful, her little face slack and soft, and it hits me all over again how much these moments have come to mean to me. I love this little girl. And I am so glad that Callie has allowed me to be a part of her life.

While tonight is my first official night living here with them, it's not the first time I've helped Callie get Sara to bed. Callie would often be up until the early hours with Sara, rocking her in her mom's old recliner.

I knew that after everything Callie had been through, the idea of letting Sara cry herself to sleep was almost unbearable. She couldn't stand the thought of walking away, so at the slightest whimper, she'd rush in, scoop her up, and hold her close. And while it was done out of love, it was taking its toll on them both. Callie was running on fumes, and Sara wasn't learning to fall asleep independently.

When I started spending more weekends here, Sara took to me putting her down without much fuss. They say kids save their hardest times for their moms because it's who they feel safest with, and maybe there's some truth to that. But the first time I spent the night here, I had a little chat with my sweet Sara. I told her that if Mommy got to be well-rested, she'd have more energy for fun the next day. Sara seemed to understand, and the bedtime struggles have eased since then.

Callie jokes that I must have made some sort of deal with the devil to get Sara to go down so easily, but I wonder if we just needed this—me being here, being a part of their nightly rhythm. It's clear this move wasn't just about convenience but building something that made sense for all of us. I've always heard it takes a village to raise children, and I'm grateful that Callie allows me to be a part of hers.

When I return to the living room, Callie is waiting, leaning against the doorframe with a warmth in her eyes that makes my pulse stutter. "You are so wonderful, Owen," she says softly, her voice sincere. "Thank you so much for everything."

I step forward and place my hands on her hips, pulling her gently away from the doorframe. She wraps her arms around my neck, drawing me in for a kiss. It's slow, unhurried—just the two of us finding comfort in the closeness. She drops her arms from my neck, lacing her fingers with mine as she leads me down the hallway to our room.

Our room.

My girl.

All mine.

After pulling me into the room and closing the door behind me, Callie turns to me, her eyes soft but full of lust. I press a soft kiss to her lips, savoring the sweet taste of her. Her warm breath dances across my skin as she starts to undo my belt buckle and begins kissing her way down my neck. I reach my hand over my head, pulling my shirt off in one swift movement before tossing it aside as she continues trailing kisses down my skin until she's on her knees in front of me.

It's a sight I will treasure forever.

The more Callie and I are together, the more I learn about what makes her tick and what turns her on. Callie is a service-submissive. Part of the way she shows affection is through acts of service, always ensuring I'm well taken care of. Callie has repeatedly shown me that she gives as good as she gets, and I am living for this moment with her kneeling at my feet.

"Can I please help you take your boots off, Sir?" she asks, her voice radiating desire as she looks up at me through her long black eyelashes.

"Yes, Kitty," I nod, taking a seat on the bench that she

placed at the end of the bed. "But you have to take your clothes off first."

She smirks at me and does as I say, slipping out of her pink cotton dress. When she gets back on her knees in front of me, she slowly unties each one of my boots, pulling them off my feet and placing them carefully beside the bench. She moves back toward the button and zipper on my jeans, freeing my now incredibly hard dick from the confines of my boxer briefs and jeans.

Jesus Christ, she is so fucking sexy.

As she wraps her hand around my cock and lowers her head, I put my hand in her hair, stroking it softly. Her warm breath against my skin is intoxicating. I'm addicted. I need more.

I tuck her long hair behind her ear as she moves her mouth up and down on my erection so I can get a better look at this beautiful goddess that is on her knees for me.

"You make me feel so fucking good, Kitty," I praise.

She hums at the encouragement and continues her movements until I pull her up to stand before me as I remain sitting on the bench. I pull off my pants and toss them aside before putting my hands high on her ribs and squeezing just a bit. I decide to have a little extra fun with her and spin her around while I remain seated before slowly pulling her down to sit on my lap.

I feel her start to get nervous as she sits back, like she's worried that she might break me. She's not going to. Before she's fully seated, I grab my cock in one hand while holding her in a half seated position with the other. Slowly stroking myself through her folds, she is soaking wet.

She whimpers as my cock passes through her pussy lips and I can tell she's trying not to beg for what she wants. I've learned that making her wait for things drives her crazy but it also makes her come so much harder. I continue stroking my cock against her entrance until she's about to come undone.

"That feels... so... good," she pants.

"Does my greedy little Kitty need my cock?" I taunt.

"Yes," she replies, almost breathlessly.

Just as the word leaves her lips, I pull her down, driving my dick deep inside her. She leans back, wrapping one arm up around my neck, pulling me closer to her. I place a kiss against the sweet spot where her neck and shoulders meet while reaching one hand down to play with her clit.

We move together, slowly, every touch intentional. I run my other hand over her belly and a wave of protectiveness surges through me. I hold her close, my lips pressed against her shoulder. I watch as the quiet connection makes goosebumps dance across her skin.

Her soft gasps fill the room as I urge her on. "Come for me, Kitty. Show me how good I make you feel."

As she starts to move up and down on my cock, I can feel my own orgasm trying to come out. She is so stunningly beautiful and this sight is enough to make any man lose their shit long before they want to.

"I love you," I whisper against her skin. Callie pauses her movements, turning her head just enough to catch her expression. Her eyes are soft and filled with warmth, sending a rush of emotions through me.

"I love—Oh God, Owen! Holy shit," she struggles to get words out as I pick up my pace on her clit and begin driving myself upward into her.

Callie's head falls back, and she surrenders to the sensation, her body moving in perfect rhythm with mine. Her moans grow louder, filling the room as she rides the waves of pleasure. I tighten my grip on her waist, guiding her as she moves, the heat between us building to an almost unbearable intensity.

I can feel her walls tighten around me, and I know she's close. Her breathing becomes ragged, each exhale punctuated with a soft, desperate cry. She's losing herself in this moment, and the sight of her like this—completely vulnerable and open—is almost too much to handle. My own release is hovering on the edge, but I force myself to hold back, wanting to watch her fall apart in my arms.

She tilts her head to the side, eyes half-lidded and filled with lust, and meets my gaze. "Owen," she breathes, her voice breaking, "I'm so close."

I press my lips against her shoulder, biting her softly while my hand still works her clit in time with our movements. "That's it, Kitty. Let go for me."

She places her hand on my thighs, holding herself steady as she cries out, her body shuddering as her orgasm takes over, her nails digging into my legs. The feeling of her pulsing around me pushes me over the edge, and I groan, my own release crashing through me with an intensity that leaves me breathless. My hips jerk as I empty inside her, every muscle in my body tensing as I hold her close, riding out the last of our shared high.

For a moment, neither of us moves. We just stay like that, clinging to each other, our breaths mingling in the quiet aftermath. The world feels distant, and all I can focus on is the feeling of her in my arms, the way her body molds against mine, warm and soft and perfect.

After I pull out of her, Callie turns to rest her head on my shoulder. Her fingers glide gently across my chest, creating invisible designs on my skin. I brush a few stray strands of hair from her face, tucking them behind her ear as we settle into the comfortable silence.

She lets out a contented sigh, her eyes fluttering closed as she nuzzles into the crook of my neck. "I love you, Owen," she whispers, the words soft and sincere, like a quiet affirmation of everything we just shared.

I tighten my arms around her, pressing a gentle kiss to her temple. "I love you too, Callie."

We stay like that, wrapped up in each other, letting the quiet envelop us. This space feels like it belongs solely to us, and for once, I'm at peace in a way I haven't been in years. It's more than just the physical connection; it's the trust, the closeness, the love that's been steadily growing between us.

Afterward, we move to the bed and lie in a comfortable silence, the gentle hum of the ceiling fan softly accompanying the rhythm of our breathing. Callie rests her head on my chest, her fingers tracing idle patterns along my skin, and I feel an overwhelming sense of contentment. Being here with her feels perfect, and I wouldn't trade this quiet warmth for anything.

I reach over for my phone on the nightstand, intending to set an alarm for the morning. But as I unlock the screen, a message from Josh catches my eye. Apprehension fills my chest as I open it.

I haven't heard from Josh since the day he chastised me for not supporting Karissa when she told me that she was pregnant. *What the fuck does he want now?*

I open the message, certain that this day will be ruined if he tries to pull the same shit this time. I consider not opening the message but decide I might as well get whatever this is over with.

JOSH:

> Hey man, I owe you an apology. I ran into Karissa at a bar last night, and she admitted she was never pregnant... She used a patient's ultrasound photo. I'm sorry for how I reacted when I thought you'd disrespected her. I should have believed you; I didn't think she was capable of this.

I stare at the screen, the words blurring as I read them over and over, trying to make sense of it all. Relief washes over me first, like a dam breaking loose, the tension that's been coiled inside me for weeks finally easing. But then there's the anger—hot and sharp, cutting through the relief with a vicious edge. The audacity of Karissa's lies, the manipulation, the sheer disregard for the truth—it all hits me at once, leaving a bitter taste in my mouth.

Callie must sense my change in mood because she lifts her head, her brows knitting together in concern. "What's wrong?" she asks, her voice soft but tinged with worry.

I hand her the phone, watching as her eyes move over the screen. She lets out a low breath, shaking her head. "Wow," she says, her voice a mix of disbelief and something else—something closer to pity than anger. "I can't say I'm surprised, but... God, what a mess."

I let out a humorless laugh, running a hand over the back of my neck as I try to process everything. "I can't believe she would go that far," I say, my voice rough with frustration. "Who does that? Who lies about something like that?"

Callie shifts closer, her hand resting against my chest in a soothing gesture. "Someone who's desperate for attention," she says quietly. "But it doesn't matter now. She's out of your life, Owen. You don't have to deal with her anymore."

I nod, her words sinking in slowly, like the gradual thaw of ice. It's over. The anxiety, the doubts, the constant questioning

—it's all done. There's a finality to it that feels like a weight lifting, and as I pull Callie closer, I let myself believe that maybe, finally, I can leave this behind.

We lie there in the dim light, her warmth pressed against me, and I find myself thinking about the future—about the rooms in this house and the lives we're building together. It's not perfect—far from it. But it's real, and it's ours, and that makes it enough. I press a kiss to Callie's forehead, feeling the soft flutter of her breath against my skin, and we drift off to sleep.

fifty-five
BIRTHDAY SEX - JEREMIH

CALLIE - AUGUST 28, 2013

The kitchen looks like a flour tornado hit, and I'm stuck in the middle of it, holding a mixing spoon like a lifeline. My pink *Chicago Bears* apron is covered in streaks of batter and flour, and Brooke, who's somehow managed to stay spotless, is watching me with a mix of amusement and concern. She's the real hero of this operation, her calm demeanor a stark contrast to my baking-induced panic. I can't help but think that this whole thing is way out of my league and I bit off more than I can chew.

I tried testing this recipe last week, so I had time to perfect it, but I could never quite get it right. The last time I tried this was the night Owen officially moved in, and I'd had to take out three messed-up batches in the garbage before he got home. Now, I'm running out of time again and called in Brook for reinforcements.

"Callie, it's going to be fine," Brooke says, her voice gentle but firm, like she's reassuring a frazzled child. She's got this whole 'calm under pressure' thing down, which is probably why she's the successful owner of the coffee shop where I work and not a perpetual mess like me. "Just take it one step at a time. They're just cupcakes. Nothing's going to explode... At least... I don't think anything will."

I laugh nervously, eyeing the batter like it's a ticking time bomb. "Yeah, except I'm the one baking them, so anything's possible. I'm not exactly known for my kitchen skills. If this goes wrong, Owen's getting a birthday frozen pizza and store-bought cupcakes."

Brooke chuckles, expertly whisking the batter as I attempt to measure out flour, managing to spill more than half of it onto the counter. The flour poofs up like a cloud, dusting everything, including my hair. I sneeze, sending a fresh burst of flour into the air. Brooke raises an eyebrow, passing me a wet towel with the patience of a saint.

"Okay, maybe try to keep the flour in the bowl," she jokes, a light laugh escaping her. "Just let me handle the tricky parts. You focus on the blow pop bouquet." She gestures to the messy but colorful lollipop project on the kitchen table.

The bouquet is a jumbled mess of blow pops poking out at random angles, stuck together with hot glue and probably some of my skin since I keep burning myself with it. The bright, crooked "32 Blows" sign is my clumsy attempt at humor, but I know Owen will love it. It's silly, sweet, and completely impractical—just like our relationship sometimes feels, but in the best way.

Brooke's daughter Lexi is playing with Barrett and Sara in the living room. Lexi, just a little older than Sara, has them enthralled with some kind of game that involves Sara's dolls riding on Barrett's toy cars. Barrett, the eldest at three and a half, is in charge, issuing commands in his toddler voice that's just shy of bossy. Watching them play together, I can't help but smile. It's Barrett's first week with us, and I've been worrying about every little thing—whether he's comfortable, if he's missing his usual routines, if I'm doing enough to make him feel at home. But seeing him here, laughing and playing with Lexi and Sara, it feels like maybe, just maybe, we're getting this right.

Brooke nudges me gently. "You're doing that thing where you zone out again."

"Sorry," I say, snapping back to reality and the flour-coated kitchen. "Just trying to keep it together. I really want this to be special for Owen."

"It will be," Brooke assures me, brushing some of the flour off my shoulder. "He's gonna love it. He's not gonna care if the cupcakes are a little... unconventional." She glances at the uneven batter blobs in the cupcake tray and smiles. "It's the thought that counts, and you've put a lot of thought into this."

We finally get the cupcakes into the oven, and Brooke helps me clean up the worst of the mess before she and Lexi head out. Lexi hugs Barrett and Sara, and they pout like she's leaving for a year-long trip instead of just going home. I take a deep breath, check the timer on the oven, and try to relax, but my nerves are still buzzing.

While the cupcakes bake, I keep peeking into the oven like I'm expecting them to morph into something else. I can't stop pacing, my mind running through all the ways this could go wrong. It's just Owen's birthday, and it's just cupcakes, but it feels like so much more. It's our first time celebrating together in our new house, with Barrett and Sara playing in the next room, and I want it to be perfect—or as close to perfect as I can manage without burning the place down. I also got him a variety six-pack of beers from BNG Brewery that I think he will enjoy.

The timer finally dings, and I pull the cupcakes out with a

mix of relief and dread. They're slightly uneven, a little over-baked on one side, but they haven't burst into flames, so I'm calling it a win. Once the cupcakes are cool enough, I smear on the Blue Moon frosting Brooke whipped up, trying to cover the imperfections with extra icing. They're not exactly bakery quality, but they smell amazing, and I'm clinging to that small victory.

The door opens, and my heart skips a beat. Owen walks in, looking worn out but grinning, and his eyes immediately scan the kitchen. He takes in the flour-covered counter, the lopsided cupcakes, and finally me, standing there with flour streaked across my hair and a sheepish smile plastered on my face.

Fuck, I didn't give myself enough time to shower before he got home.

"Wow, it smells... like a lot happened in here," he says, laughing as he takes in the scene. "And you look like you've been through a blizzard."

I laugh, brushing at the flour on my face. "Oh, this? Just trying out a new look. I call it 'domesticated disaster.'"

Owen steps closer, his eyes softening as he gently wipes some flour from my cheek. "I think you're beautiful, disaster and all. And I love that you did all this for me."

His words sink in, warm and sincere, and I feel the tension in my shoulders ease just a little. He spots the blow pop bouquet and lets out a genuine laugh, picking it up and reading the "32 Blows" sign with delight.

I'm not Martha Stewart, but if he thinks this is perfect, then maybe, just maybe, it is.

"This is incredible," he says, holding the bouquet up like a prestigious award. "I've never seen anything like it."

"I figured it was practical," I say with a grin. "You can eat it or use it as a home-defense weapon."

He laughs again, the sound filling the room, and it's like the whole place brightens. We settle at the kitchen table, Barrett and Sara still happily playing nearby. I hand Owen a cupcake, holding my breath as he takes a bite. His eyes light up, and he does an exaggerated 'chef's kiss' that sends me into a fit of giggles.

"These are actually really good," he says, genuinely impressed. "You nailed it, babe."

"Brooke did most of the work," I admit, leaning into him, feeling the warmth of his arm around me. "I was just the assistant. The messy, flour-covered assistant."

He pulls me closer, his laughter a gentle rumble that vibrates through his chest as he presses a kiss to the top of my head. The simple gesture feels like a promise, warm and reassuring, grounding me in this perfectly imperfect moment. "Honestly, Callie," he murmurs against my hair, his voice filled with sincerity, "this is the best birthday I've ever had. Thank you for making it so special." His words wrap around my heart, making all the mess, the chaos, and the effort feel completely worth it.

The moment feels cozy and perfect as we sit together, enjoying the sugary goodness of the cupcakes. The kitchen is a mess, flour still clinging to the air, and the cupcakes aren't perfect, but somehow that makes everything feel even more right. As Owen wraps his arms around me, pulling me close, I realize that this—our chaotic, beautifully flawed slice of life—is exactly what I wanted to give him. I might be a domesticated disaster, but in Owen's arm, amid our mess, I feel safer and more at home than ever.

Hours later, I tiptoe out of Sara's room just as Owen is coming out of Barrett's and I cannot help but smile. Owen spent a lot of time over the last week getting things situated for Barrett, and I know it must mean the world to Owen that we have Barrett here to celebrate his birthday.

With the kids finally asleep, we slip back into the living room and settle on the couch. Owen grabs the remote and quickly lands on reruns of *That 70's Show*. It's been our go-to comfort lately–nostalgic, hilarious, and just the kind of mindless backdrop we need after a long day.

Owen stretches out on the couch, and holds up my favorite green blanket so I can lay down on the couch in front of him. As I lay next to him, he puts his arm around me, pulling me in closer. The weight of being wrapped in his embrace grounds me with his quiet strength.

The soft glow of the TV casts a warm light over the room, and we stay like that for a while, wrapped up in each other. But the more I feel the breath on the back of my neck, the more I realize I've started slowly rubbing my ass against him like a cat in heat.

"You know, it never gets old," he replies, his voice a low rumble that sends vibrations through me. He moves his left hand down to dip lower, slipping under my shirt and brushing against the bare skin of my hip.

"What's that?" I ask, breathless.

"Seeing the goosebumps prickle your skin when you start to get all worked up for me. I love to watch it, knowing that you're mine." His touch sends a thrill of anticipation through me and I feel like my whole body aches for him.

I shift slightly again, pressing back into him, and he slides his hand up and down my side, tracing the curve of my waist and belly. I bite my lip, trying to keep my breathing steady as the heat escalates between us even more.

"You okay?" he asks softly, his lips brushing against the shell of my ear, and I nod, my eyes fluttering closed as I find myself now full on grinding my ass against his now very prominent erection.

A moan escapes me as his hand slips lower, his finger skimming the waistband of my shorts. I gasp softly and my back arches as his touch grows bolder. His movements are slow and deliberate and my body answers in the only way it knows how.

I turn my head slightly, catching his heated gaze over my shoulder, and the look in his eyes makes my pulse quicken. There's an intensity in his stare that makes me smile, feeling the same pull I always do when he looks at me like this.

His hand travels lower and I am thankful for the elastic in my shorts that allow him to slide his fingers into my wet heat, easily finding my clit and swirling two fingers there.

"Owen," I gasp, my fingers gripping the fabric of the blanket as I ride the wave of pleasure building inside me. He presses a kiss to my shoulder, his movements never wavering, and I get caught up in the rhythm of his touch.

"Good girl," he says, pushing his hard dick against the crack of my ass as he chases my climax. "Come for me," he commands.

"Maybe we should go to the bedroom," I pant, struggling to keep my voice steady.

"Shhh..." he insists. "We aren't going anywhere until after I have filled you up. And I cannot do that until you come for me."

His words are my undoing and I come so hard that my whole body tenses as he works my clit. "I need you inside me, Owen. Please," I beg.

"As you wish," he says, shifting his gym shorts down and sliding his cock between my legs until he slowly makes his way inside me.

Owen's grip tightens on my hips as he fills me, moving in slow, deliberate thrusts that make my whole body shudder. The heat between us is overwhelming, every inch of my skin tingling with the friction of our bodies moving together. His breath is hot and ragged against my ear, and I can feel the way his muscles tense, each motion sending a fresh wave of pleasure through me.

"You're perfect," he groans, his voice thick with desire. "Fuck, Callie, you feel so good."

I can barely form a coherent thought, lost in the rhythm of his thrusts and the way his fingers dig into my flesh. My head is spinning, and I grip the couch, my knuckles white as I brace myself against the mounting pressure building inside me.

"Don't stop," I plead, my voice breaking as he drives into me deeper, hitting my g-spot, making my vision blur. "Please, Owen, just like that."

He grunts in response, his pace quickening, the intensity between us growing with each thrust. The room is filled with the sounds of our labored breathing, the creak of the couch, and the desperate, breathy moans that escape my lips. It's taking everything I have in me to stay quiet. The raw urgency of it all is electrifying, pulling me under.

Owen's hand moves to the small of my back, pressing me down further as he angles his hips, pushing me right to the brink again. I cry out, the sensation overwhelming as I fall apart around him, every nerve ending alive and burning with pleasure. He doesn't relent, chasing his own release, his movements growing frantic and erratic.

"I'm close," he growls, his voice strained. "Fuck, Callie, I'm gonna—"

I reach back, clutching at his side as he slams into me one last time, his release crashing over him as he spills inside me. He groans deeply, his body shuddering against mine as he clutches me close, our bodies still joined. For a moment, everything else fades away, and it's just the two of us—breathless, tangled, and sated in the dim light of the living room.

Owen slowly pulls out, collapsing beside me on the couch, his arm draped lazily over my waist as we both catch our breath. My heart is still racing, my body buzzing from the aftershocks of our shared intensity.

"We should really use the couch more often," he murmurs with a smirk, his fingers tracing lazy circles on my skin.

I laugh softly, nudging him playfully with my shoulder. "I think we've broken it in enough for tonight."

"Maybe," he says, pulling me closer. "But I'm not done with you yet."

I turn to face him, meeting his gaze. The warmth in his eyes matches the heat still lingering between us. "Good," I whisper, leaning in to kiss him softly. I savor the quiet moments of contentment that wrap around us, binding us together even tighter.

fifty-six
ALL IN - LIFEHOUSE

OWEN - SEPTEMBER 19, 2013

Callie and I have been together for almost two months now, and it feels like we've naturally fallen into this rhythm that just works. For the first time in a long time, I feel like I'm not just treading water. Things aren't perfect—they never are—but we've found a steady rhythm that works for us. We fit, and I didn't realize how much I needed that until now.

The truth is, I wouldn't trade any of it. Not the midnight snack runs, the trips to the drug store when she runs out of antacids, or the impromptu slow dancing in the kitchen just to make her smile. Not even the anxious moments where the weight of everything hits and we just sit quietly, knowing that whatever comes next, we'll face it together.

Given Callie's cravings, I keep joking that the baby is probably made of pizza and ice cream. She laughs it off, but there's a warmth in her eyes every time, like she's glad I'm here for all the little things—even the silly ones.

I met Callie's family last week. Her mom and stepdad, Rita and Wayne Morgan, welcomed me with open arms the first time I stepped into their home. Rita is warm in her own way, but there's a formality to her that makes you feel like you've got to be on your best behavior. Her smile reminds me of Callie's, though, and I can see where Callie gets her stubbornness from.

Wayne is a nice enough guy, a retired semi-pro football coach with a big personality that fills the room. He's incredibly outgoing, the type of guy who greets you with a firm handshake and a story, making you feel like you've been friends for years even if you've just met. He's a *Bears* fan, too, so we hit it off right away on that front.

Despite his energetic demeanor, there's a certain frailty to him. Callie mentioned he's diabetic, and you can see the toll it's taken on his body; his movements are a little slower, and there's a slight tremble in his hands. But none of that dims his spirit. He's always buzzing around, making sure everyone is comfortable, cracking jokes, and telling stories that leave you chuckling.

When Barrett has come with us, they've welcomed him with open arms. Wayne even started a little tradition with my son, giving him a dollar every time he comes to see him, along with a few silly patterned neckties that Barrett loves to dress up with. Watching Barrett run up to Wayne, eyes bright with anticipation as he pockets the dollar and layers on those crazy ties, makes me realize how much the little things matter. Barrett would carefully drape each tie around his neck, his eyes shining with the thrill of these small but treasured gifts.

One thing was immediately clear—Wayne loves his stepdaughters as if they were his own, with no distinction between blood-related and blended. To him, family is family, and it shows in every little interaction. It's like he's made it his mission to be there for them, no matter what. And I hope that Callie will let me do the same for her daughters.

I met Callie's older sister Taylor too, and I could tell right away that she's fiercely protective of Callie, which I respected. Taylor has this spark—she's vibrant, funny, and doesn't shy away from speaking her mind. There's a maternal side to Taylor, something I noticed early on. She told me about how they were home alone a lot as kids, with Wayne working long hours and Rita going back to school to be a teacher. Taylor had to step up, looking out for Callie in those early years, and you can still see that dynamic in their relationship.

During our first meeting, Taylor sized me up with a look that said she wasn't going to just let any guy into her sister's life, and I appreciated that. We ended up joking about the silly things Callie does, and by the end of the night, she was teasing me like we'd known each other for years.

It's clear that the bond between Taylor and Callie runs deep. Seeing them together, sharing those inside jokes, and finishing each other's sentences made me feel like I was getting a front-row seat to something special. There's this unspoken understanding between them, a kind of closeness that goes beyond just being siblings—it's like they're each other's anchor, rooted in all those years of leaning on one another.

In meeting Callie's family, I saw how the laughter and warmth flowed so effortlessly, and I couldn't help but feel like I'd found something I hadn't realized I was missing.

A few days after meeting Callie's parents, I stopped by the coffee shop to surprise her and had the chance to meet her best friend, Brooke. I was honestly surprised we hadn't met sooner. But Callie says she's busy with her business, her daughter, and dealing with an estranged ex-husband that no one ever talks about. Brooke gave me a warm welcome, and it didn't take long for me to understand why she means so much to Callie.

When Callie told me Brooke owned the coffee shop where she worked, I didn't think much of it—until I walked into *Brooked & Brewed*. I pushed open the door to the shop, the bell chiming overhead, and was hit with the familiar, comforting aroma of freshly brewed coffee.

When I saw the rows of coffee bags lining the shelves, I stopped in my tracks as I read the label: *BB Coffee Co*. It is the same brand I've been obsessed with for years, the one I swore by every morning to get me through the day. I picked up a bag, turning it over in my hands. It felt like one of those weird, serendipitous moments where everything lined up perfectly, like maybe the universe was giving me a sign that I was exactly where I was supposed to be. I hadn't realized that Brooke's shop produced it because the shop didn't carry the same brand name as the coffee. How did I not connect *Brooked & Brewed* with *BB Coffee Co.*? It seemed so obvious now.

When Callie saw me standing there, holding the bag like I'd discovered some hidden treasure, she laughed so much it made her eyes crinkle at the corners, and her dimples pop. She shook her head, looking at me like I was the biggest nerd for getting so worked up over a few bags of coffee beans.

I looked around the shop, taking in the cozy corners where customers sipped their lattes and the faint hum of conversation mixed with the soft indie music playing in the background. Before Callie and I ever met, this shop was a part of my life, a part of my everyday routine. I just didn't know it yet. It felt like more than just a coincidence—it felt like destiny, as though my past aligned with my present, bringing everything full circle.

When we arrive at my dad's house on Friday, I'm excited for Callie to see the house I grew up in. The outside looks mostly the same—a modest two-story place my dad has made some improvements to over the years. However, I know from previous visits the inside doesn't resemble the home I grew up in anymore. Now, the walls are filled with photos of the life Dad rebuilt after he and Mom divorced. I try not to let it bother me even though this place doesn't feel like home anymore.

I take a deep breath, forcing a smile as I remind myself that tonight is supposed to be simple—a chance for Dad and Bev to meet the woman who has become such a huge part of my life. Still, the weight of unspoken words hangs heavy in the air. I haven't mentioned her pregnancy yet because Callie and I wanted to explain in person. I just hope they give us the opportunity to do so without judgment. They know she's a single mom, but I'm unsure how he'll react to the news that the woman I'm dating is pregnant.

As if she can sense my hesitation, I feel Callie's hand tighten in mine as we climb the front porch steps, Sara and Barrett following closely behind.

My stepmom makes it to the front door before we do and greets us with a warm but curious smile. "Owen, it's great to see you," she says, embracing me as we step inside. Her eyes linger on Callie's belly before she offers her hand. "You must be Callie. I've heard so much about you."

But apparently not enough. Sorry, Bev.

"It's nice to meet you, Beverly. This is my daughter, Sara." Callie smiles, but I can tell that she's already uncomfortable.

As Beverly greets Sara and gives Barrett a hug, Dad steps out of the kitchen, wiping his hands on a towel. His gaze quickly shifts from me to Callie, and I feel the air tighten, waiting for him to say something.

"Dad, this is Callie," I say, trying to keep my tone light. "Callie, this is my dad, Henry. And, Dad, this is Callie's daughter, Sara."

Callie moves closer, confidently reaching out her hand. "Hello, Mr. Klein. It's great to finally meet you."

Dad shakes her hand, his grip firm, almost too firm, and he holds it a fraction longer than necessary, his eyes scanning her like she's some kind of puzzle he's trying to figure out. "Nice to meet you, Callie. And it's Henry. No need for formalities."

The casual way he greets her gives me a glimmer of hope that maybe tonight will go okay after all. But when Callie excuses herself to grab the drink she left in the car, I can feel a shift. The kids play with building blocks on the floor in the living room and I sit with Dad at the dining room table. The door barely clicks shut before Dad turns to me, his expression unreadable but his eyes sharp as glass.

"So, is that thing in her stomach yours?"

His question lands heavy. My mind blanks momentarily, trying to ensure I heard him correctly. Then the anger hits, hot and fast. *He's got to be fucking joking, right?* I clench my jaw, trying to rein it in so I don't lose my cool around Callie and the kids. But it bubbles up.

"That's how you're gonna talk about her?" I snap, my voice low yet sharp.

He shrugs like he hasn't just thrown a grenade into the evening. "I'm just asking, Owen. You bring this girl here, she's pregnant, and you failed to mention that. I have a right to know if I'm going to have another grandkid."

I feel the heat rise to my face, my hands clenching into fists at my sides. "I wanted to explain the situation in person!" I all but shout, trying to avoid catching the attention of the kids. "Don't you dare say anything to her that makes her feel like she's got to explain herself to you. No, she's not pregnant with my kid, but that doesn't matter. She's with me, and that's what you should care about."

Dad opens his mouth to argue, but Beverly cuts in, placing a hand on his arm. "Henry, stop," she says softly, her eyes flicking between us. "This isn't the time."

He huffs and turns away, but the damage is done. Callie walks back in, her smile faltering when she senses the tension. I make an excuse about an old argument, but she can sense that something is off. She always does.

We manage to keep things civil through dinner, but I can't shake the feeling that my father's reaction–the way he spoke about Callie–may have caused damage to our relationship that won't heal anytime soon.

The drive home from Dad's is quiet, a heavy sort of silence hanging between us. Callie's hand rests on my knee, her fingers absentmindedly drawing little patterns as I steer us through the familiar streets. I can't stop replaying the scene at Dad's in my head, wishing I'd done more, said more, found a way to protect her from his bluntness. She doesn't say much, just squeezes my knee gently and leans her head against the window, eyes fixed on the passing streetlamps, lost in thought.

After a while, she speaks, her voice soft but clear. "Owen,

what happened back there? I know something was off." She turns her gaze to me, searching my face like she's trying to piece together the parts I haven't said out loud.

I sigh, my grip tightening on the wheel as I try to find the right words. "Dad...he said some things," I admit, glancing her way. "He asked if the baby was mine, and I snapped at him. He overstepped, and I didn't handle it well."

Callie stays quiet for a moment, processing. "You don't have to apologize for him," she says gently, her voice steady but edged with concern. "I just don't want to be the reason things get tense between you two."

"You're not," I say immediately, reaching over to take her hand, squeezing it tight. "None of this is your fault, Callie. I should have just told him about your pregnancy before we went so I didn't put you in an awkward situation. I'm so sorry, baby." I feel tears sneak up on me, and my voice breaks at the thought that I might have hurt her.

She nods slowly, but I don't miss the tear that falls down her cheek. "It's okay. We both thought it would be easier to explain in person. I just don't want to cause problems for you, Owen."

As I search for the right words, "All In" by Lifehouse plays softly on the radio, the familiar chords weaving through the car. The timing feels almost too perfect, and I let out a small laugh under my breath.

We're in Callie's vehicle since everyone wouldn't fit in my truck; the kids are in the back—Sara babbling in her car seat and Barrett tapping his toy against the window. But I need Callie's full attention right now. I pull over to the side of the road, slowing to a stop, and turn to her. I wipe away her tears and take both of her hands in mine, holding them firmly as the lyrics play quietly in the background.

"Callie," I say, my voice steady and sure. "I'm all in. With you, with Sara, with this baby. Nothing my dad or anyone else says is going to change that. I want this—us. And I'm not going anywhere. I need you to know that."

She smiles at me, but her eyes are still glassy from unshed tears. "Nothing and no one will ever change how I feel about you," I continue, my grip on her hands tightening slightly. "You're it for me, Callie. I'm here, and I'm staying. No matter what."

Her eyes soften, and she lets out a breath, her shoulders relaxing. She leans in, resting her forehead against mine, her voice a soft whisper. "Ditto," she says, that single word heavy with so much emotion.

For a moment, we sit there, heads together, hands intertwined, the song playing softly in the background. It feels like we're carving out our own little space in the world, a place where we're not just surviving the tough moments but building something real—together.

And just as I'm about to lean in, Barrett's voice rings out from the back seat. "You guys aren't going to kiss again, are you? Gross, Dad!" His exasperation cuts through the moment, and Callie and I both burst into laughter. I can't resist; I give her a quick kiss anyway, Barrett groaning in mock disgust. With smiles on our faces, I shift the car back into drive, feeling lighter as we head home, all of us together.

fifty-seven
YOU'LL BE IN MY HEART - BOYS LIKE GIRLS

CALLIE - SEPTEMBER 22, 2013

Meeting Henry and Beverly on Friday night was a fucking disaster, but we got through it. I didn't realize until I saw the look on their faces that Owen hadn't told them about my pregnancy. He had mentioned a while ago that he wanted to tell them in person, but then, for whatever reason, I assumed he ended up telling them since it had been a few weeks since he'd moved in with me. The way Henry kept staring at my belly, you'd think I had a flashing neon sign pointing right at it. But hey, at least no one passed out or threw holy water on me, so there's that.

Today, though, is a different challenge altogether—meeting Owen's mom, Suzanne. Owen's been reassuring me all morning, going on about how sweet and easygoing she is, but I'm still on high alert. Suzanne is making the drive here from Mount Vernon. I'm doing some last minute cleaning, vacuuming up the Fruit Loops Sara shook all over the floor this morning. The sound of Sara giggling and Barrett's animated chatter fills the air. The house smells faintly of lavender from the candle I lit earlier, and I'm crossing my fingers that this "calming scent" isn't a total scam because my nerves are about to stage a full-on rebellion.

Suzanne pulls up in her blue sedan, right on time. She steps out in one of her signature flowy boho dresses, her wild, curly gray hair framing her face like a silver halo. Owen told me her hair has always been wavy, but after she kicked breast cancer's ass, she got the tight "chemo curls" that stuck around. She's not a skinny woman, but she carries herself with this effortless confidence that makes you forget about all the stupid societal rules about how a woman should look. Owen meets her at the door, greeting her with a big hug, and I can already see the warm, inviting smile on her face. *Okay, deep breath.* I wipe my slightly sweaty hands on my dress–so gross–trying to mentally prepare for whatever's about to unfold.

Suzanne steps inside, and the first thing she does is crouch down to greet Sara and Barrett. "Oh, look at you two," she gushes, her voice soft and melodic. Barrett proudly shows off his favorite action figure, explaining its entire life story to his Nana, while Sara springs up and clings to my leg like she's gearing up for a major league peek-a-boo championship. Suzanne just smiles and waves at her, not pushing, and before long, Sara is toddling forward to hand her one of her stuffed animals—a purple octopus she's newly obsessed with, which is basically the toddler equivalent of a peace offering.

Watching Suzanne interact with them is a relief, like I'm finally exhaling after holding my breath for days. She's patient, gentle, and she's got this way of making Sara and Barrett feel like the most important people in the room. When she finally stands up, she turns to me with the same genuine warmth. "Callie, it's so wonderful to finally meet you," she says, pulling me into a hug that's gentle and comforting, like she's known me for years rather than mere minutes.

"Thank you for coming," I say, hoping my voice doesn't betray the little adrenaline surge still buzzing under my skin. Owen moves to my side, his hand resting on my back—a tiny, reassuring presence that helps me stay grounded.

Suzanne takes a look around the living room, clearly clocking the toy explosion that's taken over half the floor. I brace myself for a comment, but she just smiles, her gaze lingering on the framed photos we've put up of the little family we're building together. "Your home is lovely," she says, settling onto the couch and patting the spot beside her.

We start chatting, and to my surprise, the conversation flows easily. We cover everything from my job at the coffee shop to Sara's current obsession with only eating foods that are orange. She's genuinely interested, asking about my day-to-day and nodding along like every detail is fascinating. I almost forget that this is our first meeting; it feels like catching up with someone who's been in my life for much longer, just like her son.

Suzanne's questions are thoughtful, not invasive. She asks about my plans for Sara and how I'm feeling about the baby, clearly aiming to connect rather than pry. As our conversation flows, I decide to show her the cherry blossom tree tattoo on my arm, its delicate branches etched beautifully along my skin. Suzanne's eyes brighten as she leans in to get a closer look.

"That's lovely, Callie," she says, genuinely impressed. She gently touches the long necklace she wears daily—a Tree of Life with stones intricately wire-wrapped among the branches. "I wear this all the time—it reminds me of how everything is connected. The roots, the branches, all reaching out, just like us."

I grin, feeling an unexpected bond forming. "It's like we're all part of something bigger, even when things feel chaotic."

Suzanne nods, her smile warm and knowing. "Exactly. It's about seeing the beauty in the journey, even when it's not easy."

Owen's hovering near the kitchen, watching us with this half-smile that's somewhere between relief and awe like he can't quite believe how well this is going. And honestly, same.

When she casually mentions she'd love to babysit Sara sometime, I nearly choke on my water. Babysitting already? That's... unexpected. She says it with such sincerity, and it makes me feel like maybe, just maybe, things will be alright. God, she really is the sweetest woman, even though I can tell she definitely also has a sassy side.

The whole time, there's no judgment, no weird vibes—just acceptance and understanding. I catch Owen's eye again, and he gives me this look that says he's just as relieved as I am. Suzanne's presence has a calming effect on me, quietly unraveling the nerves still tangled inside me.

Sara climbs into my lap with her octopus, clutching it tightly. Suzanne reaches out to gently ruffle her hair. "She's beautiful, Callie," she says softly, her eyes warm. "You're doing an amazing job."

Those words hit me like a freight train. I blink rapidly, trying to keep the sudden tears from spilling over. "Thank you," I manage to choke out as tears fill my eyes. It's been so long since anyone other than Owen has told me I'm doing a good job, and Suzanne's words wrap around my heart like an embrace.

As we wrap up, Suzanne pulls Owen into a hug first, whispering something in his ear that makes him smile. She turns to me, giving me another warm hug that feels like it lingers just a bit longer than the first.

"She's a keeper, Owen," Suzanne says, not bothering to whisper this time, and it sends a rush of warmth through my chest. I want to bottle this moment, this feeling of acceptance and ease, and keep it with me for when my doubt and dark thoughts creep back in. My heart swells as I realize the only person who has accepted me quite so quickly before Suzanne is her son.

After his mom leaves, Owen wraps an arm around me, pulling me close, and I lean into him, feeling the steady rise and fall of his chest. I'm so grateful that today went better than the meeting with his dad and stepmom. I worry that his Dad's opinion of our situation might impact our relationship. A part of me is afraid that once the baby arrives, it will all be too much for him.

I've never had someone willing to endure the hard times with me. And even though Owen hasn't given me any reason to doubt him, I can't help the doubt that creeps in.

I just hope I'm wrong.

Curiosity gets the best of me, and as we sit down to watch a movie with the kids, I ask him what his mom whispered to her before she left. I know it's not really my business, and if Suzanne had wanted me to be aware, she would have just said whatever it was aloud.

He smiles, and it's almost shy, like he's not sure how I will react. For a moment, I think he's not going to tell me. But then he finally does, and it makes every worry that started to creep in fade away:

"Marry her."

fifty-eight
I WANNA BE YOURS - ARCTIC MONKEYS

OWEN - SEPTEMBER 27, 2013

I stand at the end of a tree-lined path just as the sun breaks through the canopy above. There's an overwhelming sense of peace in the air.

Then I see her.

Callie.

Walking toward me, her steps slow and deliberate. It's like she's always known where to find me. Her smile spreads across her face and I swear it lights up the world around us. She's radiant in white, her dress flowing around her as she smiles and as she gets closer, I can see the familiar amethyst glint in her eyes.

She is stunning. Absolutely stunning.

I feel my breath catch in my throat from the weight of the moment. I'm not nervous, not anymore. Callie is the direction that I've been looking for, my true north.

We don't speak. We don't need to. Everything we've been through, every risk we took to be together, every laugh, every tear, *every moment of doubt–it all led us here. The clearing feels like it stretches on forever, endless and open, but I don't feel lost. I feel found.*

The light filtering through the window is soft as I slowly stir awake. Callie's steady breath is the first thing I notice, her back nestled against my chest, the curve of her body fitting perfectly with mine. I take a deep breath, inhaling the scent of her coconut shampoo.

I'm not ready to move yet. I want to just lay here with her in this moment–the easy silence between us feels more like home than any place I've ever known. My arm instinctively tightens around her waist, pulling her closer to me. She stirs slightly, her hand covering mine.

I blink the sleep from my eyes, and for a second, I let my gaze trace the soft lines of her shoulders, the mess of her dark hair spread across the pillow. There's no doubt in my mind when it comes to my love for this woman. I'm so glad I finally took a chance on her. On us.

As I lie there, my thoughts drift back to the dream I had of Callie in a white dress. I know we've only been together for a short time–only even known each other a few months, but something deep in my soul tells me that she's my forever. The girl of my dreams. Everything I've ever been looking for.

She stirs again, a small sigh escaping her perfect pink lips as she shifts in my arms, pressing her back even closer to me. I smile against her hair, dropping a kiss to the top of her head. "Morning," I murmur softly, my voice still rough from sleep.

"How long have you been awake?" she asks, rolling back toward me and looking over her shoulder.

"Not long," I tell her, brushing her hair away from her face and kissing along her jaw. "I was just laying here thinking about us."

"Good thoughts, I hope," she says with a smile.

"Very good," I assure her, not quite ready to tell her that I was dreaming of her in a white dress, about to take my last name.

After a few more minutes of comfortable silence, Callie stretches, pulling herself away from me just enough to sit up. "I should probably start getting ready," she says. She's supposed to go to a craft show today with Taylor and Brooke.

I groan in protest, tugging her hand to pull her back to me. "Do you have to go?"

She laughs and leans down to give me a quick kiss. "You'll survive one day without me," she teases. "Besides, you have the guys coming over. I'm sure they will keep you plenty occupied while I am away."

I watch her move around the room putting on black leggings and an orange sweater. She has told me before that she doesn't like to wear orange because it makes her look like a pumpkin. But I know now she wears it because she knows it's my favorite color.

I cannot help but smile, watching her get dressed. Her ass looks perfect. Everything about her is perfect. She catches me staring and shakes her head. "You're ridiculous."

"Ridiculously attracted to you."

She throws a pillow at me, and I laugh, sitting up to catch it before it hits my face. "Fine, fine. I'll quit thinking about all the spots in this room I could bend you over," I digress.

She pulls her hair into a messy bun and turns back to look at me. "You can bend me over anywhere you like tonight," she promises. Another groan escapes as I flop back down onto the bed.

"Don't tease me if you can't please me," I joke, mocking something that she said to me when we were just friends.

"Oh, you know I can please you. You're just going to have to wait for it."

After Callie leaves, I gather Barrett's things to get him ready to go back to Sabrinas, making sure I don't forget his lions this time. Barrett sits in the backseat, his little voice humming along as he bops his head to a song on the radio. Seeing the happiness on his face means everything to me. Building a life with him, with Callie and her daughter–soon to be *daughters*.

Sabrina greets us with a warm smile when we arrive and I'm grateful there's no tension or awkwardness between us anymore. We've come a long way since our divorce. Now, it's about making sure Barrett knows he's loved, no matter what.

"See you later, buddy," I say, crouching down to his level, ruffling his hair.

Barrett wraps his small arms around my neck and squeezes me tight. "I love you, Dad," he says. "Please tell Callie I love her too since she left before I woke up this morning."

"I will," I promise my son, thrilled with the fact that he's happy with our new arrangement too. "I love you too, kid."

As I watch him run inside, I feel a strong sense of pride. Being a part of a blended family isn't easy. But we are making it work. And it's better than I ever could have imagined.

Back at the house that afternoon, Will, Luke, and Vince arrive. It's the first time they've been to the house since I moved in with Callie and we started building our life together. They step inside and I feel a sense of pride.

We settle into the kitchen, cracking open beers and tossing a bag of chips onto the counter. The conversation starts off easy, catching up on life, work, and whatever else comes to mind.

"So, how are things with Callie?" Vince asks.

I hesitate to answer because sometimes, I don't know how to put words to the way she makes me feel. It's like trying to describe something I've waited my entire life to find, only to realize it was right there all along. "She's... amazing," I finally say.

"Uh oh," Luke chimes in, leaning forward with a smirk. "Sounds like someone's in love."

Will elbows him but they are both grinning and there's no sense in trying to deny it. "Yeah," I admit, "I really am. I would marry her tomorrow if she let me."

Luke's eyes go wide and there's a moment of silence, like he's processing my answer. "Don't say that shit around Heather," he pleads. "We've been seeing each other for longer and I'm not ready for *that* conversation."

"Scares the shit out of you, doesn't it?" Vince asks me.

"Honestly, not as much as I thought it would," I admit. "I didn't think that I was ever going to find this again after what happened with Sabrina. But I'm glad I started using Flame-Finder again. I probably have Luke to thank for that."

Vince smiles, leaning back. "Good for you, man. Zoe and I, we've had our ups and downs, but she keeps me grounded. I think that's what it's about–finding someone who wants you to be better."

Will speaks up, "I think it's more about finding someone who makes you want to be better."

"That's what Vince said," Luke says, confused.

Will shakes his head. "No, man. It's about wanting to be the best man you can be for the woman you love. Not about the woman you love trying to change you."

We all let that sink in for a moment. Will might be the only single one left in the group, but he's still hit on something so real. It's not about someone pushing you to change–it's about wanting to be the best version of yourself for the person you love.

I look at my friends, at the house Callie and I have turned into our home and realize just how lucky I am. "That's it exactly. Callie's never asked me to change. Because of her, I want to be better. For her, for the kids... and for myself."

Luke raises his beer in a small toast. "To finding the ones who make us better, whether we're ready for it or not."

We clink our bottles together, a shared understanding between us. He might not be in a relationship now, but we all know it's only a matter of time before he finds someone too. One of these days, his disaster dates will have to turn into something more.

As the night winds down and the guys head out, I stand in the doorway. I pull my phone out, sending a quick text to Callie:

ME:

> Hope you're having a good time, dollface. I love you.

CALLIE:

> I love you more. 🛡️

I laugh at her ludicrous message. I'm convinced no one could love someone else more than I love this girl. I close the door before deciding to head to the shower while I wait for Callie to get home so I can show her just how much I love her.

ME:
Not possible.

CALLIE:
Yes, possible.

fifty-nine
I CHOOSE YOU - SARA BAREILLES

CALLIE - SEPTEMBER 27, 2013

It's been a good day spent with Brooke and Taylor. As we stroll through the rows of craft booths, the smell of cinnamon and freshly brewed coffee fills the air. The sun warms my skin and I take in the simplicity of the moment.

As I look at a display of funny signs that say things like "If I stirred it, it's Homemade," my phone buzzes in my back pocket. I expect it to be a picture of Sara from my mom who is watching her or maybe a message from Owen. Instead, when I glance at the screen, my stomach twists. It's not them. It's Matt.

I stare at his name for a second on my screen and I contemplate not opening the message at all but curiosity gets the best of me.

> **MATT:**
> Callie, I think I made a mistake. I love you. I have since we were kids. Please don't shut me out. I'll break things off with her if you just give me another chance.

The message catches me completely off-guard because I haven't heard from him in months and when we were exploring getting back together, he hadn't told me he loved me then.

My breath catches in my chest and I feel my throat tighten. The text brings so many emotions to the forefront of my mind–confusion, anger. After everything, Matt chooses now to say these things to me?

Is it because he's aware that I'm with someone else now–because I'm finally happy?

Without further hesitation, I swipe back to my messages and block his number–barring him from my life completely. Matt doesn't deserve to hold space in my life. That part of my life is over, and I'm not going to fall back into old patterns again. I'm not risking what I have with Owen for anything.

The following weekend when we have Barrett again, Owen and I decide to take the kids for a walk. He took the news of Matt's text to me better than I expected. It's obvious that he is grateful my first instinct was to block Matt rather than reply to him.

Today is one of those crisp fall days, the kind that makes everything feel cozy. I've been trying to walk more now that I'm getting closer to having the baby and we've been going for walks like this almost every day. Owen pulls Barrett and Sara in a big red wagon behind him.

I smile, pulling out my phone to snap a few pictures. Sara is babbling and giving me her biggest smiles while Barrett flashes me a giant grin.

"We should do this every year," I say, the words coming out before I think about the fact that I'm absentmindedly making plans for our future. Owen said he's all in with me but there's still a part of me that wonders if he's ever going to wake up one day and realize just how crazy it is to commit to someone like me–someone with all the baggage that I have.

He looks at me, his expression softening. "Yeah, I'd like that."

As of yesterday, we've been together for two months. I still get those same drunken butterflies in my stomach every time he looks at me and somehow, I know that won't go away any time soon. This is what I want for my life–him, us, the kids–this is my future. I know, without a doubt, this is exactly where I'm meant to be.

The cool breeze swirls around us as we continue walking and I feel our future unfolding with every step we take.

epilogue

HE DIDN'T HAVE TO BE - BRAD PAISLEY

OWEN - OCTOBER 29, 2013

The last month has been a whirlwind of baby prep and making space in our already packed lives. With a small three-bedroom house, we've been shifting things around in Sara's room, rearranging furniture, and squeezing in another crib and a tiny dresser for the new baby. It's a tight fit, but Callie makes it work, the same way she's managed to handle everything these past months—with very little patience, a *lot* of cursing, and the determination–or rather, stubbornness–I love so damn much.

We've been to what feels like a million doctor's appointments, and every time, we leave with a new to-do list that just keeps getting longer. Callie's beyond ready for this baby to make her debut, and I'm right there with her. Watching her try to find a comfortable position is like watching someone play an impossible game of Twister, except there's no way to win. She's exhausted, swollen, and done with being pregnant, even though she still looks like a fucking goddess to me. I've given more foot rubs in the last two months than I ever thought possible. I've always hated feet, but Callie's are different—they don't gross me out the way everyone else's do. Never thought I'd be perfectly fine with something like that, but here I am, happy to do whatever she needs.

We've been trying everything to help her go into labor—fresh pineapple, room temperature root beer, long walks around the neighborhood pulling Sara and Barrett behind us in the red wagon. We even joked that after taking a picture of the two of them in the wagon, we'd have to recreate it every year.

And let's not forget the sex—God, we've been going at it like rabbits on steroids, and I'm definitely not complaining. I did jokingly call her "Bunny" once and she didn't much care for that. Guess I'll stick to "Kitty." Callie's sex drive is through the roof; it's like she's trying to set some kind of record. She's all over me, and I'm loving every second of it. Every time, she looks at me like I'm her personal hero, but honestly, she's the real MVP here, growing a whole human while still managing to rock my world.

She's got this glow, even when she's cursing under her breath because her favorite sweatpants don't fit anymore, or she's waddling down the hallway like a penguin on a mission. I can't get enough of her, swollen ankles and all.

But then there's the reality check. Callie told me a few nights ago, in that quiet, tentative way she has when she's trying to gauge my reaction, that Adam asked to be in the delivery room when the baby is born, and she's going to allow it. She explained that he's actually been somewhat civil since their divorce was finalized—no major fights, no drama. He didn't even throw a fit when I moved in with Callie, which was a surprise considering how things used to be between them. Apparently, he and his new girlfriend, Katie, had plans to move in together as well, so I guess we're all just trying to figure this co-parenting thing out in our own ways.

It shouldn't have surprised me that she'd let him be in there—he's the baby's father, after all—but I'd be lying if I said it didn't sting a little. I know it's not my place to say anything; this isn't my kid, and Adam's been doing what he's supposed to do as a father. Still, there's this knot in my stomach that tightens every time I think about him being there for the moment Callie brings their baby into the world.

"It's not that I don't want you there," she'd said, her fingers tracing absent circles on my arm as we lay in bed. "I do. I'd love for you to be with me during the labor, but when it comes time for the delivery, Adam should be the one there." She made it clear, though, that Adam would have to stay up by her shoulder and wouldn't be allowed to touch her in any way during the delivery. "I told him, no wandering down to the business end," she added with a smirk, trying to keep the mood light. Then she glanced at me, a teasing glint in her eyes. "And you? Trust me, you don't want to see that, Owen. There are things that happen during delivery you won't be able to unsee."

I'd nodded, doing my best to keep my face neutral, to not let her see the flicker of disappointment I couldn't quite swallow. "Of course," I'd said, pressing a kiss to her forehead. "Whatever you need, I'm here."

I meant it, every word. But the truth is, it's hard. It's hard to stand on the sidelines, to be supportive without feeling like I'm overstepping. I've always been the kind of guy who jumps in with both feet, who fixes things, takes charge. This is different. This is about stepping back, about understanding that my role here is to be the quiet strength in the background, not the main event. And I'll do it, for Callie, because she deserves someone who respects her choices, who doesn't make things about their own ego or insecurity.

But damn, if it doesn't twist me up inside.

I've been trying to focus on the positives—Callie wants me with her through the labor, and that's something. I'll get to be there, to hold her hand, to help her breathe through the pain. And when the time comes for Adam to take over, I'll step aside. It's the right thing to do. It's the fair thing. I keep telling myself that, hoping that if I repeat it enough, it'll stop feeling like I'm being edged out of something that matters.

Now, as I juggle the new routine of having Barrett on weekends, it feels like another piece falling into place. Barrett started preschool recently, which means I've got him most weekends. It's a juggling act—working four ten-hour days at West Haven, then picking him up at noon on Fridays. It's hectic, but we've found a little rhythm that works.

Sabrina and I have an unspoken agreement about this schedule—it works, for now. She'll have him if she's got plans, but otherwise, weekends are my time with him. I look forward to those weekends more than anything because they allow me to have everyone I love most—Barrett, Callie, and Sara—together in one place. I've never been the picture of a perfect dad, but when I see Barrett's eyes light up every time he spots me in the pickup line, it feels like I'm doing something right.

We spend our weekend mornings at the park, and I don't believe I'll ever get tired of hearing Barrett's laughter as he repeatedly climbs the ladder to the slide, always ensuring that Sara is watching when he does.

After work, I find myself back on the porch, the sun dipping below the horizon, painting the sky with streaks of pink and orange. I've got a beer in one hand and my phone in the other, texting Callie because she's babysitting for Taylor.

> **ME:**
> How's it going over there?

I lean back in my chair, sipping my drink while waiting for her to reply.

> **CALLIE:**
> Busy, but good. The girls have been playing quite a bit and I don't know if it's just from me being up and around so much but I... uh... I think I might be going into labor.

The words make my heart skip a beat. I read them again, my brain scrambling to catch up. I sit up straighter, my grip tightening around the phone. Her due date is a week away. I shouldn't be so shocked by her statement.

I feel my hands start to tremble as I type out a response.

> **ME:**
> Seriously? Are you sure? 🙃

> **CALLIE:**
> Pretty sure. Contractions started about an hour ago. They're not super close yet, but... yeah.

I'm already on my feet, the beer forgotten on the porch railing. Thankfully, I haven't even drank half of it.

> **ME:**
> Why didn't you say something earlier?

> **CALLIE:**
> You were working and I didn't want to worry you.

> **ME:**
> Can I come get you?

I run inside the house quickly to grab her packed hospital bag and her reply comes quickly.

> **CALLIE:**
> Yes, please. I'll get ahold of Mom so she can watch the girls until Taylor gets home.
>
> I need to text Adam too since he said he wants to be there when the baby is born.

My chest tightens, a mix of anticipation, nerves, and something else I can't quite name. I've been preparing myself for this moment for weeks, but now that it's here, it feels like the ground has shifted beneath my feet. I want to be there for her, to be what she needs, even if it's just for the parts I'm allowed.

> **ME:**
> I'm on my way. I love you.

I hit send and grab my keys as I quickly head for the door.

As I drive, the streets blur past, my thoughts racing ahead of me. Callie's about to have her baby, and all I can think about is how much I want to be there, not just in the room but really there, in every way that matters. I keep my eyes on the road, my hands gripping the wheel, and remind myself that this is about Callie and what she needs. I can be strong for her, even if that means stepping back when she needs me the most.

extended epilogue

RUBY - KAISER CHIEFS

CALLIE - OCTOBER 30, 2013

The night has been a foggy blur of dim hospital lights and beeping monitors, the antiseptic scent of the labor and delivery room mingling with the faint aroma of the lavender lotion I'd slathered on before bed, hoping for a calm night's sleep. So much for that. Owen had arrived at Taylor's last night shortly before Mom got there to take over, allowing him to drive me to the hospital. The drive was a quiet one, filled with the muted hum of the truck's engine and my occasional sharp intake of breath as contractions gripped me tighter, squeezing out any sense of control I thought I had. I'm nervous and excited and so ready to not be pregnant anymore.

Owen held my hand through the entire drive, rubbing slow circles on my hand before squeezing it three times. I realize then that he's done this a few times before. Always three squeezes. Which is so strange because everything else he does is in even numbers, never odd.

When I ask him why always three, his answer makes me smile. He explains to me that it's the silent communication Barrett uses when he's nervous and needs some reassurance. Three squeezes for three words. "I love you," and two squeezes back means "I love you, too." Barrett didn't realize the difference between to, too, and two so it just stuck that way.

Moments like this make me realize how much I lean on him and how much I need him. When I look at him, there's a steadiness in his eyes that I latch onto. Once Taylor got home, Mom planned to meet me at the hospital, and the promise of her presence brought a faint comfort. Thankfully, Owen was already off work, and we had my hospital bag packed and ready—he had thought of everything. My contractions were about ten minutes apart by then, but a nervous flutter remained in my stomach, fueled by all those stories of second children arriving more quickly with no brakes, no warning.

When we finally arrived at the hospital, the fluorescent lights reflecting off the sterile white tiles felt harsh against my tired eyes. With her calm demeanor and warm smile, Dr. Everett informed me that I was about four centimeters dilated. Relief washed over me momentarily, but it was short-lived. My body, stubborn as ever, wasn't dilating on its own, and soon the pitocin was hooked up, dripping steadily into my veins. I opted for the epidural—God, I hoped it would be smooth, like it had been with Sara. But this anesthesiologist seemed hesitant, fumbling with the needle, and each attempt sent a jolt of frustration and pain through me. By the third try, I was ready to scream at her to stop, to just let me go through the rest without it, consequences be damned.

But I managed to breathe through it, somehow, gripping Owen's hand like it was my lifeline. I squeezed my eyes shut as I willed myself to stay calm. Owen's soft and reassuring voice was the anchor I clung to. "You're doing so good, Callie," he murmured. Even though I didn't feel like I was doing that well, it helped to hear it. The minutes stretched into hours. The ticking clock on the wall seemed to mock me as what I hoped would be a quick labor dragged on.

Owen has been a saint through all of this. We've been here since last night, and he hasn't left my side. He kept me distracted with stories of Barrett's latest antics and little reassurances that I was doing great, even when I felt far from it. There's a tension that thickens the air when Adam walks into the waiting room, a silent, heavy cloud that makes it hard to breathe. It's awkward having him here when all I want is Owen, the one who has been here with me through every ache, every sleepless night, every tear. Adam keeps his distance, and I'm grateful for that. His presence lingering in the periphery still feels so wrong.

The contractions are a crushing force, each one stealing the breath from my lungs, and I can only imagine what he must be feeling, standing there watching me endure this. Owen stays beside me until the nurse says it's almost time to push. I wonder if he's afraid that Adam will swoop in, play the role of the hero at the last moment, and overshadow everything Owen has been for me. Considering everything we've been through together, the thought makes my heart ache.

Before he exits the room, Owen places a sweet, soft kiss on my forehead. "I love you," he whispers, his breath warm against my skin, his lips lingering like he doesn't want to pull away. "I'll be right outside if you need me, no matter what."

"I love you too," I manage to say, my voice trembling as I watch him walk out, just as Adam enters. The shift feels jarring, like a sudden, unwanted change in the soundtrack of my life. Adam's eyes are red-rimmed, and he looks like he's been crying. For a brief moment, I feel bad for him, imagining the turmoil he must be going through. But then reality crashes back in—I didn't ask for this. He's the one who made his choices. Now, he's reaping the consequences, waiting in the wings for a moment I no longer feel should belong to him.

The doctor steps into the room, her expression a blend of determination and gentle encouragement, and I know it's time. This is it. The culmination of all the sleepless nights, the anxiety, the anticipation. I remind myself that I am strong. I have made it this far. I hear Owen's voice in my head, reminding me that I can do this. The pain is a blinding, searing force, but I push through it, focusing on Dr. Everett's calm instructions to bear down, breathe, and bear down again. Each second feels like an eternity, my body screaming, my heart racing, until finally, with one last push, she's here.

Except something is wrong. The air is thick with a tense silence that sends a bolt of panic through me. Dr. Everett confirms it's a girl, but I can't hear her cry. The quiet is deafening, an eerie, hollow void that fills my chest with dread. As the doctor cuts the cord, the baby is handed off to a nurse, and hushed whispers fill the room. My heart is in my throat, my feet are still in the stirrups, and tears are pouring down my face as I beg someone, anyone, to tell me why my baby isn't crying. Desperation claws at my insides, a primal scream building in my chest as I plead through sobs to any Gods who will listen for my baby girl to be okay.

After seconds that feel like a lifetime, I finally hear it—a small, weak cry that breaks the tension in the room and lets me breathe again. Relief and fear clash violently inside me as they whisk her away before I can even hold her—before I can even see her. The nurses quickly explain that she swallowed fluid on the way out and needs to be monitored in the nursery for a little while. I nod numbly, barely registering their words as I lie there, tears still streaming down my cheeks.

Everything blurs together in a haze of exhaustion and

emotion. Adam unexpectedly kisses the top of my head before rushing out behind the medical staff with the baby. The affectionate gesture feels so foreign. It's so out of place that I don't know how to react. A wave of nausea hits me as I'm left alone for a heartbeat before Owen comes running back in. The switch happens so quickly it's as if they've just tagged each other in during a relay race. Owen is breathless, his eyes wide with worry as he reaches my side, taking my hand in his and squeezing it tight.

In this moment, I feel completely broken. My chest aches. My body is spent. And my heart feels like it weighs a million pounds.

I don't even know what my daughter looks like.

I know she is alive, and that's what matters, but I haven't even seen her face. The weight of it all bears down on me. I cling to Owen, hoping his presence will somehow be enough to hold me together when I feel like I'm falling apart.

Owen leans in close, his hand brushing my hair back from my forehead, his eyes searching mine. "Hey, it's going to be okay," he whispers, his voice steady even as I can see the concern etched into his features. "She's going to be fine. I promise. We're going to get through this together."

"You don't know that!" The sob escapes me, and my voice sounds angrier than I intended. "You don't know that for sure." He pulls me into his arms, wrapping me in the warmth of his embrace, and I feel the tension in my body start to ease, just a little.

"You're so strong, Callie," he murmurs against my hair. "You've done everything you could, and she's here. That's all that matters. We'll see her soon, and she'll be perfect."

Owen's words seem to rescue me from the darkness that threatens to overtake me. I clutch onto him, letting the steady beat of his heart against my ear calm the frantic pace of my own. "I'm right here," he continues softly, holding my face in his hands. "And I'm not going anywhere. I love you, and I'm so proud of you."

"I love you too," I whisper, my voice cracking but full of gratitude. His unwavering support and quiet strength anchor me, and I take a deep, shuddering breath, letting myself lean into his presence. It's at this moment I realize he is the calm to my chaos, my beacon of hope in a sea of uncertainty. He is my heart, my grounding, my center. And with so much still unknown, Owen's words give me a flicker of hope, and for now, that's enough to hold onto.

I'm not sure how much time has passed when Mom quietly slips into the room, her face lighting up with a relieved smile. She looks between Owen and me, her eyes soft with maternal understanding. "Adam's been down with the baby," she says, giving us a reassuring nod. "She's doing well, and the nurses said they'll be bringing her in soon."

There's a collective sigh of relief in the room as we wait, the minutes stretching like rubber bands pulled too tight. Wayne, who had arrived shortly before the baby was born, sits quietly beside my mom, his expression a mix of joy and concern.

Brooke is here too, standing near the foot of my bed. She softly rubs my leg through the hospital blanket, trying to keep me calm. We have been through so much together over the years, and I'm grateful to have her here with me now.

As soon as I see the door to my room open again, a wave of relief washes over me. A nurse enters, pushing a small bassinet, and my heart leaps as I catch sight of my daughter. She's tiny, wrapped snugly in a soft pink blanket, her little face scrunched up as if she's not quite sure about this whole being-out-in-the-world thing. The nurse picks her up gently, cradling her in her arms as she walks over to me, a sweet smile on her face.

"Here she is," the nurse says softly, carefully helping me get situated with my daughter in my arms. The moment the baby is nestled against me, a rush of love so fierce it almost hurts floods through me. Her skin is warm, her tiny fingers curling around the edge of the blanket, and I'm overwhelmed by the miracle of her.

Owen sits beside me, his eyes fixed on her with a mixture of awe and tenderness as he rubs circles on my back. Adam stands a few feet away, visibly moved but keeping a respectful distance. I take a deep breath, glancing around the room at the faces of those who have been my rock, my family, through it all.

"I've been thinking about her name," I begin, my voice soft but clear. I meet Owen's gaze, then Adam's, wanting them both to understand how important this is to me. "We agreed that I'd get to choose this time, since Adam picked Sara's name."

Adam nods, his expression a mix of acceptance and understanding. "I'm okay with that, Callie," he says gently. "As long as she still has my last name—Graham. We agreed on that, right?"

I nod. "Yes, we did. She'll have your last name." *Although I wish she wouldn't.*

Adam seems relieved, and I take another deep breath, gathering the courage to reveal what I've decided. "I'd like to name her Ruby," I say, my voice catching slightly. "Ruby, after my mom's birthstone, because she's been such a strong, loving presence in my life."

As I say it, I can't help but think to myself that ruby is also the stone for the month Owen and I started dating. It feels like fate, a small, perfect circle closing with this little girl in my arms. I don't say it aloud—I'll tell Owen later when it's just the two of us. For now, I let the moment be about honoring my mom.

Mom's eyes well up with tears, a bright smile spreading across her face. "Oh, Callie," she whispers, touched. "That's beautiful."

I glance at Wayne, who has been silently supportive from his spot beside Mom. "And for her middle name… Morgan. After you, Wayne. I never got to share your last name, but I want Ruby to have the chance. You've been a father who didn't have to be, choosing to love your stepdaughters as your own, and this feels like a way to honor that."

The room is silent for a moment, everyone taking in my words. Wayne's eyes well up with tears, and I see him blink rapidly, his rough hands coming up to cover his mouth as he tries to compose himself. I don't think I've ever seen him cry. "Callie," he chokes out, his voice thick with emotion. "That's… I don't know what to say. That means more than you'll ever know."

Mom reaches over, placing her hand on Wayne's shoulder, her eyes shimmering with tears. "It's perfect, Callie," she whispers, her voice trembling with pride. "Ruby Morgan Graham… it's a beautiful name."

Owen squeezes my hand, his smile warm and full of love. "Ruby Morgan," he repeats softly as if testing the name on his tongue. "It suits her. We already know she's tough—just like her mom. She's going to be so proud to carry that name, Callie."

Adam steps forward, his expression softening as he looks at Ruby. "It's a good name," he agrees quietly, his voice steady.

"Thank you for letting me be here for this, Callie. I know it hasn't been easy."

I nod, feeling the weight of our past settle between us. It's messy and complicated, and there's a lot we don't say out loud, but right now, we don't need to. For a moment, it feels like we're on the same page, both of us wanting what's best for Ruby, even if we're no longer on the same path.

Adam shifts on his feet, hesitating, and I can sense there's more on his mind. Finally, he clears his throat, glancing at the floor before meeting my eyes. "Katie mentioned she'd like to come by and meet Ruby," he says, his tone careful, as if he's bracing himself for my reaction.

A pang of discomfort ripples through me, and I bite the inside of my cheek. I feel like I really cannot say no at this point, given the fact that Owen's been here at the hospital with me the whole time. She's a part of Adam's life now, and by extension, a part of mine whether I like it or not. I force myself to take a breath, steadying the sudden swirl of emotions that rise up, the mix of past hurts and the uneasy truce we're all trying to maintain.

"Yeah," I manage to say, keeping my voice even. "That's fine." I offer a small, polite smile, though it feels a bit strained around the edges. It's going to be awkward—there's no avoiding that—but this is part of the new reality we're navigating. It's not just about Adam and me anymore; it's about all the moving pieces of this extended family we're trying to piece together for our children.

Adam nods, relief flashing briefly in his eyes. He meets my gaze for a moment, and I see a flicker of gratitude there, mixed with the weariness we both share. It's been a long road to this moment, and while it's far from perfect, it's ours. He tells me to get some rest, his voice softer now, as if the vulnerability of the moment has stripped away any lingering defensiveness.

As Adam turns and walks out, the sound of the door closing gently behind him, I let out a slow breath I didn't realize I was holding. The room feels a little lighter without the weight of unsaid words hanging between us. I know Katie coming to visit will be another hurdle to navigate, but for now, I try to push that thought aside and focus on what's right in front of me.

As I cradle Ruby closer, feeling the steady rise and fall of her tiny chest against mine. I know in my heart that I've made the right choice. This little girl, Ruby Morgan, is surrounded by so much love, from her family and from the people who have become like family. And in this moment, I feel a peace settle over me, a quiet confidence that no matter what challenges lie ahead, we'll face them together.

With Owen by my side, Ruby nestled in my arms, and Sara and Barrett excitedly waiting to welcome her, I feel the quiet strength of what we've built. It's not perfect, and it won't always be easy, but as I look at my family—our family—I know that this is where I'm meant to be. We're stepping into the future, together, writing our own story, and it's already more beautiful than I ever imagined.

I'm excited to see what comes next.

TO BE CONTINUED...

acknowledgments

Saying I want to thank my late Mother-in-Law would probably be pretty weird considering this is a spicy book inspired by the relationship I have with her son. However, I am going to do it anyway. So, Sue, thank you for raising the man of my dreams. We miss you every fucking day.

To the man who inspired this story—my husband: I love you so much and appreciate you every day. Thank you for putting up with my crazy ideas and rolling with it when I said I wanted to write a book about our story. You've given me the world. Thank you for showing me what real love is. I Love You Madly.

For my Alpha & Beta Readers—Kiaya, Janie, Lindsey, MJ Bradsher, V.W. Smith, and Samantha: This amazing group of women has helped me through so much in writing this story. Thank you for your time. Thank you for your honesty. Thank you for putting up with me when I spiraled (multiple times) and for helping me select my final cover design. Thank you for putting up with the name changes and last-minute edits. Thank you for reading and rereading this story to help me get it right. Most importantly, thank you for your friendships. You all are such wonderful women, and I am forever grateful.

To Kristi Tragethon, my official unofficial editor: I will never be able to thank you enough for your time and your patience with me in this process. You, my friend, are a beautiful soul.

To my amazing cover designer, Emily Hensley from Small Fry Marketing, working with you was such a wonderful experience. I can't wait to show all these readers what the cover for Book 2 looks like sometime next year.

Finally, my ARC Readers—Thank you for supporting me and taking the time out of your day to read my story. You helped me stay motivated and your excitement for this novel lifted me up when the pressure of this project felt like it was going to take me out.